DEAL
WITH THE
DEMON

K. LORAINE
USA Today BESTSELLING AUTHORS
MEG ANNE

Permission requests can be sent via email to: authors@ themategames.com

Edited by Mo Sytsma of Comma Sutra Editorial

Cover Design by CReya-tive Book Design

Photographer: Wander Aguiar

Model: Sam Myerson

To the Spice Club mods,
Thanks for all the road flares.

Don't get too close, it's dark inside, it's where my demons hide.

DEAL
WITH THE
DEMON

Authors' Note

Deal with the Demon contains mature and graphic content that is not suitable for all audiences. Such content includes dubious consent, degradation, impact and blood play, bondage, and more. **Reader discretion is advised.**

A detailed list of content and trigger warnings is available on our website.

CHAPTER
ONE
ROSIE

Aurora Springs, Alaska

"Fake your own death, Roslyn. Save your family. Go on the run. It'll be fine," I grumbled as I trudged through the cold, muddy Alaskan terrain, heading toward my goal. Asher Henry, hacker extraordinaire.

I snorted. "Extraordinaire, my tight rear end. I found you in less than a day."

My whole body was frozen, teeth chattering, exhaustion weighing me down. If I didn't get to his forking house soon, I'd actually die, nothing fake about it.

A pang went through my heart at the romanticized version of Gavin I held onto. Him finding my note, hoping I'd be true to my word and return to him. It must've worked, or the vampire would have come and stolen me away, back to the Donoghue castle. He had to know I was dead now too. Good.

The sight of a house at the crest of the hill had me

picking up my pace. Almost there. I stepped on a root as I continued, the uneven ground sending me tumbling into the mixture of slushy snow and mud. But I was nearly to my goal. Asher would help me. He'd make sure Roslyn Blackthorne never appeared again. Give me a new name. A new life.

I reached his front door and weakly knocked, a bone-deep shiver clattering my teeth together. No answer. No lights. No sign of him.

"I'll just wait here, then," I mumbled. "You have to come home sometime."

I lost track of the hours as I sat on his porch, curled in on myself to try and stave off the worst of the wind. I may not be a human, but I wouldn't survive out in the elements like this for long. I'd already lost feeling in my fingers by the time wheels finally crunched through the snow. It was enough to make my heart stutter.

A door opened, and a deadly voice growled, "Don't fucking move."

I'd recognize that voice anywhere.

I unfurled myself, my gaze traveling up the bundled form of my would-be assailant, gun raised and trained on me.

Asher Henry, my black-hatted knight in technological armor. He didn't know it yet, but he was about to become my hero.

If I could convince him not to kill me first.

$\sim$

ASHER
One hour earlier

2

THAT WITCH WAS GOING to be the death of me after all. A hiss escaped me as a burn shot through the mark she'd saddled me with years ago. A parting gift for my unfortunate misstep.

I checked the spot on the back of my hand—just a small star right in the center. What the fuck? Was the thing growing? Instead of a single star, there was now a small cluster. Dread curled in my gut. What did this mean? How could I stop it? Whatever it was, it couldn't be good.

A loud crash behind me pulled me out of my spiral of doom. Two wolf shifters and a burly lumberjack were locked in a scuffle. I had to get the hell out of here before this turned into a full-on bar brawl.

I pulled my collar up higher as I left the Tipsy Moose behind. I hadn't even been able to enjoy my beer before those fucking Mercer twins started a fight. They had thirty other days to act like a bunch of assholes, and they chose the one night a month where I came into town for my supply run. It was my only chance to stop in for a taste of semi-normal existence, and it had been ruined by dick-swinging shifters.

Fucking typical.

The wind kicked up, sending the curly hair of my fake beard fluttering across the hollow of my throat and tickling me without mercy. Maybe one day I wouldn't have to hide my identity, but as of right now, I was still the supernatural world's most wanted hacker. That meant a life of anonymous sex, zero meaningful relationships, and way too much wig adhesive. It was all fake names, deep cover, and high security for me. Unless I wanted to get caught and become the captive of that vengeful witch.

Hard pass. She'd already done enough damage.

I scratched at my chin with an annoyed grunt, my irritation rising when I felt the adhesive give way. Great. My goatee probably looked drunker than I did—than I was *supposed* to be.

The whole thing was bullshit. My night was wrecked, and now I didn't even have a good buzz to make any of the effort worth it. I should have just waited until I got home. Then I could have cracked open one of the bottles of Jack I'd bought and found oblivion in the best way I knew. Alone.

I hated the need for these disguises, but it was the only way to maintain any sort of social life when, as far as the people of Aurora Springs knew, Asher Henry didn't exist. And I needed to keep it that way if I wanted to stay alive. In a town of one hundred seventy-three people, that was a special sort of hell.

Thus I became Joe Baker, resident hermit and curmudgeonly fisherman. No one bothered me. No one cared if I ever showed my face.

Well, almost no one.

Starting up my old beater of a truck, I waited for the heat to blast and fill the cab. Even in the spring, it was cold here. But going into hiding meant isolation in a small, nowhere town. What better place than the near wilds of Alaska?

I drove the forty minutes up the winding path to my mountain fortress, mostly muttering to myself and ignoring the sorry excuse for music playing on the radio. It was really just a bunch of static with a random guitar strum here and there, but what could you expect from a town with one fucking station?

If the night had gone according to plan, I would have slept it off at Joe Baker's houseboat or any of the other properties I owned under various names. But since tonight had shit the bed before it even started, all I wanted was to go home. That meant my log cabin in the woods. The one filled with technology so advanced not even the military had access to most of it, and no one in Aurora Springs, let alone anywhere else, would find it on any kind of map. Google Earth could fuck right off.

As I pulled past the camouflaged gate hiding my property from the prying eyes of wayward hikers, I frowned. The beams of my headlights flashed across strange tracks in the muddy earth of the dirt road.

"What the fuck?"

My pulse raced, adrenaline spiking as the path continued toward my house. Animal? Maybe. I'd encountered my share of wildlife here. They were the only creatures who breached my walls.

But as soon as I parked, I saw the culprit. A dirty lump huddled against my door. Stringy dark hair hanging in front of their—no, *her*—face.

Reaching under the seat of my truck, I pulled the revolver I kept hidden there out of its holster. You never knew what you'd come up against out here. I'd learned that the hard way.

I got out, breath tight as I raised the gun and switched off the safety. Then I cocked the hammer and said, "Don't fucking move."

Her head snapped up, and she pinned me with eyes the color of burnished gold. My heart stuttered. I knew those eyes. That face. I'd stared at them far too many times from the glow of my computer screens under the guise of "research." But she wasn't my assignment, shouldn't have been on my fucking radar at all. And yet I hadn't been able to look away even after—

"You're dead."

Her stats flashed in my memory:

Roslyn "Rosie" Blackthorne

Age: 21

Species: Vampire-Human hybrid (never turned)

Parents: Cashel and Olivia Blackthorne

Siblings: Noah and Westley Blackthorne

Status: Deceased.

Cause of death: House fire

"Not dead enough, it would seem." She got to wobbly feet, her eyes tired, face dirt-streaked and pale. "Asher, I need your help."

"Why the fuck should I help you? How did you even find me?"

A proud, exhausted smile flitted across her face. "You're not the only one with a certain skill set."

The knowledge that I'd been hacked sent a bolt of terror straight through me. If she'd been able to find me, who else could? I'd been so damn careful. There weren't any breadcrumbs, cyber or otherwise. I was as off the map as possible. Yet her presence here, the fact that she'd called me by my name, proved just how fucking wrong I was. *Christ, I was going to need to do a full security sweep.*

"Then why do you need me at all?"

"Could you put that thing down?"

I glanced at the gun I still had aimed between her eyes. "Shit. Sorry."

"And I need you because you have connections I don't."

"Such as?"

"People, papers, access to new documents."

"So you're on the run."

"Well, I can't exactly go around as the late Roslyn Blackthorne, now can I?"

"That's what this is about? You want a new identity?"

"I need to make sure Rosie stays dead and buried. God knows I went to enough effort killing her. No one can know I'm alive. Not even my family."

"What are you running from?"

Her expression went grave. "My husband."

CHAPTER
TWO
ROSIE

"Husband?" Asher's gaze sharpened, and though the gun was lowered, I knew I wasn't in the clear yet. "That wasn't in your file."

"My file? Is that like my permanent record? I thought those were made up."

The derisive snort he released was more telling than any words he could've said. I was an idiotic little nuisance.

"Are you going to let me inside?"

He took a tentative step forward, muscles coiled tight as though he was afraid I'd bite him. For all he knew, I might do just that.

"Show me your teeth first."

Bingo.

"I'm not a vampire. Don't you know how it works for born vampires? If you don't turn by a certain age, you never will. Didn't your *file* tell you that?"

He sneered, his upper lip curling beneath his flimsy mustache. I had trouble believing he thought he was fooling anyone with the sorry excuse for facial hair, but it didn't seem like the right moment to point it out.

Good side, Rosie. You're trying to charm him.

With a slight eye roll, I used my index fingers to push my lip up, giving him an exaggerated grin. After a couple of seconds, I lowered my hands. "Better?"

His eyes looked strange, a muddy brown reminiscent of pond scum. Those weren't real. Not when I could see the hint of blue beneath the brown. I might not be a vampire, but there were still perks to being a Blackthorne. I came with certain . . . enhancements. Sharper vision. Keener sense of smell. Better than average hearing. Quicker to heal, less likely to fall ill. So not a full-on supernatural, but worlds apart from a true human.

Regardless of all that, I also happened to know what he looked like. I'd found a picture of him in my research. It was dated, but I clearly recalled his sandy blond hair and piercing blue eyes. He'd been tall and surprisingly built for a man known for sitting in front of a computer all day. But either he'd let himself go, or he'd donned some sort of padding because the man standing in front of me was decidedly . . . lumpy.

"Not by a long shot." He reached out and snagged my chin between his thumb and forefinger, pulling my face close to him. Without so much as a 'how d'you do,' he shoved his finger in my mouth and began prodding my teeth.

I twisted my face free, spitting out his finger. "Do you mind?"

"If you have razor-sharp fangs and are sniffing around my house? Yeah, I do, sweetheart. I mind a whole fucking lot."

"Fair enough. Did I pass your inspection at least?"

He gave me one last suspicion-tinged once over. "I

guess. But you try anything funny, I'll shoot first and ask questions later."

"So will I," I said with a cheeky grin.

"You're not the one with a gun at the ready."

"But you are, and I move fast."

"Do you really think you could get it from me before I pull the trigger?"

One brow cocked, I smirked. "Do you want me to show you?"

For a second, I thought he was going to say yes, but he shook his head and muttered, "Fucking vampires."

"I'd thought we'd already established that I'm *not* a vampire."

"You may as well be. Especially as far as the people in this town are concerned."

"But they aren't going to find out. Not if you help me."

He shook his head and sighed, heading back to his truck to kill the lights and engine. "I'm still not sure what's in it for me."

"Karma?"

"Is a bitch. What else?"

"Um . . . my eternal gratitude."

"Worthless."

I scowled at his back as he brushed past me and moved up to the door. "I have money."

"How much?"

Ah, capitalism. "Plenty. Name your price."

With a sharp sniff, he opened the door and walked inside. For one terrible moment, I feared he'd shut me out. Instead, he nodded and muttered, "Come on in."

I glanced down at his welcome mat, or should I say unwelcome mat. "Cute."

He followed my gaze to the black rubber boldly stating, 'Fuck Off.'

"Not that it works."

"I'm not easily swayed."

"Toxic trait if ever there was one."

"Are you always this prickly?"

"Yes."

"Lovely."

Hanging his coat on the hook by the door and blocking my entry, he took his sweet time. He bent over, unlacing his heavy boots, and knocked into my hip with his bottom as I attempted to squeeze past his hulking frame. That was *not* the rear end of a man who spent all his time sitting in front of a computer screen. It was firm and tight, even from the short bit of contact.

I'm not sure what came over me because when he made no point to move, I gave it a squeeze.

"Hey. Anyone ever teach you about boundaries?"

"You were waving it in my face. What was I supposed to do?"

"So you're saying I can grab your tits whenever I want?"

"You can try," I said, giving him a simpering smile.

"I . . . you . . . ugh." He stormed away from me, heading down the hall. "Are you coming?"

I removed my coat, which had seemed like the perfect winter accessory *until* I put it to the test, and followed him inside. He turned at the end of the hallway, and I made to do the same, but he stopped me with another glower.

"What do you think you're doing?"

"You asked if I was coming."

"Into the house. Jesus, you are more trouble than you're worth." He pointed to the overstuffed leather couch in the living area. "Sit. Don't touch anything."

A little zing of heat coursed through me at the order, or more specifically, the dominance in his tone. So I sat. And I'm not ashamed to admit I watched him walk away, peeling off layers of his clothing as he went and revealing more of the sculpted body I'd gotten a feel of, until he opened a door and stepped into a different room.

A shiver of appreciation curled in my belly. "Asher Henry, who knew you were hiding all that?"

"What did you say?" he called.

Heat crept into my cheeks. "Nothing!"

Tapping my fingers on my knees, I glanced around his home, surprised by how large it was. Large and high-end. This was the type of home you saw in spreads about tech billionaires and real estate moguls. I half expected a platinum-haired Barbie doll to walk in and sell it to me.

You need to stop watching Netflix, Roslyn.

When Asher returned, he was barefoot, wearing a pair of low-slung black sweats and pulling on a Henley in the same shade. His face was scrubbed clean, revealing sharp cheekbones and a jaw of golden stubble.

Jesus Forking Christ, he was handsome in person.

He looked up, pinning me with eyes so blue they reminded me of the turquoise waters of a beach in Bali.

I think I forgot how to breathe. Or speak. Or function, because his mouth was moving, but I didn't process a single thing he said.

"Pardon?" I finally managed.

He scowled.

"So you're basically human, you've got bad manners, *and* you can't hear?" His sigh bore the weight of the world. "Tell me what you need so I can get you out of here."

"I already told you. I need a new identity and all the

documents to go with it. I need you to help me make Roslyn Blackthorne stay buried."

"I don't understand why you'd want to fake your death. You're a fucking princess. Your family treats you like the most precious thing they own." His shrewd gaze lingered on me. "Unless you're a menace. Are you a menace, sweetheart?"

"Not unless I have to be."

"Should I start calling you Dennis?"

I glared at him. "Do you always interrogate and insult your clients this way?"

"Client implies I had a choice. This feels more like blackmail."

I lifted one of my shoulders. "You're getting paid. That hardly seems like blackmail to me."

"Ah, but what would you do to me if I turned you away? Tell everyone where to find me?" He shook his head. "I can't take the risk."

"Who am I going to tell, Asher? I'm supposed to be dead. I can't call Mummy and Daddy and admit what I've done and that the big mean hacker hurt my feelings by telling me no."

His lips twitched. "Do you really call them that?"

"How spoiled do you think I am?"

"Very."

He wasn't wrong. I didn't want for anything growing up. Had a loving home and family. Had everything. Until the Donoghues destroyed it all. Tears sprung to my eyes without warning, tightening my throat and making it hard to get words out.

"Oh, God. You're crying. Don't fucking cry. I can't." He wasn't comforting me. Asher Henry just stood over me, annoyed at my emotional outburst. "Women use their tears to get what they want all the time. I'm wise to that trick."

"I hadn't realized you were an insensitive sod as well as a crazy recluse."

"You should have done better research."

"I found you, didn't I?"

His jaw clenched, and he fisted his hands at his sides, drawing my attention to some sort of tattoo along the back of his right one. He was too far away for me to make it out, though.

"How did you manage that, by the way?"

I locked my lips.

"If I help you, you need to tell me what you found so I can get rid of it. I can't risk anyone else coming across it. I'm not hiding out here for shits and giggles, sweetheart. My life fucking depends on staying hidden."

The tiniest flicker of guilt fluttered in my chest. "Deal."

He released a heavy breath and sat down in the recliner angled towards me. "So who do you want to be, Roslyn Blackthorne?"

"What do you mean?"

"The new you. What's your name?"

"I hadn't gotten that far."

"Typical."

"I had a small window. It was all I could do to take off without drawing attention to myself. But what does it matter? I'm dead as far as the rest of my world is concerned. My . . . obligations to them are gone. I can start over, and no one else is at risk because of it."

"And by obligations, you mean your husband?"

I shivered, thinking of Gavin as a stupid, misguided pang of longing hit me. "Yes."

"Is he the one putting people at risk?"

I bit my lip. "Not precisely. But his connections. The marriage came with strings. I . . ." I swallowed back my confession, not wanting to give anyone that truth. I certainly didn't owe it to Asher. "Suffice it to say we didn't end up being a good match."

He raised a brow. "That's not suspicious at all."

"It's all you're going to get."

"Should I expect *him* to show up on my doorstep next?"

"No. I covered my tracks. No one would think to look for me here. Or anywhere, for that matter."

"You're trouble with a capital T, Blackthorne."

"And you're no picnic, Henry."

He brushed his hands together like he was cleaning something off them, some imaginary bit of dirt or dust, then stood. "Well, first things first. You need a name."

"I could go with my middle name."

"No. Nothing connected to your previous life. Something boring but not too generic. Something you'll recognize when people use it."

"I had an imaginary friend when I was six. Her name was Nadia."

"Mine was Friedrich."

I smiled, picturing Asher as a child carrying on a conversation with his pretend friend. "We certainly have a knack for choosing strange names."

"Friedrich turned out to be a ghost, so . . . "

My mouth fell open. "Oh, golly." Had Nadia been a ghost?

He snickered. "Golly? Wow, princess. You better wash your mouth out."

"Not all of us like to use foul language."

His eyes widened at my prim tone. "Is that so? I quite enjoy it," he mocked. "Shit, cocksucker, cunt, motherfucker, just to name a few of my favorites. But nothing hits quite like a well-timed, nice, long fuuuck."

"I'll take your word for it."

"So what do you say when you want to curse, sweetheart? There's no replacement I can think of that's as satisfying."

"Fork with me and find out."

He held my gaze and then burst out laughing. "You do not actually say that."

"I most certainly do."

"You're missing out."

"Perhaps you simply lack the imagination necessary to find suitable replacements. Fork suits me just fine."

"So you asked your husband to . . . fork you. I can just imagine it. 'Oh, fork me. Fork me harder, Daddy.'"

I blushed at his exaggerated impersonation of me. "That's not quite how it went. We never got to the *forking*."

"Well, with a mouth like that . . ." His eyes hit my lips as his words trailed off. This time, it didn't seem intentional. Clearing his throat, he changed the subject. "So Nadia what . . . Smith?"

"Seems too obvious."

"What about Black?"

"Isn't it too close to Blackthorne?"

"I don't think so. We change the hair, the eye color, maybe your accent too . . ." He paced in front of me as he listed everything about me that needed alterations. "What accents can you do?"

"I've got a solid American I can pull out at the drop of a hat. Mum's from Seattle, so that's where I spent half of my time." I said all of that with my generic American accent, fighting a smile as his expression grew awed. "And I can do a pretty solid southern if I need to. But Nadia sounds Russian, so maybe that might be best? Or French, if you prefer. I have been told my voice is quite how-do-you-say . . . sexy like this."

He stood slack-jawed for a heartbeat before swallowing hard and subconsciously adjusting the bulge in his joggers. "Uh . . . that could work."

"Which one?"

"The sexy . . . they all could." Dragging a hand through his hair, he sighed and said, "You know what? Just stick with the British. Everyone in this town is from somewhere else, so you'll fit right in. Besides, they might catch on if you don't hit something quite right or start asking questions you can't answer. There's a whole motorcycle gang of Russian bear shifters in town. We're all here to get away."

"Is everyone here a supernatural creature?"

"Everyone."

"Even you?"

"Everyone but me." He held out his hand. "Give me your phone."

I did. "What are you doing with it? I bought a new one on the way here. No one knows this number or how to find me."

"Good. I'm giving you mine so I can reach you. Don't do anything until I text you. We can meet, and I'll get you your new papers and disguise."

He handed the device back to me, and I instantly typed him a message.

ME:

It's Nadia. *winky face emoji*

The eye roll he offered in response was so satisfying I giggled.

"What are you still doing here?"

18

"What do you mean?"

"You can leave. I said I'd text when I had everything handled."

"Where should I go?"

"To wherever you've arranged to stay."

And here it was. My last favor. The one I hoped he wouldn't deny me.

"Um . . . about that."

CHAPTER
THREE
ROSIE

"At least I can count on you for liquor," I grumbled, pulling a bottle of what I thought was vodka from Asher's bar, not recognizing the handwritten label. The writing looked Russian, though; surely they knew a thing or two about the potato juice.

"Three days and nights, you left me alone here. If you're listening in, I hope you know how lucky you are I'm not a witch, or I'd hex you." It took me a couple of tries before I could get the bottle open. "Come on, darn you," I grunted, tugging on the silver cap. Then I realized it was a screwtop, not a cork like the wine I was familiar with. "Jesus, Rosie. You're a mess."

I took a long pull as soon as the top was off, not bothering to close it again. The burn of vodka down my throat confirmed my suspicions that this was exactly what I'd thought. Homemade, strong, and the perfect choice to help me find oblivion. I was not cut out for imprisonment.

Three days. He'd left me here on my own for three forking days. At least the fridge was somewhat stocked, even if it was stale pizza and some sort of meat that I told myself was beef. For all I knew, it was venison or elk. Possibly moose. I shuddered before taking another swig.

Already I could feel the burn settling in my stomach. My limbs tingled happily, and my nose had gone numb. This stuff worked fast.

"Well, well, Mr. Henry. You seem to have acquired the good stuff."

Were my words slurred?

Holding the bottle up, I giggled at the now half-empty container. "Or maybe I'm just a lush. No matter. If I am sick on your couch, Asher, I'm not apologizing. You did this to me. It's my right to get good and pissed at this point."

I spun in a circle, laughing when some of the clear liquid sloshed out. "Serves you right. If I wasn't enjoying it so much, I'd dump the whole lot and set this place on fire."

I hiccuped. "Oops."

This brought to mind the time Noah and I had gotten into our father's Scotch. We'd been off our faces and ended up spilling half the bottle on the carpet. The study smelled of smoke and peat for weeks. And with the memory came a sharp pang beneath my ribs.

I missed them. My parents, my brothers . . . the possibility of Gavin. I missed the life I'd given up. The identity I had to let go of.

Asher's voice echoed in my head, the frustrated tone of his last words hitting me hard.

"We can fix your physical appearance however we need, but I have no fucking clue what we're gonna do about your scent. You're lucky they haven't already caught a whiff of you. This town hates vampires."

He'd left me with a warning not to go anywhere or see anyone. I couldn't even open the door. He could be dead for all I knew. It wasn't like I could check.

Then I remembered his number saved in my phone.

ME:

Are you alive?

ME:

I'm very drunk and likely about to be sick all over your home.

ME:

Have I mentioned I get quite nosy when I've been drinking? What kind of secrets do you have in this house?

ME:

Do you have a sex dungeon?

ME:

Maybe I'll wait there.

When several minutes passed with no reply, a sick sort of dread settled in my chest.

"Oh my God, he *is* dead."

Before my panic could consume me, I slammed the mostly empty bottle on the table. "Looks like you're on your own. You got this far. You can figure out the rest. What did he say we needed? A disguise, right. Easy."

I stood on wobbly legs and made my way to his bathroom, throwing open cabinets and pulling out everything I could find. There were prosthetics of all kinds, facial hair in every color, wigs, makeup, the works. Asher basically had his own costume shop.

"Thank you, Asher. May you rest in peace." I attempted to make the sign of the cross, but being that I was part vampire and not any part Catholic, I only succeeded in smacking myself in the nose. How did Father Gallagher do this? What was it Kingston had said . . . Spectacles, Testicles, Wallet, Watch?

Shrugging, I gave up. I was damned anyway, and likely so was poor Asher.

Selecting a hooked nose piece and a red beard, I found a bottle of liquid latex. I knew next to nothing about this level of makeup, but I had tried my hand at fake lashes and clearly remembered the tiny tube they came with was labeled latex. This must be his adhesive.

Frowning at the nose, I opened the bottle and squeezed a large glob into my palm, then slathered it onto my face. Graceful? No. But I wasn't going for pretty. I missed my nose twice as I tried to apply the prosthetic. Finally, after leaning in close to the mirror and giving myself a pep-talk, I landed on target . . . mostly. The beard seemed to go on easier, though something about the scraggly hair looked off.

"Ah-ha! Success! Ladies and gentlemen, the new and improved Nadia Black. Old crone. Bearded lady. Least sexy, most human, and decidedly not vampire-iest of them all."

Okay. Disguise, check. Now what?

"Scent!" I rummaged through his medicine cabinet, searching for Asher's cologne. If I smelled like him, I wouldn't be outed, right?

"No, you numpty. It's not about your outer scent. It's the blasted phermines . . . pherimes . . . pheromones."

I erupted into a fit of giggles, the hairs on my beard tickling my lips.

"If only I had a witch . . . or a demon. They could mask it like *that*." I tried to snap but wasn't successful. I ended up slamming my hand into the glass, the spiderweb cracks throwing my reflection into disorientating shards.

"Gah! Go away, old crone." The side of my palm was bleeding. The old crone was a right witch. "You can't have my blood. Everyone always wants my blood."

Sighing, I pulled off the prosthetic nose, which was now barely hanging on anyway. The beard would be enough of a disguise. I could just lower my voice and pretend I was a man.

Spotting the dark fall of hair over my shoulder, I groaned. "No one will believe you with a mane like this." I found Asher's scissors and started chopping off chunks of my hair without stopping to think about what I was doing. When the sink was filled with it, I nodded in satisfaction. There.

"Hey, I'm Chad Hardon. I'm a lumberjack." I snorted at my fantastic impression of a man. I didn't need Asher. I could do this.

"Now, how to summon a demon to fix this pesky scent problem?"

I chewed on the inside of my cheek, recalling something my Aunt Callie had said once. *"When summoning any creature, you must always represent each of the four elements. For example, demons require blood, a feather, a circle of salt with candles, and most importantly, an invitation."*

Aunt Callie knew so much more than anyone gave her credit for. Stumbling my way down the hall, I accidentally smeared blood on the wall with my cut hand. "Oopsie daisy. But hey, at least that's one of them."

I found salt in the kitchen, along with a box of matches by the stove and a fat black marker. It wasn't on my list, but I was certain it would come in handy. A taxidermy raven stared at me with his beady eyes from the mantle. Judging.

"Your opinion is not required, sir. But...I will take a feather." I plucked a shiny black tailfeather straight from his arse. "I'd say sorry, but you started it."

Tucking the feather behind my ear, I wandered through the house.

"Candles . . . candles . . . If I were a candle, where would I be? Bedroom."

I opened door after door as I meandered, stopping when I finally found Asher's bedroom. It felt like an invasion of privacy because it was. But he'd abandoned me. He was dead in a ditch anyway. This was my domain now.

The dresser was bare, the bed a tumble of sheets, but then my eyes alighted on the lone candle in the room. A pillar. Plain and black. Burned only a few times. Right next to it was a bottle of lotion and a box of tissues.

"So you *do* have a sex candle. But how sad that you're the only participant."

Just like you are destined to be.

I frowned at the unwanted internal voice. "Hush, you harlot."

I snagged what I needed and flounced out of the room, not allowing myself to remember how good he'd looked as he was changing.

Humming to myself, I clumsily set my circle, the line a titchyroo wobbly, but it was good enough. Then I took a few deep breaths as I lit the candle and stepped out of the circle.

"Intention matters more than words," I muttered, repeating my cousin Natalie's advice about spellcasting. "Okay, here goes nothing."

Holding my wish in the forefront of my mind, I closed my eyes and lifted my hands, palms facing the ceiling.

"Hail ye creatures of the night, hear my plea. I seek a bargain for . . . new smells for me?"

I expected lightning, wind, or an earthquake. Or at least for the power to flicker.

Instead, the candle guttered out. That was it. And I

thought that was more likely due to my deep sigh than anything else.

"How disappointing."

Gathering the candle and the canister of salt, I hissed as some of the white crystals splashed onto my bleeding palm. "That can't be good."

I didn't have a chance to further investigate the damage I'd caused. The front door swung open, sending apprehension through me. Asher was going to be so cross with me when he saw this mess.

"I was going to tidy up, but I thought you were . . ." I blurted, but the rest of my statement died on my tongue as I dropped the candle and salt to the floor.

An enormous demon stood in the doorway, his purple skin shimmering in the light. All he wore were tight leather breeches, but the rest of him was on full display. Rippling muscles rivaling any male I'd ever seen. A head of aubergine-colored hair that fell over one shoulder and down to his waist. He narrowed his glowing lavender gaze on me, grinning as he ran a hand over his locks and between two deep purple horns so dark they were almost black that sprouted from his hairline. A tail swished behind him, reminding me of a lion lazily taking in his surroundings.

"Well, this is . . . an unexpected treat."

"Holy forking hell. It worked."

My knees wobbled, and finally, my body revolted against all the abuse I'd treated it to. The world around me blurred, and before I could stop myself, I fainted dead away.

CHAPTER
FOUR

ROSIE

S omething warm and slightly rough slipped along the side of my palm, over and over, pulling me back to consciousness. It reminded me of a cat's tongue, but . . . forked? Wait. *Forked?*

"Ah, there she is. What the devil were you thinking, summoning a demon with a freshly bleeding wound? Did you know there are those of us who would use that to bind your soul to ours without even *asking* first?" His voice was a seductive rasp as he backed away from me, bringing his body into view as I blinked a few times to clear my vision.

"Why aren't you in the circle?" My head swam, likely from a combination of vodka and hitting the floor, and it was a struggle to make sense of much of anything.

"That's what you're leading with?"

"As opposed to?"

The demon shrugged, and I had the inane thought that shrugging was too human a movement for something so *other.* "Most people want to know my name."

"You're an uncontained demon. I'm more interested in whether you're going to kill me for summoning you."

"Oh, *ma petite monstre,* I don't mean to kill you."

"You don't?"

"Not until you make your case, ask for your dearest wish, and bargain for your life. I do so enjoy that last part. I'd hate to miss it."

I pushed myself to my feet, wanting to establish some sort of equal footing between the creature and me. My effort was short-lived, however, since I promptly sat back down on the sofa as the floor seemed to tilt.

Staring up at him, it is.

"Aren't you an adorable little morsel?" He smirked, that lavender gaze searing me. Something in his eyes said he was toying with me like a cat might toy with a mouse before eating it.

"I called you to me for help. You're right. But if the owner of this house returns to a great hulking demon in his living room, I'll have more problems on my hands than I know what to deal with—which is saying something, considering my current predicament. So give me your name, and let's get the show on the road."

The demon bowed, holding my gaze as his arms swept out on either side of his well-muscled torso. "You may call me . . . Pan."

I didn't even fight the giggle that escaped. "Pan? As in pots and?"

The curl of his lip turned decidedly sulky. "No."

"Are you going to elaborate?"

"Do you think it wise to annoy the demon holding your very life in the palm of his hand?"

"Let's not get dramatic, Potts."

"Pan."

"Peter."

"Pan."

I laughed. "Gotcha."

Anger flashed in his eyes. "And you, Roslyn Blackthorne, what shall we call you now?"

"How do you know my name?"

Brows lifting, he offered a slight huff of laughter. "I tasted your blood. I know so much about you now."

Heat crept up the back of my neck, and I shifted uncomfortably on the couch. "Such as?"

"Such as the fact you like a bite of pain with your pleasure. That you crave subjugation. That you desire punishment as well as praise. Oh yes, Roslyn, I know quite a lot about you."

"Then you already know why I summoned you. I need to disappear. I've taken every possible step. But . . . my blood, my scent, they give me away."

He reached out and tugged the scraggly false beard from my jaw. "I see the steps you've taken. Missteps, more like. Really, love, what is this?"

"I was going to pose as a man."

His eyes roamed over my figure. "Never would have worked."

I bristled. "I do a very convincing voice."

He ruffled my hair like I was a playful puppy. "I'm sure you do."

"I was going to be Chad . . . nevermind. Stop distracting me."

He raised a brow. "You're the one babbling. I merely asked a question."

"What would it cost me for you to change my scent? Make me smell . . . fae." Fae seemed to be the best choice. They were a wily sort, but they didn't change their shape or operate under any magical rules that kept them out of commission at certain times of the month. They were nebulous.

"What price are you prepared to pay?"

"Is that how this works? I set my own price?"

"No, I just want to know how much this is worth to you. That will inform the terms of the deal."

I blew out a heavy breath and glanced around the room, seeking inspiration. *How much was a new scent—a new life— worth?* Quite a lot, I had to assume. Especially if it meant my family could live without the threat of my discovery hanging over their heads. If I was found out to have abandoned my responsibilities, the Donoghues would demand a death, and I shuddered to think whose.

"Is it really that hard?" he asked when I still hadn't managed to answer.

"I just . . . what wouldn't I pay for freedom?"

Interest shimmered in his gaze. "Careful. My kind works in specifics. You don't want to give me carte blanche because I *will* take it, *ma petite monstre*."

Thoughts buzzing in my brain, I ran through the list of things of value I could give him that wouldn't end with me dead and that I wouldn't miss. I had to be careful with him. Demons were a tricky sort. One wrong move and he'd drag me to hell with him.

"A taste of my blood?"

He licked his lips suggestively. "Already had it."

"My virginity?" A few weeks ago, the thought would have repulsed me, but after Gavin, I realized just how little it meant. It would be an easy enough thing to give, if not exactly . . . pleasant.

"Tempting, but not enough."

I knew demons usually dealt in souls, but not even I

was stupid enough to offer that up freely. My nails pricked my palms as I balled my hands into fists. "Why don't you just tell me what you want from me, *Peter*."

Gritting his teeth, he let out a low growl. "I want that which no other will have. So yes, I'll take your virgin blood, but in order to grant you a new life, I'll need more than sex magic to do it. It will require life magic. The beauty of your body and the way it's made is that you, Roslyn Blackthorne, are able to create life. That is what you'll sacrifice to me."

Shock curled up in my gut, the sensation a ball of ice. "W-what?"

"You heard me. Give up your body. Your womb. Your chance at producing offspring. And in exchange, I'll make you into the person you wish to be. The woman no one can find."

I pressed my fists to my stomach, unable to process the request. I'd known the price would be steep, but I hadn't counted on this. Children weren't necessarily something I wanted at the moment, but having the possibility of them stripped from me made me mourn for a future I'd never have.

Pan took my chin between his thumb and forefinger, tipping my head back. "What will it be, Roslyn?"

What choice did I have? It was take the deal or risk being found and have to run forever. And the Donoghues showed me exactly how my body could be used against me. Like it or not, my mother's bloodline made me a target. My ability to carry it on was a burden. Did I really want to pass this curse on to a child?

"O-okay."

He clapped his hands together. "Brilliant. Shall we get started then?" And just like that, the demon in front of me stripped down, a sizable shaft hanging thick and heavy between his legs.

My eyes widened as the thing began to harden. "Now?"

"I am a very busy demon, and I haven't got all day, love."

"But I'm not ... shouldn't I be ... "

He let out a soft sigh. "Stand, Roslyn."

I rose on quaking legs, but this time managed to stay up.

He closed the distance between us, running the sharp tips of his claws through my hair and bringing his mouth to my ear. "I'm not completely heartless. I'll make it good for you. There's no enjoyment to be found in taking an unwilling woman. You will know pleasure, Roslyn. I promise." Then he nipped my neck, sending electric tingles shooting down my arms. "And pain. Just as your dark little heart desires. In fact, fair warning, you run the risk of becoming addicted to me."

My heart beat faster, my nipples pebbling at the feel of his breath on my skin. "You shouldn't make promises you can't keep."

"I don't."

His claw trailed over my shirt, cutting it down the center and baring my naked breasts as the fabric fell away. Something firm and strong ran along my spine before settling around my waist and pressing me fully against him. *Tail*, my brain distantly registered. But I was too focused on his face as he leaned close to my ear once more.

"Did you know demons have forked tongues? I can control both halves independently, darling." He shredded my leggings and used his knee to part my thighs. "Lie down in this lovely circle you made. I'm going to make you come so hard you'll forget what you're giving up. All you'll know is me, and you'll never call me by anything but my name again."

His tail trailed along the inside of my thigh and up, up, up.

"Pan," I gasped.

"Now you're getting the idea."

CHAPTER
FIVE
PAN

Oh, this little Blackthorne had no idea what she was in for. My tail continued exploring her soft skin, pulling her closer with every passing second, bringing her into the pathetic excuse for a circle she'd made. It wouldn't contain me. Not by a long shot, but it certainly was poetic. A demon fucking an angel in the trap she'd made for him.

If only she knew which of us was getting the better end of this bargain, she might have considered the terms more carefully, because it certainly wasn't her.

Fisting her hair, I yanked her head back, eliciting a soft moan to slip past those pillowy lips. "I'm going to make you beg now, *mon ange*."

Her eyes widened as I licked a trail up the side of her neck, and I relished the flicker of her pulse, slightly panicked, but I could scent the arousal coming from her cunt just as easily.

"What do you want me to do to this body?"

She shivered, her nipples tight peaks begging to be punished. "Touch me."

Giving her shoulder a little nip, I ran the backs of my knuckles over the side of one breast while my tail brushed over her already slick folds. "I *am* touching you."

"You know what I mean."

"I already told you, *ma petite monstre*, I work in specifics." Her cheeks went crimson as I nibbled my way up her neck and back behind her ear. "Tell me what you want. In detail, if you please."

"My . . . nipples."

"Yes?"

"S-suck on them?"

My cock was a steel pipe, throbbing with the need to sink inside her. That would happen sooner rather than later. But for now, I would prepare her for me. And that meant she'd give her complete submission before I took her.

This time I used the sharp points of my fangs to trace a path from her neck, down over her collarbone to the swell of her full breasts. I cupped their weight in my hands, pushing them up while I worked both halves of my tongue around the turgid peak of one, then the other. If her ragged moan was anything to go by, I was on the right track. Before the night was over, I'd leave her a quivering mess, with my cum coating her.

Fingers continuing their journey over her body, I slipped over the soft tuft of hair hiding her pussy from view. She was already wet, but I needed her soaked before I pierced her with my length.

"Oh God," she whimpered as my index finger circled her opening.

I brought my mouth to her ear and whispered, "Don't cry for him, my dirty little bitch. Cry out for me. I'm the only one who can save you right now."

"P-Pan, please."

"Please, what?"

"Touch me."

"We've been over this . . . "

"Inside. I want to feel you inside me."

I pushed two fingers into her slick heat and had to swallow a groan at how hard she gripped me. "You are so tight. I am going to rip you in half."

She moaned. "Yes."

Fuck. She *was* a dirty little bitch. My cock gave a jerk, the appendage practically screaming at me to stop toying with her and let him go where he belonged. But I had something I needed to do first. One last step to seal my connection with this creature.

I pulled my fingers from her cunt and brought them to my lips, sucking them clean as she watched with fierce hunger burning in her eyes.

"Sweet, like candy. Of course you are. Innocence always is."

"Why did you stop?"

Without answering her, I took her by the wrist, pulling her left arm toward me. Then I skated my finger along the line of blue from her palm to her heart. I wasn't done with her. Not by a long shot.

She gasped as I brought my lips to the underside of her wrist and placed the barest kiss there. Those goosebumps rose on her skin again, and she stepped closer.

"Wha—oh, my," she rasped on a groan as my teeth sank into her flesh.

Heaven. That's what she tasted like. Everything good and perfect that I would never know. And she was right here. Mine for the taking. Her blood turned even sweeter as she climaxed. The arousal singing in her veins danced on my tongue like the finest honey.

She clutched my shoulder with her free hand, clinging to me to remain upright as the orgasm rocked through her. If she was this easy to bring to climax, what would it be like when I was fully sheathed inside her? The promise of those flutters of pleasure clamping down on my shaft had my balls aching.

"I thought you didn't want my blood," she panted.

Saucy little minx. "You offered, and I intend to take everything on offer and then some."

She winced as the bite began to glow, then healed into a demonic rune unique to my name. "What is this? It doesn't even look like a bite mark."

"It's *my* mark. You're mine now."

"I didn't agree to that."

"You did. You said you'd give your blood." I pressed my lips to the faintly raised scar, and she whimpered, her eyes rolling back in her head. "You and I both know the blood of the sun is a hot commodity. Any time I need to collect, I'll call. You won't resist the urge to come to me. Not after I show you what I can do to you."

"And if I don't come to you?"

"I'll take what I need and keep your soul as my reward. I can make it hurt or . . . if you're a good girl, I can make it *hurt.*"

Her eyes widened, and she bit her bottom lip as she rubbed her fingertips across her wrist.

"Now"—I smacked her arse—"present for me."

Her brow furrowed. "Present? Like a dog?"

"No, like my sweet little bitch." Oh, but she liked when I called her that. Already the furrow was smoothed out, and her eyes were glazed with lust. Roslyn Blackthorne absolutely loved being bad. "Hands and knees. Now."

I gripped my cock and stroked slowly as she did what I instructed. A pearl of precum welled at the tip of me, evidence she affected me more than she should. But I wanted her. And I'd have her, over and over again.

Her perfect heart-shaped arse on display, she glanced over her shoulder as I knelt between her legs. "Will it hurt?"

Fuck, her voice was laced with anticipation.

"Yes."

"Good."

Sliding my palms over her arse, I spread her open, need hitting me hard at the prospect of the other tight little hole I could defile. But not yet. We had time for that; that love bite of mine ensured it.

She pushed into my hands, silently asking for me to take her. I bit back a grin. It wasn't quite begging, not by my standards, but it was close. I'd get her there. I needed to hear her say it before I would allow myself to finally slide inside her.

"If you want it, be a good girl and tell me."

"Pan, I want it."

"Once we do this, you're mine. You understand? My good little slut. You'll never be rid of the reminders I leave behind."

She stiffened but then nodded, her shoulders shuddering as my cock brushed her clit. "Do it. I . . . I want it to be you."

Arousal swept through my body, tightening my balls and making my already aching shaft swell further. She'd surprised me. There was something deliciously sordid about this sweet virgin letting a demon defile her. A twisted pleasure unfurled in my mind. *You will have this whenever you want. You can have her. She's yours.*

Somewhere along the way, this had become more than a transaction.

With a ragged groan, I pressed into her tight hole. The pressure was excruciating in the best way possible. Even with her slickness dripping down her thighs, it was a snug fit.

She cried out, but there was more pain than pleasure in the sound.

I didn't like it.

Without stopping to question the realization, I moved my tail between her legs, brushing the tip over her clit.

"Stay still, *mon doudounette*. Breathe, and don't fucking move a muscle."

This wasn't going to be over yet. I would not come like a virgin on his wedding night. I would fuck her silly for hours, *days*. I wasn't some untried youth who didn't know his way around a cunt. I was a bloody demon.

But then she clenched around me and my vision blurred as the threat of orgasm built in the base of my spine.

"I said, stay fucking still."

"I can't. It feels so good . . . what you're doing to me."

"*Putain de merde*." My voice wasn't my own; it was a harsh rasp as I gripped her hips and dug my fingers into the soft curves.

I slid deeper, finding little resistance as I continued to tease her with the tip of my tail. She was trembling beneath me, sweat beading on her skin as her climax built.

"Pan, please. Ruin me. Make me forget everyone but you."

The thin tether of my control snapped as I sank as deep as I could. "Fuuuck, *ma petite monstre*, you squeeze me so good."

She was coming as soon as I brushed against the

entrance to her womb. Her cries were an incoherent mix of pleas and my name.

"That's my good little slut. Come all over my cock like you were born for it."

I pulled out slowly, my own release barely restrained, and when I saw the streak of her blood mixed with the glistening arousal that coated my shaft, I lost myself.

"Hold on to something," I warned a beat before I gripped her hard enough to bruise that pale skin and drove back inside.

The rhythm of my hips was frenzied as I fucked her. There was nothing soft or gentle about it. It was a brutal claiming, and it felt fucking perfect. She was right there with me, pushing back and taking every thrust. She screamed out her pleasure, tears dripping down her cheeks and splashing onto what was left of the circle beneath her.

"Come for me."

"I-I can't."

"You can, and you will."

"Pan—"

I bit her, my tail working frantically between her legs as I continued with my ruthless thrusts.

She was coming again hard and fast, the flood of slick coating me in more heat, more . . . her. And this time, I was there with her, shoving in until I pushed against the end of her, pulsing and filling the womb I claimed as my prize. I rode out my climax as my new toy screamed hers, all the while knowing exactly what I was taking. She would be barren, and I would have her . . . always.

That last part she didn't know about, but she would. Soon.

CHAPTER
SIX
ASHER

"Why is the world moving?" I groaned.

I kept my eyes clenched shut as everything rocked and swayed. Fuck, I was still drunk. I squeezed the bridge of my nose, willing the earth to calm the hell down. A sudden weight shift on my chest had my head snapping up, causing another pained groan to escape.

I found myself nose to beak with a sassy-eyed puffin.

"What are you up to, bird? You trying to take advantage of a guy when he's passed out on a . . . boat?" A quick glance around confirmed that I was, in fact, on a boat. *That explains the rocking, at least.*

The mischievous waterfowl shoved its orange and black beak into my face and tilted its head. Then it hopped forward again, squaring up before squawking, the shrill sound amplifying my already pounding headache.

"Rude. Look, I don't want a fight. You might have little pufflings at home. You look like a good daddy bird. Don't throw it all away."

It squawked again, loudly, and then, to add insult to injury, something wet and warm oozed down my chest.

"Oh, you sonofa—"

The bird flew off.

"Great. Fucking excellent." I staggered to my feet and eyed the watery droppings with a grimace, grumbling to myself, "Scat is a hard limit. You didn't even ask my safe word." I let out a deep, resigned sigh. "You could have at least bought me breakfast first, you selfish asshole."

It was everywhere, all over my hoodie, which meant I'd have to walk around with bird shit on my clothes unless I wanted to end up with a face full of it if I tried to change now. It was that, or jump into the frigid Alaskan sea. No thanks.

"I really need to stop drinking."

The gentle sway of the water had my gut rolling. I was not built for the ocean. I swallowed past the urge to hurl over the side.

How the hell did I even end up here? Last night was a complete blank. I'd been working remotely from one of my safe houses, finalizing Ros—*Nadia's*—paperwork and then . . . oh right, her text messages. In my quest to avoid feeling anything for my sexy as hell houseguest, I'd ventured out to The Tip.

I stumbled off the stupid boat, whose name was *The Codfather*—of fucking course—and fell to my knees on solid ground. I would have been the worst pirate. Captain Pukebeard.

Or Shithoodie, as the case may be.

Asher, my man, what a gloriously charmed life you lead. Really . . . the stuff dreams are made of.

Casting a bleary eye around the dock, I guesstimated it was somewhere close to seven in the morning. Early enough for the sun to be up but not too many people. That was a kindness, at least. Not too many would be around to witness my walk of shame. Just the grizzled old fishermen.

I pulled my hood over my head, trying for some kind of disguise. I was getting sloppy. Too comfortable. Fuck. I probably went to the bar looking like this. Everyone saw me. But the thing about a small town like Aurora Springs was that everyone here was hiding from something. Most of the time, they were too focused on their own issues rather than anyone else's.

That was good for people like me, people like Rosie. Fuck. Rosie was home alone. How long had I been out? Did she have enough food?

I ran a hand over my face. I was not cut out for caring about other people. I had enough trouble taking care of myself. I needed this girl out of my life, stat. She was a complication I could not afford.

My dick disagreed.

He thought she was a complication we should dive right on into, head first. And now I was sporting a hard-on. Just fucking great. I was walking through town, covered in bird shit, hard for a girl who spelled danger for me with a capital D, and I was sure I looked more homeless than usual. What had she done to me? This was after only what, three, four days? Where would I be in a week?

My phone buzzed in my back pocket. Thank fuck I still had it. I wouldn't have been surprised if the thing had ended up in a watery grave after the way I woke up.

I pulled it out and stared down at the screen.

MOIRA THE GOOD(ISH):

They found her. Thank you for your help.

Relief uncoiled something in my stupid chest. I'd been

rooting for them all. Hoping they'd find Sunday alive and unharmed. I should tell Rosie. Let her know her brother's mate was safe.

I opened my text thread with my rebellious little Blackthorne and let out a short laugh, rereading her messages from last night. I suspected someone had found my moonshine.

INTRUDER:

Arte yew alovs?

INTRUDER:

Um verty drink nd lowkey abs to be sack all oven yowl come.

INTRUDER:

Have I mammogram I get quiet noisy when I've beer dry king? Ehat kinds of sects yoyo have in think mouse?

INTRUDER:

Do yew have a sexy dungeon?

INTRUDER:

Maybe I'll play with you there.

I couldn't stop my smile. She *definitely* got into the moonshine. Drunk Rosie was adorable . . . and those last two texts? Fuck.

"Why yes, Rosie, I *do* have a sexy dungeon." I was typing before I registered the action.

ME:

Stay out of the sexy dungeon. I'll be home soon.

I shouldn't have responded to her, but the need to was stronger than the fear of being hurt.

Danger, Asher. DANGER. Stay away. Far, far away. She

might make your dick feel good, but that is all. She'll leave you broken, like they always do. A little voice in the back of my mind piped up. *But she needs your help.*

And that was the fucking crux of the problem, wasn't it? I had to be the hero. I couldn't just throw her to the wolves. Literally, given the town we were in.

My stomach churned, the hangover from hell still going strong. I needed food, maybe the hair of the dog while I was at it. And Rosie? She was probably in the same shape as me.

As I approached the bar I spent too much time at, I let out a sigh. My truck was parked on the curb. Yep. I knew myself all too well.

Way to go, Asher. Establish yourself as the town drunk. Really drive that point home.

A delivery truck was backed into the alley next to The Tip, and the lights were on even this early. That meant one of the Mercers was there, and depending on which twin, it also meant food.

Adjusting my route, I turned down the alley and headed toward the back door, where the delivery driver was wheeling in boxes of something. Likely booze I'd be purchasing later.

I shook my head, disgusted with myself.

One of the Mercers stood behind the bar, rag in hand as he polished the wood. These assholes were handsome. Dark hair, bluer than blue eyes, pouty lips, and scruffy jaws. Not to mention bodies forged from years spent running wild outdoors. If there was a picture beside the word lumbersexual in the dictionary, these two were definitely it. Sexy bastards.

Hmm, maybe I could distract myself from the dark-haired beauty in my house with a dark-haired mountain man instead? Ben wouldn't be up for it, but Remi . . .

"Which one are you?" I asked, taking a stool without waiting for a greeting.

"We're closed, Asher."

"Door was open."

"The back door."

"You like it when I use your back door." His cheeks went pink, and I smirked. "So it *is* you, Remington."

"Remi. No one calls me Remington. You know that."

I shrugged. "I'll call you whatever I want. Especially when you let me—"

"Shut the fuck up, Asher. You look like shit." He eyed the mess down the front of my hoodie.

I grimaced. "I lost a fight with a puffin."

It was a testament to our *whatever-this-was-ship* that he didn't bat an eye. "What are you doing here?"

"I need breakfast. To go."

"I'm not a short-order cook."

"Could have fooled me."

Remi finally set his rag down, leaning forward with both hands pressed on the wooden bar top. "You don't get to come into my bar and talk to me like that. I've ripped men's throats out for less."

I grinned. "You wanna wrestle, big guy?"

He threw his rag in my face, which I gladly used to wipe the bird crap off my hoodie.

"Are you trying to get in my pants or piss me off, Asher? Because I'll tell you what, one of them is working."

"Can't it be both? I like you angry."

He clenched his jaw and took a deep breath. "I think you're actually hard for Ben, not me. You keep trying to turn me into the grumpy one."

"I do like them strong and silent." Something like jealousy swept across his face. I softened my voice. "Come over here, and I'll show you exactly who I'm hard for, Remi."

Heat flared in his eyes, but he looked away, swallowing thickly, shutting me down exactly as I deserved. I was such a fucking asshole. I shouldn't poke at him, especially when I was in no shape to deliver. He and I were occasional fuck buddies. That was all. We'd been playing this game ever since I arrived here. Skirting the line between friendly flirting and hate sex. Releasing tension when we needed to. Apparently, he didn't need to right now. So much for my distraction.

Remi sighed. "I can make you a breakfast sandwich, but then you have to go, okay? Ben will shit a brick if he sees you here before we open."

He walked around the bar and into the kitchen, still visible through the pass as he began cooking.

"Two," I called out.

"God, you just don't know when to fucking stop." He shook his head but kept right on working.

"It's not for me. I have . . . a guest."

"Excuse me? The hermit has a houseguest?"

Ignoring that dig, I went for it. "Actually, I need you to do me a favor."

"Making you breakfast isn't enough? This isn't fucking Burger King. You don't get to have it your way."

I laughed. "This favor benefits you and me both."

"Now that I find difficult to believe. When are you ever interested in what benefits me?"

"I can name plenty of times I—"

"*Asher.*" Even tinged with exasperation, I loved how my name sounded coming from his mouth. He and Ben were the only ones in town to ever use it. Well, until Hurricane *Nadia* blew in.

"Fine. Look, you still need a new bartender, right?"

Coming around to me with two breakfast sandwiches wrapped in waxed paper, he frowned as he placed them in front of me. His eyes narrowed in that way he had when something smelled rotten.

"Yes. Why? What are you up to?"

"She's here to stay. My guest. I need to get her out of my life before I lose my mind."

"That sounds more like the Asher I know and somewhat tolerate."

I rolled my eyes. "Can she have the job? Is the apartment upstairs still empty? That could be part of her pay."

"Does she know her way around a bar?"

"Sure." I mentally shrugged. She was a spoiled princess. I was sure she knew how to pour a cocktail for Daddy and his friends. A . . . blood cocktail.

"What's her name?"

"Ro-Nadia. Nadia Black."

Remi caught my slip and raised a brow. "One of your runaways?"

"Something like that."

"She gonna get us into trouble?"

"No?"

"Is that a question?"

"Look, once you hire her, she's your problem. I'm just covering her tracks. My services don't extend beyond papers. I'm not fucking witness protection."

"So you want me to be her bodyguard."

I smirked. "You look the part. Just . . . get her out of my hair, will ya?"

"Fine. Bring her by tonight, and we'll get her all set up."

Snagging the sandwiches, I got up from my chair and

offered him a cocky wink. "Thanks, lumberjack. See you later."

"Can't wait." The sarcasm would have hurt if I hadn't earned it. Or if I had a heart.

I blew him a kiss, but my smile faded as I walked out the door. I'd taken care of my unwanted houseguest and fulfilled my obligation to her, so why didn't I feel better, or at least relieved?

But more importantly, why was I jealous of Remi Mercer?

CHAPTER
SEVEN
ROSIE

BLACK-HATTED KNIGHT:

> Stay out of the sexy dungeon. I'll be home soon.

"What?" My pounding head throbbed even harder as I tried to make sense of Asher's message. But then I scrolled through my previous string of texts to him. Drunken incoherent ramblings. "Mammogram? Sexy dungeon? Oh dear God, I'm never drinking again."

I'd been awake for the last hour, much to my chagrin. I never could sleep off a hangover. But it was *where* I'd woken that had sent me into a panicked frenzy. Asher's bed.

I closed my eyes against the flash of memory from last night. Pan placing me on the mattress, parting my thighs, tasting me. He was right. That forked tongue had been very useful. I'd had no idea. The demon might have ruined me for regular men. How could they compete with *that*?

The bundle of freshly washed sheets I'd been clutching slipped from my arms, and I eyed them with a wince. Bending over was hard. Muscles I didn't even know I had were sore; my inner thighs were bruised from his broad shoulders and strong hips. I'd thought he'd leave after the first time, but no. He'd taken me over and over, making me scream his name until my voice was nothing more than a ragged thing.

"Pull yourself together, Roslyn. You're not doing yourself any favors by standing here like a lovesick fool. He was using you and it felt good. Full stop."

I was having trouble summoning any regret at the loss of my virginity. It wasn't like I'd been saving it for any special reason. I just hadn't ever gotten a chance to part with it. And then after what Gavin had awoken in me . . . it seemed more a hindrance than anything. And now . . . after a night spent with a demon who more than knew his way around a female's body, I think I might be addicted. Even sore, bruised, and with a steel spike rammed through my head, I could feel the slick gathering between my legs. I wanted more.

The front door opened with a whir of automatic locks, and I spun around, eyes slowly catching up with my motion. I needed some forking water if I was going to survive my first official morning after. No walk of shame for this girl. I was trapped at the scene of the crime.

At least the sheets were clean.

And my summoning circle.

Dear God, what the hell had I been thinking?

"You look . . . hungover," Asher grunted.

He had something white smeared across his jumper. "So do you."

"What the hell happened to your hair?"

I touched the uneven mess at the back of my head. Yesterday it had hung long and straight down to the base of my spine. Now it . . . didn't. "You don't like it?"

"Don't you know the first rule of makeovers? No cutting your own hair."

"At least I didn't go for a fringe."

"Small mercies."

We stood there awkwardly, eyeing each other.

He raised a brown bag. "I brought you breakfast." And then he held up a file folder. "And your documents."

My stomach growled and simultaneously rolled. "I'm not sure eating is a good idea."

The slight smirk that twitched up one side of his lips had my thighs clenching. "Eating is exactly what you need after searching for my sexy dungeon with a bottle of moonshine as your companion."

"Is that what I drank? I thought your vodka tasted a little dodgy."

"Well, technically it *is* vodka. The Russians distill it, and then I add my own special ingredient."

"Death?"

He snickered. "Something like that."

"I'm sorry to be the bearer of bad news, but I seem to have polished off your supply."

My heart jumped into my throat as Asher stepped closer to me, reaching one hand out as though he was about to gently touch my cheek. Did I want him to touch my cheek? Yes.

Squinting, he moved in further, and I tipped my chin up

without conscious thought. But instead of kissing me like my stupid heart assumed, he rubbed at my cheek.

"You're . . . molting." He frowned as he pulled something off my face.

Jesus, Rosie. You lose your virginity and automatically start assuming every bloke is trying to get a leg over.

"You might also be out of liquid latex."

He pulled back, eyeing me more carefully. Then he grinned and plucked off a few wayward strands of red beard. "Why didn't you use the spirit gum?"

"The what now?"

"Amateur."

"Well, what was I meant to be doing for three whole days while you were off gallivanting and doing God knows what? I used the resources I had at hand."

Backing away, he leaned against the wall and continued smirking. "And how did that work out for you?"

"Swimmingly."

"It sure looks that way." The sarcasm dripped from every word before he lifted the bag of food. "I'm gonna heat these up and make some coffee. Then we need to get you . . . handled. You can't go anywhere looking like that."

I bristled at the words, even though I knew he was right. I just didn't appreciate hearing how shit I looked. Not when he somehow managed to make dirty sweats look sexy.

Bastard.

Thirty minutes later, we'd eaten our breakfast—delicious and, as he'd said, exactly what I needed—and now I was sat in the bathroom as Asher tried to make something salvageable of the disastrous haircut I'd given myself. In the moment, I thought it looked quite fetching, but that moment was full of alcohol-soaked lies.

"What the hell did you do in here?" he asked, waving a hand at the spiderweb of cracked glass on one side of the mirror.

"Gave myself a makeover."

"Uh-huh. Looks like a bomb went off."

"Sorry?"

He shook his head and began rooting around in his cupboard, likely searching for supplies for whatever he had planned.

"So, who is Nadia Black?"

"Uh, me?"

"No, I mean, what type of woman is she? This is your chance to reinvent yourself. To become who you've always wanted to be. Is Nadia a sexy siren? A smoldering temptress? A librarian who rescues puppies but is secretly DTF?"

"What the hell do you know about smoldering temptresses? And what is DT—oooh."

He waggled his eyebrows. "Down to fu—"

"I've got it. Say no more."

"Okay, so we're going with the *virginal* librarian who rescues puppies."

"No."

Not after last night. My cheeks heated, and I couldn't hold his gaze in the mirror.

"I don't want to be any of those." The thought of giving up the pieces of me, the things that made me *Rosie,* didn't sit right. I wasn't sure how to express exactly what those things were, but I *did* know I didn't want to spend the rest of my life playacting as a stranger. I wanted to become the woman I was meant to be. "I just want to be my true self."

"And who is she?"

"I don't know. I'm still getting to know her."

"Are you asking me to surprise you? Do you trust me that much?"

"I came to you for help, didn't I?"

Instead of laughing at me, as I'd half expected, he turned serious. "All right, sweetheart, buckle up and prepare to be amazed. The master is going to work."

I looked on as he started mixing up product and pulling out a velvet roll containing shears and other hairstyling tools. "Do you moonlight as a hairdresser or something?"

"I've been on the run for the better half of a decade. Who do you think does all my haircuts?"

"A bowl and your mum?"

He yanked on a long chunk of my hair, exasperation tinging his voice. "Cute."

I bristled at the word. I'd been called cute, precious, a porcelain doll my whole life. Fragile. Breakable. Ornamental. Not anymore. "That's what they all say. I don't want to be cute anymore, Asher. Make me into someone you'd fantasize about."

Those blue irises he rarely let me stare into locked on mine, and for a moment, I fell into them and the promise of what he could do to me if I let him. His jaw tightened, a muscle ticking there just under the surface as he took in a sharp breath. "Easy." He placed both palms on my shoulders. "Say goodbye to Roslyn."

Instead of managing the flippant wave I'd been aiming for, my lower lip trembled. I wasn't ready to leave her behind, but I knew I had to. A tear escaped, slipping down my cheek, and before I could wipe it away, Asher caught it, stroking my face gently.

"Don't worry, you'll always be her."

"Do you think sometimes I could be her for a little while, just with you?"

His expression went soft with understanding, but his voice was firm. "No. It's not safe for either of us. From this point on, you have to be Nadia. Even in here." He tapped my temple.

"Right. Of course." I shook my head, feeling stupid. "Forget I asked."

Several hours later, I barely recognized the woman in the mirror. My once amber eyes were now dark brown, thanks to the contact lenses Asher had taught me to put in. But the haircut made all the difference.

I'd never done much with my hair, just let it grow and wear it down. It always suited me, but the style was undeniably girlish. There was nothing girlish about the woman in the mirror. Her bob was edgy, brushing her nape in the back, and hanging in perfect points just above her sternum, with a feathery fringe that made her eyes appear huge. Asher had also dyed the ends, so they were now a deep purple. Just a hint of color, but it was a statement nonetheless. This was a confident woman. Not a wilting flower.

She was the woman Asher had helped bring to life.

Nadia Black.

I had to say it in my mind over and over.

Turning around, I found Asher staring at me, just as entranced as I'd been.

"Do you like her?" I asked.

He had to swallow twice before he could answer. "Yeah, she's fucking hot."

Blame it on the hairstyle, or the newfound confidence brimming in my veins, but I pushed up onto my tiptoes so I could look him in the eye. "Thank you, Asher. For everything."

And then, without another thought, in a gesture of pure instinctive gratitude, I pressed my lips against his.

CHAPTER
EIGHT

ASHER

She was kissing me. Why the fuck was she kissing me? And why the fuck did I want to keep going? Her lips were plush, warm pillows against mine. Everything about her was soft, sweet, perfection.

My hands settled on her hips as I breathed her in, not kissing her back, but not *not* kissing her either. I just stood there, taking it in. Memorizing her shape, the fit of her against me, the way she smelled, the way she tasted. And when she broke the kiss, wrapping me in an embrace, I wanted more. So much fucking more, but I held myself still. Forced myself not to act on the impulse to pick her up and sit her on the counter, shove my hips between her legs, and rock into her like she was the only place I'd ever call home again.

With a controlled gentleness, I pushed her away. "You're welcome," I murmured, working to keep my voice calm and unaffected even though internally I was a wild storm of conflicted emotions.

"Make me into someone you'd fantasize about."

If she only knew. I'd been dreaming about her ever since

I found her picture. No makeover required. But now that I knew what her lips felt like against mine? I internally groaned. I was absolutely fucked.

I'd called it, known from the second I recognized those amber eyes gazing back at me from my doorstep that she'd bring me nothing but danger and heartache. Here was the proof.

I could *not* get attached. I didn't do relationships. I barely did friendships. The Mercers were as close as I got, and that was risky enough. I had to be ready to run at a moment's notice. No roots. No entanglements. Nothing permanent.

The last thing I should do was fall for her. Nadia Black was off-limits if I wanted either of us to stay safe.

"Pack your shit. We're going out."

Her eyes went wide, confusion swirling in them. "What do you mean? I thought I couldn't leave."

"Fuck. Your scent. I forgot about that." How could I have been so stupid? Oh, right, the pretty girl had sent the rest of my careful attention to detail scattering with one drunk text about a sexy dungeon. "I need to see a shaman about a spell for that."

The thought of talking to any kind of witch made my skin crawl, but there was no way around this. Nothing else would mask her Blackthorne pheromones.

"Oh, that. I took care of it."

She said it breezily, but I caught the sudden tensing of her body, the frenetic energy she was trying to hide.

"What did you do?"

"Just a little something I learned from my Aunt Callie."

"Care to elaborate?"

"Can't. Family secrets and all that."

"Uh-huh."

And there was the other reason I had to get rid of her. She was clearly keeping secrets. Not to mention the fact that she was technically fucking married. Jesus, I needed to get her out of here and pass her off to the Mercers. Then she could be their problem, and I could go back to my hermit ways. Or maybe I'd find a different pretty girl at The Tip tonight and take her back to one of my safe houses to work off my tension first. Maybe I could get her to let me call her Rosie while I railed her.

Bad idea.

"Whatever. You say it's fine, then I guess I have to trust you. It's your ass on the line, not mine. Get your stuff together. We're leaving in ten." I huffed and left the bathroom, dragging my hand through my hair and forcing myself not to look back at her.

She stared after me, and I could still picture the hurt clouding in her eyes. The kiss had been as innocent as they came, and here I was, running away like she'd just told me she loved me. No wonder she was confused. I was overreacting—big time. But it was self-preservation, because if I stayed in there with her for one more second, I was going to say fuck it all and give in to the urge to take her. To keep her.

She. Is. Not. For. You.

Ten minutes later on the nose, she stood at the front door with the small bag she'd had when she arrived. Without a word, I escorted her to my truck, holding open her door and helping her in. Once she was settled, I moved around to my side and jumped in, barely buckling my seat belt before throwing my truck in reverse.

"Am I allowed to know where we're going?"

"The Tipsy Moose."

"I beg your pardon?"

"It's a bar. You work there now."

She went a little green. "Asher, I never want to drink again."

"So don't. You'll be serving the drinks. No one said you have to drink them."

"Okay, let me clarify. I never want to smell alcohol again."

"That'll pass."

"So you just went out and got me a job?"

"And a room. There's an apartment above the bar. You'll stay there from now on."

"By myself?"

"You'll be safe. I took care of security personally." The edge of panic in her voice made me thankful I'd planned so meticulously for her care. She wasn't used to being alone. She probably never had been until I'd abandoned her for the last three days. Or, I guess, her trek across Alaska was probably the first time. That only made me feel marginally better about abandoning her again now.

"Will you . . . can I call you?"

"Text me. I'll check in. Don't worry, I'm never far. And the Mercers will keep their eyes on you."

"The Mercers?"

"They own the bar. Good guys. Well, as good as you'll find up here. Better than me, certainly."

"That's not much of an endorsement."

I shrugged. "It's them or the biker gang. Take your pick."

"If you're sure."

"I'm sure. Trust me, you're safer with them. I'm . . . a liability."

I glanced down at the stars inked into my hand, the mark left on me by that witch. Something wasn't right with me inside. I could feel it there, taking root. I couldn't take focus away from Nadia's safety for my own issues. This was the right thing to do.

The *only* thing to do.

For once I was thinking straight, being responsible, not just for my own shit, but for someone else's as well.

I'd done my part. Gotten her new identity established. The rest was up to her. She was the one who faked her death. Now she needed to live with the consequences.

The rest of the drive to town was filled with tense silence. She tried a few more times to start a conversation but eventually gave up when I wouldn't give her more than one-word answers. Asshole Asher was in full effect. Better she get used to him. This is how it had to be between us.

I couldn't have her getting any ideas about a meaningful or long-term friendship between us. She might accidentally out me at the bar, and then my one refuge in this godforsaken town would be lost. Then I really would have to move. Again.

"Here you are. Remi will let you in. He knows you're coming."

Fuck me, I was such a dick. I didn't even let myself get out and walk her to the door. Could I have been worse? I guess. I could have kept driving and told her to jump out of the moving vehicle. That would have been an even bigger dick move.

She hesitated with her hand on the door handle. "Uh, thanks again. For everything."

"Don't mention it. Seriously."

She bit her lip, nodding. "Goodbye, I guess."

"See ya."

Fuck, I hated myself. Especially for causing that pinched, worried expression on her face. She almost reminded me of a little kid going off on their first day of school. Part of me wanted to hug her tight and promise to beat up anyone who looked at her funny. The other part was ready to shove her out the door and never look back.

As soon as she was on the sidewalk, I slammed on the gas, telling myself I was watching in the rearview to make sure she went inside, knowing it was a lie even as I did. I just wasn't ready to leave her. I needed one last glimpse of her, like an addict needed that final deadly fix. If I could just stop thinking about her, I'd be fine.

And after I turned the corner and lost sight of her, my phone buzzed, a text from her popping up on the screen.

INTRUDER:

Thank you for bringing me back to life.

Well, fuck.

CHAPTER
NINE

BEN

Fucking Remi. The sheer number of boxes my brother left for me to unpack said he'd done the bare minimum this morning when the delivery guy arrived. Now I got to take care of customers *and* put all this shit away.

I inwardly seethed as I pulled the liquor bottles from their boxes and back-filled the shelves. We couldn't keep operating like this. Perpetually behind. Short-staffed. Running ourselves ragged.

The Tipsy Moose was hardly a hot spot, but it was the only bar in town, which meant we were always busy. Too bad the people of Aurora Springs were more interested in being patrons than employees. It was a good thing tourism wasn't popular here. We weren't a stop on any cruise line's itinerary—thank fuck—and we sure as shit didn't plan on advertising the town's charms.

I grunted as I lifted two cases of tequila and lugged them toward the store room. This should have been done already. I had plenty of other things to do, and Darla was late. As usual.

Mondays. No one likes Monday for a reason.

After depositing the boxes, I dusted off my hands and made my way back to the bar, daylight stealing inside as the front door opened.

"Y-you're late," I grumbled at my waitress.

"I'm sorry. I didn't know what time I was supposed to show up."

I stopped dead in my tracks at the unexpected British accent. Who the fuck was this? She sure as hell wasn't Darla. I shifted, giving the woman my full attention, and it felt a bit as though the wind had been knocked out of me as my gaze roamed over her. She was tiny, probably just a hair over five feet tall, with these enormous eyes I wanted to inspect closer and a sweet kissable mouth—kissable? What the fuck?

I blinked a few times to push aside thoughts of kissing her or anything else when she turned around, clearly trying to gauge where she should go from here. I nearly groaned when I glimpsed a full, round ass encased in tight denim.

She was definitely new in town. I would have remembered her. This woman might be hotter than anyone I'd seen in a long time, but she didn't belong here. She was an outsider. Aurora Springs wasn't a place for outsiders. They were going to chew her up and spit her out.

"W-who t-t-the f-f-fuck are y-you?"

Smooth, Bentley. Real smooth. Trip over your words like this is the first goddamned time you've spoken English.

"A-Asher sent me? H-he s-said you were expecting me?"

Is she making fun of me? I bristled instantly at her stammer but immediately dismissed the assumption as I caught a whiff of her nerves. She wasn't being an asshole. She was just nervous. And . . . fae?

"Sit," I told her.

She did, her bag dropping to the floor next to the stool she chose.

"Name?"

"Ro-Nadia. My name is Nadia Black. Asher told me you have a job for me. And a flat."

Fuck. That fucking nuisance of a hacker. If he thought just because he had something on us, he could push people into our lives . . .

I grumbled, reaching under the bar for an employment application, then thinking better of it. If she was getting help from Asher, she didn't want anyone to know where she was. This would be best handled under the table. Instead, I snagged my phone.

"Number?"

Her eyes went wide, but she figured it out quick enough. She pulled out her own phone, swiped the screen a few times, then rattled off her digits.

I quickly entered them into my phone and then messaged her. "S-save that."

She opened her mouth like she was going to ask a question, then thought better of it.

"W-worked i-in a b-bar b-before?"

Guilt swept across her face.

"D-don't l-lie."

"No," she whispered, biting her bottom lip.

This was just like my asshole brother. Hire some hot piece of ass without even checking to make sure she knows what the fuck she's doing. Sure she's gorgeous, but can she be of help? Clearly not. Now I'll have to spend days training her. She probably doesn't even know how to pour a beer.

I sighed and gestured for her to come around the bar. "P-pay at-tention."

I hated how anxious she made me, how tight my

throat was, that my tongue wouldn't let me get my words out. My stammer hadn't been this bad in a long time. Granted, I hadn't met anyone new in a long time either.

Usually I got around it by rarely saying much of anything at all. A few well-aimed glares tended to get my point across just fine. Was it a healthy coping mechanism? No. But it was better than the alternative—the sneers, or worse, looks of pity.

Character building, my brother said.

More like it taught me to use my fists at an early age. Kids loved to pick on the weak, so I made damn sure they knew Bentley Mercer was far from fucking weak.

I had to be strong because we didn't have anyone else to protect us. Our Alpha died. We had no pack. It was the Mercer twins against the world. I might struggle to speak, but I didn't have any problem laying someone out if they crossed us. Remi did all the talking, then I cleaned up his messes.

Like this one, standing next to me, smelling like citrus and sugar cookies and looking like a fallen angel. *Why is my mouth watering?* Jesus, I needed to get laid. It had been months. *Fuck, months?* I did a little mental math, and yes, six months, to be exact, since Remi and I shared a night with Darla.

"What should I do?"

Her question pulled me from my thoughts before I did something stupid, like try to taste her. Crossing lines with employees had proven to be a stupid choice.

I snagged a pint glass and pulled a beer, tilting the glass just right to avoid too much head on the top. I set the drink on the bar, then moved aside to watch her try.

"Like this?" She followed suit, pulling on the tap but not

tilting the pint enough, so I reached out and helped her adjust the angle.

Touching her skin was a bad idea. My arm broke out in goosebumps from the contact, and I had to force myself not to jerk away. My dick had his own reaction to her. He did *not* want to separate from her. Not at all.

The pint glass overflowed, and I smacked the tap to cut off the flow.

"C-close enough." I sighed before taking the beer and downing it in four long swallows. "Y-you can s-s-start tonight."

Her eyes lit up. "Thank you. Truly." Then she glanced around again. "Where should I put my things?"

I pointed at the ceiling, and the confusion on her face had me fighting a sigh. Stalking around the bar, I grabbed her bag and waved for her to follow me. When we reached the staircase, I let her go first. *Wrong move, Mercer.* Now her juicy ass was right in my face. My wolf was raring to take a bite. He wanted me to let him out to play so she could run and he could play chase.

Pulling my keys from my front pocket, I shouldered past her as we reached the door to the upstairs apartment. I needed to stop looking at her like she was my favorite dessert. She was one of Asher's lost causes. She needed protecting, not a sex-starved werewolf panting after her.

I dropped the bag at the threshold and gritted my teeth against the urge to follow her inside.

Before she could say another word, I headed downstairs, her scent permeating everything inside the bar, the knowledge she was here leaving me rock hard and tense. The thought of her upstairs, alone and probably wondering what the hell she'd gotten herself into, had something like possessive instinct gnawing at me.

Without stopping to think, I pulled out my phone and sent her a text.

ME:

Your shift starts at 7.

ME:

If you want to eat, be down here by 6. Dante will be in the kitchen. He'll take care of you before it gets busy.

ME:

Let me know if you need anything.

ME:

Actually, make a list. We'll take you grocery shopping tomorrow.

OFF-LIMITS:

Thanks.

OFF-LIMITS:

And thank you for taking care of me. I'm a quick study. I promise I'll pay attention to whatever you teach me. I'll do it exactly like you want.

Exactly like I want.

Fuck me. The images *that* brought to mind.

I rested my elbows on the bar and dropped my head in my hands, groaning.

It was going to be a long fucking night.

TEN

I could already hear my twin's annoyed grunts as I barrelled through the bar's back door.

"I'm late, I know."

"What else is n-n-new?" He huffed under his breath, frustration seeping from him.

Fuck, he was upset about something. Ben rarely ever struggled with his words around me unless he was worked up.

"What's wrong?" I asked, stopping my mad dash to the office. *Damn, it smelled good in here. Did Ben bake cookies?*

"N-N-Nadia."

"Who?"

His brows pulled together as he focused hard on a spot he was polishing on the bar. Breathing long and slow, he worked to calm himself, searching for his words. I knew this process well.

"The w-woman you hired."

"I didn't hire a . . . oooh. Yeah, I meant to tell you about that. Asher called in a favor. Shit, I forgot he was bringing her by this afternoon. Is she here?"

"Upstairs."

"I take it she doesn't have any experience after all?"

"W-what gave it away?"

"My porcupine of a brother. You're always prickly when it comes to training the staff. Or, you know, dealing with people in general. You really are a natural barkeep. So warm and loving."

He threw his dirty rag at me. "Fuck you."

"There he is. Proving my point. Do your spines grow back when you hurl them at people? You wouldn't want to run out."

"Watch it. I-it'll be a b-bottle next."

I laughed. "Consider me warned. I take it I'm on babysitting detail tonight?"

"She's your mess. Y-you should be."

"What's she like?"

Ben's face twisted. "Pretty."

I did a double take. "Excuse me? Did Bentley Mercer just call a girl *pretty*?"

"Wait." He narrowed his eyes. "You hired her without ever meeting her?"

The words were there this time, just the barest hint of a stammer threatening. He was coming back to himself a little bit at a time. Good. I didn't need to deal with him being pissed at me all night.

I shrugged. "We needed a bartender. Asher needed to get her out of his hair. She needed a job and a place to stay. Win-win-win. I do love a three-way."

"No."

"No?"

"Hands off."

"You calling dibs?"

"No more employees. We a-agreed."

"*You* agreed. I just didn't have the energy to fight you on it."

"No, Remington."

"Remington? Wow, you must really mean it to go for the whole mouthful."

"Asshole."

"I know you are, but what am I?"

"Child."

"Listen, what's the point of being the boss if we can't reap the benefits? Just because you're a grumpy motherfucker who's allergic to fun doesn't mean I have to be. And if she's hot enough to make you look twice, I'm definitely up for a little fun." I waggled my eyebrows. "Speaking of fun, did you make cookies or something? It smells like—"

"It's her."

That stopped me. "What?"

"Sh-sh-she smells so fucking g-good."

Oh, fuck. She was off-limits *and* smelled like that when she wasn't even in the room? This might've been a bad idea. But I couldn't tell Ben that. There was no way I'd admit to making a mistake. He'd never let me live it down.

"Christ, we're going to have to beat the regulars off with a hose when they get a whiff of her."

Ben groaned. "J-just what I f-fucking need."

"Maybe we can capitalize on it and make some hot new merch. We could get some masks made up with our logo. *Just the tip* right over the mouth. It's like an advertising double entendre. It's that or find some nose plugs. Or just learn to live with it, I guess. It's way nicer than having to smell your BO all day."

"Are you s-sure that's not your own p-pits you're smelling?" He smirked, just a ghost of one, but it was there.

"Ah hell, I think I just spotted a dimple. Bentley Mercer, you charmer."

"I hate you."

"Love you too, big bro."

"Best two minutes of my l-life."

"Rude. You would have made a terrible only child."

"G-go check on her? Oh, and g-give her this." He tossed me one of our shirts. "S-she didn't have much with her."

My stomach did a stupid little flip-flop thing I didn't like. Why the fuck would some lost little bird make me nervous?

Because she smells like everything you love the most, and your mouth is watering already, dumbass.

Dragging a hand through my hair, I pretended I wasn't preening—I totally was. Then I squared my shoulders, took a deep breath, held it, and marched up the stairs like a grown-ass man should be able to do.

I took the stairs two at a time, trying to ignore the way my heart hammered in my chest. I went to open the door out of habit but caught myself and knocked instead.

"Be right there," a sweet and feminine voice called.

Fuck she has an accent? No way was I keeping my hands to myself. Off-limits, schmoff-limits. If this chick gave me the green light, I was going for it. Accents were my wolf-nip.

She pulled open the door, and my stupid heart skipped a beat.

Pretty? No, this woman was fucking stunning. She had this cute nose I wanted to boop just so I could make her smile. And a sexy little beauty mark I wanted to lick. And . . . motherfucking shitballs, this was going to be an epic failure if I had to keep my word.

She smiled quizzically. "Did you need something? You could've simply texted."

I held up the shirt. "I, uh, brought you a uniform."

"There's a uniform?"

"Yeah, there's a uniform, baby girl. And I'm sure you're gonna look perfect wearing it."

She unfolded the black cotton, her nose scrunching adorably. "Just the tip?"

"The Tipsy Moose. The townies call it The Tip for short. Just the tip? Get it?"

"I, um . . . it's lovely."

Heat crept into my cheeks. Why the hell was I embarrassed? That was a world-class pun. "Damn right it is. I designed that logo myself. See, the antlers are the words."

"Very clever."

Now I was annoyed. "You clearly don't appreciate my marketing genius. I bet you like to steal little kids' balloons for fun too."

She batted those long as fuck eyelashes at me. "Oh, it's one of my very favorite pastimes. I like to pop them with my teeth too."

Saucy. I liked it. "Do you enjoy biting things?"

"When the need arises."

"Me too." I leaned on the doorframe with one arm and hit her with my best smolder. "Does it *arise* often for you too?"

She blushed and cleared her throat. "I'm glad to see you're in a better mood."

"What?"

But then it hit me. It happened too frequently not to.

She thought I was Ben. She didn't know we were twins.

Oh . . . this was going to be fun.

"It's been a weird day. This asshole Asher—you might have heard of him—wandered into my bar at the butt-crack of dawn, covered in bird shit, and demanded I make him breakfast and give some new friend of his a job. And then I had to do inventory and lost track of time, and well, you know the rest."

"You were the one who made the sandwich. It was really quite good. Better than your design skills." Her smirk told me she was teasing.

Man, did I like this little firecracker of a woman. She was going to keep us on our toes. Ben was in for it. Fuck, so was I. It was a good thing we liked sharing.

"Would you like to come in? I don't have anything to offer you, but it seems rude to leave you standing in my stairwell like a lost puppy."

My wolf gave a little snarl at the comparison. We were so *not* a puppy, but if she wanted to rub my belly, I'd let her call me her good boy.

"Oh, so it's yours now?"

"I suppose we share custody."

"Do you like to share, Nadia?"

She flicked her gaze from me, her cheeks turning pink and that sweet scent growing stronger. Yes. She did.

I stepped over the threshold, though stalked might have been a better word. Instinct was winning over sense the closer I got to her. I was usually better at controlling myself than this. It wasn't like I was hard up, but the way my wolf was acting, inching close to the surface, sucking in deep lungfuls of her scent, he was just as drawn to the lovely Nadia as I was.

I shut the door behind me, forcing her to take a step back.

"What are you?" I growled, all seduction, no threat.

"What?"

"You smell . . . other."

"Oh, I'm fae. Half-fae," she babbled. "No magic to call my own and all that."

That made sense. She didn't smell like a full-blooded fae. I'd met a few of those prissy fucks. They thought they were so high and mighty with their proper manners and accents—well, the accents I liked.

"What's the other half?"

She swallowed. "Human."

"We won't hold it against you. Though we'll probably tease you about being prey. Don't be surprised if we try to chase you."

"We?"

"The other shifters in town. We love a hunt."

"What if I don't want to be hunted?"

"Metaphorically, baby girl. Besides, no one else will get a chance. I'd get to you first."

The way her eyelids went half-mast and she leaned a little closer had my cock coming to life. I mean, more than it already was. I'd been sporting a semi since I caught her scent earlier.

Her phone chimed, and she glanced at it with a surprised frown. "How are you texting me when you're standing right in front of me?"

Jig's up. That didn't last nearly as long as I'd hoped it would. Ben and I could have had so much fun teasing her.

"What's your stance on identical twins?"

"There are *two* of you?" The way she said it told me she was appreciative rather than frustrated with the idea.

"Allow me to introduce myself." I took her hand,

dipping down to brush a kiss on the backs of her fingers. "I'm Remington Mercer. You can call me Remi. And the grumpy asshole you met earlier is my brother Ben—Bentley. Don't worry, he's mostly bark. Just a little bite."

"And you?"

"Oh, baby girl, I'm all bite."

CHAPTER
ELEVEN
ROSIE

I stared at my hand resting on the back of the door as Remi stomped down the stairs. The place where his lips had touched my skin tingled even now. It promised wicked things in the quiet of the night. Just like I'd gotten from Pan. Lifting my palm from the door, I rotated my wrist and stared down at the five-pointed star the demon had left behind. I let my fingertips graze over the raised skin, shivering and clenching my legs at the pulse of arousal the slight touch caused.

That couldn't be a normal reaction. It was too intense, too primal, and the flood of need that rushed between my thighs too obvious. I prodded the mark again, and a moan fell from my lips as the answering throb hit me. Oh, no. No. No. No. I couldn't possibly survive a night working at the bar without running the risk of touching this forking mark. What if Remi brushed across it? What if *Ben* did? Would I orgasm right there in front of all the patrons? Only two creatures had seen me in the throws of my pinnacle before. One a demon, the other . . .

An image sparked to life in my brain, a memory of Gavin, of his words in my ear.

"Have you never touched yourself, petal?"

"No. Not like this. It's never felt like this when I—"

"When you come. Say it."

His fingers curled upward, sending me hurtling toward release. *"When I c–come."*

"Oh, yes. Even if my fingers weren't buried inside you, I could smell how wet you are for me. Come for me, wife. Show me just how tight this cunt can grip me. Show me how you'll milk my cock."

My heart gave a pathetic twist in my ribcage. Just like it did every time my thoughts returned to Gavin. I did my best not to think of my abandoned husband, but it was harder than I'd hoped. Especially when I was in . . . *need* like this. He was the one to wake this part of me. He was the one who should have been my first everything. The one to take this writhing desire and release me from its grasp.

I huffed out a bemused laugh. Married for over a month and only a single kiss on the lips to my name. And not even from my husband . . . or my demon lover.

Did that make me a slut? Or the opposite of a slut?

Pan's words rushed through my mind. *"Once we do this, you're mine. You understand? My good little slut. You'll never be rid of the reminders I leave behind."*

Looks like he was right. I brushed my thumb over his mark once more for good measure and had to brace myself against the wall as my eyes rolled back in my head and a vision of what he'd done to me came roaring back.

"What do you want me to do to this body?"

"Touch me."

His teeth grazed my shoulder as his tail did unspeakable things. *"I am touching you."*

"You know what I mean."

"I already told you, ma petite monstre, *I work in specifics. Tell me what you want. In detail, if you please."*

Taking a shaky breath, I let my fingers drift across my lower belly to toy with the waistband of my jeans. Did I have time to take care of myself before my first shift? Perhaps if I released this tension I wouldn't be so worked up when I went downstairs.

Memories assaulted me. Some real, some mere wishes.

The ghost of Asher's lips against mine and the scrape of his nails over my scalp. The press of Ben's chest against my back as he corrected my pour. Remi's heat as he breathed over my knuckles. Gavin's scent. Pan's wicked tongue.

My hand drifted lower.

A sharp vibration in my back pocket had me jerking upright.

I let out a shaky breath and pulled my phone out.

MR. MERCER:

Are you coming?

My eyes went wide and my gaze darted around. *Are there cameras in here or something? Forking Asher.* He said he took care of the security. I wouldn't put it past him, slipping a few in my room so he could spy on me.

MR. MERCER:

Last call for dinner before your shift.

Relief hit me sharp and strong. He wasn't watching me stand here as I panted for five different men at once. The grumpy, sexy git was bossing me around.

> **ME:**
> I'll be down in a tick. Just changing into my uniform, boss. *smiley face emoji*

I could see he was typing; those little dots dancing on the screen told me so, but nothing came through. I pulled off my top and tossed it onto the couch before slipping the uniform tee over my head. Like a glove. Glancing at myself in the long mirror on the wall next to the door, I grinned. I looked good. Not at all like Roslyn Blackthorne.

Then another terse note appeared.

> **MR. MERCER:**
> I'm not holding dinner for you so you can do your makeup.

> **MR. MERCER:**
> If you're not down here in three minutes, it's going in the garbage.

> **ME:**
> You're a very grumpy goose. You know that, right?

> **MR. MERCER:**
> Get used to it.

> **ME:**
> I've won over grumpier. You'll love me before long.

> **MR. MERCER:**
> Two minutes.

I glanced around the loft-style flat with its open floor plan, staring at the kitchen and its handful of appliances I barely recognized. Ben didn't realize what a gift he was giving me by providing dinner. Growing up with an army of staff at our beck and call, I'd never had to learn how to fend for myself. Even if I knew how to turn the stove on, there wasn't a meal I was prepared to make. Cereal perhaps? That seemed simple enough. Anything more than that, I'd be in trouble.

I was going to starve if I didn't sort myself out. But that was tomorrow's problem.

Glancing back at my phone, I typed another text because I couldn't help but sass him.

ME:

Keep your shirt on. I'm coming.

MR. MERCER:

It's you who needs your shirt on.

ME:

Imagine the tips I could make without one.

More of those dots floated on the screen. I was openly smiling as I waited for his reply to come through.

MR. MERCER:

Don't even think about it.

MR. MERCER:

The last thing I need to worry about is beating the shit out of my regulars because you're a walking distraction.

MR. MERCER:

If I have to chase off Tom, Dick, and Harry for staring at your tits, it's going to cost me money, and that will really piss me off.

MR. MERCER:

You don't want to piss me off, new girl.

Butterflies took flight in my stomach at the thought of him coming to defend my honor. Not that he'd actually said it, but I could read between the lines. His subtext was coming through loud and clear.

ME:

> Aw, Mr. Mercer. You're a regular hero, looking after me and my tits like that.

MR. MERCER:

> One minute, Nadia.

I hadn't had this much fun since I left home. Stubborn curiosity held me in place.

ME:

> I'm just making certain my . . . assets are properly displayed so I can take advantage of those tips I mentioned.

MR. MERCER:

> I'm holding your plate over the garbage.

ME:

> And typing with one hand? You are a man of many talents.

MR. MERCER:

> It's going in.

Then a photo came through of a basket with black and white waxed paper lining, a perfect-looking burger with chips on the side, fried and golden, nestled within. I recognized the hand holding the food over a large rubbish bin. Of course, my hormone-addled brain focused more on the muscled forearm in the picture rather than the possibility he'd really toss my food. What was it about a forearm? It was like the male equivalent of a Victorian lady displaying her ankles. Just one glimpse set me all a quiver.

My stomach gave a hungry gurgle, reminding me I

hadn't eaten since Asher brought me a sandwich that morning. It felt like ages ago.

Not wanting to risk missing dinner and knowing I would go back to study said forearm in detail later, I threw open the door and rushed down the stairs.

"Put the food down and nobody gets hurt!" I cried as I skidded to the bar.

Ben's dark brows rose as he assessed me. His hands were empty.

"You didn't. Please tell me you didn't waste that meal simply because I was winding you up."

He stepped to the side, revealing a familiar basket filled with food beneath the warmer.

"Saints be praised," I said, pressing my hand to my chest. "It's a miracle. I'm so glad I don't have to kill you and then go diving in your rubbish bin to rescue my poor innocent burger."

Soft snickers rang out, alerting me to the fact my performance had an audience of more than one. Three burly men were seated at the far end of the bar, watching me with unabashed glee.

"N-Nadia, m-meet Tom, Dick, a-and Harry."

IT TOOK A FEW HOURS, but eventually I found my rhythm. Thankfully no one here was interested in margaritas or other frilly cocktails. The most elaborate drink I'd had to mix was a Jack and Ginger; otherwise it was whiskeys on the rocks or beer. Even I could manage that.

Something you'd think my new boss would appreciate, but Ben just kept glowering at me from the other side of the bar. Scowling, more like. What had I ever done to him for him to hate me so? Did I smell bad?

"Here you go, lads," I said, setting down three fresh pints for my new favorite people.

Tom, Dick, and Harry had been providing running commentary for me all night. They were a riot and harmless so far as I could tell. Though as the drinks continued to flow, the gargoyles had grown a bit more rowdy.

"Come on over here, love, and give us a smile," Dick slurred in his thick Cockney accent. Even I could barely understand him. "You're far too fit to be hiding behind that bar."

"Leave her alone, mate. It's her first day. Don't want to scare off the pretty little bird before she has a chance to get to know us. You're ruining it for the rest of us." That was from Harry. His Scouse lilt had me smiling, reminding me of a tutor I'd had as a child.

My voice was bright as I laughingly informed them, "I can hold my own, gents. I assure you, I'm no wallflower."

"Damn right, ya can. Pretty lass like you," Tom chimed in, his Scottish brogue delightfully charming. I could stand here chatting these three up all night. At least they *wanted* to talk to me. "Maybe ye'll take a wee break and come sit over here with me."

"I-I d-didn't h-hire y-you to flirt, Ms. B-Black."

I rolled my eyes at my three new friends.

"Technically you didn't hire her at all. I did," Remi said, swooping in and giving my hair a playful tug. "How's it going so far, Nadia?"

"It was going quite well until a dark cloud came over to spoil it." He reminded me of that one character from a child's story. The one with the storm cloud always chasing him around. I had the sudden urge to buy a bow for his tail.

Ben snarled. "Y-you're s-s-supposed to be w-working. N-not trolling f-for a d-d-date."

The three gargoyles stared at Ben with wide eyes and slack jaws. Then they shared knowing glances between them.

"Sorry, mate. We didn't mean no harm. We didn't realize she was yours," Harry said.

"Yeah, she's not wearing a ring or nothin'. No mark." Dick glanced at my hands and then my neck.

Tom shrugged. "It was an honest mistake, lad. We wouldn't have chatted her up if we knew you'd laid claim already."

Ben's brows slanted down in a fierce glare. "She's n-n-not m-m-mine."

The vehemence of his denial had my back snapping straight. "You would be so lucky, Mr. Grumpy Pants. I am a delight."

"Yeah, you are. C'mon, Nadia. I think you need a smoke break." Remi put an arm around my shoulders.

"I don't smoke."

"Mr. Grumpy Pants doesn't need to know that."

Sealing his mouth shut tight, Ben stared daggers at us.

Remi laughed. "I'll bring her back in fifteen. That'll give you time to get whatever you've shoved up your ass either into a position that makes you smile or remove it. If you're taking suggestions, I'd go for the prostate stimulation. Might do you a world of good."

"Fuck off."

"Trying to, you cockblock."

Ben stormed into the kitchen.

Remi laughed. "Isn't he fun to play with? I love pulling his tail. He's like a lion with a sore paw. All grumpy snarls and mean stares. Really he just wants a big cuddle. Maybe for someone to rub his belly."

"Not it," I said, laughing as he took me to the back alley. The cool air felt good after the heat of the bar.

"Wolves are easy creatures, Nadia. We just want someone to rub up against and to give us scritches behind the ears. Maybe let us nip on them a little."

"Hump them, you mean," I said, recalling the only male shifter I had any sort of relationship with. Kingston Farrell always seemed to be ready to hump something. Namely his mate.

"That too."

Ben didn't seem like he wanted to hump me. He wanted to get as far away as possible. But Remi . . . that was a different story. He was hard to figure out. Flirty and full of easy smiles, but there was a distance in him too. He wasn't the serious kind. Remington Mercer was like a golden retriever. Always ready for attention and affection. Even now, he was touching me gently as we breathed in the bracing chill of the night. His arm was pressed against mine as we stood together. I wasn't used to casual contact, so I was hyperaware of him. We Black-thornes had always been more . . . separate. Not to say my life was lived without affection; there was just less of it.

"So you all settled in yet?"

"It doesn't take long to unpack a single bag," I said with a light laugh.

"Oh, that reminds me. Asher dropped off some stuff for you, and I ran out and got you some essentials too. Figured you'd appreciate having some groceries to hold you over until we can do a proper stock up."

"Oh . . . thank you." That was unexpected. His brother

had offered the same, but the easy kindness when I was little more than a stranger was way above and beyond.

For as alone as I felt, I sure had a bunch of people looking out for me. Even the ones who seemed more inclined to poke me with a stick most of the time.

"Don't worry about Ben. He'll come around. He just has to growl and snap first. Eventually, you'll like him almost as much as you like me."

I grinned. "Almost?"

"I can't have anyone else be your favorite, baby girl. I'm claiming that spot now."

"And what if it's already taken?"

He put a hand over his heart and feigned being shot. "Bullseye. Right through the chest."

"I do have expert aim."

"Do you now?"

I bit my cheek, wondering if it was safe to reveal that part of myself. How much of my past did I have to let go of? My skill with a bow and arrow seemed safe enough to keep. I couldn't keep the smug pride out of my voice as I admitted, "You're looking at Spirit Lake Summer Camp's archery champion two years running."

Remi whistled and held up both his hands, taking a step back. "I didn't realize I was in the presence of royalty. Excuse me."

"Then you must kneel before me if I'm royalty."

He smirked. "I'd get on my knees for you anytime you asked, my lady."

My heart gave a little flip. "Good to know."

If my reply was more breathless than usual, Remi thankfully didn't call me on it.

The back door opened with a creak, and Ben's stormy face appeared. "B-break's over, you two."

"Uh-oh, the fun police found us." Remi shoved off the wall and took my hand. "Back to the workhouse."

Instead of letting go of me, Remi kept our fingers laced as he led me back inside. All the while, I felt Ben's hot gaze on my back, the tension in the hall thick enough it was hard to breathe. Was this going to be how it was? Ben glowering, Remi flirting, and me not sure which way to turn.

What had I gotten myself into?

TWELVE

BEN

"Come on. Open up for me." I grunted as I slammed the ax back down on the massive oak round. Sap and water sprayed everywhere as it cracked halfway on the first strike.

The sunlight filtered through the new growth of the trees surrounding the house Remi and I shared. Did I need to be chopping wood? Not exactly, but I couldn't fucking sit around and do nothing. I was edgy, totally keyed up, uneasy.

Why not just turn into a wolf and run to blow off steam? Because a wolf couldn't compulsively check his cell phone. What if she texted me? What if she needed me? What if something happened to her and I was too busy playing in the forest?

The huge log split down the middle after my fourth swing, and I let out a groan of satisfaction. "That's right. Part like a whore's thighs, right down the middle."

I tossed the ax to the ground and took a moment to catch my breath and shake out hands that were still humming from the force of the blows. Maybe I needed a fight?

Or a fuck.

That little voice in my head prodded at me, sending a visual of Nadia right along with the suggestion.

No. I didn't need to fuck her.

But you want to.

Shut up.

Thank God our next fight night was coming up. I always felt better after beating the shit out of some smug underworld asshole.

My phone let out a shrill ring.

The alarm.

I fucking knew it.

I pulled out the device with shaking hands, checking the notification with my heart in my throat.

Fire?!

I was off and running before I stopped to think through my next steps. Would the truck have been faster? Possibly, but that would have required me to go inside and grab my keys. Should I have put on a shirt? You betcha, but again, time. She could already be dead.

"Not on my fucking watch."

I tore through the woods until I burst out the other side, onto Main Street and into a surprised-looking Tom who was dressed for a hike.

"Och, what do ye think yer doin', Ben?"

I didn't answer him. There wasn't time. Checking the sky for any sign of smoke, I raced to the bar as fast as my legs would take me. When I reached the doors, they were locked, of fucking course, and I hadn't brought a damn thing with me besides my cell phone.

"Fuck it," I grunted, tapping into my wolf's strength as I

slammed my shoulder into the wood and broke it open in one move.

"N-Nadia!" I shouted over the shrill alarm. "N-N-Nadia!"

I was always stutter-free when I was alone, but now that she was nearby and my emotions were raised, it was back in full force. She set me off. Worse than I had been in a long time.

I pounded up the stairs, taking them three at a time and bursting through her door with no care for my own safety. When I got inside I got a lungful of burnt . . . toast?

Nadia ran into the room, a towel loosely draped around her slick skin.

"Bugger it!" she cursed, spying the smoking toaster with a dark scowl. "What the devil are you doing in my living room, Ben? Or are you Remi?"

I hated that she didn't recognize me. Which was stupid. Remi and I were identical. People mixed us up all the time. But I wanted her to know me on instinct, which was completely unfair.

"B-Ben." I took a breath and forced myself to calm the racing of my heart, then I held up my phone. "Alarm."

"Would you mind turning it off? It ruined my shower."

I stared at her, stupefied. Ruined her shower? The woman nearly burned my bar down, and she was worried about an interrupted shower? Stalking into the small kitchen, I unplugged the still smoking toaster, then tipped it on its side until the blackened chunk of what used to be bread spilled out. The toaster was a goner. We'd never get the smell out.

She wrinkled her nose. "I'm sorry. I've never had to fend for myself like this. I'm trying to learn."

And she couldn't manage toast?

Throwing open one of the small windows above the sink, I scolded, "N-no m-more cooking."

"How am I supposed to eat?"

"Cereal. S-sandwiches. Yogurt."

"That will get old fast."

"I-I'll t-t-teach you."

Fuck, what was I getting myself into? I could barely string a sentence together in front of her. How the hell would we get through a whole fucking lesson?

Her brows flew up. "You'd do that?"

I lifted my shoulder in a shrug. Apparently I would. "N-not hard."

She gestured to the mutilated appliance in the sink. "Really?"

"If y-you kn-know w-what you're d-doing."

"Which I clearly don't."

I really needed her to get out of that damned towel. All I could think about was what she was hiding under it.

"G-get d-dressed."

She finally seemed to realize what she was wearing. Or rather, what she wasn't wearing. Her entire body flushed.

"Oh my God." Mortified, she hurried out of the room. "Back in a tick!"

She returned dressed in tight black pants and a loose top that hung off one shoulder, exposing the place my wolf would mark her if he had the chance.

Mark her? What the hell?

"Okay. I'm dressed. When is my first lesson, professor?"

I was quickly coming to learn that Nadia was playful and more than a little mischievous. She was quick-witted and had a sharp tongue. I'd spent more time than I should've last night listening to her exchanges with the regulars, wishing it had been me. Hating that it would never be me.

Even with Remi, I couldn't snap back like that. I had to think through and fight for every word.

I was already regretting my offer to help her.

Turning away from her, I pointed to the toaster. "L-lesson o-one. O-only p-push it d-down once."

"Got it."

"T-two," I said, gesturing to the microwave. "N-no m-metal."

"Good to know."

My throat was tight as I worked up to the next bit of instruction I wanted to give her. "W-w-w . . ." I trailed off, frustrated as hell I couldn't get the word to come out.

She picked up her phone and began typing on the screen, bored with me already. Fucking rude. But then my own cell chimed.

> OFF-LIMITS:
>
> I don't mind texting if it's easier.

Another came through right on its heels.

> OFF-LIMITS:
>
> And this way I don't even have to take notes. *winky face emoji*

Relief hit me hard, right in the chest, where everything was constantly tight and heavy at the same time.

> ME:
>
> It's a whole lot easier. And now I can make sure you don't burn down my bar.

Her nose wrinkled as my text came through.

"Sorry about that."

ME:

You owe me a new door too.

OFF-LIMITS:

How did my little toaster snafu hurt your door? It looks fine to me.

ME:

I broke it trying to get in and make sure you were alive.

Her eyes went round.

OFF-LIMITS:

You're a regular Lancelot, aren't you?

ME:

Sure. Call me whatever you want, new girl.

OFF-LIMITS:

Do you want to explain why your shirt is missing? Did you break that too?

I glanced down at my bare chest, a low chuckle escaping.

ME:

I was chopping wood.

OFF-LIMITS:

Shirtless?

ME:

I get sweaty. And I was in a hurry. You know, trying to save your life.

OFF-LIMITS:

Do you charge admission?

ME:

What?

OFF-LIMITS:

To the gun show?

I laughed, shaking my head at her flirty message. I had to admit, I was eating it up too. I never got to talk with anyone like this. Least of all women. I couldn't resist a flirt of my own.

ME:

Why? You want to come?

Her cheeks burned pink, and then I realized what I'd said and quickly added:

ME:

Watch me chop wood?

OFF-LIMITS:

What's the going rate? I don't have much money. My boss is a cheapskate.

ME:

I hear he's a real hero. Took you in. Offered you a job. A place to stay. Even played firefighter.

She batted her eyelashes and took a step closer, then glanced down at the phone.

OFF-LIMITS:

A shirtless firefighter who moonlights as a lumberjack. My teenage self would never believe her fantasy has mostly come to life.

I was dying to ask her more about said fantasies, but I reined myself in. Barely. I only managed because my jeans were getting uncomfortably tight and I really didn't feel like getting teased about being shirtless and sporting a boner.

ME:

> Okay, lesson three. Don't leave anything cooking unattended.

OFF-LIMITS:

> Oh, are we done flirting now? Okay. Schoolgirl mode activated.

The image of her in a plaid skirt and button-down had me damn near groaning.

ME:

> Also, hot burners and flammable things don't mix. No towels or paper near them, okay?

OFF-LIMITS:

> Got it, boss.

ME:

> How are you with a knife?

OFF-LIMITS:

> Are you asking if I know how to shank a bloke?

ME:

> More like the proper way to slice vegetables. Maybe table that until I can make sure you know the right way to do it so you don't accidentally cut off a finger or something.

OFF-LIMITS:

> Are we going to do this again? Like, regularly?

The prospect of being near her like this, teaching her to cook, had me excited. I *wanted* to help her. I told myself it was only because she needed someone, but that was a bald-faced lie. I was excited because she needed *me*.

ME:

> Somebody has to make sure you don't burn the bar down. Might as well be me since I have a vested interest in the place.

Sure, buddy. That's why.

OFF-LIMITS:

> Will you always be shirtless?

ME:

> Only if you're good.

She snorted in disbelief, her head snapping up so she could look at me. "Like a reward for passing my exams? Or is it more like strip cooking? I saw a film like that once. Nudity as an incentive for learning. I was a big fan."

Her eyes widened as the words hung in the air.

"I didn't mean to say that out loud."

ME:

> Too late.

She bit her lower lip, embarrassment radiating off her, so I let instinct guide me and closed the distance between us. Reaching out, I touched her chin and tilted her face up so she had to look at me. I didn't want her to be ashamed of anything she said to me. In fact, I wanted her to feel safe telling me anything . . . everything.

Her mouth was so close. All it would take would be for me to drop my head a few inches, and I could taste those lips and see if they were as soft as I'd imagined them. I could feel her go pliant in my arms, coax a moan from her, make her beg for more.

I dipped my head, and the little hitch in her breath

urged me on. But then my fucking phone rang, and I knew it was Remi by the ring tone.

We broke apart as I answered.

"What?" I barked.

"Dude, where the fuck are you? We were supposed to be on our way to Midnight Falls ten minutes ago. You know if we're late, Pablo won't give us a discount on his new tequila."

A low growl rumbled through me as I flicked my gaze at Nadia. "P-pick me up at th-the T-Tip."

There was a beat of silence, and then my brother laughed. "You sonofabitch, you're with her, aren't you? Sneaky. How is our little houseguest this morning? As *pretty* as ever?"

"F-fuck you."

I hung up. Then shot a glare at Nadia she didn't deserve. "I h-have t-t-to g-o. D-don't t-try to c-cook anything."

She held up her hands. "Lesson learned. It's cheese and cold bread for me until I get the Bentley Mercer seal of approval."

Oh, she had my seal of approval. Just not the one she was talking about.

"L-later, N-Nadia."

"Later, professor."

My dick twitched. Fucking traitor.

After running downstairs without letting myself look back, I snagged a spare shirt and tugged it over my head. How was I going to explain my reaction to Remi? Why I didn't just call the fire department. Why I tore through town like a bat out of hell and rode to her rescue. Because for the life of me, I didn't understand it either.

Hopefully I'd figure it out soon. I didn't think we could afford it if I kept breaking down doors to get to her.

Remi honked and I hurried outside, sliding into the cab of the truck. "W-we need to stop by the hardware store."

He raised his brow. "Oookay?"

Groaning, I rested my head back on the seat. "Don't ask."

CHAPTER
THIRTEEN
ROSIE

"I've missed the scent of your sweet cunt, petal. How dare you run from me." Gavin's voice was a sensual rasp across oversensitive skin. I broke out in goosebumps at the threat lingering in his words.

"I'm sorry, my lord."

He trailed the handle of his whip along my spine, making me shiver. "Are you really?"

"Y-yes."

He pressed his lips against my ear, his warm breath fanning down my neck. "Then why did you run? You had to know I'd find you. I'll *always* find you. Is it because you *want* to be punished?"

I gulped, shame and need coiling in my belly. "Yes."

"If it's a punishment you want, that's exactly what you'll get. Hands on the bedpost, petal. Don't touch anything, and don't let go. But please, do feel free to scream."

I gripped the bed, the same bed in the same room I'd been unintentionally privy to at the Donoghue estate. But this time, instead of Daniel being on the receiving end of

Gavin's domination, it was me. That was how I knew it was a dream. He hadn't really found me.

But here, in my darkest fantasies, it didn't matter. Here he was mine. Here we could finally be together.

"Are you ready, petal?"

"Yes, my lord."

The whip cracked down, and I arched forward as a harsh sting radiated through my body. It burned and throbbed, but I immediately wanted another taste of its sharp bite. The pulses of pain echoed in my clit, an answering flood of arousal dripping down my thighs. I was twisted, and I loved it.

"More," I moaned.

His dark laugh filled the room, coating me in his own lust. I needed him. God, how I needed *this*.

"You don't get to demand things of me. Not here."

"Please, my lord. I deserve to be punished."

"That you do, and punish you I shall. Perhaps by denying you the very thing you crave."

"No," I sobbed.

He ran his nose along the side of my neck, breathing me in. One of his hands ghosted around my hip, a barely there touch that had me squirming.

"But if I deprive you, I also deprive myself."

His hand continued its journey, gliding up my stomach until his knuckles caressed the underside of my breast.

"And where's the fun in that?"

His voice was a seductive whisper, but his grip on me turned punishing. He pinched the straining peak of my nipple between his fingers and gave a cruel twist, forcing a scream to tear free of my throat.

"Gavin!" His name slipped out without permission, but

I couldn't hold it in. I needed him to know how much he affected me.

"Yes, my darling little flower. Now you remember who you belong to."

"I never forgot."

"Pretty little liar. Yes, you did, but you won't now. Never again. Because I'm going to find you and fill you so full of my cum, no one else will be able to mistake you for theirs."

He continued to twist and pluck my nipple, tears pricking my eyes and making incoherent pleas fall from my lips. I squirmed under his attention, needing him in more ways than just this. I wanted him to do what he threatened. To claim me and fill me and call me his.

"Spread your thighs and let me see how wet you are."

I did.

His free hand skated across my bare arse, between the cheeks, and down until he found my slick folds. Then those talented fingers sank inside me in one hard thrust, spreading me, making me cry out.

"What a needy little cunt you have. So hot and ready for my cock. You'd let me do anything to you right now, wouldn't you, petal?"

"Y-yes."

"Yes, what?"

"Yes, my lord."

"Good girl."

He pulled his fingers from me and began working my clit as he pressed his lips to the base of my neck, then kissed a path to the side, where my shoulder and throat met. Sparks burst through me as he sucked on the skin there. It shouldn't feel like he was sucking directly on my clit—it wasn't a spot that usually made me feel anything—but now that he was touching it, I was more aware of it than any other place on my body. Except perhaps for the place between my legs desperate to be filled.

"Mine," he growled, just as his teeth sank into my flesh.

I was so close to the magical finish line. Just a little longer. One more flick of his fingers and I'd ...

The jarring chirp of my cell phone shattered the dream just before I fell over the edge. With a frustrated huff, I reached blindly for the device as texts continued to roll in one after the other, telling me who it was before I even saw the screen. *Ben.* I sat up and tossed the covers off my legs.

LANCELOT:

Be ready in an hour.

LANCELOT:

Cooking lesson.

LANCELOT:

I'm going grocery shopping.

LANCELOT:

You're coming with me.

LANCELOT:

No arguing.

ME:

Fine. Also, I hate you. Bring coffee.

LANCELOT:

I'd tell you to make your own damn coffee, but you can't be trusted.

ME:

At least you're learning.

LANCELOT:

You're the one who's supposed to be learning.

LANCELOT:

57 minutes.

LANCELOT:

Don't make me come up and get you.

LANCELOT:

I WILL make you go to the grocery store in whatever state I find you.

ME:

I doubt you'd let me run about in public with my bits flapping around. You were pretty opposed to the idea when I suggested it for the bar.

LANCELOT:

Try me.

LANCELOT:

I dare you.

LANCELOT:

55 minutes.

I smirked at my phone, flopping back on the bed with a groan. Unfulfilled need still surged through my veins, and I restlessly pressed my thighs together, trying to alleviate the ache as thoughts of my sadistic husband danced in my mind.

"Well, he said I have an hour . . ."

I trailed my fingers down my belly until I reached the soft hair hiding my . . . my cunt. I tried out the word in my head, remembering how Gavin's voice sounded in my ears. It was dirty and perfect all at the same time.

"I can do a lot in an hour."

FOURTEEN

I was a sick bastard. I knew that. But I didn't fucking care as I watched Rosie—*fuck*—Nadia fall back into bed and slip her fingers between her thighs. I'd forgotten I left the feed running after my check-in with her last night, but when I heard her moaning, I stumbled to my desk and told myself I was just checking to make sure she was okay.

Turned out she was more than okay. She was horny.

And dammit, so was I.

Just the sound of her moans had been enough to have my cock standing at attention, straining and poorly concealed behind my boxer briefs. I couldn't want her, but fuck did I ever. I couldn't stop thinking about her. Instead of getting easier as the days passed, it got worse. I wondered what she was doing every fucking minute.

I tried to chalk it up to finally having a house guest after all the time I spent alone, but I wasn't stupid enough to buy my own bullshit. It was all her.

"Stop watching her, Asher. You're not a voyeur."

Yes, you are.

"Do not take that dick out of your underwear. Turn off the feed and get to work on something else."

Or don't.

The demon on my shoulder was decidedly without an angel counterpart, and all I wanted to do was listen to him.

"Yes," she moaned. "Just like that. Touch me."

See, she wants you to play with her.

When she peeled up her shirt and started tweaking her nipples, I lost the battle. My palm shot down to my erection, the crown already poking out above the waistband of my boxers, and I groaned along with her. Shoving the fabric down, I released my hard length and gave a slow stroke.

"Come on, sweetheart, make yourself feel good for me."

You could zoom in. See how she likes to be touched. See exactly *how she gets herself off.*

"No," I gritted out, drawing the line at being that much of a fucking pervert. But goddamn was it tempting.

Her breaths became harsh as she dipped her fingers inside, and I thanked my past self for installing the camera with the focus centered on the bed. Especially when she widened her thighs and let me see the glistening puffy lips of her pussy. One hand cupped her breast while the other now circled her clit.

She wasn't gentle with herself either. The closer she got to release, the more she squeezed and plucked at her breasts. The rougher her hand between her legs.

"Good to fucking know," I grunted, feeling my orgasm build in my balls.

When she dipped her fingers inside and then pulled them out and brought them up to her breasts, rubbing her arousal over her tightly furled buds, I groaned, the unexpectedly dirty move sending my own need ratcheting.

"Fuck, Rosie. Who knew you were such a dirty girl? What else do you want to rub into those perfect tits?"

The thought of coming all over her, of rubbing it in and getting her off with it, had me nearly cross-eyed holding back my O.

"Come for me, sweetheart. Come so I can. Fuuuck."

I was so damn close my legs were shaking.

She bucked on the bed, letting out a ragged moan, and her perfect brows drew together as her pleasure was written all over her face. A story I never wanted to forget.

"God, Rosie. Yes." I hissed as my balls tightened, and the orgasm finally broke free. I reached for the box of tissues on my desk, but it was too late. My cum splattered across my chest and dribbled down my stomach. One jet of it hit me on the chin. Fuck. I hadn't come like that in a long damn time.

I would have been embarrassed if I wasn't so relieved.

Christ, I needed that.

From the satisfied smile on Rosie's face, so had she.

I stared down at my cum-soaked chest and was hit with a wave of guilt and shame. I shouldn't have done that. I was a creepy fuck. This was a line I had never crossed before. I smacked my keyboard, shutting down the feed and sending my main monitor to black.

"Never again, Asher. No more. From now on, you keep your fucking distance."

FIFTEEN

The sharp bite of citrus filled my nose as I cut into a fresh lime. Ben had put me on restocking duty, which was fine with me. It gave me time to practice my knife skills. I was determined to impress him during our next lesson.

Harry burst through the door. "There's been a murder!"

Tom and Dick spun in their usual seats to face the shouting man.

The trio had been permanent fixtures at the bar every night. Perched on the same three stools as though carved of stone most of the time. With their burly builds and gruff voices, I would have pegged them as the sculpted sentinels even without knowing they were actual gargoyles. I could see Ben assigning them watch duty.

"Oi. What the bloody hell are you on about? Are you off your rocker? A murder? Here? Nothing happens here." Dick rolled his eyes, annoyed by the outburst.

"You think I'd lie about something like that? I'm telling you, there's been an honest to God murder," Harry shot back with a scowl.

"Well, don't leave us in suspense. Who is the unfortunate murdered bastard?" Tom demanded, asking the question that had been burning my own tongue.

Remi came out from the office he shared with Ben, a towel tucked into his back pocket and an unbuttoned flannel showing off the fitted Tipsy Moose tee hugging his muscled torso. "What's this about a murder?"

Darla sidled over to me, listening as intently as I was. It was my first time working with the pretty shifter. She was a biker babe through and through, but you'd never know it talking to her. Her sweet voice was a complete contrast to her tattooed arms and leather-clad body. I had more than a small girl crush on her. In another life, I'd have wanted to be just like her. Confident, self-assured, bad-arsed.

"Bill Pritchard." Harry said it like he was dropping a bomb, but no one seemed surprised.

"Are you sure he was murdered? Or did he just drink himself into the path of a moving car?" Darla asked.

"I don't know about you, but I've never heard of a car draining someone of all their blood and leaving them on the pier."

"Sounds like a vamp," Remi said.

The energy in the room turned tense. Apparently Asher hadn't been kidding when he said they hated vampires here. I shifted nervously behind the bar.

"You'd think so, wouldn't ya? But if it was, this vamp wasn't well versed in feeding. The marks on him weren't anything like a vamp's bite." Harry dragged a hand across the back of his neck. "He was—"

The door burst open, and a tall, heavily muscled cop walked in. Well, he swaggered in, his aviators hiding his eyes, tan cowboy hat on his head. "There's been a murder, y'all."

"Yeah, we know, Dallas. Harry already told us." Remi leaned against the bar next to me, his body close enough that I could feel the warmth radiating from him. "You're about two minutes too late."

"Well, shit. Way to steal my thunder."

"Sorry, Sheriff," Harry said.

Dallas pulled off his glasses, revealing a pair of heavily lashed amber eyes. With all that sun-kissed skin and golden hair, he reminded me of a . . .

"Lion," Darla supplied, her voice low. "He served in the military, then moved up here after some kind of scandal. We made him sheriff because he was the only one with the necessary skill set. Scarlett is his deputy. She's a cute little thing. Pixie. Direct descendant of the notorious Tink."

My eyebrows lifted at the wealth of information.

"I'm not a gossip, I swear. Just sparing you the agony of listening to her tell you all about it herself. That girl's a talker. Once she starts . . ." She held up a hand and mimed a talking puppet. "It's exhausting."

"Do you have any idea who might've wanted him dead?" I asked.

Darla snorted. "Who didn't? That drunk was a festering boil on this town's otherwise unblemished behind."

"That's a . . . colorful description."

"Asshole's been in and out of jail so many times they should've just given him his own cell. The last time I saw him, he'd badly beaten his wife, Aimee. Sweet as sugar, that one. Ben helped her, come to think of it. She showed up here one night covered in bruises, could barely walk. Ben took one look at her and stormed off. I don't think I've ever seen him so pissed."

I could picture it so easily. Especially after he came to my rescue the other morning. Ben was a protector through and through. He was truly a good man, even if he was prickly.

"Look, I know there was no love lost between Bill and most of this town, but the fact of the matter is, I've got a dead body chilling in the one drawer we have at the morgue. We need to figure this out so we can get him laid to rest." Dallas's gaze swept the room, landing on me. He narrowed his eyes and stalked across the floor until he was directly in front of me. "You. You're new."

He braced his elbows on the bar and leaned forward, sniffing me. "Fae?"

Realizing I was still clenching my knife, I forced my fingers to relax so I could set it down and appear as non-threatening as possible. I knew I was innocent, but as the only newbie in town, I also knew I was a clear suspect.

"Yup." I gave him my sweetest grin. "I'm Nadia. Moved here last week."

"Which fae court are you from?"

Panic gripped my heart. *When in doubt, be vague.* "I don't know. I was a changeling. Raised with humans."

"What powers do you have?"

"None aside from some enhanced senses. The rest of my power never manifested."

He pursed his lips, leaning closer. "You have an alibi for last night, Nadia?"

"Hey now, stop interrogating my new bartender," Remi said, coming to my defense. "You're barking up the wrong tree."

Dallas backed away, crossing his arms over his chest. "All right, fine. But I'm keeping an eye on you, girlie. It's too convenient. A newcomer rolls into town just before a crime spree."

"Is one murder really a crime spree?" Tom asked.

"It is when the worst we usually deal with is a parking violation."

"What about the bears?" Darla asked. "You know Ivan and his boys are involved in a lot more than distilling."

The hairy mountain of a man in the back corner stood up, his expression thunderous. "Why is it always us? We make your vodka, and you don't complain. But when someone ends up dead, you blame the bears."

Dallas shrugged. "Settle down, Ivan. Y'all haven't given me a reason to suspect you, but I *will* follow any lead."

"You'd know if it was us. We'd leave our calling card."

"I don't doubt it."

A chill ran down my spine. The tension in the room was thick enough to slice through, just like I did the limes.

"It's okay, baby girl. They do this all the time." Remi's voice was a gentle murmur in my ear as he rested a palm on the small of my back. "Posturing. Alpha against Alpha. Comes with the territory when you live in a town of supernaturals. You'll get used to it."

"Do we need to worry about some mass murderer running around town?"

He locked eyes with me, and his brows pulled together. "Bill probably got caught with another shifter's mate. I'd bet it was a crime of passion, maybe even self-defense, not a serial killer."

"Oooh! Speaking of serial killers, did you hear that guy in London struck again? They're calling him the supernatural Jack the Ripper."

I glanced at Darla; her excitement about the topic was a hair unnerving. "He's going after prostitutes?"

"Well, no. Just supernaturals, but the crime scenes are grisly. *And* in Whitechapel. Also, we call them sex workers now."

"Everyone knows Jack was an exiled fae. Who's to say it's not the original? He's likely still alive. The fae are very . . . challenging to kill." The bear's cool gaze landed on me, and I stiffened.

Great. Fae was supposed to be the safe choice. Now I was linked with a serial killer. A British one at that. Fork me.

I raised my hands, my laugh shaky. "Not it."

The three gargoyles chuckled in unison, Tom raising his pint glass at me before drinking it down.

Remi wrapped his arm around my waist, giving me a squeeze. "Of course it isn't you. You've been working here every night this week. Besides"—he booped me on the nose—"you wouldn't hurt a fly."

"A fly, no. But I draw the line at spiders. They don't deserve to exist in my space. With their beady eyes and hairy legs. Honestly, who needs eight eyes?"

"I'm glad to see the *murder* we're investigating hasn't dulled your sense of humor, Miss . . ." Dallas said, sarcasm dripping from every word.

"Black."

"Miss Black, I'd like you to stay close to town the next few weeks, you understand? I might need to ask you more questions as the investigation continues."

I cringed.

"And Remi, where's that brother of yours? I need to talk to him too."

Remi shifted his position, standing taller. "Ben's camping. He needed some time to run and let his wolf out."

"Alone?"

"Yeah."

"Didn't he have an altercation with Bill a few months back?"

"Who here hasn't?"

Dallas let out a harsh laugh. "Ain't that the truth." He made a show of grabbing his belt and pulling his trousers up a little. "Well, tell him I need to holler at him when he gets back, you hear?"

"Will do."

The sheriff nodded, then eyed me one last time. "Pleasure meeting you, Miss Black. I'll be in touch."

"Can't wait."

He sauntered back out, sucking all the air out of the room with him.

"Crap on a cracker. He really has it out for you, Nadia." Harry shook his head. "You should have offered him a drink."

"Wouldn't that look like a bribe?"

"Well, sure, but who doesn't warm to a pretty woman after a pint or two?"

"You need a pint or two to appreciate her? You need your eyes checked." Tom frowned, then stared at me. "She's probably using some sort of faerie magic on us."

"Okay, fellas. That's enough. Stop ogling my bartender." Remi put me behind him, but not before I caught his cheeky wink. "That's my job."

A flutter built strength in my belly. I could not be feeling this way about both of the Mercer brothers, Asher, *and* dreaming naughty dreams about Gavin. Especially not when I let a demon take my virginity not even a handful of days ago.

Life sure had gotten exciting all of a sudden. A girl fakes her death, and suddenly the whole world as she knows it goes tits up.

The mark on my wrist began to tingle, the sensation sending my heart racing, arousal hitting me hard and fast.

What the blazes was this? The need built to a swell I could barely contain, and I didn't miss the stiffening of Remi's shoulders. Oh, please don't let him be able to scent my arousal. That would be terribly embarrassing for my boss to be able to do right now.

"You okay, baby girl?"

"I uh . . . ungh," I moaned as I was hit with a pulse of pleasure. I reached out and grabbed his forearm on instinct. "Cramps. I, erm, need to go lie down."

"Sure, it's slow tonight. Take the rest of the night off."

"Thanks, Remi."

I couldn't have gotten out of there fast enough. I'm pretty sure smoke flew out from beneath my feet as I raced up the stairs and into my room.

I'd only just shut the door and rested my head against it as a new wave of lust flowed through me.

"Hello, *ma petite monstre*. Miss me?"

Speak of the demon.

SIXTEEN

Roslyn stood in front of me, her cheeks flushed, eyes bright, nipples pressing against the fabric of her T-shirt. *Looks like my mark did the trick.* Bully for me.

"I'm glad to see my summons worked without issue. I did try to ensure it would be pleasurable for you."

"That . . . *this* is you?"

"I said I would summon you when I had need." To demonstrate the point, I plucked the invisible tether that connected us, biting back a grin as she moaned and slid down the door onto her plump arse.

"Stop it, you . . . you . . . oh God."

"What was that? You want me to make it worse?" A thrill ran through me as I gave the thread another tug and she devolved into a puddle of need.

"N-no. P-please no," she stuttered, struggling to form words through the haze I built within her.

"I know your preference for pain. I could make it hurt, if you'd rather."

"Just, just stop. Please. I'm here."

I released the hold I had on her, dropping the connection instantly. It wasn't as much fun if she was well and truly forced. I wanted her begging on her knees for me. Of her own free will.

That reminded me why I was here.

"You've been a naughty girl, Roslyn."

"What do you mean?"

"I did warn you that I owned you, did I not?"

She bit her lip, looking every inch the adorable puppy. I wanted to break her. Shatter that innocent facade. Turn her back into my perfect little slut.

"You are mine. Plain. Simple. Not up for debate. But your cunt is wet for someone else." I stalked over to her and crouched down so I could grip her face in my hand, pressing hard into her cheeks. "You touched yourself thinking of him . . . of *them*."

"How do you know that?"

"Oh, *mon ange*, I know everything. You belong to me now. There's no part of you that you can hide. Not your body, not your thoughts. So long as our deal is in place, the connection cannot be broken. Which means . . . you've been a very . . ." I leaned close. "Naughty . . ." I licked a line up her cheek before giving her a nip. "Girl."

Her tongue darted out to wet her lips. "What are you going to do to me?"

There it was. That flash of heat in her gaze. The interest . . . and the fear.

"Teach you a lesson, of course." I pulled her to her feet, loving the feel of her hot breath as it escaped in a rush against my chest. "Perhaps I should make an amendment to our deal. Some sort of chastity agreement. What do you think?"

"What else can you give me that's worth me letting you control who I . . . give myself to?"

Rage burned in my veins, and I wrapped my hand around her throat, shoving her against the wall. "Don't you understand? You'll never give yourself fully to anyone now. It's me who owns you. Me who commands your body. Who owns each and every one of your orgasms." I reached between her legs, pushing my fingers past the band of her pants and straight to her dripping center. Then I sank two of them into her without warning, growling against her lips, "Mine."

Her head fell back, hitting the wall hard enough that I wondered if those stupid shifters would hear. What would they think if they burst in here and saw their precious princess being railed by a demon? The thought made my cock harder than it had ever been. I'd show them exactly who was in charge. Spoiler alert, it wasn't them.

I whispered in her ear, "This cunt only flutters for me. It only wants my cock."

"You can't control that."

"Oh, can't I? Did you think I was joking about the chastity amendment?"

I couldn't actually enforce it, but she didn't know that. I was a consummate liar. It was practically in my job description. Hello . . . demon.

"No," she gasped.

"Oh yes, *ma petite monstre*. In fact, from this moment on, if you let anyone else into this perfect pussy, something terrible will happen to them."

"You're lying."

"Maybe I am. Is it worth the risk to test me?" I winked. "Shall we call one of your prospects upstairs for an after-work shag?" I tapped my chin with my index finger, the one I'd just pulled from her slick cunt. Fuck, it smelled good.

"Which one is more disposable? The grumpy lumberjack or the playful puppy?"

"Neither. Leave them alone."

"It's you who needs to learn how to do that, my sweet little whore." I sucked her off my fingers, and my erection throbbed behind my pants. Fuck, I wanted to be inside her. But she needed to be taught not to set a toe out of line again.

She was mine. For as long as I wanted her.

And I would not share.

Dropping to my knees, I grabbed the waistband of her jeans and pulled them off her. Knickers too. I needed to taste her, to bring her to the edge.

"What are you doing?"

"If I recall correctly, you were a fan of my tongue's many skills. I'm going to lick up every drop of you." I slapped the swollen lips of her pussy, drawing a gasp from her. "Spread your thighs. I want a snack."

She did as I asked, her legs parting as I cupped her round arse in both hands and held her up, kneeling in front of her and burying my face between her thighs.

"Pan, oh, yes."

I licked along her entire, sopping slit. She was a whore for me. At my beck and call. Open and ready, clenching in anticipation of what I—and I alone—would be giving her. I worked her over, my tongue making her writhe and squirm, one side laving her clit, the other filling her hole.

"Pan!"

I grinned, pulling back so the vibrations of my voice rumbled over her sensitive flesh. "Promise me you'll behave and I'll let you come."

"Stop toying with me."

"Never."

She wriggled. "I need you."

"Do you, now? Whatever for?"

Before she could answer, I sank my tongue inside her and fucked her, flicking the tips upward and pressing on that special spot women often were taught was a myth. Fucking patriarchy.

She cried out, but I used my tail to stuff her mouth full. No need to alert the shifters that she was in any kind of distress. Surprisingly, she sucked on the end, causing my eyes to roll back in my head as she curled her tongue around it.

Few realized just how sensitive a demon's tail could be, but the nimble appendage was every bit as responsive as my dick. More so, in fact. The only thing it couldn't do was cover her in my cum, but despite that particular downside, there were so many other fun things I could use it for.

"The devil take it," I grumbled, pulling my actual dick out of my pants and giving it a stroke or two. I could bury myself inside her heat right now and nail her into the fucking wall, make her come around me, mark her with my seed, brand her with it.

"Say it, Roslyn. Say you're mine. Promise me."

Who the ever-loving hell was this desperate wanker? Why did I care if she was fucking anyone else? I wasn't her bloody boyfriend. I was a demon of the first order. I'd been roaming the earth for centuries, and never, not once, had I craved a human's possession like this.

I hated what she'd reduced me to. Hated *her* for this power she held over me.

My grip on her turned brutal. Pulling my tail from her mouth, I curled it around her throat until she gasped for breath. I got to my feet and pressed the head of my cock to her opening. Her eyes were wide but glazed with pleasure as I ran the tip along her folds.

"I want you to remember this moment, Roslyn. Remember who it is that is allowing you to continue to draw breath. *I* gave that to you. *Me*. And I can take it away anytime I want to."

With the control of a priest, I slipped the tip of my dick inside her. I didn't move past that kiss of her lower lips around my crown. But my fingers drifted until they toyed with the rise of her clit, and she rocked her hips back and forth, searching for the penetration I promised but withheld.

"Oh, oh God, I'm going to—"

I pulled out of her and immediately ceased playing with her. "Not so fast, *mon ange*. I didn't say you could come yet."

"What are you doing?" she panted, her eyes filled with accusation.

"You need to listen when I speak to you, darling. Because I already told you. I am teaching. You. A lesson." With each word, I flicked my index finger over her clit, causing little whimpers of need to puff out of her lips.

"Please, Pan."

"Now," I murmured, continuing to edge her as I denied myself everything I wanted. "What do we say when someone asks who you belong to?"

She shook her head. "I don't belong to anyone."

I rocked my hips. "Wrong answer."

Pulling away, I shoved her to her knees.

"Now, you'll get no reward, dear one." I stared down at her and began stroking my thick length. "Open for me, darling. Unless you want it all over your sweet face."

I watched as she tried to slide a hand between her legs and immediately caught her wrists with my tail, halting the movement. "I own your pleasure. I am the only one who gets to decide if and when you get to come."

"I hate you."

"Good. Hate me all you want. It doesn't change the fact that I am the one who gives you what you crave. Now open up for me, and perhaps I'll change my mind."

Her cheeks were a fetching shade of pink, frustrated tears brimming in her eyes. She could not be more perfect, except perhaps if she was stuffed full of my cock and covered in my cum. But we would get there. Eventually.

"I can fill your mouth or your cunt, or maybe even your tight arse. Which one would you like?"

"All of them."

Oh my, the little slut had a mouth on her when she wanted. "That can be arranged, but you have to give me what I want first."

"Fine. I'm yours. No one else gets me . . . there."

"Where?"

"My flower."

A dark laugh escaped me. "No, no, no. That won't do. If you won't say cunt or pussy, we'll call it Pan's box." I smiled. "Oh, yes. I love the sound of that."

"You can have it. Now give me what I need."

"All right, then. Take off that ridiculous shirt and lie back. Let me have what's mine."

She did. Her legs fell wide, her glistening pussy open and ready for me. Poor girl. She didn't even know what kind of creature she was letting control her. I was about to show her.

Fitting my knees between her thighs, I stroked my cock hard and fast, watching as realization dawned on her face.

"Mine," I growled as pleasure shot through me, and I

came all over her lower belly in hot spurts of blissful release.

She watched with wide eyes as I sank back onto my heels and then rose to my feet.

"W-what are you doing?"

Smirking, I tucked my still hard cock back into my pants.

"You really need to work on your listening skills. I grow tired of repeating myself."

She sat up on her elbows, her tits swaying provocatively and making my cock give an appreciative twitch. "That's it?"

"I told you before we started you needed to be taught a lesson. Now you have."

Her gaze narrowed, and she laid back down, trailing her fingers through the streaks of cum covering her belly.

"Have I?"

I was too entranced by the sight of her playing with my spend to stop her when she reached her cum-soaked fingers between her thighs.

"What are you playing at, *ma petite monstre*?"

"Technically it's *you* making me feel good, Pan. It may be my fingers, but it's your cum, after all."

My lip curled. One thing a demon could appreciate was a technicality. "Go on."

I watched her roll her clit, slickened with my release, and my dick throbbed in answer. Then she came with a whimpered cry, and as soon as she was finished, I dropped back to my knees and dove in face first, cleaning her of our combined desire and loving the taste of us.

She came again beneath my tongue, so I bit her, just to give her a hint of pain along with her undeserved pleasure. I bit down harder, piercing the sensitive flesh and lapping up the drops of blood I'd come to collect, the taste of her sending a rush of euphoria through me. I should have known better; the pain only sent her spiraling higher. I would have to be more clever in my punishments because one thing was abundantly clear: my little monster hadn't learned a fucking thing.

Oh well, there was always next time.

SEVENTEEN

ROSIE

Glancing at the clock, I fought the wave of nerves as I realized Ben would be here any second. With a week of cooking lessons under my belt, I'd had the bright idea to invite him over for dinner to show off my new skills. Currently, those consisted of cooking pasta without setting the house ablaze.

I used a spoon to scoop a few of the yellow noodles out of the simmering pot. Pinching one end between my fingers, I pulled it free.

"Oh, fork me, that's hot."

"W-what are you d-doing?"

Spinning around, I flung the noodle, not at the wall as I'd originally intended, but straight at my dinner guest.

He glanced down at the string of pasta hanging from his black button-up shirt—an upgrade from his worn tees and flannels, which I couldn't help but appreciate, knowing it was for me. There was a mixture of confusion and amusement on his handsome face. "W-w-when you invited me over f-f-for dinner, I thought w-we'd be eating it, n-not wearing it."

"Does it count as done if it sticks to you instead of the wall?"

His lips curled up, the hint of a smile making my heart flip. "S-sure."

"Oh, thank God. I've gone through half a box of spaghetti just trying to test for doneness."

His attention flicked up to the wall behind the stove, liberally splattered with the stringy pasta in various stages of clinginess. Most had already fallen to the counter. Brows drawing together, he took a deep breath, then sighed before muttering, "Baby steps."

"Have a seat. It'll be ready in just a tick."

I gestured to the perfectly set table. Well, as perfect as I could make it with the hodgepodge of items at my disposal. Mismatched plates, a tablecloth made of the thin blanket usually draped over the back of the sofa, and a battery-powered candle in the center all rounded out the decor. Was it elegant? No.

I heard a hitch of laughter. My shoulders lifted defensively. I might not know much about cooking, but I'd eaten at enough high-end restaurants to know what belonged on a table.

"What?"

He shook his head.

"Are you laughing?"

"N-no," he lied.

I put my hands on my hips. "Bentley Mercer, I made you a lovely meal, and you're *laughing* at me?"

He gestured to the table. "N-not you, but h-how many c-cups d-do we need?"

I bit my lip, taking in the two wine glasses, two water glasses, and the chipped coffee mugs I'd set out for us. Then the numerous forks, spoons, and knives set around the dinner, salad, and bread plates.

Okay, so maybe I went a little overboard. I was just trying to make it nice. "It's supposed to be elegant. This is how I grew up. I'm afraid I don't know any differently."

"I g-grew up eating T-TV d-dinners."

I couldn't hide my disappointment. I'd gone too far, and he didn't like it. I should've kept it simple. Stupid girl. Reaching for the extra silverware, I began gathering them up, but his warm palm on the back of my hand stopped me.

"Hey, d-don't do that. I l-like it." His brows dipped, and he wrinkled his nose. "I-is something b-burning?"

"Oh, sugar! The bread." I spun out of his hold and shot across the small room to the oven, grabbing a towel to help pull the smoking garlic bread out. "It's ruined. I'm cursed when it comes to bread."

He shook his head and walked over. "W-we can s-save it." Then he grabbed a bread knife from the block on the counter and, using an oven mitt, held the loaf with one hand as he scraped the charred edges off the top. "See? G-good as n-new."

I was a bit more dubious, but he was the expert, so I was going to trust his judgment. He sliced the bread and placed it in the small basket I'd set aside for exactly that purpose.

"Why don't you sit, and I'll bring you a plate?"

His lips lifted in that half-smile I was coming to love and dread in equal measure. It made me stupid. I couldn't think straight when he smiled at me.

I swore I could feel his heated gaze on me as I moved about the kitchen, plating food for him, adding freshly grated cheese to the top of the mound of pasta and red sauce. The distinct sound of a cork popping followed by the glug-glug of liquid being poured told me he'd taken the liberty of opening the wine and serving it. I liked the idea of him serving me anything. Of him ensuring I had what I needed. Ben made me feel safe. Protected. Cared for in a way not even my family had ever managed.

Hands full with our two plates, I brought them to the table and sat across from him.

"Oh, blast! I forgot the salad."

I jumped up from my seat and raced to the fridge. Grabbing the salad bowls I'd prepared, I pulled them out and dashed on the homemade vinaigrette I'd prepared. When I turned back to him, he was sitting patiently, that grin still on his face.

"Okay," I said, handing him a bowl. "Eat up."

He lifted a fork and dove into the pasta first. I couldn't help but watch intently, my stomach twisting with nerves as I waited for his verdict.

Rosie, you twit, it's boiled noodles and store-bought sauce. Why do you care so much?

He took a big bite, his expression shifting from excited to confused, then rapidly schooling itself to an even sort of acceptance. "Mmm." He gave a tight smile as he chewed. Was the pasta crunchy? Why was I hearing crunching?

I took my own tentative bite, nearly spitting it out. Perhaps I shouldn't have kept adding noodles to the water after all my tests. The texture was all over the place. Some were mushy, while others were definitely crisp. And why did the cheese taste funny? There was a spiciness to it I didn't recall tasting before.

God, Rosie. You couldn't even get this right.

I took a sip of my wine, watching with bated breath as he went for the salad. I knew the instant he put it in his mouth I'd mucked that up as well. He coughed, eyes widening, then as soon as he could, he downed his entire glass of wine.

"It's terrible," I said, my shoulders slumping, cheeks burning.

"N-no."

"Don't lie to me, Ben. It's dreadful. Bloody awful."

"I just w-wasn't p-prepared for the p-p-pepper."

I scrunched my nose. "I followed the recipe. It said to add two teaspoons of pepper."

He was trying so hard not to smile. I could see the battle warring in his eyes. "W-which m-measuring spoon d-did you use?"

I got up and snagged the spoon off the counter, holding it up. "This one."

"Th-that's a t-tablespoon, baby."

Tears sprung to my eyes. Embarrassment, frustration, and absolute irritation at my helplessness. I couldn't even measure correctly. What had I learned in the twenty-one years I spent as a Blackthorne that would help me live life out in the real world? Nothing. I was an absolute menace to society. A burden. And now I was poisoning one of the few people trying to help me.

Horrified, I reached for his plate, intent on chucking this travesty of a meal in the bin, but he stopped me, holding onto the other end and keeping it in place.

"N-Nadia, s-stop."

"No. Please. You can't possibly want to eat this. I should never have thought I could do it." I gave the plate another tug, but he held fast.

"Baby, stop."

His voice was so soft, so filled with kindness I didn't deserve. There wasn't an ounce of his stutter in the words.

My grip on the plate went slack as I blinked up at him, only to watch on in horror.

He hadn't expected me to let go because the plate shot toward him and dumped down his shirt into his lap.

I burst into tears.

Ben was on his feet and tugging me into his arms before I could push him away. "Don't cry, baby. I love th-that you c-cooked for me."

His hand trailed down my back, lips pressing to the crown of my head.

"I just wanted to do something nice for you," I said through sobs. "I can't even do that without dumping your food in your lap."

"It's fine. I can change."

I looked up at him then, at the affection in his eyes. My breath caught when he cupped my cheek and brushed away the tears.

"These jeans are new anyway. They need a few good washes."

I swallowed back a little hiccup, too stunned by the gesture and the crystal clear words. "Your stammer . . . "

His gaze went thoughtful. "I d-didn't even n-notice."

But I knew why. He'd been too focused on me. On making me feel better. Pointing it out made him self-conscious, which is why it must have returned. That's when I realized the more comfortable he grew around me, the more it had faded. We hadn't needed to text much at all over the last couple of days.

Warmth exploded in my chest. I didn't know why it mattered that Ben could relax enough around me that way. But it did. It mattered a lot.

"Ben . . ."

The pad of his thumb, still wet from my tears, brushed

over my bottom lip. He just stared at my mouth, an intense expression clouding his features.

"Ben?"

"I'm gonna kiss you." My shocked gasp brought his eyes to mine, then uncertainty flashed in his. "All right?"

No one had ever kissed me. I'd never pressed my lips to another man's, with the exception of Asher that day in his bathroom. And that didn't really count since it hadn't been more than a quick brush of my lips over his. I couldn't even recall whether he'd kissed me back.

I would know if he had, wouldn't I?

Even still, I nodded.

And then Ben's lips were on mine, and all other thoughts flew out of my head. He tasted of spice and wine. Of so much undiscovered desire between us. The soft moan he let out against my mouth had me reaching up and threading my fingers in his dark hair, bringing us closer.

The sensation of being kissed by Bentley Mercer was not unlike free falling. It reminded me of the time my father had rented out an amusement park so we could attend in the middle of the night with the rides at our disposal, just after Noah had turned. My first rollercoaster. Ben's kiss made my stomach flip the same way as the first big drop. My head went dizzy, my legs tingly and weak, and adrenaline followed.

His hold on my face stayed tender. It was so different from the way Pan touched me. Gavin too. They wanted to own me. Ben wanted to cherish me.

I lifted up on my toes, ready for more, wanting everything, but his lips feathered over mine, gentling and then going still. He pulled away and I chased him, feeling his soft chuckle wash over me.

"Fuck, baby. I w-wanted to do that all w-week."

"You did?"

"Yeah."

"What stopped you?"

"R-rules."

I stared at him, confused. "You're the boss. What rules?"

"My own s-stupid ones." He shook his head. "I sh-should have known I w-wouldn't be able to r-resist you."

Why did those words make me want to burst into song? For the first time, it felt like I'd met someone I could give my heart to. Someone who might actually want it. Like I'd found a place where I belonged. That place just so happened to be a person.

Except, I'd made a deal with a demon I couldn't renege on. Pan would ruin Ben if I took things farther. I knew he wasn't lying either. The look in the demon's eyes had been vicious and filled with promise. If I gave myself to anyone, Ben included, Pan would make him pay.

With immense effort, I pushed away from the man holding me close. "I . . . We should go slow." I should have said we needed to stop altogether. But I was a selfish coward.

"Whatever you want," he agreed, pressing another soft kiss to my lips. "I'm n-not going anywhere."

That was what I was afraid of. I'd never been good at resisting temptation.

"There's still t-time to eat before Remi and I have to l-leave." He tucked some hair behind my ear. "Come on. Let's s-see what we can r-rustle up for d-dinner."

CHAPTER
EIGHTEEN

ASHER

I knocked back another gulp of the moonshine in my glass as I finished pulling data on my newest client. A high-born vampire with a penchant for cheating. One of his *friends* was feeling chatty. He wanted me to see what I could find on her so he could blackmail her into silence. Buying her off seemed like the smarter approach to me, but I supposed mutually assured destruction was just as effective. As long as I was getting paid, it wasn't my place to judge.

I clicked a couple of windows closed and started encrypting my findings when one of my burner phones buzzed with an incoming call. A soft hum of interest vibrated in my throat as I realized it was my local line.

"Hmm, which one of you wants to torture me now?"

There were only three people who had the number. Ben, Remi, and Rosie. My cock twitched at the thought of those last two. And then there was the idea of them both . . . at the same time.

"Christ, you need to get laid," I grumbled, hitting the screen and accepting the call. "What?"

"Oh joy, it's grumpy Asher. My favorite." Remi's voice skated across my skin, a mixture of sarcasm and playfulness. He was keyed up, energy at a high. That meant one thing. Fight night.

"You know how I like to switch things up. Keep you guessing."

"Oh, there's no guessing. You're an asshole. End of story."

"Yeah, but I sure am pretty."

"There is that. Unless you're sporting one of those stupid beards. Seriously, who do you think you're fooling?"

Given the number of times I'd sat right in front of him without so much as a flicker of recognition in his eyes, I'd say everyone. But pointing that out wouldn't win me any favors. And if I played my cards right, I might just get my dick sucked tonight. Remi always came back from these fights raring to go. Either with the urge to continue sparring or to get railed. I liked both options, but door number two was my favorite.

"Is there a reason you called me? I'm not in the mood for a booty call, wolf."

Lies. I was definitely up for a booty call. From the smirk I could hear loud and clear in Remi's voice, he knew it too.

"Yeah, actually, there is. Ben and I are heading out of town for the night."

"How is that my problem?"

"I figured you'd want to know since your little project is gonna be unsupervised. Just a week ago, she almost burned the place down, but Ben was able to get to her. This time she just might succeed."

Christ. So far I'd managed to keep my promise not to spy on her again. But knowing she'd be at the bar . . . all alone once it closed . . . surely tonight I got a pass?

It'd be fine. I'd keep an eye out and keep my hands off my cock. Simple.

There you go lying to yourself again, Asher.

My frustration with my own weakness made my voice come out as a harsh growl. "And what do you expect me to do about it? I'm forty fucking minutes out of town."

"You could . . . come down to the bar and hang out with her?"

I laughed. Hang out? I didn't hang out with anyone. I fucked, I watched, and I took notes. That was it. It had been a long ass time since I did the first.

"I don't hang out. I'll keep an eye on her, okay?"

"Don't let anything happen to her."

"Aw, look, Remi has a crush."

"Fuck you, Asher. She's your charity case."

I sighed. "Don't get your panties in a bunch. She'll be fine. She's more capable than you think, but consider Babysitter Asher on duty." I hung up and tossed my phone on the desk.

She was stronger than they gave her credit for. Anyone who could fake their own death and make it to my hideaway had to be. I'd already gone to town for my monthly supply run and visited more than I liked in order to get Rosie taken care of. Now I was doing it again? What the fuck was wrong with me? How could I keep my ass alive if I put myself out there in plain sight all the damn time? Unless maybe I really was paranoid.

I could've chosen any of my disguises for tonight, crusty old fisherman, one of my season hunters passing through town, but I didn't want to be a smelly old man around her. That only left me one option. Tonight I had to be Henry.

It was the persona I used when I was on the prowl. Complete with shifter pheromones to disguise my true scent. They wouldn't do me any good long term—like whatever spell Rosie used to make herself smell fae—but they'd keep my secret for the evening. That was the goal. Nothing more than a night.

More importantly, Henry was someone the locals were familiar with, so I wouldn't draw any unwanted attention, which was important after something as major as the town's first murder in a decade. No one would look twice at the handsome loner wolf shifter with his glasses and emo tattoos. Well, they might, but even so, no one bothered him because he was always working on his novel. It also gave me a reason to bring my laptop and headphones. I could hole up in the corner and pretend to be working while keeping Rosie in my sights.

Pulling out a few items from my temporary tattoo stash, I selected two sparrows to apply to my neck and a set of knuckle tattoos that spelled out FUCK LOVE. Henry was a broody motherfucker. In another life, he probably played guitar and was lead singer for some rock band. Maybe the next lead for the Apocalyptic Unicorns. Maybe he was working on poetry or lyrics instead of a novel. The mental image made me snicker. I'd been a hermit for so long that the idea of doing anything in the spotlight was fucking laughable. I'd probably piss myself from stage fright.

After applying the neck art, I moved to tackle my fingers, but the sight of the star pattern on my left hand stopped me.

"What the fuck?" I murmured, tracing the ink-like markings. "You cannot be growing. Moira stopped this." My chest hurt. I wasn't interested in calling the Belladonna witch again, but fuck, if this curse kept moving up my goddamned arm, I'd have to.

Ignoring it for now—because really, what the fuck

could I do about it?—I finished applying the tats and then grabbed Henry's go-to black hoodie and leather jacket. They were his pussy bait. Or dick bait, depending on the night.

One liberal dash of pheromones, and I was good to go. Except for the pièce de résistance. I snagged Henry's dark-rimmed glasses and settled them on my face. "Clark Kent, who?" Then I winked at myself like the smug prick I was. "I'm always Superman, baby."

Why was I fucking excited to drive into town and watch Rosie? Oh, right, because I was a disaster and a glutton for torture.

I did it anyway, and in forty minutes on the dot, I pulled Henry's Jeep behind the boatshed a few blocks from The Tip. Grabbing my beat-up backpack, I slung it over my shoulder and made my way through town, clocking her the second I stepped inside.

She was a fucking wet dream standing behind the bar, making drinks and flirting with the regulars in those skintight jeans and belly-baring crop top. She had her hair tucked behind one ear, exposing the long column of her throat, her makeup far heavier than anything I'd seen her wear before. Those ruby red lips curled up in a sexy smile, giving life to a dozen images of them wrapped around my cock. Just that fast, I was hard.

"Motherfucker," I growled down at my dick. "Really?"

Her eyes found mine across the room. Even with her contact lenses disguising the color, they sent my body humming. Shock was quickly replaced by pleasure, and I knew she'd recognized me. I'd be lying to myself if I said I hadn't hoped for exactly that. If I didn't want her to know who I was, I would be here as Hank, the ice road trucker.

I gave her a slight nod and made for the corner table

Henry preferred. A few patrons waved but didn't say anything to me as I found my seat and began pulling things from my bag.

Before I even had my laptop fired up, Rosie stood in front of me. "I haven't seen you in here before . . . "

"Henry," I supplied.

Her lips twitched. "Nice to meet you, *Henry*. What can I get you?"

Tom let out a chuckle and shouted from his spot at the bar. "Don't waste your time on that prick, Nadia. He's a lost cause. The only thing he loves is his book."

"You a big reader, Henry?"

"Writer," I corrected, enjoying this playful, flirty side of her way more than I should.

"Oh? What kind of book? I'm a fan of romance novels myself."

Oh, I could play this game with her all night. "Steamy ones?"

"The spicier, the better."

"Then that's what I write. So hot your toes will curl."

"My favorite. Can't wait to read it."

"Maybe you'd like to spend some time brainstorming with me after your shift . . ." *What the fuck, Asher?*

"Are you asking me to be your muse?"

"Maybe."

"Hmm, I'll have to check my schedule. Things are pretty tight."

God help me, I palmed my dick under the table. "Are they?"

"I don't know if I can squeeze you in."

Jesus fuck. I choked on my own words before I got them out. "I bet I can make it fit."

Her cheeks bloomed with color. "Oh my . . ."

"Come on then, Nadia. Stop fannying about with the writer and come over here and let a real man entertain you."

Harry was officially on my shit list. I shot a glare his way, but the brawny fucker only smirked.

There's no contest, buddy. This one's mine. Back off.

The possessive thoughts were followed by a slew of others. *Mine? Back off? What the hell is wrong with you? We don't play for keeps, Asher. One and done, remember?*

"What do you want to drink, Henry?" she asked.

I cleared my throat. "Whiskey. Neat."

She winked. "Right. I'll be back in a tick."

"Thanks, Nadia." The name felt wrong in my mouth, but it was there for a reason. I kind of loved sharing this secret with her.

It took more effort than it should to return my eyes to my laptop. It was going to be a long night, but at least it was shaping up to be a fun one.

Hours later, the bar was more full than normal. Every single member of the North Star MC seemed to be here. The place was loud, filled with raucous conversation, cheers, and shouts from the Russians, and Rosie was handling them better than I expected. I was pissed she'd been left alone, though. Because it was a weekday, she didn't even have Dante the cook to back her up. What the fuck were the Mercers thinking?

That's why Remi called you, asshole.

The reminder wasn't enough to blunt the edge of my temper. What the hell was I supposed to do against an entire pack of drunk bears?

As Rosie continued slinging drinks and smiling at customers, I felt the atmosphere change from jovial to tense. The shifters weren't laughing now; they were growling at each other, each shot they knocked back ratcheting up the emotions and loosening lips.

"Come over here, pretty little one. Come keep me company," Alexi called from one of the tables.

"I'm sorry, mate, I'm a bit busy at the moment." Rosie's brow was furrowed now, fatigue showing clear as day. "Maybe another time, yeah?"

She carried a tray filled with shot glasses to another table and delivered them to the five hulking MC members, then moved toward the bar once more. But Alexi snagged her wrist, pulling her onto his lap.

"Come on, don't be so cold. You've been working hard. You deserve to take a little break. I've got something nice and hot for you."

Unease washed over her face, but she covered it up with a laugh that didn't quite ring true. "There's no one else to take care of your brothers. I don't think they'd appreciate me taking a break."

"They'd get over it quick enough. They love to watch."

Shoving back my chair so hard it fell on the floor, I stalked over to the Russian. "She said no, dickweed."

The bar went silent, every eye in the room trained on me. *Fucking perfect.*

Alexi looked me up and down and laughed. "What are you going to do about it, pipsqueak?"

I wasn't a pipsqueak by any means. While I might be a nerd by some people's definitions, I was cut. I knew how to defend myself, and I could kick ass if I needed to.

He leaned close and sniffed me. "Little beta wolves don't scare me."

"Oooh, I'm shaking. Are you and your cousins gonna get me with your Scare Bear stare? Which one are you? Limp-dick Bear?"

The sound of chairs scraping against the floor and knuckles cracking filled the room.

Good job, Asher. Piss off the whole damn MC. Great idea.

Thankfully, no one else seemed ready to jump in.

"Nothing limp about me. Isn't that right, Nadia?" Then he slid his tongue up Rosie's neck, and she jerked away from him before slapping him across the face.

"There's nothing under those pants you should be proud of."

She was hot as fuck when she was angry. But Alexi stood, all six-foot-six of him, and snarled as he lashed out, his open palm connecting with her face before I could get between them. He hit her so hard that she dropped to the floor, and everyone in the space seemed to stop breathing for a moment.

"W-what the f-fuck is th-this?" Ben shouted as he and Remi burst through the door.

"Everyone get the hell out of here. Right fucking now." Rage filled Remi's voice, and his accusing stare landed on me, eyes gone a feral icy blue. His wolf was at the surface, barely leashed and spoiling for a fight.

Remi sported a split lip, and I couldn't help but notice Ben's bruised knuckles as he rushed to Rosie's side, carefully helping her stand.

I only caught his whispered words because I was right there.

"I-it's okay, baby. I-I got you."

Without another word, he picked her up, cradling her body and taking her upstairs.

"I said now!" Remi roared when the patrons didn't immediately start filing out.

"What about our tabs?" Harry asked.

"NOW!"

Alexi crowded me, poking me with a finger in my chest. "This isn't over, pipsqueak."

"It's fucking over because I said it's over. Get out," Remi said, putting himself in front of Alexi with nothing but fury on his face. "Don't test me. I'm not afraid of you or your brothers."

"What are you going to do to me, little wolf?"

"Alexi. You heard him. Let's go." Ivan Romanov, the North Stars' prez, growled low—an animalistic and not remotely human sound—as he came up behind Alexi. "Don't make me force you out. You won't like what happens."

That was the only thing that made the bear back down. Slowly, everyone filtered out of The Tip. Everyone but me.

I knew I was in for it the second Remi spun around.

"You had one fucking job."

NINETEEN

REMI

The look on Asher's face when I rounded on him only added fuel to the fire burning in my blood. All he'd had to do was take care of her. That was it. Instead, we got back to find her on the floor, bleeding and scared, with fucking tears in her eyes. I didn't care what the reason for it was. It never should have happened.

If I'd been here, it wouldn't have.

Instead of cowering, which a smarter man would have done when faced with six plus feet of snarling Alpha wolf, Asher went toe-to-toe with me.

"Oh yeah? And what exactly did you expect the *human* to do against a whole pack of drunk Russian bears, dumbass? You're the shifter. You're the one who is supposed to be protecting her, not running off like a piece of shit and leaving her at the mercy of those fucking animals."

"You know I had to go."

"Sure. Whatever. Just don't blame me for your bad decisions. Where was Darla? Or Dante?"

"It's a Tuesday. It was only a few hours. How was I supposed to know the entirety of the North Stars would show up? Goddammit." I ran a frustrated hand through my hair, tugging on the strands as I felt my wolf battle me for dominance. "This is ridiculous. She wouldn't have even been here in the first place if not for you. You're the one who brought her here. It's as much your responsibility to keep her safe as ours. If not more."

"I'm a *human*," he enunciated the word, slowly drawing it out like I was a four-year-old with a hearing problem. "How many times do I need to remind you that while I am a fucking savant when it comes to technology, I can't keep her safe the way you're supposed to be able to. If you don't abandon her, that is."

"Fuck you, Asher. You and your stupid ass disguises and paranoid bullshit." I hated knowing he was right.

Fuck.

Fuck.

Fuck.

If something had happened to her . . .

My wolf clawed at my control, fangs making my gums tingle with the need to slip free. I was either going to have to calm the hell down right now or fuck some shit up.

Instead of saying another word to Asher, who stood there, glaring at me in that judgy as fuck way he had, I stalked into the back office. Tearing open the top drawer of the desk, I pulled out my copper case filled with exactly what I needed to wrangle my beast.

"Come to daddy," I murmured, opening the box and snagging a pre-rolled joint. Could I use a vape? Yeah, but it didn't have the same ritual. I liked the process of rolling joint after joint. Almost as much as the crackle of burning paper, the glow of the cherry, and tang of the smoke when it came time to partake.

"Are you serious? This is how you deal with your problems?"

"That's rich coming from the guy who drowns himself in moonshine. You're not my preacher, Asher. Don't fucking act high and mighty with me."

Asher's tall frame filled the doorway, arms crossed, anger radiating from every cell. The scent filled the air, mixed with something else. Another wolf's pheromones. What. The. Fuck?

"I see you've moved on. Bending over for another wolf now? I thought you liked to top," I snarled.

"Why do you care?"

"I don't. You can fuck whoever you want."

"Like I need your permission. Besides, from the looks of things, you're desperate to get Nadia under you."

"And you're not? Do you even know what the truth is anymore? So many lies spew from that fucking mouth of yours it's hard to tell."

"You love my mouth, *Remington*."

I took a long moment before I brought the joint to my lips and lit the end. Then with my gaze locked on his, I sucked in a deep pull. My cock was throbbing at the mention of his mouth, of getting Nadia under me, of fucking. It had been one high after another tonight. First we'd won our fights, then we'd squared off with the North Stars, and now this. Even with the effects of the smoke in my bloodstream, I was too keyed up to be trusted.

"Get out of here," I warned. "I'm not under control, Asher. I need to let this out, and there are only two ways I can do that."

Instead of backing away, he stepped further inside the office. "I'm not afraid of you. You think you're some big bad wolf I should bow down to. All it would take is one anonymous email, and all your secrets would be out in the open, Mercer. I have as much on you as you do me."

I saw straight through the bluff. I could out him as easily as he could out me. "Try me."

Instead of saying anything else, I took another draw, holding the pungent smoke deep in my lungs before leaning forward, gripping him by the neck of his hoodie, and exhaling straight in his face. He sucked in the smoke, his lips so close I could feel the energy crackling off him.

"Fuck you, Remi."

"Maybe this time I should fuck you, Asher."

"Never gonna happen."

I smirked. "You only top because I let you. You really think you could tame me if I didn't? I'm a wolf, Asher, and as you seem to enjoy reminding me, you're just a puny little human."

His lip curled back, but it wasn't just anger blazing in his eyes. The rough growl of his voice sent a flood of need straight to my dick.

"Is that what you think? You'll be singing a different tune when my cock is deep in your ass, and you're begging me to let you come."

This had taken a turn in a direction I wasn't expecting. But at this point, I was so on edge, I needed something to tip the scale one way or another. If I didn't get some kind of release, I was going to hurt someone.

So what was it going to be? Fuck or fight?

Both were fun.

One felt infinitely better.

"Prove it."

"Beg me and maybe I will."

I slipped my palm down his chest until I cupped the bulge behind his fly. He was just as hard as me. Thick and ready. He knew what we both wanted, but the two of us had to play this game first. This dance of loathing. Usually it was pretend, but right now, the instinctive need to protect Nadia had true hatred burning in me. Why? Why was I so angry with Asher over something that shouldn't matter this much?

She's mine.

My heart gave a stutter as the words flashed in my brain.

She's mine, and I trusted him, and he let her get hurt.

"Fuck off, Asher. You're trying to distract me from the real issue, as usual. You brought her here and dumped her on us. Now we're attached, and you have to deal with the consequences of your fucked up deals."

"You're the one who has his hand on my cock, Mercer. I'm not trying to distract you from anything."

"You're lucky it's not gripping your balls."

"That could be fun."

I growled. "You don't even care that she was hurt? Why help her at all?"

He shrugged. "Money talks." But I saw the flicker in his eyes.

"Liar."

"It's not your business."

I squeezed his dick. "Is this for me, or for her?"

"Does it matter?"

Yes? No?

Asher dragged his nose along my neck, lifting his lips to my ear. "You're the one I'm with."

Fuck. He had to know what he was doing to me. Every time we were together like this, all it took was one well-timed word, and I gave in to him. Let him have his way with me. Begged him to make me see stars. Submission was a heady experience for an Alpha like me. It went against my very nature, which made it almost taboo. But with Asher? I craved it.

I let out a soft groan, and that was all it took. He gripped me by the throat and shoved me back against the wall a second before his lips crashed against mine in a furious clash of livid desire. He wanted me. He hated me. And I loved it all.

We were frantic and fiery as we devoured each other. All traces of the rage and pent-up urge to shift converged into one impure need. Lust. I wouldn't be hurting anyone but myself tonight.

"I told you you were hard for me."

"You talk too much," he growled, taking his hand off my throat and sliding two fingers deep into my mouth. "I like you so much better when your mouth's full."

I made an annoyed sound in the back of my throat, which only had him pressing down harder on my tongue to keep me quiet.

"Suck them like you would my dick, Remi. Earn it, and maybe I'll give it to you."

Fuck me. I forgot what a dirty mouth he had.

I closed my lips around the digits, did as he said, but wished they were the real thing. Maybe he'd let me suck him if I was good. His eyes fluttered closed as I trailed my tongue between the two fingers and hummed. My own hands were busy working his belt until I could reach inside his jeans to find the thick cock I craved. He was just as worked up as me, but somehow, he had more control.

The low grunt he released when skin met skin had my hips jerking, my own dick needing attention. Then he was gone, his fingers, his heat, the press of his chest to mine.

Until he spun me around and shoved me hard against the wall.

"What was that you called me? A puny human?" He growled low in my ear. "Does this feel puny to you?" He shoved his cock against my ass and rolled his hips, making me moan. "Because I promise, once I'm balls deep inside you, you won't. Remember how I can destroy your fucking ass, Remi? How you begged me to do it again and again? You're going to fucking love it, just like you always do."

"Do it," I gritted out.

"Not yet."

The scrape of his teeth along that special spot on my shoulder had me gasping. It was the one that made me shiver in a way I wasn't used to, one he shouldn't know about. Then his hands undid my belt, tearing at my fly and pulling me free as he shoved my pants to my knees. He took me in his hand and slid his large palm down my length. I couldn't quite help the whimper of relief that bit of friction caused as I thrust into his hand. Already my balls were pulled tight, my jaw clenched with the need to come.

"More," I begged. "I need more."

He shoved his fingers into my mouth again. "Get them wet for me, Remi."

I sucked him deep while he continued his languid strokes up and down my shaft. It wasn't nearly enough, but I was so fucking close. It was always like this with Asher. Unpredictable. Explosive. Raw.

I rolled my hips, silently pleading with him to move faster, but he stopped, instead squeezing me tight at the base.

"You don't get to do that. You come when I make you come, Remington." Then he pulled his fingers from my mouth and slid them between my ass cheeks until I felt the pressure of one against my rim.

"God, please," I whispered.

"Look at you, already begging. It's my favorite sound."

The things this man could do to me were unnamable.

"Asher," I groaned, needing to feel him inside me more than I needed my next fucking breath.

"You want my cock? Are you sure?"

He bit down on the back of my neck, holding me hostage as he sank one finger into my ass, testing, teasing, opening me. But even with the lubrication my mouth had provided his fingers, I needed more.

"There's lube in the left drawer," I bit out. "Fuck, Asher. I need more."

"Oh . . . the desk. That sounds like fun." He slapped my ass as he took a step back. "Bend over the desk, Remi. Ass up. Get ready for me to wreck you."

God, he would. He always did. That's why I always came back like a fucking puppy desperate for attention. Asher owned me in ways no one else did, in ways I never let myself examine too closely. As much as I wanted him to be, he wasn't a casual fuck. He was a toxic addiction I couldn't quit.

Maybe because I didn't really want to.

Usually I had no trouble letting people go. I was used to them being temporary. But not him.

Only one other person in my life caused the same sense of twisted panic at the thought of losing them. And it was way too fucking soon to be thinking that way about *her*. Especially with Asher pressing me flat against the desk as he flicked open the bottle of lube and poured some straight down my crack.

"One finger or two, Remi?"

His voice was dark and domineering, and I knew he wasn't really asking. He'd use two. He always did.

"Two."

"Good boy. Now let me open you up."

There it was, the promise of everything he could give me. I swallowed a moan as his slick fingers sank into me, curling and tapping that perfect spot hidden inside.

"Fuck, Asher. You feel so fucking good."

"I haven't really started yet."

I know. And that's what made it so damn perfect. If he could reduce me to this with a couple of fingers, I would be an incoherent mess when he finally gave me his dick. I needed that release. I needed to let go.

"Fuck, I'm gonna come," I whimpered.

"Not yet. You're not coming until my cock is deep inside you."

"Then get a fucking condom on and give it to me, Asher."

His dark chuckle had me walking a tightrope, threatening to fall at any second. "I thought you'd never ask."

TWENTY

"H-here."

Ben handed me the bag of ice he'd insisted I place on my slightly swollen cheek. It didn't even hurt anymore, but I took the offering anyway. I couldn't deny him this small thing. Not with the concern and frustration blazing in his eyes.

The scene in the bar was a blur. One second I was about to be felt up by a handsy bear, the next Asher was there defending my honor and I was on the ground. Before any of that made sense, the twins were back, and Ben was hauling me into his arms and up into my room.

As grateful as I was for the rescue, I was more worried about what was happening to the two men still downstairs. I'd heard their snarled words. The threats from the MC. I needed to know they were okay.

If they'd come to blows because of me . . .

"Are y-you okay?" Ben asked, hesitantly reaching for me and brushing my fingers with his.

"I'm perfectly fine. I'm not the delicate flower you think I am."

"Maybe n-not. But you're s-soft and sweet, like a petal."

My heart gave a squeeze at the innocent word. *Petal.* It slithered over me in Gavin's voice, haunting me with its rough and domineering echo. Not at all the way Ben said it.

I couldn't help but wonder what he was doing. If he still thought about his 'dead' wife. If he missed me . . .

Stop it, Roslyn. That girl is dead. It doesn't matter anymore. Besides, you have your hands full enough between your demon lover and the swoony shifter. Shifters.

And don't forget Asher.

I didn't have the handsome hacker. Not really, but my heart protested his lack of inclusion. I didn't recognize this woman. The one who wanted to keep all of them. I blamed my sister-in-law. Until her, I wouldn't have ever imagined the possibility of multiple love interests.

Why should I choose? Sunday bloody well hadn't.

If I'd learned one thing about myself during my *reinvention,* it was that I had spent far too long playing the wallflower in a cast of peacocks. I could take what I wanted. Just like Sunday had. If that was truly what I desired.

A little thrill raced down my spine and settled between my legs at the thought of all those hands and mouths on me. There might have even been a tail . . .

"Is Remi . . ." I wasn't sure how to finish that question. *Is he okay? Is he coming upstairs? Is he going to be jealous if I fall for you, Ben?*

"He's fine. P-probably feeling the s-same as m-me."

"And how's that?"

"K-keyed up. W-worried about you."

I pressed my hand against his cheek. "I'm fine. Look, the bleeding's already stopped, and it doesn't even hurt."

He gave me a dubious look.

"I promise. I'm going to pop down and check on him." I needed him here with us. I didn't like leaving him alone.

"I d-don't think that's a g-good idea."

I popped out my hip and shoved the bag of ice into his chest. "Are you thinking to try and stop me, Mercer?" I used the same snarky tone I would if I was talking to my overbearing brothers.

Ben's lips twitched. He wasn't intimidated in the least. He probably thought me a kitten swatting at a big mean wolf. He wouldn't be that far off, really.

"I should, b-but I won't." He slid his knuckles over my unmarked cheek and leaned in to whisper, "Don't be g-gone long, baby."

A twinge of need made itself known in my belly, but with it came apprehension. I'd made a deal with Pan, and I needed to remember that. Things couldn't go too far with Ben, not without putting him at risk. But the man made it quite the challenge to stop myself.

Only because you don't want *to resist him, you strumpet.*

You don't want to resist any *of them.*

"Back in a tick, I promise."

"I l-love the way y-you talk."

My nose crinkled, and I stopped in the doorway. "What do you mean?"

"Th-the things you say. 'In a t-tick, forking, oh sugar'," he imitated me, his smile making my belly swoop. "I've n-never met anyone l-like you, Nadia."

Something uncomfortable wrapped around my heart, like thorns piercing the muscle and twisting. That name was wrong on his lips. I wanted him to call me Rosie. To know who I really was.

Stop it. Nadia is just a name, as is Rosie or Roslyn. If he knows your secret, he's in even more danger, you little fool.

I forced a smile I didn't quite feel. "The feeling is entirely mutual, Bentley. I assure you."

Then I darted down the stairs before I could do something stupid, like fling myself at him and beg him to take me to bed.

My steps slowed as I neared the main floor. The lights still blazed bright, but it didn't sound like anyone was down there until a strange noise came from the office. A scrape, a thud, and grunts of pain.

Oh, no.

Were they fighting? Had Alexi come back to get his revenge? With quick but quiet steps, I followed the sounds, ready to do . . . something to defend Remi. Instead, my entire body ran hot at what I saw through the mostly open door.

Asher had Remi bent over the desk. I couldn't make out much, but it was abundantly clear they were *not* fighting.

My mouth fell open as Asher pressed one hand flat on the desk and leaned forward to growl in Remi's ear. "You're so good at taking my dick, Mercer. So. Fucking. Good."

Oh. *Oh.* I should have turned around the instant it registered, but I couldn't. It was Gavin and his submissive all over again. I was captivated, a slave to my own raging desire. Tingles built between my legs, the hot rush of arousal only amplified by the sight of Remi, eyes closed, brow furrowed, pleasure flickering across his face.

I should go.

My inner voice was such a killjoy. But then another voice curled through me. Pan. "*Stay and watch. They would've closed the door if they didn't want you here.*"

A quick glance around confirmed I was alone. The voice urging me on was in my head. Who was I to resist a demon on my shoulder?

"God, Remi. Fuck," Asher grunted, his arm wrapped around Remi's waist, moving in time with his deep thrusts. "You ready to give it to me?"

"Yes."

The gritted out words, equal parts need and desperation, had me pressing a hand between my own legs. I mouthed the word *yes* as well, but I wasn't sure if I was ready to join them or if I just wanted to watch. It was *that* good. I couldn't look away now if my life depended on it.

Asher's pace turned frantic, the intensity between them nearly crackling in the air as Remi groaned and tensed. He arched his neck back, teeth sinking into his lower lip, veins straining. God, he was beautiful, his dark hair and stubbled jaw a sharp contrast to Asher's golden tresses. They almost looked like two fallen angels wrapped in a carnal embrace.

"Touch yourself. It's okay." Pan's words whispered through my mind.

My fingers slipped under my waistband and toyed with my clit, sending sparks shooting through me. Before I could stop myself, a soft whine escaped me, and Remi's gaze found mine. The wicked smirk on his lips made me squirm with the urge to join them both. I couldn't break the eye contact, and neither did he.

"Fuck. I need to come. Don't you want to?" Remi gritted out, winking at me just before he groaned.

Asher must have done something with his hand because Remi's eyes rolled back and he let out a guttural moan that curled itself around me. I wouldn't forget the sound of his climax for as long as I lived. Asher was right behind him, his expression a mix of pleasure and pain as his orgasm crested.

"So good. Fuck, Remi."

I was on the edge, but I couldn't bring myself to take it

further, especially not when Pan's sharp, *"Don't you fucking come,"* shot through me.

Remi stared at me once more, that cat who got the canary grin on his face. I knew he wanted me to give in, but there was something about being caught that made me self-conscious. I'd save my climax for later when I was alone and reliving this moment for the first of which I was sure would be countless times.

Asher hung his head, his breaths coming in harsh pants as he stayed in place behind Remi. "This is the last time, Mercer."

"That's what you always say."

"I mean it this time. If anyone finds out and can connect me—the real me—to you, I'm as good as dead. And so are you."

Remi didn't look remotely bothered. His smile stretched, and I knew what he was about to say before the words left his lips.

"Hate to break it to you, Asher, but your little rebel already knows about us."

"Are you deaf? There is no us."

"He says while his dick's still inside me."

Asher pulled out, making both men groan. He turned away, cleaning himself up. "Doesn't matter. She doesn't know anything."

"Wolf's out of the bag, buddy. She does now."

Asher's head snapped up and back, finding me in the doorway.

Oh, sugar. Why didn't I leave when I had the chance? Forking Pan and his devilish words.

I took a step back, then another, stumbling over myself in my haste to get away.

"Ro-Nadia, wait!"

Nope.

Nope. Nope. Nope.

There was no way I'd be able to face him. Not after I'd watched him rail Remi into the desk and touched myself like a wanton heroine from a bodice ripper. My cheeks flamed as I ran up the stairs, desperation to get back to the safety of my room fueling me.

I collided with a warm wall of man on my way, Ben's arms wrapped around me and kept me from falling backward.

"Where's the fire, baby? D-did you make toast again?"

Something about my expression must have tipped Ben off because his teasing smile faded, his gaze sharpening as his nostrils flared, breathing me in. His focus flicked behind me and then landed on my face. It wasn't hard to tell he had a pretty good idea of what I'd been up to and why. My cheeks were on fire. And my lady business was wet. Not just wet, forking drenched.

Without a word, he reached for my hand, lifting it up to his face. Holding my gaze, he ran his nose along the seam of my fingers, which had been buried between my thighs minutes prior.

The deep inhalation and flick of his tongue sent a rush of need right to my core. Wet again. It seemed to be a real problem around the Mercers . . . and Asher.

"Nadia," he groaned. "What are y-you doing to me?"

I didn't have a chance to answer before he wrapped his lips around my fingers and sucked hard. A primal growl of satisfaction rumbled low in his throat. His blue irises trained on mine, a flash of his beast in their depths. The wolf liked the way I tasted.

My knees buckled.

He released my fingers before dipping his head low, lips

at my ear. "You taste so m-much better th-than I could have imagined."

Hand trailing over my hip, he toyed with the waistband of my pants.

"Ben . . ."

"I know you w-want to t-take it slow. But please, baby. Let me take c-care of you."

Oh, great balls of fire.

CHAPTER
TWENTY-ONE

BEN

Jesus, Nadia smelled so fucking good. Everything about her called to me in a way I didn't really understand. All I knew was that I could make her feel good. I'd be the one to give her release. And if she said yes, I would.

I was desperate for the chance to prove I could give her everything she needed. Not just me, but my wolf. He was clawing at the barrier between us, begging to be let out.

His interest was new. My wolf had never cared about any of the women I hooked up with.

Nadia was different. Special. *Mine.*

My gut clenched at that word. It meant something.

"P-please, baby." I wasn't above begging.

She took in a shuddering breath. "Yes."

As I dragged my lips down her throat, a growl escaped me, but it wasn't one of warning or anger. This was feral. I wanted to tell her to run so I could chase her, catch her, pin her, and mark her.

Fuuuck. My cock could have been cut from stone, it was so hard.

189

I could have let her walk, but that would've taken too much time. I needed her writhing against me, to devour her mouth, feel her skin on mine. The urge to touch her was impossible to resist.

Sliding my hands down her back, I gripped her ass and hauled her up.

She let out a startled gasp.

"W-wrap your l-legs around me, baby."

She obeyed without question, locking her arms around my neck and trailing kisses up and down my throat. *Bite down, fuck, please.*

She grazed her teeth along the kiss-slick skin, but didn't take it farther than that. It was probably a good thing, because just that much had my whole body shaking, ready for release. She couldn't know it, but that was the exact spot she'd claim me if she'd been born a shifter.

"You're m-m..." I began, but faltered.

Shit. I'd almost said something I couldn't take back. I couldn't call her mine—not out loud. Especially when I hadn't been the man to make her wet. I knew what she'd seen. Remi and Asher. As soon as I left her apartment, I heard them going at it. But I was going to enjoy the fuck out of being the one who got to taste her as she came on my tongue.

She pulled back to look at me, a question in her eyes.

Before she could ask what I was about to say, I kissed her. Pouring all the words I couldn't utter into it. Telling her with my body what I wasn't ready to admit.

I deepened my kiss, adding my tongue and giving her a tease of what was to come. The way she sucked on it had me wishing it was my cock instead. And then she let out a little mewl of pleasure and ground her denim-covered cunt along the ridge of my erection.

Fuck, if this is how good you feel with clothes on, what will it be like when I sink inside you with nothing between us? When I give you my knot?

My steps faltered.

Where the fuck had that thought come from?

I'd never gone bare inside a woman, and I'd certainly never wanted to *breed* one. After what happened to Remi and me as kids, I had zero interest in starting a family. But Nadia had me twisted inside out. With her I wanted everything. I wanted to give her everything. My knot. My seed. I wanted to fill her full of me until I was dripping out of her and had to push it all back inside.

I groaned, my hips kicking up and pressing into the cradle of her body of their own volition. I was about two seconds away from dry humping her right here in the damned hallway.

Breaking our kiss, I ran my nose along the column of her throat as I pressed her against the door.

"Fuck, Nadia. Y-you smell s-so good."

She shivered and bared her throat to me. She couldn't know what it meant, but my wolf did. Even if I wanted to, I couldn't stop myself from accepting what she was offering. I bit down on that special spot where my mark belonged.

That's right, baby. Let me make you mine.

I clamped down a little harder as the thought rolled through my head.

"Oh, God, Ben."

Her moan nearly had me coming in my pants. I needed to get her under me, right the fuck now. Reaching blindly for the doorknob with one hand, I opened the door and walked us inside until I found the couch.

"The bedroom—"

I cut off the breathy words with another kiss. I wouldn't

191

be able to keep myself under control if I got her in a bed. It would be hard enough to keep my dick in my pants in the living room. But this wasn't about me; it was about her. She'd asked to take things slow, and I respected that. I wouldn't put either of us in a situation that had her going further than she was comfortable with just because we were swept up in the moment.

But fuck did I want to.

"N-no, baby. This w-will do just f-fine."

Leaning down, I laid her on the couch, her limbs still wrapped around me. It didn't take much for me to get her to untangle herself, though, because she wanted my lips to explore her. If her little breathy moans were any indication, she was starving for my touch.

Resting my weight on my left forearm, I trailed kisses along the side of her neck while my other hand ghosted down the front of her body. She pressed up into the touch, craving more, silently begging me for it.

I'll take care of you. Fuck, I'll take such good care of you, you'll forget all about Remi and Asher.

At least for now. The last thought was an unwelcome intrusion, but I wasn't naive enough to think it wasn't true.

As I ran my fingers between her perfect fucking tits, I had to stop, just for a moment, so I could feel the shape of her, the softness in my palm. And she instinctively arched into me in response, sending every possessive bone in my body into action. My wolf was right there, ready to take charge, begging me to mark her.

No. It's too soon. She doesn't even know what it would mean to be claimed by me like that.

It would be the mortal equivalent of marrying her while she was drunk. Except it would be permanent. There wasn't a way to break a mating bond without doing permanent damage to both of us. And if I mated anyone, it would take death to get me to let her go.

"Ben, please."

Her fingers curled into my hair, tugging on the strands and sending tingles of pleasure racing across my scalp and spine.

Goddamn, I wanted her to pet me.

But not as much as I wanted to pet her.

I moved my hand lower, desperate to discover her most intimate secrets. The way she liked to be touched. The sounds she made when she came. To find out just how fucking wet she was and feel the slickness I brought out in her. Because by the time I was done with her, there was no way she'd be anything but drenched.

My fingers found the button of her jeans, making quick work of it and the zipper so I could press inside. She groaned and rolled her hips into my hand as I slid it between her thighs.

Fuck, baby. Your panties are ruined. I have to taste you.

She couldn't hear me, but I didn't mind. Our bodies were communicating just fine on their own.

I shifted my weight, pulling back so I could tug her pants off before returning to her. I didn't think I could wait any longer to have more than just the hint of her pleasure I'd sampled on her fingers earlier. Not when I felt that heat when I coated my own digits in her arousal and knew it was right there, ready for me.

"Spread w-wider for me."

The little hitch in her breath had my dick protesting being locked behind my jeans. I ached for her. I wanted nothing more than to free myself, sink inside, and claim every part of her.

Sliding down between her thighs, I grabbed her and

adjusted us so I was kneeling on the floor and her perfect pussy was at eye level.

"What are you doing?"

I grinned up at her. "What's it look like I'm doing, baby?"

I was proud that my voice didn't falter. The way her lips parted and her eyes went glassy told me she found her answer and very much approved of my plan.

Though she'd spread her legs for me, I wasn't a small guy. My shoulders were broad, and I needed more room. I had to fit between those thighs if I was going to explore her as fully as I intended.

"Open up for me," I whispered, grabbing her knees and widening her stance. Then, I gave up all pretense of letting her have control and tugged until her ass was at the end of the cushion and those smooth, supple legs of hers were wrapped around my head.

I took a minute, just staring at her glistening slit, trying to decide whether I wanted to attack her clit or if my tongue belonged inside her first.

"I'm so sensitive your breaths are bringing me to the edge."

The whispered confession had me grinning in primal satisfaction. I blew directly on her clit, loving the flood of slick that dripped out of her in response.

"Ben, you wicked wolf. Eat. Me." She squirmed in my hold, bringing her cunt even closer. "Please?"

I laughed at the frustration tinging her words. She even managed to make her dirty demand sound prim and proper. I had the sudden urge to see what it would be like if I could make her truly lose that last shred of her control. I wanted to hear what naughty words would sound like coming from her lips. To break through the restrained and reserved way she carried herself. To make her come apart so hard she'd lose all hold on her manners.

"So sweet." I brought my face a breath away from her pussy, one finger trailing the outside of her lips, not touching her hard little clit. "Do you taste like sugar too?"

"I don't know. You tell me, you bloody tease."

I licked up her seam, nearly coming from the sound of her moan. *Oh God, she did.* I knew it. Just one taste and I was already addicted.

"Fucking perfect," I breathed, moving my hand so I could sink two fingers inside her. She clamped down on me, and my dick gave a happy jerk, begging me to let him replace my fingers.

"B-Ben, oh . . ."

Curling my fingers, I coated them in her desire and then pulled out, holding the glistening offering up to her.

"Taste yourself."

She opened her mouth, and I swore under my breath when her tongue touched my fingers. What would it feel like to have her sucking my dick instead of this? She cleaned herself off me, her eyes going half-mast and my cock throbbing behind my fly.

"Sugar," I whispered. "Sweet. Perfect."

Mine.

I couldn't help myself. I pressed my palm against my aching dick for just a second. I needed some friction, even if it was just a little. I was dying. For her.

"Please, Ben. Please."

Unable to draw it out any longer, I buried my face in her pussy, coating my lips in her sweetness and giving myself what I wanted—giving her what she *needed*. Taking care of my . . . I didn't let the word take root in my brain. Not now. I could feel it there on the horizon, pushing at me, looming.

Big. Important. Life-altering. But I wouldn't allow it to fully form.

It wasn't long before her cries grew frantic, her hips grinding against my face as she chased her release.

A growl slipped free, my wolf encouraging her.

The vibration sent her over the edge, and she came with a whimpered cry of my name, her thighs clamping hard around my ears, her fingers clenched in my hair as she ground herself against my mouth. My tongue speared her, fucking her in a way I'd never done to anyone. I didn't even care that it wasn't my cock. I just wanted those walls fluttering around me, any part of me.

Pulling away as her legs went boneless and she sagged in pure bliss, I used the back of my hand to wipe my lips clean. I knew full well that as soon as I hit the shower, I'd be reliving this moment, her scent clinging to my face and hands, as I got myself off.

"Your turn," she whispered, attempting to sit up.

My dick really liked that idea. But she wanted to go slow. Going from a single kiss after a disaster of a dinner to oral sex on her couch was far from slow. Me fighting the urge to mark her was even farther.

Slow was the right choice. She needed to know what she was getting into with my wolf and me. It wouldn't be a one and done with her. Nadia woke something much more primal and possessive inside me. When I fucked her, it would be so much more than that. Which was why I needed to get out of here before I did something permanent.

Something she wasn't ready for.

Leaning forward, I cupped her face in my palms and kissed her. "N-not tonight."

"But why? I want to taste you as well. Feel you in my mouth."

I groaned, resting my forehead against hers. "Th-this was about y-you."

I had to get out of here before I caved. If she touched me, I wouldn't stop.

She reached for me, but I grabbed her wrist. "N-no, S-sugar. Not th-this time."

Fuck, my stammer was back and worse than ever. With all this tension building inside me, something was about to come to a head. I was spiraling, and my control was razor thin.

Releasing her, I stood and adjusted myself.

She was so beautiful sitting there looking up at me, hair a mess, cheeks pink, lips plump from biting them as I'd made her come. "So you're saying there will be a next time?"

I ran my thumb down her cheek, tipping her chin up and stealing one last kiss before I made myself walk away. "You've got me n-now, baby. There's n-never gonna be a l-last time."

CHAPTER
TWENTY-TWO

ROSIE

I stared, eyes unseeing, as I gazed down at the sofa where Ben brought me to a blistering climax less than twelve hours ago. My, how quickly things change in only a couple weeks. My grumpy, rugged boss had turned out to be a—what was the term, cinnamon roll?—with a really talented tongue. A grin stretched across my face as I let my thoughts drift to revisit *everything* that happened last night.

Remi staring straight at me as I watched him come under Asher's attention. Ben . . . doing what he did. To say nothing of what kind of pleasure Pan brought me whenever he called. And unbidden, a flash of memory hit me, Gavin pressing me against the wall at the Donoghue estate as he fed from me and filled me with his fingers.

My thighs clenched as a flutter of desire hit my belly. I bit my lip, flushing as I realized there was no knowing which of the men it was for. And that I didn't care.

Was this what it had been like for Noah before he found his mate? Enjoying himself with whomever caught his fancy, promised to no one and free to take pleasure wherever he saw fit? If my overbearing big brother knew what I was up to, he'd lock me in my room and go on a rampage.

Why was it men could sow their wild oats and be applauded for it, but single women were expected to be chaste little virgins? No thank you. That was the patriarchy trying to keep us from learning about the power of good sex and demanding it for ourselves. If a woman didn't know better, she'd stay shackled to a man that wasn't good for more than a few mindless pumps and no thought of her own orgasm. I would never marry again if that was my fate.

Although Gavin certainly had known how to touch me. If his plotting family hadn't wanted to use me as their pawn, I might've stayed and found happiness in what had started out as a desperate arrangement. But now, as far as I was concerned, we weren't married any longer. He was a widower. And I, a free woman. What better time in my life to explore my newly discovered sexuality? I'd run off to start over, and now was my chance to discover who the new Rosie—sorry, Nadia—was and what she wanted for herself.

A sudden banging on my door made me jump and stare at the wood panel as if it were a wild animal about to spring into action and maul me.

"I know you're in there, Adele."

Darla's voice caught me by surprise. Why was she popping over for a visit?

As if she plucked the question from my mind, she gave me the answer. "Open up. We're going out."

I unlocked the door and pulled it open. "My name is Nadia. You know that, right?"

"I know." Darla shrugged, shoving her way inside. She looked like she belonged in a music video, not in a small town in nowhere, Alaska. Her dark hair was pulled up into two fun buns, and she had a cropped Black Sabbath T-shirt that might've been vintage, paired with skintight leather pants and motorcycle boots I coveted more than a triple chocolate ice cream sundae.

"But it's a stupid waste of your British accent to be named Nadia. Adele is freaking awesome."

"True, but I don't have the pipes to back up a name like that."

"Fake it 'til you make it, princess."

"Why do Americans insist on the royalty nicknames?"

She booped my nose. "Because we don't have any."

She had no way of knowing how accurate her nickname was. My father was the king of the North American vampires, so technically, she was spot on. But I couldn't mention that or explain to her that I'd also lived half my life as an American. My heart gave a little pang at the thought of my parents and Blackthorne manor. I missed them more with every passing day. And if I let myself, I'd be dragged down by the overwhelming guilt of knowing how much my "death" hurt them. They'd be grieving me as much as I'd grieve the loss of any of them.

Shoving thoughts of my family aside, I assessed the woman who'd apparently decided we were friends now and found a spark of envy building inside me. She was so beautiful, her confidence radiating from every cell. I missed the certainty that came with knowing exactly who you were and your place in the world. With all the changes in my life lately, it felt a bit like learning to walk all over again.

"So, what are we doing today, then?"

Darla's wide smile was blindingly white. "We're going shopping. You can't just hide in this godforsaken bar all damn day. The boys think they can keep you here all to themselves, but that's not happening."

"They're not keeping me."

"Oh, please, I know a Bentley Mercer sex bubble when I see one."

Heat crept into my cheeks, combined with jealousy. *How did she know?*

"If we're going to be friends, you should probably know I tapped that. Both of them, actually . . . at the same time."

"What?" Had I heard her wrong? I didn't think so. Fantasies battled for attention in my mind. Had I just discovered a new twin kink?

"The Mercers like to share."

Darla's words confirmed it. Yes. Yes, I had. And knowing that it wasn't off the table just made it even more tantalizing.

"They were a great distraction to help me scratch the itch after I moved back here. It was never serious, just sex. I don't think I'll do serious again after losing Jax. But that's old news, so in the past it's not worth bringing up, except I didn't want you to think I was hiding anything."

My mind was reeling from the info dump, but it was mostly stuck picturing what it would be like to have both twins. "Thanks?"

"Ben's got a huge—"

"Okay, that's enough. Let's not discuss our boss's anatomy on our first time out, yeah?"

Mirth danced in her eyes. "And they're identical. Everywhere. Just so you know. In case you decide to ride the Mercer train all the way to the station."

I laughed. I couldn't help it. What could you really say to that? "Darla, you're a breath of fresh air."

"I told you. It's no fun being locked away in a tower. Sex bubble or not. Come down and party with the rest of us troublemakers."

"I thought we were going shopping?"

"We are. For the Howl at the Moon party this weekend. If you want the full Mercer experience, you have to look utterly bangable. Not that you don't already, but I mean . . . who doesn't love an excuse to dress like a sex kitten, am I right?"

Sex kitten. I'd never in my life been called that, or been given the opportunity to dress like one. The closest I've ever come would be Pan referring to me as his dirty little bitch, and somehow I didn't think that was quite the same thing.

"How does a sex kitten dress?"

Darla's gaze traveled down my denim- and sweater-covered form. "Not like that. We need more drag queen and less girl next door." She cocked her head toward the exit. "Come on. Get your shit, and let's go before the Mercers catch us."

"Drag queen? Really?" I glanced around the room, not wanting to admit I had nothing to take with me, save perhaps the lone key I used to lock the apartment. How depressing.

"Yeah. Have you ever met one? The most beautiful creatures you'll ever know. They're prettier than mermaids or even the fae. Everything is sparkle and sass. You need a dose of that."

Sparkle and sass . . . I liked the sound of that.

"Brilliant. Give me the works, I suppose."

She winked. "Oh, I will. When I'm done with you, the whole town will want to fuck you."

"Is that a good thing?"

"It is if you want to make Ben jealous. He won't be able to keep his hands off you if he sees anyone else sniffing around his territory. Remi either, for that matter. The only ones they play nice with are each other. I can't wait."

"But I thought Remi was . . ." I stopped myself, unsure if his relationship with Asher was secret for more than one reason.

"Oh, honey. Remi swings both ways. He's a sexual connoisseur. Sometimes he drinks red wine, sometimes white . . . maybe even a rose."

"That's from Schitt's Creek."

"Still true. Bisexuality is more common in shifters than those toxic Alphas want to admit."

Oh, the things I was learning this morning. Darla should pop around more often. I was getting one hell of an education. Not even Ms. Esther's School for Young Ladies had been quite so informative, and those girls were the biggest gossips I'd ever met. Also, I was no stranger to bisexuality. There were more girls hooking up with each other than not. Then they'd sneak off to see their boyfriends on the weekend.

"Okay, enough boy talk. Let's go. I want to show you around Aurora Springs. I doubt any of them helped you get your bearings."

She was right. I'd seen the inside of the bar and Asher's house. Aside from my cold, sodden trek through town, I had no idea where I was.

A warning voice in my head reminded me that was likely for the best. I was technically in hiding.

"Stop being such a goodie two shoes. You're safe. Rosie is dead. Nadia doesn't have any enemies." Pan once again whispered in my ear, urging me to give in to my true desires. The old Rosie might have been worried about how often his voice seemed to roll through her mind these days. Nadia didn't particularly care.

"All right, babes. Lead the way."

~

"Hungry?" Darla asked as we wandered the downtown area.

Aurora Springs was small, which I figured out very quickly after my arrival here, but the main thoroughfare was charming, filled with little shops and a quaint café. There was even a barber shop with a traditional red and white pole outside.

"I could go for a bite."

"Duke's is open. Teddy makes the best apple pancakes. The eggs benny are pretty fantastic, too, if you're more of a savory girl. He uses asparagus and just a dash of smoked paprika."

A little pang tore through me, my thoughts turning to Gavin. *My duke.*

I hope it didn't sound forced when I murmured, "Sounds perfect."

As she led me toward the diner, I caught a ruggedly handsome Mercer profile out of the corner of my eye. I stopped, smiling at the sight of one of the twins draped with a black cape in the barbershop. I couldn't tell which one it was until Remi turned his head and gave me that slow, wicked smirk.

The swoop my belly did had me gritting my teeth. I couldn't let myself get turned on in the middle of my new hometown. Especially not with more than half of the population being shifters. They'd know.

"Uh-oh, trouble just got you in his sights," Darla murmured.

Trouble indeed. I hadn't seen Remi since he caught me watching him go to Poundtown with Asher. My cheeks burned at the memory of the look on Remi's face when he came. His grin turned knowing, and he bit down on his lower lip, still holding my stare. With no more than a twinkle in his eyes, Remi sent the promise of pleasure at his hands through me.

A flood of arousal filled my belly, and I instinctively pressed my thighs together.

"Let's go." I had to tear my gaze from him, but I couldn't stand here like a twitterpated fool either.

We'd just turned away when the soft chime of a bell told me I wasn't getting off that easily.

Remi's warm fingers curled over my wrist, his voice low and husky in my ear. "Where do you think you're running off to, baby girl?"

Before I could respond, Darla's huge handbag slammed into his chest. "No. Off. Bad."

She continued to wail on him like an elderly lady fending off a mugger until he released me. The shock on Remi's face had me doubling over with laughter.

"Go sit, Remi. Leave her alone. God, you've still got shaving cream on one cheek."

He ran a hand along his smooth jawline, his lips twitching in amusement. "She was trying to make a break for it. Nadia always seems to be *running* off." The way he enunciated the word left no doubt he was referring to my disappearing act the other night.

God, would I ever be able to look at the man without immediately picturing some depraved sex act?

He licked his lower lip. "Honestly, I can't tell if she's *coming* or going."

"She *is* coming . . . with me, Remington."

Remi's eyebrows shot up. "Is she now?"

Darla smacked him with her bag once more. "Not like that, you pervert. We're having girl time. You know, brunch, a mini shopping spree, mani-pedis. a.k.a. no Mercers allowed." She snagged my wrist.

He leaned close, his lips a breath from my ear. "Have fun today, baby girl. Anything you want, put it on the Mercer account. But you have to model it for me later."

I gulped, imagining Remi peeling off whatever new garments I might bring home. Before I could answer him, he'd turned away and headed into the barbershop, sauntering through the door like a pirate swaggering across the deck. A sex pirate.

"Okay." It was all I could manage, as I found myself agreeing to his terms even though he was already gone. These forking Mercers played havoc with my head. I could barely form coherent sentences around either of them these days.

Just wait until you have to face Asher again.

I was surprised the voice was my own and that Pan hadn't called me out on my raging horniness. It was as if my thoughts were planted firmly in the gutter these last few days. But I hadn't broken his rules.

Technically.

And everyone knew demons and fae both dealt in technicalities.

"You think I don't know about what you did? Just wait until I get my hands on you, ma petite monstre. *I'll make sure you forget all about him and his tongue."*

It was like thinking of him had summoned the ghost of Pan to my traitorous brain.

"Nadia? Hellooooo? Come back down to earth, girl. Remi Mercer is hot, but he's not *that* good-looking."

I blinked a few times, clearing my head as I returned my focus to the here and now. "Sorry. What's in the water here?" I asked with a laugh. "It's like everyone is super-model gorgeous."

Darla grinned. "You're not wrong, but the Mercers are a special breed. All that tragedy in their past only ups the mysterious, broody bad boy thing they have going on."

I wasn't sure I'd classify Ben as a bad boy, but he certainly had the broody thing down. Remi, on the other hand, was nothing but bad. In all the very best ways.

"Tragedy?" I asked, not wanting to pry but also painfully curious.

"It's not my story to share, but I can tell you they lost their parents young, leaving the twins in their own little pack of two. No one else gets in."

How sad for them. I felt a strange kinship knowing they only had each other to rely on. In a lot of ways, we were alike, except I was the one who died and was forced to abandon my family.

"That's enough of that. Time to eat and then get you some new clothes. I heard Remi say he was buying. We should make sure he regrets that decision."

CHAPTER
TWENTY-THREE
ROSIE

Arms laden with the spoils of our shopping trip, Darla and I walked toward The Tip, smiling and laughing together. It was honestly wonderful to have someone I could talk to who didn't have any notion of my secrets. They hadn't mentioned it, but Ben and Remi knew something was amiss with me. There was no way they didn't suspect due to my connection with Asher.

Even back home, I didn't have many opportunities to just be 'one of the girls.' I was a Blackthorne first and foremost. And with as many enemies as my father had, well . . . let's just say protective barely scratched the surface when it came to him.

"Darla, what's that?" I asked, pointing to a steeple jutting from a thatch of trees on a nearby hillside.

She followed my finger, her shoulders drooping a little when she saw what I was looking at. "You've discovered Aurora Springs's secret heartache."

I wasn't sure what I expected her to say, but that certainly wasn't it. "What do you mean?"

"Ever wonder why vampires aren't welcome here?"

"I hadn't realized they weren't, to be honest." I was aware of the town's dislike of vampires because of Asher's insistence on my bloodline being a problem, but I didn't know why. I needed more information from her. This seemed like the perfect opportunity.

"Picture it. The year was 1997," she began, gesturing dramatically. "Christmas Eve, the ground blanketed by newly fallen snow, the moon bright and glowing in the sky."

Wow, she was really going for it with the storytelling. I stared at the steeple, catching sight of the scorch marks that blackened the windows.

"Families gathered together with their priest, ready for midnight mass. And then, she came."

"Who?"

"Her name is Aisling."

The hair at the back of my neck stood on end. Why did I recognize that name?

"The wicked bitch vampire who slaughtered the entire congregation, save the two who escaped."

"She killed the others?"

"Without mercy."

"Alone?"

"The two who survived"—she gave me a pointed look —"they were too traumatized to share much. It seems like there may have been a small nest of vampires who attacked, but no one knows for sure."

"Jesus."

Darla nodded. "There may come a time when vampires are allowed to walk these streets again, but Aurora Springs has a long memory. I doubt that night is coming any time soon."

I gulped. "What happens to them if they wander into town?"

"We kill them." It was the first time I caught the beast lurking beneath Darla's skin. She hated my kind as much as the others.

My stomach churned. I supposed that deal I'd made with Pan was more helpful than I could've imagined.

"Were you there . . . when it happened?" Given her age, she very well could have been, though she would have been a child at the time. But the depth of loathing in her voice made me wonder.

Her gaze lost its hard edge, and her eyes dropped. "No, but my mother was. I was little and had fallen asleep, so my dad stayed home with me. It . . . we left two days later. I only moved back here last year. After I lost Jax, it felt as though something was calling me back. I wasn't about to question it. I wanted to get as far away from the memories of him as I could. It's hard to stay in a place filled with the ghosts of your happiness, knowing you'll never be complete again. I have more than one reason for hating vampires."

Well, wasn't that just lovely. I couldn't win. My kind had a terrible reputation amongst humans and creatures alike. The Blackthornes themselves were notorious. All the better reason to keep my true identity under lock and key.

"It seems a lot of the town's residents find themselves here for one reason or another."

"Yeah. They should have called it Lost Souls, Alaska, rather than Aurora Springs. But I'm glad I came home. This town saved me." A faraway look filled her eyes. "Remi and Ben saved me. Those two are good men, no matter how much shit I give them."

We stopped at The Tip, and I tried not to flinch when

she pulled me in for a hug. I still wasn't used to these affectionate wolves.

"Thanks for making me go out today. I really needed it."

"Of course. Anything for a chance to get under the Mercers' skin. I can't wait until Ben sees the tab we ran up."

I bit my lip, not nearly as excited by the prospect as she was. Every time I'd tried to put something back, she'd grab two more items in its place. It was an expensive lesson. Thankfully I wasn't footing the bill. I just hoped the Mercers could afford it; otherwise I would be returning everything when I wasn't under Darla's watchful eye.

As soon as I closed the door behind me, I felt his eyes on me. It was Remi. I don't know how I knew; I just did. Only a couple weeks ago, I hadn't been able to tell them apart, but now . . . each of them had a different energy, a pull I couldn't deny.

"What's the damage, baby girl? How mad is my brother gonna be?" He stood behind the bar, black leather jacket and tousled hair making him look like the pirate I'd envisioned earlier. Especially when he poured two shots of dark rum and slid one shot glass toward me.

"You don't want to know."

He winked at me. "That bad, huh?" Then he downed his shot and sighed. "You're gonna have to show me for real. I need to be able to justify everything."

"What, here?"

"Why not? Bar's closed for a couple more hours. You can use the stage and give me a proper show."

"What stage?"

He gestured to the corner where a few tables had been cleared out of the way. "The stage. Where the performers set up and play."

"I thought stages were raised."

Remi smirked and walked around the bar, grabbing a chair in one hand and stalking around the room to drop it in the previously empty area. "There you go. Feel free to stand on it while you give me a twirl."

My cheeks were warm under his attention. Then I killed the shot, relishing the burn. "Where do I change?"

"The office. If I'm not mistaken, you know where that is." The cocky bastard winked, and a flutter built in my belly. If he kept looking at me like that, he was going to walk back there and find me humping his desk.

"Only if you promise to stay put."

He laughed. "I promise not to wander where I'm not wanted. But just so you know, an open door is always an invitation."

As I walked past, I half expected him to slap me on the arse, but he didn't. He kept his gaze trained on me but made no move to touch me. Part of me was sad about that.

Entering the office, I allowed myself one moment to relive the memory of Asher thrusting into Remi over the desk. My fingers trailed the smooth wood top, and I swore I could hear their moans of pleasure echoing off the walls.

"Pull it together, Roslyn." I shook my head and closed the door.

I could've gone for one of the more demure choices, like my new black jeans and off-the-shoulder top. I didn't. If Remi was going to make me give him a show, I'd bloody well better give him a show.

I snagged the crop top and leather mini skirt Darla picked out. I'd never actually wear this skirt in public without tights or something beneath them, but for Remi . . .

I smoothed the leather over my hips, the cool silky lining brushing the bare skin of my arse. Even that contact affected me. The flickers of arousal that Remi had ignited with his smoldering gaze and flirty words turned into a full-on blaze inside me.

"You want him to know you're wet for him, don't you, ma petite monstre? One cock isn't enough for my dirty, insatiable little slut."

Pan's voice made my nipples tighten, the stiff nubs pressing hard and persistent against the satin of my bra, begging for some sort of attention.

"Go on, do it. You know you want to."

With my demon's ever seductive croon in my ear, I quickly peeled off my bra and dropped it behind me on the desk, too in the moment to consider what I was doing. The need for some kind of relief was too strong to resist, so I reached up and tweaked my nipples, biting down on my lip and swallowing a groan as I imagined Remi doing the same.

"Are you sure you want that pesky lace pressed against your dripping cunt?"

Forking hell. I couldn't go out there braless *and* knicker-less. Could I? They were already sodden. Besides, Remi asked to see new clothes. These undergarments weren't really new.

Shimmying out of the thong, I laid it neatly atop my bra and took a deep breath. Before I could talk myself out of striding into the bar, I opened the door and stepped into the hall. I was aware of my nudity beneath the barely there garments as my thighs brushed together. I was already wet, the slickness coating my inner thighs.

The way Remi's shoulders stiffened as I came up behind him told me everything I needed to know. He turned, one brow cocked and his eyes burning a bright blue, that smirk I loved missing from his mouth. Instead, feral hunger was written in his every feature.

"Fuck me, baby girl. We should let Darla pick out your clothes every damn day."

"So I guess you fancy it?"

He took my hand and helped me onto the chair so I could give him his twirl, as requested.

"I mean . . . I'd *fancy* it more if it was on my bedroom floor."

I snickered, the line so cheesy but somehow still so forking hot coming from him. There wasn't a shred of irony in his words.

I blushed hot when his fingers trailed the exposed skin of my waist, that intense stare trained on my throat.

"I fancy this." His lips traced a path along the V of my shirt's neckline. "And this." Talented fingers slipped across my hip and down to the edge of my skirt until they found bare flesh. "And if you let me, I know I'd fancy . . . this."

He shifted his hands so they skimmed up my legs, his thumbs brushing the sensitive skin at the juncture of my thighs.

"Fuck, baby girl, you're bare. Are you trying to kill me?"

I sucked in a little gasp as his thumbs ghosted over my swollen lower lips.

"Wet. Hot. Ready," he groaned. "Did you like watching me with him? I saw you touching yourself. It only made it hotter for me. It made me come so hard to see you biting your lip, desperate for it. For us. Were you imagining what it would be like to join us? What it would feel like to have me inside you while he was inside me? Or were you hoping both of us would fill you?"

The mouth on him. I couldn't take it.

"You want us both?" I asked through a tight throat.

"Baby girl, my hand is between your legs, and my cock

is a fucking piece of steel in my jeans. Is there any doubt I want you?"

Widening my stance, I hoped he got the invitation. When his fingers sank inside me, I cried out and had to steady myself by holding onto his broad shoulders.

"Tight and slick. I knew it."

He pulled his fingers out and brought the glistening digits to his nose before sticking them into his mouth and sucking. When he removed them, a slow smirk curled his lips.

"So that's why Ben changed your name to Sugar in his phone. Guess it wasn't cookies he was eating the other night."

Oh, goodness. I wanted him to put more than his fingers inside me. My body ached for it. I'd only seen a glimpse of his manhood, but from the bulge in his jeans and the comments I'd heard from Darla, he was blessed with sizable assets. Assets that would wreck me.

I desperately wanted to be wrecked. But since he'd mentioned Ben, I felt it only fair to ask, "Is that going to be a problem?"

"You and Ben? No. Not as long as there can be a you and me, too. So . . . what do you say? Should we start on the bar? The pool table? Upstairs?" He winked, his voice a sexy whisper, "Bent over the desk?"

"Yes."

"Which part?"

"All of it. Any of it."

He laughed, grabbing me by the waist and pulling me off the chair, dragging me slowly down his body.

"My, my, you are a naughty girl. I thought you'd heed my warning. Honestly, I expected your pathetic little bleeding heart would be enough of a reminder for you to keep your legs closed.

But I suppose those wolves are expendable. When he fucks you, call out my name."

My chest tightened and fear stabbed straight through my gut. What was I doing? These Mercer men turned me into a cat in heat. I had to stop this. The last thing I wanted was to hurt either of them. I'd done enough of that to the people I cared about already.

"I-I can't. I'm sorry." I spun out of his grip and raced up the stairs to my room.

"Nadia? Nadia, wait!"

I hated that he probably assumed he'd done something wrong. He hadn't, not even close, but I couldn't let this go any further. I couldn't put their lives at risk because I was devolving into some sort of sex addict.

You let a demon take your virginity. Did you really think there weren't going to be any consequences? What did you think was going to happen, you twit? You'd go on with your merry fake life as if everything was the same? Of course he left you with these . . . these urges!

Instead of being cowed by the prissy, self-righteous voice in my head, I snapped back, coming to my own defense. *Technically, Gavin started it. Him and that whip of his.*

Reaching my room, I slammed the door behind me and rested against its cool surface, my heart hammering wildly even as the ache of unfulfilled desire throbbed inside me.

I had to put a stop to whatever was building between the Mercers and me. They were too important to me, and I was far too dangerous to them.

What the fuck?

I stared after her, my wolf primed to chase her down and finish what we started. God, I was so hard it hurt. I pressed my palm to my crotch, needing the friction, the pressure, some kind of touch.

Hearing the echo of her door slamming shut, I winced, knowing I was at fault. "Idiot. You never go for the threesome before you've had the twosome. What are you, fucking new here? No wonder you scared her off."

I had to swallow a moan at the mental image of Nadia taking my cock while Asher fucked me. My dick gave a happy twitch as if to say, *'Yes, please!'* God, I wanted that. I wanted it so fucking badly it made me stupid. It was the only excuse. And after the way she'd watched us, I knew she wanted it too.

I sighed and looked down at my bulge. "What are we going to do now, buddy?"

As if expecting him to talk back, I waited. Goddamn, I could still smell her. It wasn't doing me any good to stay in this room, bathing in her scent. Her flavor lingered on my tongue, coated my fingers, and told me she needed me. But she'd run.

I was a cocky bastard.

No. I was insatiable. Drawn to her. Desperate to make her come and give her pleasure. I frowned. When had that happened? When did Nadia become a focal point in my world?

Frustrated with myself, I headed toward the office, thinking a little accounting might just help me get my head on straight. Or bore me to fucking tears. Either way, it would take care of my raging hard-on. Math could kill anything. It was better than fire. There were other, much more enjoyable ways to deal with it, but it was Nadia I wanted. Her slick heat. Her cunt gripping me tight. Her cum coating me. Rosie Palmer and her five friends were a sad fucking substitute.

"Fuck, Mercer. Stop thinking about her." I dragged my hand through my hair and gritted my teeth as I rounded the corner to the office, her scent still in my nose. "Profit and loss. That's all you need to focus on right now. Profit and fucking loss. Taxes. Expenses. Payroll. Oooh, better yet, *inventory*."

As soon as I opened the door I knew I was screwed. Right there on the desk, left like a fucking offering, were a tiny pair of black lace panties draped across a matching bra.

"Did you leave this for me, baby girl?"

She must have.

She wanted me to find it.

I picked up the scrap of fabric, the dampness making me growl.

Fuck, she'd been wet when she'd taken them off. Because of me. *For* me.

God, the things that did to me, to my wolf. I felt fucking

feral as the need to mark her, mate her, claim her roared inside me.

Mine.

I lifted the lace to my nose, dragging her scent deep into my lungs. Wishing she was the one I was inhaling. That it was her pretty cunt pressed against my face instead of a sexy pair of underpants. My cock didn't seem to care. All he wanted was to shoot his shot.

"I got you, buddy. Nadia left us a little help too." Kicking the door shut, I tore open my fly and pulled my length free, breathing in Nadia's arousal as I stroked long and slow.

"Fuck, yeah, baby girl." I threw my head back and brought those panties away from my face, running them lightly over my cock until I could cover myself with them as I jerked off.

The soft scrape dampened by her slick felt like fucking heaven. It wasn't her mouth or her cunt, but it was close. Beads of precum leaked from the tip, a musk solely mine mixing with her scent until the room was filled with a combination uniquely *us*.

Oh, shit.

I lost it. I fucked my fist with an intensity generally reserved for when I had someone in my bed and our only goal was to get off.

"Goddamn, Nadia," I gritted out as my orgasm built. "Take it."

Tingles collected at the base of my spine, the rush of pleasure hitting me hard and fast as my toes curled and I pumped my cock. I came with a deep grunt, painting the desk with jet after jet of my cum. The only thing that would've made this better was if Nadia had been here to lick it clean.

If she'd been here, you would have planted your cum inside her. Where it belongs.

I'd barely tucked my dick away and pocketed Nadia's naughty souvenir when the door burst open. My twin took one look at me, then the desk, and let out an annoyed growl.

"You're c-cleaning that up."

I smirked. "I wasn't gonna leave it for you."

"W-why does it smell like N-Nadia in here?" His brows pulled together. "Where is sh-she?"

"She left me a little worked up earlier. So I came in here to take care of the books, but she forgot her clothes and . . ."

Ben glanced down, noticing the bags from her shopping trip.

"By the way, we bought her some clothes."

He raised a brow. "*We* did?"

"You'll thank me later."

Ben gave me a considering look, crossing his arms over his chest. "Sh-she's important, Remi. I n-n-need her."

That statement made my heart lurch. I stared at him, at the desperate plea in his eyes. He was saying, *don't fuck this up for me. Don't take her away.* But now that he'd said it, one word echoed in my head again.

Mine.

It was quickly replaced by another.

Ours.

No wonder my twin's stutter was so much more pronounced than usual. His heart was a mess, just like mine.

"She's important to me too."

Ben's expression softened, going thoughtful as a truth I was only just coming to understand poured out of me.

"I've never fucking felt this . . . this pull. I want to be

around her all the time. To touch her, to be able to look at her, make sure she's safe."

Ever since she set foot in the bar and I caught her scent, my thoughts had been consumed by her. I took every opportunity to be in her orbit. But until this moment, I hadn't realized the truth. It wasn't a crush or something as insignificant as attraction. It was deeper than that, primal. She was in my blood. I couldn't quit her now if I tried. I wouldn't give her up. Not for anyone. Not even my twin.

"It's the s-same for me. I w-want her all the time."

"Ben . . . I think she's our—"

He finished my sentence. "Mate."

"Have you heard of that before? Shifters having the same fated mate?"

He lifted one shoulder in a shrug, the wild energy I'd sensed swirling in him seeming to calm in the wake of my truth. "We shared a womb. Why n-not a mate? Makes p-perfect sense to me. N-not like it'd be the f-first time we s-shared a woman."

"This isn't any woman, though. She's *our* woman." I shook my head at the novelty of that. "Fuck. We found our mate."

"Yeah."

"Now I see why you've been such a grumpy fucker. I swear to God, I thought you were going to tear off Alexi's arms and beat him to death when we saw what he did to Nadia."

He chuckled. "I almost d-did. Kinda hard t-to do that w-with her in my arms."

"What should we do next? How do we tell her?"

"W-we need to g-go slow. She's n-not ready."

"Do fae have mates? Would she even understand a mate bond?"

225

"I th-think s-so."

I released a heavy breath. Now that I'd realized what my wolf had practically been shouting at me this whole time, all I wanted to do was make things official. "I'm not the best at being patient."

"I kn-know."

"She wants us both. There's no way she doesn't if her reactions have been any indication. But so far she's only dealt with us one on one. We need to get her comfortable with both of us. Get her used to the idea that she doesn't have to choose, that we're hers."

Ben nodded. "Y-you're the expert."

"Sexpert."

He grunted, but a slight twitch lifted his lips. "Wh-what do you suggest?"

"Movie night. You, Nadia, and me on the sofa together."

In the dark.

Snuggled up.

My twin grinned, picking up on my unspoken thoughts. "S-set it up."

CHAPTER
TWENTY-FIVE

ROSIE

" **I**s every resident of Aurora Springs here tonight?" I asked as the music surrounded us. Something hypnotic wrapped around me, making me move to the beat as if on instinct.

Darla glanced around. "Just about. Everyone loves a reason to party. And with so many of us being shifters, the full moon is as good a reason as any. That's why we call it the Howl."

A burly lumberjack next to her threw back his head and howled, followed by nearly every other person in the crowd, including Darla.

"Go on. Your turn."

I blushed, my cheeks hot. "I'm not a shifter. I don't howl."

Darla poked my belly. "You are tonight. Go on."

"Maybe I need a little liquid courage . . ."

She laughed at me, took me by the shoulders, and spun me around until I was facing a little bar manned by Mr. Bentley Mercer. The Tip was providing the hard stuff tonight, and Ben was playing barkeep. I pulled my two drink tickets from the pocket of the leather miniskirt Darla had chosen for me. That, paired with fishnets and shit-kickers—Darla's words—plus my deep purple top, made me look about as far from Roslyn Blackthorne as possible. I'd done my makeup to match, selecting a heavy black eyeliner and a deep plummy lipstick that matched the tips of my hair. I had to admit, the look gave me more confidence than I'd had in a long time.

"Be right back," I called, heading in his direction.

I'd kept my distance, but I wasn't sure either of the twins noticed since they'd both been acting . . . off ever since my shopping trip with Darla earlier in the week. Remi, I understood. I'd all but asked him to take me right there in the middle of the bar before pulling the rug out from under him. But Ben . . .

Maybe Remi told him what happened, and he thinks you're a shameless harlot and wants nothing to do with you.

I grimaced. It would be what I deserved. No promises had been made between any of us, but somewhere along the way, feelings had developed. What started off as harmless flirtation and sexy times had turned into more. And that was a bit terrifying, knowing Pan was out there, ready to swoop in and destroy the two people who'd made this town home. I'd hoped giving them space from me would help us all go back to an easy friendship. Instead, it seemed to do the opposite for me. I craved them. Not just physically. I wanted their smiles and laughs, to talk and joke with them. To feel like I was part of their . . . what? Their pack?

Watching Ben move behind the table as he mixed drinks for Tom, Dick, and Harry, I let my heart run away with me a bit. He was striking tonight with his black and white plaid shirt and denim jacket. The way the blue material made his eyes seem brighter had me licking my lower lip. And that hair. Slicked back, neat and tidy, just like him. I wanted to drive my fingers through it and muss it up.

He finished pouring the drinks and laughed at something the gargoyle trio said. But everything died when he turned his eyes on me. The friendly smile faded into a guarded expression as I approached.

"Oh, be still my heart, lass, you're a vision, and my heart cannae take it," Tom said, pretending to stagger back in my presence.

"Let her alone, you stodgy old man. Can't you see she's got her eyes on someone else?" This from Dick, a twinkle in his eyes.

Harry spoke up before I could. "It's not my fault I'm irresistible, lads. Step aside so I can push this bird around the dancefloor."

"Sh-she's m-mine," Ben growled, his eyes narrowing in warning, and God help me, my belly fluttered. The intensity in his voice gripped me by the heart and squeezed. He'd laid claim to me in front of them, and I liked it but feared the consequences at the same time.

The gargoyles exchanged knowing looks. "Pay up, chaps. I had money he'd get his head out of his arse by the end of the month," Dick said, holding out his hand, palm up.

Meanwhile, my heart did somersaults. "Yours?" I whispered.

Ben's expression softened as he looked back at me, color tingeing his cheeks. He opened his mouth, closed it, and let out a soft sigh before shutting his eyes and steeling himself. Then those blues were locked on mine, fierce and determined as he said, loud and clear, "Mine."

"That's our cue, lads," Tom said, slapping the others on the shoulder.

"But you . . . you're cross with me."

I didn't know what I was supposed to say. I was too confused by this unexpected declaration. Here I was thinking he was done with me because I couldn't keep my legs closed, and the whole time he'd been . . . what, exactly? Wrestling with his feelings for me?

"We need to talk about some things," I said as soon as the coast was clear and curious ears weren't listening in. "I have a few confessions to make."

"I kn-know. N-not here, okay?" He poured me a pint without me asking and shoved it at me. "H-here. H-have fun, N-Nadia. I'll f-find you later."

I knew his dismissal was for the best. Everything with Pan meant I should keep my distance, no matter how badly I wanted to stay.

I turned around even though all I wanted was to stay next to Ben, to take in his comforting scent and warmth, to feel his protectiveness. Darla caught my eye and waved me over, a drink in her hand she hadn't had before. While she wasn't looking, a tiny blonde waved her fingers over the glass, little sparkles pouring from the tips. *Pixie dust.*

The blonde caught me watching and her mouth rounded in a little O before she giggled, winked, and held a finger up to her lips as if to say 'It'll be our little secret.' Then she went on and did the same to a few other unsuspecting saps.

Before I could warn her, Darla took a long sip, then sighed with a smile. "Scarlett . . . playing the green fairy tonight, are you?"

The pixie woman flounced up to us. "Shh. Don't tattle.

Dallas will make me leave, and you know nothing fun ever happens around here without me."

I frowned and was about to protest; she'd drugged everyone, after all.

But she leveled her gaze on me, grinned, and blew me a kiss. Pixie dust hit me square in the face, not landing in my drink in a small dose like everyone else.

"Scarlett!" Darla said with a laugh, but the pixie was already sauntering off into the crowd. Looking back at me, she pressed her lips together and shook her head. "Nothing for it now but to enjoy the ride. Come on, let's dance. Maybe you can sweat some of it out before it really kicks in."

In response, I sneezed.

"Oh, that's another way to get it out." Darla linked our fingers. "But dancing is much more fun." She downed her drink, then took mine away from me, handing it off to a woman who looked like she might be a sea nymph.

"Wh-what does it do?" Apprehension twisted my gut. "Am I going to hallucinate or something?"

"Relax. It's just a little inhibition blocker. You'll loosen up, have some fun, take what you *really* want." She waggled her eyebrows, then glanced pointedly behind me at Ben. "No worries. No consequences. Just let it out and howl, baby."

Howl. Take what I really wanted.

The pixie dust already humming in my veins, I smiled and tipped my head back as I let her words sink in. The best I could manage was a fit of uncontrollable giggles as she spun me around and ground up against me. The music took on a life of its own, no longer something happening around me but something happening *to* me. I felt the melody in my bones. I couldn't have stood still if I wanted to.

Everything felt so *good*. The way my hair brushed against my neck sparked little tingles of pleasure across my skin, the thump of the bass guitar radiating through my cells. God, I was euphoric. I never wanted this to end. It would only be better if Ben . . . or Remi . . . or Asher, for that matter, were here, touching me. Gavin's dark gaze flashed in my mind, unbidden and unwelcome but resonating just the same. He wouldn't dance with me, but he would watch. For a second I wondered if Pan would dance with me, but then, I was pretty sure a demon on the loose in the middle of town would be a bit of a mood killer . . . so probably not.

Faintly, the thought of Pan sent a warning through me, but my pixie dust-addled mind didn't care. Not one titch.

Warm palms slid around my waist from behind, pulling me against a broad, firm chest. His lips brushed my neck as he murmured, "Goddamn, baby girl, you dance like you want someone to fuck you."

Remi.

"Maybe I do."

He turned me in his arms, his tall frame causing me to tilt my head back so I could stare into his eyes. His pupils were blown. So he'd been visited by the pixie too.

"Can I volunteer as tribute?" His voice was rough with need.

"What would your brother say about that?"

"He'd ask if he could join us."

A bolt of pure arousal shot through me, and I moaned, not doing a thing to hide my reaction to his words.

Remi's grin turned wicked. "Like the sound of that, baby girl? You want to be worshiped, don't you? Hands, lips . . . cocks"—he lingered on the word, his fingers ghosting over my skin—"everywhere."

My nipples were painful points, begging for his touch.

Come to think of it, so was my . . . pussy. Good lord, even in my mind that word made me blush.

"I can smell you, Nadia. You're ready to let me claim you."

"Don't call me that," I said on instinct, and I had no idea how to walk it back or make sense of it except that hearing my fake name on his lips was wrong.

"What should I call you, then?" His mouth was at my ear, teeth grazing the lobe.

"I don't care. Just not Nadia."

He feathered kisses along my neck. "Whatever you say, baby girl."

I let out a little whimper, and I could feel his smile against my skin.

"Fuck, I want to mark you." He ran his teeth along the cord of muscle joining my neck and shoulder. "I want everyone to know you belong to me."

I wasn't opposed to the idea. But I knew that was a big step. An important one, filled with meaning for shifters and vampires alike. Everything below my waist tingled in anticipation of him giving me something so sacred.

If I was in my right mind, I might have stopped to ask myself if it was something I really wanted. There was no taking back a mating mark. I'd only just met Remi. This should feel sudden. I had feelings for other men. But none of those thoughts held any weight. I was too swept up in the pixie dust-induced euphoria.

"Uh-oh, we're in trouble." Remi's words could have been ominous, but the amusement in them made me giggle.

"Why?"

"Because I f-fucking can't w-watch him with you and n-not be here too." Ben came up behind me, pressing his strong body to mine, sliding his hands over my hips as we moved.

Remi came closer, sandwiching me between them. I forgot how to breathe; all I could think about was the feel of their heat surrounding me. The rough scrape of their stubble as they kissed along either side of my neck. The brush of their hands . . . everywhere.

Ben's lips were at my ear as he whispered, "I need you, sugar."

"I need you too. Both of you." I barely recognized the sound of my voice. It was all sex and need and want.

Remi grinned. "Your wish is our command, baby girl."

I knew people could see us, but I didn't care. There wasn't anything I wanted more than them touching me in this moment.

"Looks like the pixie dust is working. We're not the only ones nearly fucking on the dance floor." Remi's hips ground into mine, his hard length pressing against my belly, promising more if I'd let him out to play.

Ben's fingers tightened on my waist. "P-pixie dust? Fuck."

He stopped kissing my neck and put a little space between us, so I took that as my opportunity to turn around and wrap my arms around the back of his neck. I could look into those fathomless blue eyes and run my fingers through his hair all day.

He was so handsome.

"Come on, man. Don't ruin this for us. It'll be fun."

Ben glared at his twin over my head. "Not like th-this."

I wasn't sure what they were talking about, only that I needed him to move in close again. I was still thinking about what Remi said . . . about those other couples. I wanted us to be one of them. Or would we be considered a throuple? It didn't matter. I wanted it.

Them.

What happened to keeping your distance, Rosie?

Shut up.

Are you really doing this, then?

I didn't hesitate as I quickly answered the only sensible brain cell left in my body. *Yes.*

Well then, you better freshen up. No one likes a swamp crotch!

Good point!

"I'm just going to pop to the loo and powder my nose. Be right back!" I chirped, moving before either of them had a chance to say anything.

If we were about to get freaky on the dance floor, I needed to make sure I was prepared for them. That meant these knickers needed to go.

TWENTY-SIX

BEN

"What the f-fuck, Remi?" I rounded on my brother as we watched Nadia walk away. I hated that she was leaving us, but fuck, what a sight.

"You scared her off!"

"What were y-you thinking? W-we can't claim our mate w-when she's high o-off her ass."

"Why not? It's going to happen eventually. And a little pixie dust will make it feel even better."

I squeezed the bridge of my nose, knowing it was useless trying to talk sense into my twin when he was like this. I released a breath and tried anyway. "B-because it's too fucking important. S-she can't regret it."

Or us.

The thought of her hating us in the morning made my chest tight. I wanted to make her happy, not take advantage of her and force her to bond with us. Because no matter what Remi thought, doing this now would be wrong. She had to choose us, stone cold sober.

"She wants it as bad as we do. Pixie dust loosens inhibitions. It doesn't turn you into a different person. It's not like what she's feeling is fake. She's our *mate*, Ben. She will always choose us in the end. Drunk. High. Sober. Horny. We're *it* for her."

"Exactly w-why we should w-wait."

"I don't think you're listening. She. Wants. Us." Remi got in my face and took time to enunciate each word. "Maybe if you'd let Scarlett dose you too, you'd be more fun."

"One of us has to b-be the grown-up."

"Oh fuck you, Bentley."

"You're just p-pissed you'll have to deal with b-blue balls."

"Damn straight I am. A mate means we don't have to go without."

"I don't th-think that's what that means."

"It's part of it."

I dragged a hand over my nape, sighing. "It m-means you take care of her. F-forever."

Remi's expression slipped, his desperation cutting through his high. "I need her. The wait is killing me. Do you have any idea how hard it's been to keep my hands to myself?"

"Y-yes."

He groaned. "But you already got to taste her. It's not fair."

"H-how old are you?"

Rolling his eyes, he said, "Thirty-one, same as you, fucker."

"G-good. I thought you f-forgot. This tantrum of yours m-makes you look like a child."

"You gonna put me on timeout, dad?"

"Keep it up. I j-just might."

"I'd like to see you try."

Remi was saved from my answer by the buzz of my phone in my pocket. My brows dropped at the sight of Asher's name.

ASHER:

What are you idiots doing? You're supposed to be watching her. Instead, that bear just followed her upstairs.

My body tensed. I didn't bother asking myself how Asher knew that when he wasn't even here. He was a nut. The guy probably had cameras everywhere. Without another word, I bolted, heading toward the bar, my heart in my throat.

"What are you doing? Going to watch her pee? You better not mark her without me! We do this together or not at all!"

I gave him the finger as I sprinted away. If my brother hadn't been partying with the green fairy, he might have realized something was wrong and come with me. Just went to prove I made the right call putting a stop to things.

I ran through the bar, my pulse racing when I caught up to him. I recognized the fucker's scent immediately.

"Alexi," I snarled, my wolf in my voice.

The bear froze, then turned with a shit-eating grin on his face. "Oops. Is this not the way to the bathroom?"

"Stairs are off-limits." Fuck, I was proud I didn't stammer through that sentence.

"Not when there's a bitch in heat, panting for it up there."

"Keep your p-paws off her."

"You're pathetic. Can't even talk like a man. She needs a real shifter to claim her."

241

My claws extended as my wolf slipped free. "Get. The. Fuck. Out." *How's that for not stuttering, asshole?*

His eyes widened slightly before his own animal took hold. He swelled in size, his bear making him tower over me. That was okay. Size didn't mean shit. I was protecting my mate. This fucker didn't stand a chance.

I shifted, my clothes shredding as I welcomed my animal form and sprung into action, launching myself at the bear. He was overconfident and didn't move to slap me away, so when my teeth sank into his throat, he let out a grunt of pain. I had him tumbling down the stairs in seconds, his huge form rolling end over end until he landed on the floor with a thud.

The fucker wasn't dead. He was barely wounded, and when he got to all fours and locked eyes with me, I planted my feet and stared him down, hackles raised as my deep growl filled the air.

She was mine. He wasn't getting anywhere near her, but he was welcome to try. I'd kill him without a second's remorse. No one threatened my mate and lived.

Alexi morphed back into his human form, blood trailing down his chest from where I'd bitten him. "This isn't over, Mercer. I'll be back. You can't watch her every moment."

I didn't stop growling until he was gone, my limbs trembling with the adrenaline surge as I transitioned back into a man.

Panic twisted in my gut, making me nauseated. He was right. As long as she was here alone, she was at risk. What would have happened if Asher hadn't texted me? Remi and I had been right here, and we were still almost too late.

"Well, isn't this a lovely surprise? I didn't realize the party was coming back to mine. And you've started without me, I see," Nadia's voice hit me straight in the heart . . . and other places.

I was hard as a fucking rock, but so damn scared for her I couldn't control my reaction. In two strides, I had her pressed against the wall next to her door, my large frame caging her far smaller one.

"Get your ass inside," I growled. "Y-you're so fucking h-high you didn't even r-realize you w-were in danger."

"What?" she breathed, her eyes rounding.

I pointed toward the door. "You w-were f-followed. Alexi c-came to finish w-what he started."

Her mouth fell open.

"You can't be t-trusted to take care of yourself, so I'll d-do it for you. P-pack your shit. Y-you're coming home with me."

Eyes swimming with tears, she blinked a few times. "I . . . I just. I'm sorry."

Ah, hell. Now I was making her cry.

I pulled her into my arms, holding her tight, resting my cheek on the top of her head. "I d-don't know w-what I'd d-do if s-something . . . h-happened to y-you." My words were a mess, my stutter the worst it's been in years as I battled through the emotion clogging my throat. "I w-was s-so s-scared, sugar."

Her arms went around my waist, fingers trailing up my spine and easing some of the fear that had controlled my reaction. She breathed me in, and it wasn't long before her lips pressed against my skin, right over my heart. "Nothing will happen. You took such good care of me, Ben. I'm right here, safe in your arms, because of it."

Dipping my head, I met her gaze as she looked up at me. "Y-you're mine, sugar. I'll die before anyone t-touches you."

She might not have been a shifter, but her words were

every bit as fierce as my wolf's as she cupped my cheek and promised, "I'd do the same for you."

One thing I would say about pixie dust, the effects wore off quickly. Her pupils weren't as wide as they had been, eyes clearer, speech less slurred. She was my Nadia again, almost. I cradled her face between my palms and crushed our mouths together. I needed this from her, just a kiss, a reminder of our connection.

Lifting her up, I urged her to wrap those sexy legs around me so I could carry her to her room. A hiss escaped me as her slick heat rubbed over my erection. "Christ, sugar. Where are y-your panties?"

"Oops."

With each step toward her room, that sweet cunt slid against me until I was practically seeing stars.

Don't come.

Don't come.

Don't come.

My wolf was begging me to slide inside her. Just for a second. It wouldn't hurt anything. Instead, I set her on her feet next to the kitchen table and growled, "Bend over."

She did, tossing me a look over her shoulder. "What are you up to, Bentley Mercer?"

"I know you w-want to go slow, and I'm n-not going to f-fuck you while you're still high."

"I'm not—"

I shook my head. "You are. B-but I'm g-going to make us both f-feel good, sugar."

Sliding my cock between her slick thighs, I held her hips in place and began a slow thrust, gliding along her swollen lower lips and hitting her clit with my dick.

"Ben," she moaned, rocking back into me. "More."

"Greedy."

"Inside, please."

"N-no. I can't. Not yet."

She whined, but didn't argue. "Faster, then. Please."

That I could do.

My fingers tightened on her, and my hips picked up speed as I continued thrusting between her legs. Her whimpers of pleasure every time I hit that sweet spot were my new favorite sound. And then Nadia, the temptress that she was, clenched her thighs tighter, squeezing me and tilting her ass up. It was too much. The delicious rub of her cunt against me, the pressure of her legs, the sight of her. I reached around and pulled her skirt higher so I could rub at her clit with my fingers because hell, I wasn't going to last.

"Come for me, sugar. Please."

A flood of warmth coated my cock as she obeyed with a ragged cry. I reared back, jerking out from between her thighs so I could spill my cum across her perfect ass.

"Fuuuck, Nadia. Goddamn."

She was breathing hard, looking back at me over her shoulder with a sexy smile. "I could listen to you come all day."

"Same."

I have no excuse for what happened next; it was pure instinct driving me. While Nadia watched, I scooped some of the cum off her ass and slid it down between her legs. I stopped, locking eyes with her and waiting, silently asking, *is this okay? Am I taking it too far? Do you want this as bad as I do?*

She bit down on her lip and nodded. "Do it. Put it inside me."

I groaned and slid my cum covered fingers inside her tight little cunt. The fact that she might not be on birth control or that up until this second I hadn't ever wanted kids didn't even cross my mind. I just knew my seed belonged inside her. Fuck the consequences.

She groaned and tried to take my fingers further, welcoming my gift.

"That's where I belong, sugar."

"Yes."

"Are you fucking kidding me?" Remi's voice dragged my attention from Nadia to the doorway, where he stood, fuming.

"You c-couldn't knock?"

He only had eyes for Nadia. "What did I tell you about open doors?"

She giggled. "Looks like it was my turn to get caught while bent over."

"That's not . . . I wasn't . . . I didn't even get to watch."

"You s-snooze, you lose. S-should have come with m-me."

Remi's eyes blazed with annoyance. "We need to have a serious talk about sharing, Benji. This"—he gestured to Nadia and me—"is not what sharing looks like."

I laughed. "I d-don't know. W-we shared my cum j-just fine."

"I hate you."

"Settle down, lads. I'm sure we can figure something out."

Remi crossed his arms. "By my count I'm behind by at least two orgasms. You owe me some alone time"—he pointed at Nadia, then turned his gaze on me—"and *you* can fuck right off."

I should have felt bad. But I didn't. "Oh, go j-jerk off in the shower th-then."

She stood up, pushing me away gently. "Shower seems like the right idea. Then I'll pack."

"Pack?" Remi asked.

"Sh-she's moving in."

His brows rose. "Really?"

"Your brother was most insistent. Something about me being unable to take care of myself and needing you to look out for me."

"I mean, I'm not going to complain, but that seems a little harsh, bro."

"Alexi tried . . ."

Remi's jaw clenched, his wolf flashing in his eyes. "Take your shower, baby girl. My twin and I need to catch up."

Rising on her toes, she pressed a sweet kiss to my lips, then turned away and strolled into the bathroom.

"Alexi? How much trouble are we in?" Remi asked as he closed the door.

I blew out a breath, realizing that tonight was only the beginning of what would likely turn out to be a war. "A w-whole fucking lot."

TWENTY-SEVEN

Remi's hand was a light weight on the small of my back as we walked through the door of The Tip with Ben right behind us. We were late. But last night had been eventful in more ways than one, and lucky for me, they were in charge.

Darla's eyebrows flew up into her hairline as she spotted us. She comedically looked from the stairs leading up to the apartment and back to me, a small smirk playing on her lips.

"Well, I guess that pixie dust *really* worked out for you."

I couldn't stop the blush burning its way up my neck. Instead of answering, I shot her a death glare.

"I wish," Remi grumbled. He'd been very vocal about his jealousy since discovering his twin and me in the kitchen, using every opportunity to point out that Ben got what *he* wanted.

Ben slapped the back of his head. "Shut it."

"Maybe if I was the one who—"

"I s-said, shut it," Ben interrupted, the snarl of his wolf in his voice.

"You know, for someone who got his jollies last night, you sure are grumpy today."

"Remi, I s-swear to fucking g-God, if y-you d-don't—"

"I moved in!" I said, a little too forcefully, desperate to stop their bickering.

"What?" Darla's shocked expression was followed by a sly smile.

Remi's arms wrapped around my waist as Darla watched. He nuzzled my neck and placed the sweetest kiss there. "I'll let you get her all up to speed." Then he added in a low whisper, "And tonight we'll make up for lost time. I promise."

Before I could do more than shiver in anticipation, Ben was right there, placing a soft kiss on my lips. "H-have a g-good day, sugar." And then he was off, moving after his brother into the back office.

"Well, you work fast." Darla whistled, stalking toward me and pulling at my neckline and leaning close.

"What are you doing?" I asked, slapping her away.

"Checking for mate marks."

"No, it's not like that. Well, it's sort of like that. The guys had me move in because Alexi followed me up the stairs last night and would've tried something if not for Ben."

"Jesus, are you okay?"

I nodded, joining her behind the bar and getting to work slicing up limes and adding them to their respective container. "Ben got to me in time. Thank God. But the twins don't want me staying here alone anymore."

"I don't blame them. Well . . . good for you three. You'll be so cozy all *snuggled up* in their cabin." Something in the way she said it hinted at nights filled with sexy orgies.

I picked up one of the bar towels and slapped her arm.

"Behave," I hissed, not ready to admit my heart was secretly hoping for the same.

"It looks like I'll be the only one of us behaving for a while. Two Mercers in one little house. How ever will you manage, Nadia?" She leaned close, whispering, "Better stock up on lube. They're not lacking anything below the belt . . . though you know that now."

It didn't seem appropriate to mention I'd only gotten to sample the goods of one of the Mercer brothers. What was the protocol for talking about your sex life with your one and only friend when said sex life involved both her bosses? Whom she'd also slept with? Probably not a good idea all around. Best to keep my mouth shut about any and all nocturnal activities.

Before I finished my prep work, Tom, Dick, and Harry burst through the door, all three of them trying to squeeze through at the same time. Unfortunately for the burly gargoyles, they were too wide and got lodged in the doorway, the trio turning into one snarling tangle of curses and limbs.

"Oi, you tosser! Get out of my way." Harry's brow was so deeply furrowed I could barely see his eyes.

"Get out of *my* way, ye fat bastard."

Dick elbowed both of them from his position in the middle and popped free of them. "It's the both of yous who are in *my* way, ya gobshites. Wait yer turn."

Darla and I did nothing to hide our snickers of amusement as we watched them work their way free of each other.

"Who needs the telly when we have you handsome lads to keep us entertained?" I asked, grabbing three clean pint glasses and setting them up for our regulars.

The gargoyles preened at the compliment. "Didja hear

that? The bonny lass thinks I'm handsome," Tom said, slapping Harry on the arm.

"She was talking about me, ya arse," Dick grumbled.

They all took up their places at the bar, and I slid one pint to each of them.

Tom leaned forward, waggling his bushy brows. "C'mon, lass, enough of this stringing 'em along. Tell 'em you've chosen me and get it over with. Put these poor bastards out of their misery."

"How can I choose between you?"

Darla elbowed me. "Careful, Gargoyles mate for life, just like Mercers."

I cast a glance over my shoulder in the direction of the office. It was laughable thinking I would have been able to keep my distance. I missed those two even though they were in the same building.

"It's true," Dick confirmed with an emphatic nod. "The ritual is something to see. Only happens once a decade."

I raised a brow, waiting for him to fill me in. He didn't disappoint.

"The clans all get together and reveal their wings."

I blinked at him, wondering what I was missing.

Harry picked up the explanation. "Fated mates have matching wing patterns."

"Ahhh." Seeing my way out of this, I offered them a sweet smile. "So you sadly cannot be my mates, lads. I am not a gargoyle, and I don't have any wings."

"Bugger," Dick grunted.

"We won't hold it against ye," Tom added.

"That's right, luv," Harry agreed with a lascivious wink. "But I'll let you rub mine anytime you want."

"Careful," Ben growled at Harry, having popped out of the office to grab something from the stockroom.

The gargoyles raised their hands in surrender.

"Just having a bit of fun, nothing to worry about." Then Tom mumbled something that sounded a lot like, "Except I don't see a mark on her claiming her as yours."

"W-what was that?" Ben asked, abandoning the stock-room and heading for us.

"I said, ye havenae marked her."

"Yet." It was one word, but it was full of promise, and the shiver it sent down my spine was impossible to ignore.

Darla just laughed, the witch. She was enjoying watching me squirm entirely too much.

"You th-three, behave. You t-two, b-back to work." Ben pointed at us in turn, though his fierce expression softened when he looked at me. He left with a slight smile playing on his lips, and I'd be lying if I said it didn't feel like he took a piece of my heart with him.

"Oh, look at that, boys. She's got it bad."

I picked up the hunk of lime I'd been working on and chucked it at Darla. "Enough, you. Leave me be."

Blessedly, they relented in their teasing, and we went about our shift, a steady stream of patrons coming in and having drinks. I kept hoping I'd see *Henry* again, but the tattooed, bespectacled version of Asher never appeared. We hadn't spoken since he caught me watching him and Remi. I missed his snark. *Liar. That's not what you miss.* It was the level of understanding we shared. He was the only one who knew the real me. The only person I trusted fully with almost all of my secrets.

"Nadia, break time!" Remi called from the kitchen. He was covering for Dante, who'd called in sick. No one bought the excuse. We all knew he'd had a little too much fun the night before.

I blew him a kiss as I pulled off my apron and headed

toward the alley for a little fresh air, pulling my phone out of my back pocket as I did.

Without stopping to think about what I was doing, my fingers tapped out a message to the hacker.

ME:

Take a break from your isolated computering and come to the bar.

His response came through immediately.

HENRY:

No.

I laughed at the brusque response that was so distinctly him.

ME:

Please?

HENRY:

No.

ME:

Why not?

HENRY:

I don't like people.

ME:

You like me.

HENRY:

Debatable.

My lips hitched up in a smile. I jumped onto a stack of crates, making myself comfortable as I settled in to continue our chat.

ME:

That's not a no.

HENRY:

It's hardly a yes.

ME:

You don't know me well enough not to like me.

HENRY:

. . .

ME:

You only know me on paper. The real me is very different. I'm quite mysterious. Very surprising.

HENRY:

Oh, you think so, do you? I bet you're on a break at work. Probably hanging out in the alley just to get some quiet before you have to head back in. And you can't resist trying to win me over, so you had to keep texting me.

I sat up a little straighter. How could he possibly know that?

ME:

Okay, Houdini. What am I doing right now?

I scrambled for something ridiculous and childish I could do, like stick a finger in my nose or flip him the bird. But then Pan's voice sounded in my mind like the mischievous demon he was.

"Don't be shy. Do what you really want, ma petite monstre. *Show him what he's missing."*

I dropped my phone in my lap so I could cup one hand over my breast and slide the other down my belly and past the waistband of my leggings. Heart hammering in my throat at the illicit nature of what I was doing, I let one finger graze my clit as I moaned.

Asher's response came in almost immediately.

HENRY:

Dirty girl. At work?

The only way he could know that was if he was watching me right now. Instead of surprise, I felt an answering wave of arousal. I loved knowing he was out there, watching over me like some techy version of a guardian angel on one of his secret surveillance cameras. He'd warned me once he had them everywhere. I guess not even The Tip's back alley was off-limits.

"Can you hear me too?" I said into the empty alley.

Another text came through.

HENRY:

Yes. Does that make you wet?

I bit my lower lip and nodded, trying to contain the tempest of surprise and hunger swirling inside me at his dirty response. Where had that come from?

HENRY:

Good. It's going to drive Ben and Remi fucking crazy, not knowing who did this to you.

A little flicker of guilt wormed its way through me at the mention of the twins. What would they say if they knew what I was doing right now? That this little show wasn't for them? Sure they shared, but only with each other. Would they be angry? Disappointed? Hurt?

We were going to have to have a chat about their expectations . . . and mine. Because I wasn't quite ready to give up on the possibility of exploring things with my hacker.

Pan's voice whispered through my mind. *"What about me, mon trésor? Are you ready to say goodbye to me?"*

No.

"That's because you're my dirty little slut. I think you're due another visit. That cunt of yours needs a reminder of who it belongs to."

I shuddered, my fingers working over my clit a little faster.

HENRY:

I love your face when you come.

That stopped me. He what?

Pulling my hand free of my leggings, I stood and searched the space for his camera.

ME:

How do you know what I look like?

HENRY:

. . .

ME:

Asher Henry, have you been spying on me in my most private moments?

HENRY:

It's for your own good.

The thought of him being privy to everything. Him watching every single time I touched myself when I thought I was alone, my time with Ben . . . A flood of arousal pooled between my legs. I shouldn't be so turned on by the realization—frankly, I shouldn't be turned on by his breach of my privacy at all. But I was.

I absolutely forking was.

His next string of messages proved just how closely he'd been watching.

HENRY:

You have a really pretty pussy. So pink and perfect.

HENRY:

Just wait. Remi will offer to shave it for you. You should let him. There's nothing like a hint of danger along with pleasure.

HENRY:

Fuck . . . I'd pay to watch that. Good thing I've already got the VIP access.

Oh, God in heaven. I liked this far too much.

HENRY:

Not so cocky now, are you?

HENRY:

I bet you're fucking dripping.

HENRY:

Show me.

ME:

Sorry, my break is over. Say your goodbyes, Hacker. I'm living with Remi and Ben now. You won't be seeing anything again unless you bring yourself out of your hidey-hole.

HENRY:

You think I'm not already there? I'm very good, sweetheart.

HENRY:

You should sleep naked, by the way. It'll drive Remi crazy.

Smirking, I couldn't resist sending one last message.

ME:

Remi, or you? But don't worry . . . I'll make sure we put on a good show for you. After all, you gave me such a good one in the office.

I silenced my notifications and stood. Then, even though I was turned on beyond belief, I marched back into the bar, praying for Remi or Ben to pull me into the back room and give me some relief, or hoping I could ignore the lust. I wasn't sure which.

Neither option happened. Instead, I was greeted by a bar full of patrons, a frazzled Darla, and Sheriff Dallas Walker standing at the door.

He puffed out his chest and announced gravely, "There's been another murder, y'all."

CHAPTER
TWENTY-EIGHT

PAN

What the fuck was my little toy up to now? I could sense her need. Feel the gnawing hunger building in her body. It had been too long since I'd had a taste of her and she was so quick to forget me. A whisper in her mind was all I could do until I had the strength to come to the surface once more.

With the seals of Armageddon still open, the veil between our realms was thinner than ever, making it easier for my kind to walk in the mortal world. That didn't mean it came without a price, even for an archdemon like me. Sometimes power wasn't all it was cracked up to be.

Okay, that was a lie. Power was everything, especially for a demon, but the stronger you were, the higher the price. Those little trickster shites could cross back and forth as easily as cockroaches crawling in the dark. But me? It wasn't that simple. I wasn't an imp.

I hated not being able to access her at all times, especially since every day that passed meant we were closer to the gateway closing. Every seal was like a lock, and if the humans managed to close all seven of them, it was 'Cheerio and fuck right off' for dear old Pan. I needed to figure out a way to stay earthside.

Permanently.

Rosie was my ticket. She just didn't know it yet.

Fucking hell, just thinking of her had my cock hardening. She wasn't supposed to be a drug to me; that was my job. I was seducing her. Stealing her away from all that was good and light and beautiful and opening up her dark side. Corrupting her. *Using* her.

So why was I the only one suffering? She should be over here. On her knees. Lips parted. I shouldn't have to resort to servicing myself when I had my own personal sex toy on loan.

The more I thought about it, the more I warmed to the idea.

I might not be able to go to her . . . but I could make her come to me. The rules were different for humans. All they needed to cross into our realm was a willing heart and a sponsor. I'd sponsor her. Oh, yes, I'd sponsor her so hard she'd cry and come around my cock.

Lips curling in a wicked smile, I tugged on the thread binding our souls together, pulling her consciousness to mine. Did you know demons have souls? We do. Dark though they are. I doubt the sweet Roslyn would have ever agreed to our deal if she knew just how connected we were. But then, she did say *anything,* and I warned her I would take *everything* if she let me. So . . . it was her own fault, really.

"*Ring around the Rosie . . .*" I sang soft and slow, drawing it out and changing the nursery rhyme into something much more sinister. As it was meant to be originally when I'd created it back in the 1300s, whispering the song in the ears of children as the plague ravished the world.

"Pan?" Her sleepy voice sounded in my ears, as innocent and sweet as a tiny kitten begging to be loved. It made me want to do despicable things to her. I didn't like my toy sweet. I wanted her as depraved as I was.

"Come, *ma petite monstre*. I'm ready to play."

I could sense her becoming more alert. I didn't need her alert. I needed her compliant.

"No . . . not in your realm. Tonight, you're coming to me."

Why did I like the idea of her in my space so much? Because maybe then I could keep her here and never have to share her with any of those other idiots. I hated them touching my toy. I'd never been cut out for sharing. Unless it was . . .

My thoughts were interrupted by her voice.

"How?"

I plucked on the thread again, knowing she felt it when the answering flood of her arousal came back through our connection loud and clear.

"Just think of me. I'll do the rest."

Her sigh rolled over me, sending sparks of electricity racing in my blood. As soon as she obeyed, I felt the thread building strength, pulling her through realms, and impatience overtook me. I didn't want to wait for her any longer. Grasping onto it, I tugged, grinning when Rosie materialized on the ground right in front of me. On her hands and knees. Just the way I wanted her.

"Oh, I like the look of you at my feet. Did you miss me?"

She lifted her head, staring up at me, her eyes the beautiful golden color those ridiculous contact lenses hid. *Bloody hell, stop saying she's beautiful. She's only pretty when she cries. Or when she's choking on your cock.*

"Where are we?"

263

"In your dreams, obviously." We weren't, of course, but she didn't need to know that. "You do love dreaming about me, don't you, *mon ange?*"

She dipped her eyes away from mine but didn't deny it.

"Oh, you thought I didn't know about that? About you begging me to fuck all your holes and fill you with my cum? Dirty girl, I loved it. I took notes."

She swallowed and moved to get to her feet.

"Oh, no, no, no, little one. That won't do. You caused me quite a problem a few minutes ago, and I need you to remedy it."

"Problem?" she asked, her face scrunching in confusion. "What did I do?"

The sweet little lamb. She needed someone to toughen her up. I reached under the waistband of my pants and pulled my cock free, shoving the fabric down my hips. Leaning forward, I grasped her by the wrist and jerked her up until she was cupping my rigid length. "You made me hard. Fix it."

Her eyes widened, zeroing in on the glistening drop of precum at my tip. As if speaking to her, my dick twitched. "Fuck, your mouth is so perfect. I can't wait to see it wrapped around me while you swallow me down."

She licked her lips before leaning forward on her knees like the greedy little slut she was. She lived for my cock. She just didn't like to admit it. That was okay; I didn't need words. Just her cunt.

And her blood.

"Open," I commanded.

She did, but I was far too large for her tiny delicate mouth.

Fuck, this was going to feel amazing. She'd be crying and choking and begging and ...

I was going to lose my grip on control and spill myself all over her face if I kept letting my thoughts run away with me.

"Wider." I slapped her face with the head of my cock, and she moaned in response.

She tried to open her mouth wider, but it was clear there was nothing for it. I simply wouldn't fit. Just because I *could* adjust the size of my cock didn't mean I wanted to. But in this instance, to get what I wanted, I was going to have to. There was no point in breaking my toy beyond repair.

"I didn't know you could do that," she breathed, watching as I shrank my size just enough to accommodate her, but not enough that it wasn't going to be uncomfortable. I wanted her to feel me in her throat for days. To wake up tasting me, wondering just how much of this dream was real.

All of it, little one. Every fucking second.

She wrapped her mouth around me and sucked me deep. I couldn't help myself; I threaded my fingers in her silky hair and gripped hard.

"All the way. To the fucking root, *ma petite chou.*"

She backed away, and I let her, those big eyes blinking up at me. "Did you just call me your little cabbage?"

"Oh, I'm sorry, did that offend you? Shall I just refer to you as my filthy little slut instead?"

She blushed, but not with shame. Desire made her eyes a molten gold. "As long as you call me yours—"

The words made my chest tighten in panic, so I shoved my dick past her lips, stopping her from saying whatever else she'd been about to as I forced myself down her throat. Her surprised moan vibrated around me and had my eyes rolling back in my head.

"This is a much better use for your mouth. Less talking. More sucking."

Without warning, her palm cupped my balls and squeezed while she took me all the way, until her nose was pressed hard into the flat plane of my lower belly. Her breath fanned out against my skin, and there was a suspended moment where she looked up at me with perfect trust shining in those big doe eyes.

Without conscious thought, I skated my knuckles over her cheek, the caress far more tender than any I'd ever shown her. Or anyone, for that matter. I didn't *do* tender.

I owned her.

But she also owns you.

Fuck. Where did that thought come from?

Then she fucking swallowed, the muscles in her throat constricting and I all but collapsed, barely keeping my senses as an indescribable pleasure took me. The woman might not be literally holding me by the balls, but it fucking felt like it.

"Again," I demanded, my voice a rasp.

She was quick to obey. This time I couldn't help but rock my hips forward, sliding deeper down her throat. Her eyes welled, and it was the most perfect fucking sight. Her lips stretched obscenely around my cock. Teardrops hung like diamonds from her eyelashes. She was the most painfully stunning creature.

She was mine.

And I was going to destroy her.

My fingers tightened in her hair, tugging hard and pulling a muffled gasp from her. "You let them touch you. You let him paint you with his seed. And somehow you still avoided breaking our bargain, Roslyn."

Her answer was a moan as she wrapped one hand around the base of me and began stroking in time with the now steady bobbing of her head. She didn't know it, but I wouldn't be able to hold out much longer at this rate. She had me. I was nearly there. Putty in her hands. But did I want to come down her throat or in her perfect cunt? That was the dilemma I faced.

Both.

There was no reason I couldn't take her a second time. Or a third . . .

There were no rules here. Only my ownership. Only my pleasure. She was mine to use however I saw fit. And I would not be finished with her any time soon, so I might as well enjoy myself in the process.

Without warning, I thrust into her mouth, chasing my climax.

"Keep it all in your mouth, *mon chaton*. Don't you spill a fucking drop," I growled as I pulsed and throbbed inside her.

She whimpered in what I took for assent as I began shooting jet after jet of cum into her mouth. Her eyes went wide, tears streaming down her cheeks as she worked to keep herself from swallowing what I gave her.

"Show me." I reached down, holding her mouth open as I slid out, my cock glistening with strands of her saliva. "That's a good toy. So obedient. You were made to take my cum."

Her lip quivered beneath my hold, the only outward sign that she was struggling.

"Swallow."

Her throat bobbed, and it took her a few tries, but she drank every last fucking drop.

"My turn," I growled, picking her up and carrying her to

the bar, laying her out on the onyx marble like my own personal buffet.

Without giving her a chance to protest, I tore the shirt and leggings from her, baring her body to me. She smelled like sin, and I wanted to bathe in it. "Look at you, positively dewy with want for me."

"You're the only one who gives me what I need."

"Quite right, *mon chaton*. Now shut the fuck up while I'm making you come."

Her eyes went wide, but she pressed her lips together as I spread her thighs. Gripping her so tight that my nails pierced her skin, I slammed inside her.

"Pan!" she screamed, her eyes falling closed.

"Look at me," I snarled. "You fucking look at me when I'm inside you."

Her gaze snapped to mine, a little panicked, a lot aroused.

"Good girl. Now watch me."

Sheathed to the hilt, I expanded until she writhed on my dick, her keening cries telling me she both loved it and was stretched as far as she could handle.

I leaned forward, murmuring, "Can your pathetic wolves do that?"

"N-no," she stuttered, the lone word breathless and filled with need.

"What about this?"

As my cock began to vibrate inside her, she let out a wanton moan and arched back, her body trying to take me even deeper. "Oh God, Pan."

"Just Pan. God doesn't live here."

"OhmyPanthatfeelssogood."

"Yes. Your Pan." Fuck, I needed to keep myself under control. I shouldn't love hearing her call me *hers*.

"Take me, please. As hard as you can."

"Do you want me to make it hurt?"

"Yes," she hissed, too gone to feel any shame at her request. "I want to feel you for days. With every step, I want to know I'm yours."

The way those words hit me sent a deep ache straight to my balls. She wanted the pain. I was pain personified. We were a match made in Hades. I would rail her so hard she'd have bruises inside when I was done. But first . . .

"Eyes on me, *ma petite monstre*. Watch me mark you."

Her gaze was hazy with need, but she kept it locked on me as my claws lengthened into sharp points. Using my thumb, I pressed my nail down into the pillowy mound of her breast until a bead of her blood appeared. Then I drew my nail down over the pebbled tip of her breast and lower. An angry scratch, just deep enough to break the skin, was left in my wake, crimson trailing over the swell and making my mouth water as my cock twitched inside her.

Her pussy fluttered with an impending climax. She was already so close.

"Oh, Pan," she moaned. "Please . . ." then she bit that full lower lip before adding, "more."

Holding her gaze, I leaned down, letting both halves of my tongue gyrate before I licked up the line of ruby drops. Her perfect flavor burst on my tongue, wine and spice, but under that, sugar sweet . . . like a cookie.

"Do you have any idea how good your blood tastes? I think I might be addicted to . . . it."

You was the word that tried to come out. Thankfully I caught myself in time. All the good that did me.

"The other, Pan. Mark the other."

"Do you want something more permanent this time?"

"L-like what?"

With a wicked grin, I gave a cursory thrust, reminding us both we were fully joined still, and then I brought her fingers up to trail along my chest to the platinum rings adorning my nipple. "I would part with one of these. But only if you'll wear it as a reminder of me."

"Okay," she breathed. "Do it."

I unclamped the hoop and set it down on her quivering belly. Then I reached for a bottle of liquor and pulled the cork free with my teeth, splashing the contents all over her chest and soaking the jewelry for good measure. Safety first, after all. Then I licked my way up her body, letting my fangs fill my mouth.

"How are you—oh!"

I bit down, piercing her with my razor-sharp teeth, fighting the urge to suckle from her nipple as she cried out under me. Lapping up the combination of blood and alcohol, I canted my hips forward and fucked into her deep and slow.

She was so lost to the pleasure-pain I had her trapped in that she didn't even notice when I slid the jewelry inside. Something about seeing that primal claim sent me over the edge. I sank my teeth into her breast, drinking more of her blood as I was reduced to little more than a rutting beast, fucking her with abandon, knowing she'd be ringed with bruises and loving it. Just the thought of her pussy swollen and sore from my rough treatment made my orgasm rise again, right on the heels of the last one. If I could, I'd fill her until her belly was distended and she looked like she was three months gone with my spawn.

I might not be able to walk on her plane at the moment, but make no mistake, Roslyn belonged to me.

As I pulled back, eager to watch her face as she came,

the soft glow of the ring on my finger drew my attention, reminding me of my duty.

Roslyn's blood was the key.

I was merely the vessel of her destruction.

But so long as I kept her mindless with pleasure, she'd never see the trap until it was too late. With as possessive as she made me, perhaps I should be more worried about being caught in *her* snare. She wasn't mine to keep, but what would happen if I could never let her go?

TWENTY-NINE

REMI

Was it normal for girls to moan and grab their tits while they were dreaming? Because Nadia sure the fuck was. Jesus Christ, the woman could turn me on in her goddamned sleep.

I lost track of how long I stood there watching her, but when her breathing changed as she blinked her eyes open to find me hovering over her like a fucking pervert, I didn't even have it in me to feel ashamed.

"Remi? Did you need something? Why are you standing over me watching me sleep? Is this a new thing I'm going to have to get accustomed to?"

"You were crying out. I came to check on you."

It wasn't exactly a lie. She didn't need to know I'd been standing here for almost half an hour, staring as she moaned and writhed and felt herself up.

"How . . . protective of you."

I shrugged. "That's me."

Her lips twitched. "I would've pegged you for more of a Jacob than an Edward. You seem more like a pace at the door kind of guy than you do a stalker who watches people sleep."

"Surprise?"

God, what the fuck was wrong with me? I didn't even know how to talk around this girl anymore. Ever since I realized she was my mate, I'd become an absolute fucking sap. I was second-guessing everything. What to say. What to wear. How to act. I was fucking suave. What was this stupid Twilight bullshit? She was right. I was standing over her like a stalker vampire who glittered.

Not that there was anything wrong with a little glitter. Wouldn't be the first time I sparkled.

Fuck. Focus, Remi.

Nadia slowly sat up, biting back a smile as the blankets pooled in her lap. "Are you okay?"

"No. Not remotely," I admitted, taking a seat on the edge of her bed. "You cried out, and I turned into a hot mess. I'm not used to . . . this."

"Monday mornings?" she teased.

"Having a girl living in my house."

It was the *living* part of this that really got to me. She wasn't just a random girl. She meant more to me than just a good time in the sheets. She was gifted to me by fate. Christ, she was *the-fucking-one*.

I never thought there was a solitary *one* for me. I mean, if I felt this way about her, what did that mean for Asher and me? He was never supposed to be more than just a hookup. But the thought of giving him up . . . that didn't sit well either.

But she was my mate . . . so what the fuck did my anxiety over letting him go mean?

"Hey, Remi . . . if this is weird for you, I can find my own place."

"What? No. No," I said a little softer. "Sorry, my thoughts are just sort of spiraling."

"Do I make you uncomfortable?"

"Well, when you lie there moaning and grabbing your tits, yeah."

Her eyes went wide. "I was . . . moaning?"

"It's why I came to check on you."

"And . . ." she lowered her voice to a whisper, "touching myself?"

"It sounded like some dream you were having."

"It must have been a nightmare."

"If *that's* what it sounds like when you have a nightmare, I can't fucking wait to experience a wet dream."

Her eyes went owlish. "What?" she laughed.

"You know. A sex dream. One where you wake up all turned on and ready to go? Sign me up for one of those."

"What happens when you have one of those? I don't think I've ever experienced one."

She had to be kidding. But I'd play along. "Well, it's called a wet dream because of the . . . you know . . . fluids."

"Fluids?"

Fuck, now I was embarrassed. "Cum. All over your PJs. Or sheets."

She went adorably crimson. "Does that happen often?"

I laughed at how shocked she sounded. "Have you really never had one?"

"I'm pretty sure I'd remember"—she gestured in the direction of my crotch—"fluids."

"Maybe it's easier for girls to ignore. Not so much for guys. I wake up in a cold puddle of jizz, I remember."

She wrinkled her nose.

"Annnnd, I've killed the mood. Cool. Now that I've

275

crossed *light stalking* off my to-do list for today, do you want some breakfast?"

She bit her lip, trying not to laugh. I appreciated the effort, but I'd obviously royally put my foot in it.

Just add 'slam your head into a wall' to that ol' to-do list of yours, buddy.

"Breakfast sounds lovely. Any chance you might have some beans or stewed tomatoes on the menu?"

I gaped at her. "We don't do that weird British shit here. You'll get your eggs and toast and love it. Maybe even some bacon and . . . coffee."

"Bean water?" She sat up and held her palm to her chest, scandalized. "Please, spare me the dreaded drink of the rebellion."

"Please don't tell me you're a tea and crumpets girl because, sweetheart, I hate to break it to you, but we're fresh out."

"I don't know about crumpets, but I wouldn't turn down a scone."

"Scon? You mean a scone?" I emphasized the *correct* pronunciation of scone. "One of those lumpy biscuit things?

"A *biscuit* is a cookie. A scone is a scone."

I shook my head at her. "Agree to disagree, baby girl."

"I'll have you know, I am actually half-American, and I love a good strong black coffee."

"Thank God for that. I thought we might have to deport you."

"Ah, lucky for me, I can claim dual citizenship."

"Alaska is like its own country anyway. You can claim asylum here with us."

"Would you keep me safe, Remi?"

Everything suddenly went from playful to a pinpoint

focus on her as I stared into eyes I hadn't realized were such a startling gold color. "I would. I'd do anything to protect you."

Her smile slipped, but it didn't feel like I'd upset her. More like the opposite. I'd taken her by surprise, and she was touched. Or at least I was hoping that's what the soft mist of tears in her eyes meant.

Aw hell, Remington. Now you're making her cry.
Abort. Abort.
Get the fuck out of here before you fuck it all up.

"All right, so . . ." I jerked my thumb toward the door. "I'll just go make breakfast while you . . ."

"Shower."

"Right." I snapped and pointed at her, wondering when the fuck I'd started using finger guns. Christ. "See you out there." My voice fucking cracked. Jesus H. I was regressing into a teenager. Had a witch laid a curse on me? Was I going to wake up tomorrow in my seventeen-year-old body?

Eyes still on her, I nodded and turned on my heels, walking straight into the wall. I hit the plaster so hard a photo fell, and she jumped to her feet. "Oh my God," I grumbled. "I'm fine. I'm fine." I held up a hand. "Pretend you didn't see anything."

As I left the room, all I could think was that she'd never want to go anywhere near my dick now. I'd successfully placed myself in the friend zone without even trying. Way to go, Remi.

NADIA and I had just settled onto the couch for the second movie in our Ghostbusters marathon—I was still baffled how anyone made it to their twenties without seeing at least one of them—when Ben walked in.

"Don't you t-two look c-cozy?"

"Join us? We made snacks," Nadia offered, holding out the big bowl of popcorn I'd helped her make. "You've been gone all morning."

"Let me c-clean up f-first."

"I'll save you a spot," she said with a big smile. Then she snuggled close to me, and I swear I preened at the attention.

My fingers trailed along the curve of her shoulder, down her arm, and back. I just wanted to touch her all the damn time. "So, does bustin' make you feel good?"

Ben just laughed and shook his head as he walked away while Nadia shifted her position and faced me.

"What? Busting? I didn't do any busting." Her cheeks turned crimson, and embarrassment hit me hard at the realization of what I'd just said. Out of context, that was a really dirty question.

"Ghostbusting. You know . . . I ain't afraid of no ghosts." The longer she stared at me without a clue what I was talking about, the more awkward I felt. I swear I had game. I'd never felt so stupid talking to a woman in my entire life. Not even when I was a preteen hoping to cop my first feel. She'd broken me. I was broken. I finished with a pathetic, "Who ya gonna call?"

"Oh, that kind of busting. Yeah, I liked it. Although, someone should tell them ghosts look nothing like that. My aunt is a ghost, and she's lovely."

"Your aunt is a ghost?" I was riveted. "A real one? I've never seen a ghost in real life."

"Really? They're everywhere. You can't see them?" She smirked. "Not even the one standing right behind you?"

"Wait . . . are you serious?" A chill ran down my spine. "Nadia. Is there a fucking ghost behind me? Is our house haunted?"

She erupted into giggles, falling back on the couch and pointing at me while she held her stomach, wincing a little as something clearly hurt her. I wanted to ask what was wrong, but she brushed it off and said, "Oh, you should have seen your face. You're positively ashen."

I glanced behind me, seeing nothing but the room as it always was. "That was mean."

"Perhaps, but I will never forget it."

"Me neither," I warned her. "Payback's a bitch, baby girl."

"W-what did she d-do now?" Ben asked, striding into the living room fresh from his shower in sweats and a T-shirt. I didn't miss the way her gaze ate him up. My brother might be a surly fucker, but he knew how to make women pant for him. Asshole.

"She told me we had a ghost."

Ben snickered. "A-and you f-fell for it? S-serves you right."

I flipped him off. "You would have too, dumbass."

"I w-wouldn't be s-scared. That's the d-difference."

"Easy to say after the fact," I muttered.

Nadia curled into my side and pressed a soft kiss to my cheek. "I'm sorry, Remi. I was just teasing."

Staring down at her, it was hard to hold on to my butthurtedness. *Yes, it's a word. I used it in a sentence, so it counts . . . I think.*

"Hey, your eyes aren't gold anymore. I never knew fae could change their eye color at will. Or is it like a mood ring kind of deal? Gold when you're horny, chocolate-colored when you're being a brat?"

Her mouth opened and closed as panic shot through her expression.

"I . . . I—"

Realizing I'd outed her somehow, I tried to backpedal. "Hey, it's all right. I love them whatever color they are."

"They're naturally gold, but I . . . Asher, he gave me contacts so I could . . ." The way she trailed off, like she didn't know how much to tell us, hit me in the chest.

"S-so you could hide. M-makes sense. Your eyes are d-distinct."

She stiffened at Ben's words but relaxed when it was clear there was no judgment coming from either of us. "I hate lying to everyone."

"Trust me, baby girl. You're not the only one in town with secrets. Hell, I'm pretty sure all of us are running from something in one way or another. We assumed that was the case for you the day Asher dropped you off on our doorstep. You fumbled over your name like you were still getting used to it."

"Every time you call me Nadia, I cringe. I hate it." She couldn't look at me while she made her admission, playing with the blanket in her lap instead.

I twirled a piece of her purple hair around my finger, tugging a little until she met my gaze. "I already told you I'll call you whatever you want. If Nadia keeps you safe, be Nadia. If you want to be my baby girl, that's fine by me. Or . . . if you want to know what it sounds like when we call you by your real name, fire away." I gave her my most charming smile. All big bad wolf and sex.

"I want to be myself when I'm with you both."

Ben sat next to her, his palm on her thigh. "B-be who you w-want. We'll be here either w-way."

She took a heavy breath, then nodded. "Rosie. Call me Rosie when we're here together."

"Nice to m-meet you, Rosie," Ben said, giving her one of his rare smiles.

I leaned in close, running my nose along her neck. "Hi, Rosie," I purred. "Your name is lovely, but I'm still going to call you baby girl."

She shivered. "That's . . . fine. I like the way you say it."

"Are w-we watching a movie, or should we m-make other plans?"

"Uh . . . I think maybe we should stick with the movie." Rosie made a face. It was the second time she seemed like she was in some sort of pain.

"What's wrong? Who hurt you?" I surprised myself with the fierceness of my words.

She shook her head. "No one. I slept funny. My . . . *twins* hurt."

Ben and I exchanged a look. "We're fine."

"Not *you* twins. *My* twins. Mary-Kate and Ashley." She cupped her breasts with another soft wince.

"Baby, are you telling me you actually call your tits Mary-Kate and Ashley?"

She turned bright pink. "Only when forced to refer to them at all."

"Why not call them your boobs? Or tits? Or breasts? Or fuck, I don't know *anything* else?"

"What would you rather I call them? My nunga-nungas?"

I snorted. "Or your dirty pillows. Chesticles. Bacon hangers. Milk monsters . . . snuggle pups?"

"Hot f-floppies?" Ben offered.

"Where on earth did you hear these?" She had tears in her eyes from laughter.

"We're guys. It's handed down from generation to generation."

"Is there some sort of sacred ceremony?"

I laughed. "Oh, wait! We forgot my favorite. A classic."

She eyed me. "Go on."

"Fun bags." I waggled my eyebrows.

"My friend Moira has a party tit," she admitted. "Though mine don't feel up for a party right now."

"Do you need me to massage them for you? I volunteer as tribute."

Ben let out a grumble.

"You snooze you lose . . . right, Benny boo-boo?"

He reached around Rosie to slap the back of my head. "Knock it o-off."

"Benny boo-boo? Oh, that's precious."

He pointed a finger at her nose. "No."

"No? I think yes, Benny boo."

He growled at her but ruined the effect by smiling. "Don't m-make me spank you, sugar."

The way she adjusted her hips and clenched her thighs made me very aware she liked the idea of a spanking. I could get on board with that. Definitely.

"Hmm . . . maybe we save that for later. Once 'the twins' are up for it."

"You're going to spank my girls?" she asked, her eyes huge. But not with horror. I could smell how into the idea she was.

"Well, I was picturing you over a knee so they'd be smooshed into our legs or the bed or something, but I mean . . . if that's what you're into, I'm always down to try new things."

"Do you want me to call you Daddy too?"

Ben's low hum of approval surprised me. But then, he

was the responsible one, the caretaker. I was the idiot who was admittedly barely a functioning adult most of the time.

"Do you *need* a daddy, baby girl?"

She bit her lower lip, considering. "Perhaps . . . or, is there a more wolfy honorific I should be using?"

"Alpha," Ben growled almost instantly.

Fuuuck. The thought of her calling me that did things to me.

She gave us each a soft smile. "Yes, Alpha."

We growled in unison, my dick jerking to painful attention. In true horny teenager fashion, I discreetly grabbed a pillow and settled it on my lap.

She wasn't up for sexy times, so we needed a subject change. Right the fuck now, or she was about to find herself with those yoga pants down around her ankles and my face between her legs. Or my cock. Or my face, then cock . . . *dammit, Remington. Focus.*

"All right, time for the movie. I know you're dying to see them save New York again."

Her light laugh warmed me, and she surprised me when she laid her head on the pillow I'd placed over my aching dick. Ben put her feet on his thighs and one hand on her hip while the opening credits rolled, and I couldn't help myself; I stroked her hair, loving the feel of the strands. She was asleep before Vigo the Carpathian spoke to the creepy art gallery guy for the first time.

My phone buzzed in my pocket, and I carefully shifted so I could get to it without waking her. Glancing at the text, my heart lurched.

SHE-BITCH:

Tomorrow night.

ME:

No. The deal is once a month.

SHE-BITCH:

The deal is whenever I say it is. Be there tomorrow.

SHE-BITCH:

Or else.

I swallowed back a scream of frustration. I hated this. Hated the sword hanging over our heads because of my fuck up.

"W-what?" Ben asked quietly.

"She wants us tomorrow. No arguing."

"Fuck. We barely m-made it out last time."

"We have to go. The debt is never going to be paid if we don't."

"You and I b-both know the d-debt will n-never be paid. She's n-not going to l-let us go until we're dead."

I sighed, knowing my brother was right. Aisling had us by the balls. "I hate this."

"C-call Asher. R-Rosie needs protection."

Glancing down at the sleeping beauty on my lap, I nodded. Asher was an asshole of the first degree, but he would keep her safe. I trusted him with my life, and looking at Rosie, I realized that included her.

CHAPTER
THIRTY
ROSIE

A lie of omission was still a lie. That meant the twins were lying to me. I knew I shouldn't be upset about it, but . . . just last night, I shared one of my biggest secrets, and they immediately turned around and started keeping things from me. They thought I'd been asleep while they spoke about some messages Remi had received, but I'd heard everything.

My shifters were in danger. Something about a woman and a debt. I knew that was the reason they had to beg off tonight, but Ben was trying to sell me some story about a supply run. I hated knowing he wanted to fill my head with things that weren't true. That he thought I didn't deserve the truth. If I was honest, it hurt.

I trusted them. Why couldn't they trust me?

Perhaps because they've only just learned your name . . . Nadia.

How could I be cross with them when they knew so little about me? I was such a hypocrite.

But it didn't change the fact that it was still painful.

Seeing the flicker of unease in his eyes as he lied to my face was like a dagger in my heart.

How is what he's doing any different from him thinking you're fae?

"For starters, mates tell each other the truth. How can we possibly be mates while we're exchanging falsehoods left, right, and center?"

"We'd tell you if we could." Remi's voice caught me off guard. I thought I was alone in the house.

Spinning around, I smacked straight into him, my breasts pressed against his firm chest. Pain radiated from my nipple—definitely pierced by my not-so-much-a-fantasy demon lover—and I winced in response but tried my best to hide it. That blasted Pan had done far more to me than I'd thought possible for someone who was supposed to be a figment of my imagination.

Because it wasn't a dream, you soft-headed ninny.

I still wasn't sure how he'd managed it, but the arse had found a way to visit me in my sleep. With every interaction, it seemed his hold on me grew stronger. I should be more concerned about that—I *was* concerned about that. I just didn't know what I could do about it.

I preferred problems I could actually solve. Like getting to the bottom of the Mercer boys' secret.

"I don't like the way this makes me feel," I admitted, my gaze darting everywhere but to him. "You two keeping things from me. What if I could help?"

He curled a finger under my chin, forcing my eyes to meet his. "I'm sure you could, baby girl. But even if we wanted to—and we do, I promise—it's not safe. The last thing we want to do is put you in danger when you came up here to get away from it." A wicked smirk curled his lips. "Besides . . ." Reaching out, he flicked my nipple lightly.

"You're keeping plenty from us. You won't even tell me how you hurt yourself."

I let out a little gasp, more from surprise than anything else. Also, the slight flicker of pain sent a curl of hunger through me, but we weren't going to talk about that. "How very dare you, sir? What did poor Mary-Kate do to you? You two haven't even been properly introduced yet."

"I know. And whose fault is that? Because it's sure as hell not for lack of trying."

I giggled at his thoroughly put-out expression. "How about you stay here with me, and we see about arranging a proper play date for you two?"

"Can Ashley come too?"

"I'm more interested in whether Rosie and Remi get to come, but sure."

He gaped at me. "That might be the dirtiest thing I've heard you say."

"You're rubbing off on me."

He winked, giving my nose a quick kiss before exhaling heavily and taking a big step backward. "You have no idea how tempting your offer is, but I can't. Asher will be here soon to keep you company while we're gone."

"Maybe I'll introduce *him* to Mary-Kate."

"Before me?" The pout in his voice was adorable. "That's not fair."

"Then stay."

His balled-up fists showed me how much he wanted to give in to my request, how he was fighting the urge to break whatever rules he was up against so things could be different.

"Remi, is someone making you do something you don't want to do?"

"In a manner of speaking."

"Are you being blackmailed?"

His expression was pained. "I *really* can't talk about this, baby girl. You've got to take my word for it."

I opened my mouth and then shut it as a possible explanation floated through my mind. What if the Mercers were spelled? A powerful witch would certainly be able to force such an arrangement. *I should call Moira.*

Wait. I'm dead. I can't call Moira.

But Asher can.

"I see the wheels turning in your head, Rosie. What are you thinking?"

Ben came through the door at that exact moment, rescuing me from the lie I'd have to tell if I answered Remi. These two would be the death of me with their broad shoulders and penetrating stares. And they smelled so good. Like . . . sex and cedar. Sexy cedar. I almost laughed at myself.

"W-what's got you smiling like that, sugar?" Ben asked, sliding one hand around my waist and tugging me close.

"I've decided to go into the fragrance business. I'm going to start by bottling a cologne inspired by the two of you. It shall be called"—I waved my hand as if painting a picture—"sexy cedar. Or perhaps Mercer Woods."

"That sounds like a dick joke."

"Wait 'til you see the bottle. Ten inches and as wide as my wrist."

Remi snatched my hand and inspected my wrist. "Your wrist isn't very thick."

"Yours, then."

"H-how would you know what he's got behind his f-fly?" Ben pulled me back against his chest, then brought his lips to my ear. "He hasn't shown y-you, has he?"

"Not yet. But I was told you're *identical.*"

A little nip on my ear had me longing for them to stay even more fiercely than before. "If y-you're a good girl, m-maybe we'll sh–"

Asher burst through the kitchen door, his expression stormy, as per usual. "Fuck, you guys, what the hell is going on with the people in this town? Is Mercury in retrograde? Has Persephone escaped Hades again, and he's taking it out on all of us? I spent the last five minutes trying to keep from running Tom, Dick, and Harry over. The drunken idiots kept falling off their rooftop perches. Has anyone told them they're only gargoyles when they're stone?"

"They were perfecting their poses," I answer with a laugh, recalling the bet they'd made the day before. "Tom said he was the fiercest, and so they all set out to show each other up."

"Of course they fucking d-did," Ben said, shaking his head with a laugh. "Those assholes are going to k-kill someone one day."

"I take it this sort of thing happens often?"

"At least twice a year. We've had t-to b-ban them from anything higher than one s-story."

"Fucking idiots," Asher grumbled, heading to the cabinet and pulling out a pint glass. "You got any beer?"

Remi looked from Asher to me, then to Ben. "Are you sure we should leave her with him?"

"W-we have t-to."

"Oh, wow, thanks for the vote of confidence, assholes. I'm sure Nadia and I will be just fine."

"Rosie," Ben said without missing a beat.

Asher slowly turned around and prowled toward me, finger pointed at me like a forking wand. "What was the first rule, *Nadia*?"

I pressed my lips together and looked away.

"What did you ask me to do?"

"Help me hide," I mumbled.

"And how can I do my job when you can't even last two fucking weeks without backsliding? Rosie is dead."

I stomped on his foot. "Stop picking on me. I can tell them my name if I want."

"That's it. Put him in his place, baby girl," Remi said with a proud smile.

Asher ignored him and growled at me. It was pretty impressive, considering he was one hundred percent human. "Not if you want to stay hidden. Fuck, Rosie. Every person who knows your name is a liability. Now you have three of us."

"I suppose that also means I have three strong allies then, doesn't it? The way I see it, none of you will let anything happen to me. You're mine . . . *my* pack, for lack of a better word."

"It's a fucking fantastic word," Remi said.

Ben pressed a kiss to my temple. I assumed that was his way of showing he agreed with his brother.

Asher threw his hands in the air. "Why am I the only one who cares? You didn't pay me enough for this. When it all blows up in your face—and it fucking will—don't come crawling back to me making those dopey sad eyes at me." He mimicked crying, rubbing two fists under his eyes and putting on an over-exaggerated frown and baby voice. "I'm scared, Asher. They're coming for me. Please help me. Save me. I need you. Wah wah fucking wah."

"Are you done?"

"No."

I raised a brow. Ben must have done something similar behind me because Asher's eyes flicked to him and then back to me.

"Yes."

"Good." I poked him in the chest. "Also, I haven't paid you yet, so don't get too cocky."

"I know! What the fuck is that about?"

"I hate to break up such a love fest, but we have to go, or we'll be late." Remi put a hand on Asher's shoulder, and the look my black-hatted knight gave him was a mixture of loathing and lust. *Hello, nurse.*

I couldn't tell if those two loved or hated each other.

Apparently, neither could they.

"B-be nice," Ben said to Asher before turning toward a billowing electric blue orb.

"What's that?"

"Our ride," Remi answered.

The orb stretched until it resembled a watery door. Panic clutched my heart as the twins approached the shimmering magic.

"Wait!" I raced to them, flinging myself into Remi's arms first. "Whatever you're doing, be careful."

The self-satisfied grin that lifted one corner of his mouth was so confident it bordered on arrogance. "You do like me best. I thought so. Well, give me a good luck kiss, then."

I tipped my head back and pressed my mouth against his, losing myself to the play of his lips on mine. He groaned and grabbed my arse, pulling me close until I could feel his erection pressing into my belly.

If not for Ben reaching out and grasping me by the nape of my neck, I don't think Remi would have let me go.

"D-don't forget me, sugar." The man kissed me breathless, a promise on his lips.

"If I'd known this was an orgy, I would've worn better underwear," Asher grumbled.

Remi winked at him. "Or none at all."

Then Ben released me, and the two of them walked through the portal, leaving me alone to deal with a grumpy, possibly horny, hacker.

THIRTY-ONE

GAVIN

"My, my, look at this, poppet. The duke has finally returned. I thought we'd lost you after your sweet virgin bride perished." Lilith Duval stood in front of my table, her svelte figure surely enticing to most, only serving to irritate me now.

Her dark-haired companion gave me a once over, his gunmetal gaze not remotely friendly. "Oh, joy. I'll alert the media, shall I?"

"Quiet, pet. This is grown-up time, remember?"

I sighed. "Lilith, I didn't realize you'd taken to harassing your patrons. If your services are required, I will let you know." Bringing the tumbler to my lips, I took a deep pull of the smoky Scotch.

"Do you hear that, love? I do believe the duke told us to kindly fuck off."

"In your own establishment, Lilypad? How very ballsy. Maybe the popinjay is more interesting than I gave him credit for."

"Will you please stop speaking about me as if I'm some exhibit in the zoo?"

Lilith's laughter was dark and sensual, as was her way. "Oh, darling. But you are. The ruined duke. Quite the talk of the town once that pesky Apocalypse was taken care of. The Donoghues disgraced, the Blackthornes once again the heroes."

I gritted my teeth, my hand spasming on my crystal glass. "I wouldn't call them heroes."

"Well, they did help repair my beloved *Iniquity* after that dreadful attack. So forgive me, but they are certainly *my* heroes. Though sadly down one family member. Such a tragedy, losing Roslyn like that."

I winced at the name, my eye twitching a little.

Lilith cooed, missing nothing. "Oh, but that cut deep, didn't it? I can taste your agony, Gavin. How exquisite. A sadist's pain is such a rare vintage."

"Is there something you need, succubus? I'm not paying for your scintillating conversation."

"Prickly. I like you like this." She ran a hand over my shoulder, and I couldn't help myself. I snatched her wrist and stopped her.

"Watch it," her companion growled, his hand around my throat, tugging my head back. "I'd think very carefully about your next move. I'm quite territorial over my Lilypad. I would so hate to spill your blood over a misunderstanding. Okay, I wouldn't. But I might feel a pang or two of remorse at the mess. We only just reopened. No need to start *breaking* things again so soon."

Releasing her, I stared him down as he removed his fingers from my neck. "Who the fuck is this, Lilith?" I leaned in and took a long inhalation. "Fae?"

She rested her palm on his chest, curling into his side. "This is Crombie. He and I have an . . . *understanding*. He scratches my back, and I—"

"Tickle my balls?"

Ignoring him, she trained her gaze on me, power pulsing in those blue irises. "You should understand our arrangement better than most. Is that why you're here, darling duke? Are you in need of a new submissive? I can provide you one, surely. I even have a few girls who look just like Ros–"

"No."

Why did my fucking chest ache at the thought? I couldn't replace someone I never truly had. Fuck. What was happening to me? Had Roslyn really etched herself into my bones so quickly? It had been over a month. I should be over this by now, but losing her haunted me as much now as the day I got the news. I couldn't even see a rose without thinking of my sweet, innocent petal. The staff thought I'd gone mad, forbidding the flower's existence on our property.

Shoving to my feet, I knocked back the rest of my drink, then slammed the glass on the table so hard it cracked. "Add that to my tab," I grumbled. "I assume the door is open?"

She smirked, one brow lifting. "Back to the fights, are we?"

"It's better than being here. You're looking a little tired, Lilith. Get some rest."

Her eyes flashed with true temper before a dark smirk curled her crimson lips. "Haven't you heard the saying, Gavin dear? There's no rest for the wicked." She waved her hand toward a corridor to my left. "The door is open, yes. The *rose* room will serve you this time."

That bitch. She knew just where to cut.

The pleasure rippling across her face as she breathed in my pain told me she was more of a sadist than even me.

Then again, she was a born hedonist. She'd find pleasure in anything.

And she did.

I flicked a final glance at her companion, still unclear why a fae radiating that much power would willingly submit to the Demon Queen herself, but then . . . who was I to judge?

After a month of isolation, of working through a spiral of dark depression I shouldn't have felt over someone I barely knew, I stepped through the door and back into the life I'd known before Roslyn Blackthorne ruined me.

Only it didn't fit anymore.

Everything was familiar. The air coated in the heavy scent of sweat and smoke, the faces of creatures all sharing the same secret, the pulse of violence that hummed just beneath the surface. It had been my siren song for years. Now it left me feeling . . . empty.

Nothing could fill the void that Roslyn's death had created within me.

I'd never experienced grief like this. It didn't make sense. The woman had barely been more than a blip in my life. She shouldn't have this much power over me. Especially not in death.

I hadn't even fucked her, for Christ's sake.

Maybe that was the problem. She'd always be the ghost of what could have been. The mate I never got to claim.

"Oh, goody, the Mercers are here." Lilith's godforsaken voice curled in my ear, making me shudder. Of course she'd followed right behind me. Feeding with every step I took.

The electric blue magic that swirled in the portal they'd opened pulled my gaze to them. The two identical men still stood on the other side, but there was no mistaking them. Them or the woman in their arms.

"Hello, what's this?" Lilith purred. "If I didn't know better, I'd say that was—"

"Roslyn."

My voice was a harsh rasp of utter disbelief, and with one word, I changed the course of my entire life.

THIRTY-TWO

ROSIE

"Looks like you couldn't Asher Henry your way out of babysitting me this time."

Asher let out an amused huff as he stretched out on the sofa, long legs taking up the entirety of the cushions. He was ridiculously good-looking, and I wasn't sure he knew it. He didn't get the opportunity to spend a proper amount of time with people as his real self. What a lonely way to live.

"What?" he grumbled. "Why are you looking at me like that?"

"I have no idea what you mean."

"Like I'm a puppy you want to rescue."

"So what if I do? I quite like puppies."

"I can see that. You've adopted two of them."

"More like they adopted me. But you were the one that saw to that, weren't you?"

Sitting up, he dragged a hand through thick golden hair. "I didn't ask for their help so they could get you into bed."

A surprised laugh escaped before I could stop it. "Is that what this is, then? Are you jealous?" Did I want him to be?

"Maybe."

"Of Remi or me?"

His expression was unreadable, but there was a lot happening behind those blue eyes of his.

"Both?" I offered, trying to make it easier on him. Getting Asher to open up was about as easy as trying to crack an oyster with a foam pool noodle.

Brows lifting, he pinned me with an intense stare. "You aren't ready for the things we could do to you. Don't joke about that."

"Who says I'm joking?" I waited, holding my breath to see if he'd try to call my bluff.

"You have your hands full with the wolves, and you're seeking a third? Weird choice for a woman in hiding."

The dismissal left me unexpectedly disappointed even though he was absolutely right. I was supposed to be keeping a low profile. Messing around with three different men—not to mention my demon—didn't exactly fit the bill. So why was I so hung up on him?

But logic rarely factored into matters of the heart. Which is why I snapped back, "This from the man who thinks any connection is a bad thing. Asher the Hermit."

His focus drifted from me to the floor between his feet. "Can't get people killed if you don't have connections with them. You of all people should know that."

The words pierced my heart more effectively than a stake. Thoughts of my family, of the people I'd left behind, poured salt on an already open wound.

"You can be a right twat, you know that?"

"It's been brought to my attention once or twice."

I opened my mouth to fire back some cheeky barb of my own, but something about the way he held himself stopped me. As if he was braced for it. Like he was picking a fight on purpose.

"You're pushing me away. Why?"

"I've already broken so many rules, Rosie. Fix them and forget them. That's the extent of what I do. Except you turned me on my head, and now I can't seem to get away from you. I need to cut ties. I'm cursed."

"Well, that's a bit dramatic, don't you think?" When he didn't crack a smile, I faltered. "Wait, cursed? Like . . . *cursed?*"

It was the first he'd mentioned this, and I immediately jumped on it. Taking a seat across from him, I rested my elbows on my knees and leaned forward, eager to hear more.

"Fuck," he growled, blowing out a heavy breath. "I shouldn't be talking to you about this. The more people who know about me—the real me—the worse off for all of us."

"Well, I'm technically already dead, right? Surely I'm a safe bet."

He didn't smile. Instead when his eyes found mine, they were intense and deadly serious. "You need to stop joking about that. You act like your life is worthless, like you don't have anything to lose. But so far all you've done is ditch a name, and not all that well with the way you're still throwing it around. It won't take much more than a few well-aimed questions before someone connects the dots. I mean, shit, you found me. If you can track me down, what's stopping that husband of yours from coming after you?"

My gut churned at the thought of Gavin. "It's complicated. All of this is. But we're not talking about me right now, Asher. What did you mean about being cursed?"

"I suppose Moira told you about my aversion to witches when she pulled me in to help your brother?"

"Yes, she said you helped the wrong person."

He let out a bitter laugh. "That's one way of putting it."

"What do you mean?"

"What started off as a routine trace turned out to be the worst mistake of my life. Something about it felt off from the jump. I probably wouldn't have even taken the job if not for Sam."

"Sam?"

"Samantha. My girlfriend."

A bolt of jealousy went straight through me, strong enough that I had to clench my teeth for a moment before I said something snarky or stupid. "Y-you have a girlfriend?"

"Not anymore."

The harshness of his reply made me wince. "What happened to her?"

"She turned on me. Set me up. Then left. Proof positive everyone lies. Don't trust anyone."

"Ouch." Considering the number of lies I'd been forced to tell recently, the condemnation in his voice hit home. Hard.

"Oh, those are just the headlines. What dear 'ol Sam failed to mention was that she was a witch. And that the man I was helping find for her was a witch hunter she'd hired to go after some coven she had beef with. When it all went to shit, she pointed the finger at me." He held up his hand, the back facing me. "And now I'm stuck with this."

I was on my feet and walking toward him before I could think twice. My fingers traced the delicate constellation of stars that started on the back of his hand, then branched up to wrap around his forearm.

"A tattoo?"

"More like a death sentence."

I dropped his hand like I'd been scalded. "What?"

"It used to be a single star. A few weeks ago, right around the time you showed up, actually, it started to spread. Like a fucking rash." His laughter was a coarse rasp. "Or maybe a plague. I wasn't exactly given a pamphlet about the details, but nothing good will come out of this new development."

"How do you break it?"

He let out an annoyed grunt. "What?"

"The curse?"

"How the fuck should I know? There isn't a manual that comes with these things."

"Well, there were quite a few children's tales that hinted at true love's kiss. Maybe you need to find a damsel to fall in love with you?"

He snorted. "I tell you I'm a dead man, and your response is that I need to find my faerie princess and beg her to kiss me back to life?"

"Or prince."

Eyes smoldering, he snatched my hand from where it continued moving up his arm. "Or both?"

My breath caught at the smirk twisting his lips.

He tugged on my wrist, pulling me forward and on top of his lap. "You think you could be my cure, Rosie?"

I licked my lips, suddenly parched. "You never know until you try."

His smile was pure sin as he reached up and tucked a piece of hair behind my ear. The soft brush of his skin against mine sent pure heat through my veins. This was the first time he'd closed the gap between those flirty texts and real physical connection. I wanted more.

Leaning close, he brought his mouth to the corner of

mine, nose rubbing the slope of my cheek as he moved to my ear. Tingles shot through me at the slight hitch in his breath as he wrapped one hand around the back of my neck and held me in place. "There's just one problem. You're not a real faerie. Remember?"

"No," I agreed, my voice matching his rasp. "But I *am* a princess."

His nose grazed mine, and for a second I thought this was it. I was finally going to get a proper kiss out of him. But then he pushed me off his lap and onto the cushion beside him like so much rubbish. Shifting in his seat so that he leaned back against the arm of the sofa, he drawled, "That's right, the little Blackthorne princess. What would your daddy think if he knew the kinds of things his darling daughter was doing?"

"Probably go on a murderous rampage and behead the lot of you. Then again, he's rather tame these days. Perhaps he'd simply invite you all over for a drink so he could size you up in person. Shall we ring him and find out?"

Asher growled low. "Don't even think about it."

"Okay, I was just joking. Blimey, you'd think you were an Alpha too."

He didn't take the bait. Instead, he surprised me by changing the subject. "I'd always wondered what it would be like. Growing up in a mansion with a family that doted on you."

"It was pretty normal, I suppose. Mum and Dad loved us, we fought like . . . well, like children do. But I always knew they'd care for me."

His eyes took on a wistful quality as he listened. "You always felt safe?"

"Yeah. Parents tend to do that. It's kind of their job."

"I wouldn't know. I never had any."

The admission sent a wave of sadness through me.

"Don't."

"I didn't do anything."

"You're giving me that look again. The poor puppy look. Stop it."

"I'm not."

"You are. I didn't tell you so you'd pity me. I don't want your fucking pity, Rosie."

He stood and took a few steps toward the kitchen, seeking physical distance to go with the emotional distance he was trying to reconstruct, if I had to guess. But I didn't want to let him off that easily. Now that I finally had a glimpse of the truth. I wanted it all.

"Then what do you want, Asher? Do you even know? Would you even let yourself have it if the opportunity was right there within reach?"

He spun back around. "What do *you* want? Freedom? A new life? A new name? That's all window dressing. What about you? Who do you want to be, because as far as I can tell, you're living a half-life right now. You can be in or out, but not straddling both worlds. It's not too late. Rosie Blackthorne could magically show up after a few lost months. You could go back."

It was a tempting offer, even if it was impossible. I could *never* go back. Nothing had changed. Gavin and his family were still out there. And so long as they lived, they were a threat to mine. This was the only way to keep them safe. But still, his question burned.

What did I want?

"I want to be in control of my life. To make decisions based on my desires."

"You have to know what you desire first."

"I'm still figuring that part out."

"Is that what all this is? You trying on men for size until you find one that fits?"

"Don't you dare judge me, Asher. I saw you trying Remi on just a few weeks ago."

His jaw ticked. "Who says I'm judging?"

"That judgy tone, for starters." I pointed at his face. "And that wrinkle betwixt your eyes."

One brow lifted. "Betwixt? Shall I find you a broom? Maybe a cute pointy hat?"

"I thought you hated witches."

"I might not if they looked more like you."

The frank admiration in his gaze had the breath whooshing out of me. I never seemed able to get my footing with Asher, and the unsteady ground left me reeling.

"Why do you feel the need to toy with me if you don't want me?"

"I toy with you *because* I want you. The problem, princess, is that I can't have what I want. I never fucking could."

Sweet lord. "I didn't tell you no."

"I wish you would."

"No."

His lips twitched. "Are you actually telling me no, or are you telling me you won't?"

"The second one."

"Jesus, you're trouble."

"The name is Nadia."

"No," he said with a slow shake of his head, stalking toward me. "Not to me. Never to me. I see you, Roslyn Blackthorne. Maybe better than I see myself. You will always be Rosie to me."

I swallowed back a sigh of pure happiness at hearing that. I needed to feel seen after trying so hard to be invisible. The problem with disappearing and killing off my past was that it wasn't something I'd ever wanted to do. I liked Rosie. She was a bit naive and more than a little pampered, but I loved my life. Giving it all up left a gaping wound inside me that nothing would heal. Except, perhaps, someone who truly knew and appreciated me. Someone who *saw* me.

Someone like Asher.

THIRTY-THREE

ASHER

"Why do you feel the need to toy with me if you don't want me?" Rosie's question was met with a cold pit in the center of my stomach. She was so hurt.

The truth exploded from me without conscious thought. "I toy with you *because* I want you. The problem, princess, is that I can't have what I want. I never fucking could." Wasn't that the entire reason I'd exiled myself here in the first place?

Those big beautiful eyes of hers stared into my dark, twisted soul. Breaking my walls bit by bit. "I didn't tell you no."

"I wish you would." It would be so much easier to stay away if I didn't know she wanted me as much as I wanted her. Need for her fucking consumed me. I'd never wanted anyone this way. It was driving me crazy, making me break my own damn rules, putting my life on the line just for a glimpse of her. Goddammit, I wish I'd never been pulled into the Blackthornes' web. I'd been a goner the moment I saw her picture. Now there wasn't any going back to the way things were.

"No." Defiance looked good on her, and my dick took notice, thickening in my jeans.

It didn't escape me that she'd given me what I asked for without giving me anything at all. She was a clever one. As smart as she was beautiful. A deadly combination. My own brand of kryptonite. "Are you actually telling me no, or are you telling me you won't?"

"The second one."

"Jesus, you're trouble." I hoped to God she didn't hear the desperation in my voice.

"The name is Nadia."

The name had never suited her. Not when she picked it, and even less now that I knew her. Nadia was detached, jaded, cold. Fake. A fucking lie. But Rosie? She was sugar sweet and perfectly made. An innocent creature with a heart as pure as freshly fallen snow—even if she did have the body of a siren. Walking temptation for a man as fucked up as me. She represented everything I'd ever wanted. Everything Sam had stolen from me when she set me up as the fall guy and sent me down this path. Now I was destined for nothing but loneliness, and fuck if that wasn't a bitter pill to swallow.

There was no way she'd be anyone other than the woman I wanted. And even if I couldn't keep her, I couldn't let her believe I saw her as anything less.

"No," I said, suddenly needing to be close to her. "Not to me. Never to me. I see you, Roslyn Blackthorne. Maybe better than I see myself. You will always be Rosie to me."

Her breath hitched just the barest bit, and those cherry red lips parted, beckoning me. Fuck, I wanted to taste them. Once hadn't been enough. I wanted to drown in her kisses. I wanted to remember what it was like to be with someone who craved my touch—me, Asher, not just a fumble in the dark. Even with Remi, that level of intimacy was missing. But that was my fault. I kept him at arm's length. I wasn't strong enough to do the same with her. If I gave in now, I'd be a goner. But even worse than that, I'd take her down with me.

The realization was a punch to the stomach. Instead of closing the distance between us, I reached down and grabbed the remote, blindly turning on the TV and staring at the screen. My heart raced in my chest, the truth hanging between us even as the moment was lost like a balloon floating away. I could see it. It was right there and forever out of reach.

Just like her.

Fuck my life.

The episodes played one after the other, but I wasn't paying attention to the screen. Every breath she took, every inch she crept closer, registered within me until she finally dropped her head on my shoulder and that contact made me relax.

I ran my fingers through the silky strands of her hair, my eyes drawn to her profile. Even asleep, she looked like an angel, dark lashes fanning over the cream and roses of her cheeks. My fingers had a mind of their own as they traced the arch of her brow and the slope of her nose. Memorizing her and this moment.

My need to taste her was as strong as ever.

Do it.

She's asleep. She doesn't have to know.

Just this once. Take what you want.

The door crashed open, Ben and Remi staggering in,

covered in blood and bruises. It was impossible to know if they'd won or lost their fight, given the state of them.

Rosie jerked awake, body tense as she stood and faced them.

"Oh my God, what happened to you?"

She was terrified for their safety, but I knew they'd be fine. They were already healing, the cuts on Remi's face knitting together as I stared at him. It was the gleam in his eyes that twisted me up inside. Wild. Hungry. Feral.

Their wolves were close to the surface. The adrenaline of their fight turning into a different kind of hunger. Ben's eyes were a mirror of his brother's as they raked over Rosie.

"Mine," he snarled, shoving his twin off him and prowling forward.

Rosie sucked in a breath, a little whimper escaping as she took a few defensive steps backward.

"Don't run unless you want them to chase you, princess," I warned her, my voice low, my eyes locked on Remi.

"We do love a chase," Remi agreed, his voice threaded with the gravelly undercurrent of his wolf as he closed the distance between himself and Rosie. "But you don't have to run, baby girl. We're gonna claim you either way."

Fuck. I palmed my erection as the tension in the room grew. I hated the jealousy burning through my veins. But not because they had her, or she had Remi. I wanted to be part of it all, and I was stuck here on the outside, just like I always was and always would be. This life, it would never be mine. She would never be mine.

I started to take a step back, ready to see myself out and leave them to it, but I couldn't seem to make myself look away as they sandwiched her small body between them,

Ben crowding her from behind while Remi cupped her head and ran his nose up the side of her neck.

"Are you ready to be ours, baby girl?"

Ben chose that moment to nip that tender spot where her neck and shoulder met, leaving no doubt what Remi was asking. Rosie's eyes flicked up and met mine.

"No."

I wasn't sure which of us was more shocked by her answer. Me, Rosie, or the twins.

Ben looked absolutely gutted, his eyes wild. "W-what?"

Remi's head turned, following Rosie's gaze and finding me standing there like some kinky voyeur.

"Oh . . . I see." He stepped away from Rosie and came at me with the grace of a wolf stalking his prey. "You. Every. Fucking. Time. Why is it you ruin everything just when it's getting good? Can't you ever let me have anything I want? Or are you determined to make me as miserable as you?"

If he'd had a knife, he couldn't have cut me deeper.

"Well, that's my cue," I said, my voice giving nothing away. No way in hell was I going to give Remi the satisfaction of seeing how completely he'd just eviscerated me.

"Wait. Asher, please don't leave."

Fuck me, her plea hit me hard. "I shouldn't be here. This is . . . between you three."

"But that's just it. You should be here, Asher. With me. I can't say yes to you"—her eyes darted between Ben and Remi—"not unless you understand that I need him too. I can't explain it, and I didn't expect it, but I know it deep in the heart of me. I need all of you."

God, that one sentence changed everything and nothing all at once.

My heart lurched as her amber irises found mine. All I had to do was stay. But there was too much at risk if I did, and

Remi had made it clear. I didn't belong, even if she wanted me. Even if being near her calmed the tumultuous storm in my head and heart. It wasn't just her body I wanted. It was *her*.

"I'm not sure what to do here. I'm just a human. This mate stuff seems like a wolf thing. Or, fuck, I don't know . . . just way outside my comfort zone."

Remi scoffed. "Of course it fucking is."

Ben, on the other hand, vibrated with rage. He hadn't managed another word. I wasn't sure he could at the moment; he seemed to be on the brink of shifting.

"I n-need to m-mark you, sugar. F-fuck, it's t-too hard t-to hold it off." His hands slipped up her torso, between her breasts as he held her close to him, lips at her ear.

"Ben," she whispered.

"You can't," Remi said. "You heard her. She doesn't want it."

"She doesn't w-want *you*. She d-didn't say no to me."

"Yes, she did. She said no to both of us. She doesn't want to be our mate. She wants to string us all along."

I wasn't used to Remi being the angry one. I mean, he gave as good as he got with me, but this was different. He was a wounded animal, backed up into a corner, ready to fight his way out.

"I'm not getting in your way, boys. Nothing's gonna happen with Rosie and me. I'm no good for her anyway."

The wounded look on her face was too painful to bear, and the wolves weren't much better. I dragged a hand over the back of my neck and forced myself to look at the floor rather than into any of their eyes. Now was not the time to challenge the Mercers. Not when they were on the brink of shifting into wolves capable of tearing me to ribbons.

"That's right, Asher. Run away like you always do. If you

were half the man you claim to be, you might actually stay and fight for what you want for a change. You don't deserve her. Not if you can't sack up and take her."

"Wait, do you *want* me to toss my hat in the ring?"

"It'd be a nice change. Rosie deserves to have men in her life that are worthy of her."

"Like you?"

"I seem to be the only one here actually respecting her wishes. Those involve all of us. Isn't that right, baby girl?" Remi smirked and moved closer to her again, causing Ben to tense and release a warning growl from somewhere deep in his throat.

"Careful, Bentley. Your wolf isn't in charge here."

"M-my wolf is a-always in charge."

"Rosie needs the man right now."

"My mate needs me," he snarled, his eyes flashing an electric blue as his beast took over.

I had the unexpected urge to put myself between her and them. It'd be the last thing I ever did, but fuck if I wasn't halfway to doing it anyway.

Before I could, Remi gave her wrist a quick tug and pulled her away from his brother, shoving her into my arms. "She needs you to be the man she wants, not the beast who'd take her without consent, Ben. Don't ruin everything."

Ben growled, low and menacing, as his teeth elongated into dangerous fangs.

"Get out of here. Go!"

I wasn't sure which one of us Remi was talking to until Ben stepped up to him, pressing his forehead against his twin's. "No."

Completely unfazed by the posturing, Remi shoved Ben.

"I said take a fucking hike, Ben. Go for a run. Work it off and get yourself under control."

The Alpha command in his voice was unmistakable, and I was embarrassingly hard for it.

Ben's glare could've turned us to stone on the spot, and he very nearly took another challenging step forward, until Rosie broke from my hold.

"Ben, stop. Please. I'm not . . . you don't understand." She could've been a wilting flower in the face of his wild need, but she stood tall. "I can't be your mate. I can't be anyone's. It doesn't change how much I want you."

His brows furrowed, hurt flashing in his eyes and giving an indication that the human half of him was still in there somewhere, fully aware of what was happening. But then he spun, his clothes tearing to shreds as he welcomed the change and bounded out of the house through the still open door.

Remi sighed, walked to the door and shut it, then turned to face us with the smirk I fucking loved painted on his face. "So . . . who's up for a threesome?"

CHAPTER
THIRTY-FOUR

REMI

"You know, when I said threesome, this wasn't what I had in mind." I laid down another card. "Fucking Uno. It could've at least been Twister. Naked Twister."

Rosie snickered. "Or strip poker."

"Exactly," I said, throwing my hands in the air and likely flashing my cards, not that I remotely cared. "I'm the injured party here. I should get to pick."

Asher cocked a brow. "How do you figure? Your injuries already healed themselves."

"I'm talking about emotional damage. Pain and suffering. Blue balls. Take your pick."

Rosie's laugh was free and easy, and I loved it. "I know one way you could take care of the blue . . . erm . . . balls. I've heard it's quite effective, even."

"A blow job?" I asked, waggling my brows but also hoping maybe she or Asher would volunteer.

"No. But a proper wank session in the shower never hurt anyone."

I pouted and pressed a hand to my chest. "It would hurt me, right here. In my heart parts. Help a guy out, baby girl."

"You're a horny bastard, Remington." Asher tipped back his beer and did that manspreading thing with his legs, like he didn't have enough room for his junk. Fuck, why was that hot?

"And this is news to whom?"

"Literally no one," Asher said with a sigh. "Though a little growth would be nice."

"I'm a shower, not a grower." I threw a pillow at his head. "Besides, you're one to talk, kettle."

"Now, now, children." Rosie's smile didn't quite hide the worry in her eyes. She'd been glancing at the door every couple of minutes since Ben took off. If I was being honest, we all had. I'd hoped he would have come back by now.

"He'll be back, I promise. He just needed to work off some of this crazy tension. All this is new to us."

"All what?"

"The call to mate. Neither one of us ever thought we'd find our mate. And we definitely didn't think she'd be for both of us. Or anyone else," I added, frowning a little.

I wasn't a stranger to feeling a pull to more than one person. Hell, I was currently playing the bologna in the sandwich of my dreams. Well, it would have been a dream sandwich if we were all naked and engaged in an activity that got us a hell of a lot sweatier, but there was little that would make me happier than being in the middle of Rosie and Asher.

Annnd I was hard. Again.

The urge to pull her against me and kiss her silly warred with my wolf's own need to claim her, only serving to ramp it all up again. I stood and shrugged out of my leather jacket as I prepared to shift.

"I'll find him, okay? We'll talk. He'll come back to us."

She nodded, her eyes shining with unshed tears. "I don't want to hurt him—or you."

"I know you don't. Doesn't change the fact that it happened."

"Remi . . ."

Before I could stop myself, I slammed my mouth down on hers, kissing her hard and fast. "It's not all or nothing, Rosie. Even if Ben thinks it is right now."

I glanced at Asher, not sure if it was wishful thinking on my part when he tilted his chin up slightly as if he was asking for a kiss too.

But that wasn't Asher's bag. We fucked. End of.

"You'd better be gone by the time I get back," I warned. "Once I talk him down, the last person he'll want to see is you. Not until he's had time to think this over."

Asher slapped his fan of cards down on the table in a messy stack. "Yeah, dibs out on being werewolf bait." He stood and then leaned down to press a kiss to the top of Rosie's head and, by the looks on their faces, surprising both of them with the gesture. Asher recovered first, gruffly clearing his throat before saying, "See you later, princess."

"You don't have to leave," she whispered, and even though I tried not to be jealous, the longing for him in her voice had something aching inside me.

I wanted her to want me like that. But I wasn't going to play games with her. All my cards were on the table. She knew where I stood.

"Okay, I won't go far. I'm just gonna step outside and give you two some space." Asher flicked his gaze toward me. "I'd tell you to behave, but I hate to waste my breath."

I flipped him off. "Behave on this."

He raised a brow. "How old are you?"

"Old enough to fuck like a champ."

"Jesus Christ."

"I think I've made you say that a time or two."

Asher laughed. He actually laughed. "Yeah. You might've." He started for the door, ruffling a hand in my hair as he passed. The casual touch made my stomach swoop.

That was new.

Then he walked out without another word.

As I returned my attention to Rosie, I knew we'd be having a conversation about Asher before I left to get my wayward brother. There was no avoiding it now.

"So . . ." I began, unsure what to say.

"So?"

"How about them Seattle Cyclones?"

She smiled. "Are you ever serious?"

"Only when it can't be avoided."

"Is there more between the two of you than sex?"

An alarm buzzed in my brain. My instant reaction was to say no, but that fucking swoop . . . it had me confused. "We're kind of friends."

"You know it's okay for you to fancy him, right?"

"Fancy him? Is that what we're going to call it?"

She gestured with her hand. "You know . . . like him, like him."

I laughed and pressed both palms to the table, leaning close to her. "For a woman with a sexual appetite like yours, you sure have trouble saying the words."

"I'll have you know I've only done the deed with one person . . . erm, creature."

"Lucky bastard. Who is he?" My wolf was ready to hunt him down and kill him.

She mimed locking her lips. "I know better than to fall for that one."

"Okay, fine, so you fucked one beast and got a taste for it? How do you go from basically a virgin to needing multiple mates to keep you satisfied?"

Was it my finest moment? Perhaps not, but the question was an honest one.

"I've no bloody clue. But I want you all. I'm drawn to you all. I can't deny it, and I don't want to. I spent my life denying myself the things I wanted so other people could soar instead of me. I'm not going to do that again."

"I wouldn't want you to," I admitted with a sigh. "My wolf doesn't understand it. But I get it."

"You know what it's like to be pulled in by more than one person," she said softly, without an ounce of judgment in her tone.

"Not until recently, but yeah . . . I guess I do."

She rested her hand on top of mine. "I happen to know for a fact that it's possible to love more than one person at a time. What you feel for one doesn't diminish what you feel for another."

"Been through this before, have you?"

"Not personally. But my bro—" she caught herself and corrected, "friends of mine have a . . . group dynamic."

"And they make it work?"

"Quite successfully, after a few false starts."

"Is that what happened tonight? A false start?"

She laughed quietly. "It certainly fits. But, if I learned anything from them, this kind of relationship can only work if everyone is honest about what they need." Her eyes flicked back up to mine. "And I do mean everyone. There's no room for hidden resentment or jealousy."

"You telling me no one gets jealous?"

"I didn't say that. I'm sure they do from time to time, that's just in our nature. Especially for possessive Alpha wolves." She gave me a pointed look. "The only way around that is to regularly talk about your feelings."

"Gross," I teased.

Her sweet smile made my heart swell, and other parts too. Ben needed to get on board with this. He was fucking everything up by running from us, from what we all could be. The only way we could fix it was to do exactly what she said. If being open about my emotions was what she needed, I'd be first in line. Even if the thought of it made me want to squirm, I had enough trouble admitting them to myself.

"Then let me go find our grumpy wolf so I can get him to *talk about his feelings* with me, okay?"

Looking relieved, she rose, then lifted on tiptoe and pressed a gentle kiss to my lips. "Okay."

I stripped right then and there, not wanting my clothes to be sacrificed for the cause, and couldn't fight my laugh at her assessing gaze. She liked what I was packing. Of course. I winked at her. "Save that thought. Once the Ben situation is sorted, I plan on being creature number two."

"Creature number . . . oh." Her cheeks went pink. "I might hold you to that, Remington."

"That's right, baby girl. Practice saying my name. You'll be screaming it once I get this fixed."

Her eyes went glassy, and the scent of her arousal flooded my nose. Fuck. I was cock blocking my own damn self.

"Don't you dare do anything to ease the ache. Let me take care of you when we get back."

"Then hurry."

~

IT TOOK LONGER than I thought to hunt my brother down. He'd run far. He always ran far. Ben wasn't the guy who stayed and worked through his feelings. He was the one who punished himself until his mind was clear enough that he could handle his shit. My brother would push his body until he was broken and bruised before talking about how he felt. Maybe that was because of his stammer or simply due to the things he'd had to see when we were little.

Not that I blamed him. I was the lucky one, really. We both lost our parents, but at least I didn't have the visuals burned into my memory. All I dealt with were the remembered sounds of screaming, the scent of blood, the scraping of claws on the wood floor above us. The little *drip* as the warm liquid squeezed through the floorboards we'd hidden beneath and splashed down onto us. It had been years before I could stand being out in the rain. Even now, my skin grew tight and my breathing uneven if I spent too long in the shower.

Some things you just never forget.

"Don't look up, Remi." Ben had pulled me close, pressing my face into his chest. Protecting me, even as he trembled in terror. He took that on for me. Stood sentinel for the both of us. Made sure, even as everyone we'd ever loved died, that he and I were safe. His soul bore the scars of that day so that mine could remain whole. Or as whole as it could ever be after living through a slaughter like that. From that night on, he barely spoke, and when he did, it was a stilted, halting, painful struggle for him. All because he'd kept me safe.

Well, now it was my turn to protect him. Before he fucked up our chance at a happy ending beyond repair. I wouldn't let Rosie slip through our fingers because I knew if she did, he'd regret it for the rest of his life. Just like I would.

I found him in his human form, sitting on a jagged boulder at the edge of a cliff that overlooked the rushing glacial river below. Even from this distance, the slick sheen of blood on his bare skin glowed in the moonlight.

"What was it this time? Grizzly? Mountain lion?"

Ben didn't look at me, just lifted one shoulder in a wordless shrug. It told me everything I needed to know. He'd let his wolf have free rein. Anything that happened after was likely a hazy blur of random images that didn't quite make sense.

"Do you at least feel better?"

A grunt was all I got.

"Cool cool cool. Good talk. Glad you made time for one of our infamous heart-to-hearts."

"Fuck off, Remi."

"Hey, look at you. Not even a hint of stutter."

He glared at me. Sure, it was a low blow, but at least he'd looked my way.

"You're a real asshole, you know that? I thought it was Asher, but it's you."

The low growl that left his chest was a warning. So was the flash of neon blue in his eyes. He was still on a razor's edge.

"You're such a jealous fuck. Threatened by a human? Come on, Ben. You'll share her with me, but not anyone else?"

He jumped up, his chest heaving. "You d-don't c-count. Y-you're j-just an extension o-of me."

Ouch.

I don't think my twin had ever said anything in his life that cut me as deeply.

"Wait, let me get this straight. You don't mind sharing Rosie with me because I'm just some copy of you? What kind of narcissistic bullshit is that?"

"Remi—"

"No. I get it now. Thanks, bro. So glad to finally learn how little you actually think of me."

"S-s-she shouldn't w-want anyone else. W-we are the s-same, Rem. That's why it w-works."

"I'm not you. I'm so fucking different from you, I don't think anyone who knows us would ever mistake us for each other. Like it or not, even if we look alike, she wants me . . . *me*. Not another you. One stuttering, emotionally anemic asshole is more than enough."

Hurt flashed in his irises, but I refused to acknowledge the burn of guilt in my belly. He'd more than earned that one.

"It's n-n-not the s-same as her w-wanting Asher. W-we're p-pack."

"She's not pack. She's not even a wolf."

"She fucking should be!" His shout echoed off the rocky mountainside.

"Ben, she's our mate. The fact that she wants him doesn't change that."

"How c-can our m-mate want to b-be with someone else?" He sounded so broken, so defeated, I didn't know what to do with that.

"Love isn't all or nothing." Rosie's words spilled from my mouth, echoing the truth she'd handed me earlier. "You *can* love more than one person at the same time. It doesn't mean you love the other one less. Love expands. It's not finite. Trust me."

I wasn't sure where that last bit came from, but now

was not the time to dig too deeply. This was Ben's come to Jesus moment, not mine.

"Don't push her away because of this. Don't fuck up our chance to claim our mate. She's ours. There's no other explanation for the way we feel about her."

I didn't tell him how my instinct had been screaming *mate* through every cell of my body. Rosie had etched herself on my bones without even trying. My wolf begged to mark her with an intensity that almost hurt. That shouldn't be happening this early in the game. Unless she was fated to be mine . . . ours.

"S-she s-s-said no." I opened my mouth to object, but he kept going, his dark eyes shot through with a glowing blue as his wolf snarled, "She r-rejected us."

"No, she didn't. She needs time. She's not a wolf. Who knows how the fae deal with mates. Do they even have them? And I know for a fact, it's pretty commonplace for them to have more than one lover." I thought back to the stories of the Shadow Queen and her men. At the time, I'd been intrigued, but I never considered that same arrangement being my fate.

I seemed to be getting through to him. His brow furrowed. "Y-you t-think Asher could be h-hers too?"

I shrugged. "How the hell am I supposed to know? But if she feels for him even a fraction of what we feel for her, how can we deny her? Our job is to give our mate what she needs. If that's him, who are we to stand in her way?"

"Fuck. I'm an asshole." He dragged a hand through his hair.

"Tell me something I don't know."

Ben's lips twitched up.

"So does this mean your head is now safely dislodged from your ass? Can we go home now? My balls are frozen, and so help you, if I end up with frostbite I'm coming after yours as payment."

"I c-can't promise n-not to kill him for touching her. But I'll t-try."

"What a vote of confidence. I'm sure that'll make him eager to join in."

"It's all I c-can give you."

"Well . . . it's something, I guess."

Ben rolled his eyes and shifted, bounding back the way I'd come without another word.

"Cool, so I'll just follow you then," I shouted after him, annoyance vibrating through me. He might be my twin. And he might have saved my life. But he really was a fucking asshole. He was lucky I loved him.

"And if anything, *you* look like *me*," I muttered, shifting and making my way back to our cabin and the woman waiting for us inside.

THIRTY-FIVE

GAVIN

Her voice floated out from the window, each perfect melodic note slicing straight through my heart. Roslyn was alive. There was no doubt now that I'd heard that sweet sound. On the heels of my relief came the fiery burn of anger.

She left me. Pining. Mourning. Heartbroken. And it had been a lie.

How. Dare. She.

My palm twitched at the thought of what I was going to do to her when I got my hands on her.

"Did you really mean what you said? About wanting us all? About wanting me?" The man's voice grated on my every nerve. I'd tear out his throat and bathe in his blood. He was a dead man.

"I wouldn't have said it otherwise."

Jealousy ignited in my veins. Roslyn was mine. *My* wife. *My* mate. *Mine.*

"I've never felt like this."

Devious little liar.

The denial was right there on the tip of my tongue. I

knew for a fact that my wife had burned for me. I'd tasted the truth when I pulled my fingers from her dripping cunt. My cock swelled at the memory of her distinct flavor. She haunted me.

I shook with the need to blur inside and steal her away. *Control yourself.*

"How would it work? A schedule? I get you on Hump Day and alternate Sundays?" The man's voice was filled with amusement, but there was hesitance in it too.

"I don't think that's how it typically goes in arrangements like these. My brother . . . his mate has three others. They all exist together. No jealousy, no schedule."

"That's right. I remember. They also almost ended the world."

"Almost. But we won't talk about that."

"So you think we all say yes, and it'll be just one big happy orgy, huh?"

"Something like that. Why . . . are you considering it?"

My jaw was clenched so tight my teeth throbbed.

"I am. Fuck, I want you, Rosie."

At the soft rustle of fabric and her hitched breath, I lost my precariously balanced control. I crept closer to the window, desperate to see her.

The American tosser had her in his arms, his lips molded to hers, his hands in her tresses as he defiled what was mine. Who the bloody hell was this wankstain? He certainly wasn't one of the Mercer twins.

My fangs ached, hands tense with the need to tear off his cock and feed it to him. But I couldn't give in yet. There were two others trying to take what belonged to me. I needed all the players in place before I made my move. No one could know I was here until it was time.

Plucking out the slim tungsten case from my jacket

pocket, I flicked it open and selected one of the hand-rolled opium cigarettes. I needed something to calm the beast inside me before I lost hold of its leash and left a bloodbath in its wake.

I never claimed to be a good man. The only person I'd be good to was kissing another before my very eyes. He would pay.

"Asher," she breathed, pulling away, "I think we should take things slow. Until we know where the others stand. I don't want to hurt anyone, and Ben . . . he's not—"

"I know. He'll come around, but I can wait for you. I've spent twenty-eight years without you. I can wait a few more days."

"What brought about this change in you?"

He sighed, and I wanted to reach into his chest and pluck out his still-beating heart. Maybe I'd go the way of my ancestors and feast on it for good measure.

"No one has ever done what you did for me, Rosie. No one. You claimed me as yours even though it might ruin your relationship with Ben and Remi. No one has ever wanted me before."

"That's not true. Remi wants you."

"No, not like that. I mean *chosen* me. All anyone has ever done is give me up. Made me feel disposable. Left me. It's why no one ever noticed when I disappeared. It made it easy to keep everyone at arm's length. Until you. You're the first person who's ever wanted to keep me."

Oh, for fuck's sake. Stray dogs are less clingy.

"You deserve to be wanted. I'm sorry you ever felt anything less." My Roslyn cupped his face and kissed him, and I died inside as I watched her mold her body to his.

He was about to feel nothing. Forever.

But two hulking naked men burst through the back

door, and I crushed the cigarette under my foot as I recognized them. The Mercers were home.

"Looks like we're just in time," Remington said, his cock swinging in the breeze.

Roslyn slipped out of the American's arms and turned around, her eyes wide as she took in the other twin's blood-streaked form. "Good God, Ben, what did you do? Must you always come back home covered in bruises and soaked in blood? I'm too young to die of a heart attack, and seeing you like this on a regular basis is sure to send me into cardiac arrest."

"W-worked off some frustration. I'm g-good now." He didn't touch her, and I was grateful. I didn't think I could stand here another minute if they all began taking liberties with my wife. I'd burn their fucking house down and paint her in the ashes.

"Go take a shower, man. You smell like death." Remington shoved his brother toward the hall before winking at Roslyn. "I'm gonna go get some clothes on. Then we should probably talk. Unless you want to take care of that problem of yours first."

The sensual promise in his words left little confusion as to his meaning.

"That's my cue. You two have fun. I'm going to head home. I'll text you tomorrow, princess."

A low growl slipped free from my throat, and Remington's head snapped up, his eyes glowing with neon fire as he stared intensely out the window.

I blurred away, knowing I'd bring on a confrontation I wasn't quite ready for if I stayed. Three on one—two really, the mortal didn't count—wouldn't be a problem. But I didn't want my fragile petal caught in the crossfire. I'd take them out, one by one, starting with the human. There was no need to rush this. I'd bide my time. Savor it. Silence each voice whispering in her ear until the only one she heard was mine.

I never said I was the hero of this story. I was one hundred percent the villain, and this time, I'd win.

THIRTY-SIX

I started my truck with a lightness in my chest I'd never experienced before. Was this what happiness felt like?

Whatever it was, it was a one-eighty from what I'd been feeling on the drive down a few hours ago. If I'd known this was the way the night would go, I might have been a little more eager to spend time with the Mercers. I've spent my life alone, but now . . . the possibility of not having to wake up to a cold bed, of having someone to share a morning conversation with, of being sort of . . . normal, made me yearn for more.

Jesus, I was screwed. I didn't know how to do normal. What if I fucked it all up? What if she changed her mind once she got to know me better and realized what a fucking mess I really was? What if she left? Everyone always left.

I was so focused on my meltdown that the soft bump and jerk of my truck had me snapping back to reality with an adrenaline-fueled lurch. It almost felt like I'd hit something, but a frantic check in my rearview didn't show any wounded deer or bunnies. Must have just been a rogue branch or pot hole.

"Get it together, Henry. This is so not the time to have a fucking crisis. Do you want to drive off the side of this damn mountain?"

Rain began pelting my windshield, gently at first, but building in intensity. Before long, I had to turn on my wipers and had to slow down so I could see through the torrential downpour. I took the turn out of town, the one-lane dirt road already a muddy mess, and had to slam on my brakes as my headlights flooded the road and revealed a large branch lying in the path.

"Fuck," I grumbled, knowing I wasn't getting home without dealing with that first. "At least you have no one to look pretty for right now."

Resigned, I left the truck running and jumped out, grabbing a set of work gloves I left in the side of the door for this exact scenario—fallen trees came with the territory when you lived in the middle of the woods.

"Fucking trees. Goddamned Alaska. If this curse doesn't kill me, I'm buying myself a damn island in the tropics." The thought of Rosie in a string bikini sipping one of those umbrella drinks did a lot to improve my spirits as I pulled the heavy as fuck branch to the side of the road, water running from my hair into my eyes.

"I'm afraid you're not going to live long enough for either of those things," a deep resonant voice said from behind me, his British accent sending a chill down my spine.

I turned, reaching for my gun and cursing myself for leaving it in the holster under the seat. I was getting sloppy. "Who the fuck are you?"

"Doesn't matter. You won't be around to tell anyone."

I couldn't see his face through the rain and the brightness of my truck's headlights. But he was large, formidable, and everything about him screamed one word. Run.

"Get out of my way, man. I don't have time for your intimidation tactics. If I pissed you off, join the queue. I've got a list of enemies a mile long. You're not new."

"Maybe not, but I'm here, and they're not."

I doubted my mouth would be much use to me, but it made me feel a little more in control, which was all I really had. "You want a fucking cookie?"

I was thankful my voice didn't betray the panic burning in my gut. I was just a human. Genetically I was nowhere near a match to this guy. Whatever he was. If he got his hands on me, it was all over. Just when I'd finally found something worth sticking around for.

Fuck.

That.

"I can smell your fear, boy. It's going to make your blood even sweeter."

Motherfucking vampire.

I didn't have any defense against him. If I ran, he'd catch me. My gaze raked the ground and lit on a jagged piece of wood that had splintered from the branch. If I could get it, I could stake him. Maybe.

"You smell like her," he murmured, the words nearly unintelligible.

"What was that? You kind of mumble. Has anyone told you that? E-nun-cia-tion is your friend. You should try it sometime. We could practice it a little right now if you want. It's really common for vampires to have speech impediments. All those teeth."

As expected, he didn't respond, but it was worth a shot, right?

The vamp was a blur as he rushed me.

My heart stuttered, my entire body coming alive as if it knew death was here and was protesting the inevitability of it. I was aware of every breath, every tickle of wind and rain against my skin, the rise of each individual hair on the back of my neck. I'd never been this keyed into my own existence before. It was electric, like lightning rather than blood coursed through me.

On instinct, I lifted my hands and turned my face away.

Blinding light erupted around us, blasting both of us apart. My arm tingled, and my focus instantly went to the limb to make sure the asshole hadn't ripped it off. Shock did things to people. I might not realize it was gone if I didn't check. But no, my hand was solid, intact, and the stars creeping up my forearm were . . . fucking glowing? Jesus Christ. Had I done that?

Frantic, I stumbled to my feet and cast my gaze around the area, searching for my attacker, but he was gone. Did I kill him? Had he been vaporized? Was I a superhero now? Fuck. I didn't remember any radioactive spiders, but stranger shit had happened. It was possible . . . especially in a town like this one.

I flexed my hand, and the glow disappeared. Everything in me settled back to normal.

"What the hell was that?"

Knowing that the vampire could come back any second, I didn't waste time standing around to figure it out. I needed to get the hell out of Dodge.

Then something the fucker said ghosted through my mind making ice skate down my spine.

"You smell like her."

There was only one *her* he could be referring to.

I scrambled into the truck and searched for my phone where I'd tossed it on the passenger seat.

My fingers shook from the adrenaline surge and rain, meaning it took me a few attempts to unlock the damn thing and pull up Remi's number. I hit call, my heartbeat ratcheting up with each consecutive ring.

"Pick up, pick up, pick up."

"Hey–"

"Remi–"

"This is Remi. No one leaves a fucking voicemail anymore, but if you're going to, do it after the beep. If you're persuasive enough, I'll call you back."

"You motherfucking narcissistic asshat," I growled, listening to his cocky-ass message. When the beep came, I gripped the phone so hard I worried I might crack it in two. "Listen to me very closely, Remington Mercer. This is not a fucking joke. There's a vampire in town. And I think he's coming after Rosie. Do not let her out of your sight."

THIRTY-SEVEN

BEN

"Ben, we need to talk."

The constant weight on my shoulders eased the second I threw the deadbolt, closing the bar for the night. Rosie narrowed her eyes at me as she wiped down the last of the tables, her gaze full of questions.

Her statement would have had me tucking tail in any other circumstance, but I knew exactly what she was getting at. Since Asher's message a couple nights ago, Remi and I had been so far up Rosie's ass she'd barely been able to pee without one of us standing over her. Not that we'd mentioned the reason for our obsessive behavior to her. She probably thought it was related to the whole uncompleted mate bond thing. She couldn't be more wrong, but the last thing we wanted was to scare her. We'd protect her with our last breaths, so there was no need to tell her about the rogue vampire. He wasn't going to get anywhere near her. If he tried, I'd end up wearing his fangs on a necklace.

"About w-what?"

"I don't like the way things feel. You're everywhere I

am, but you won't talk to me. I . . . need to know we're okay."

"We're f-fine, sugar."

She threw her hands up. "Oh, okay then. Since we're *fine,* I guess I'll just let it go."

I blew out a breath. How did I explain everything without fucking it up? I'd gotten my mind wrapped around the idea of sharing her body with someone other than Remi—at least in theory. We'd see what happened when we put it into practice. The sex wasn't the issue. It was my wolf. He didn't know how to be around his mate without marking her. My biological instinct begged to claim her. It was all I could do to draw in a full breath when my throat felt like it was closing in on itself and my body shook with the need to make her mine. Permanently.

She breezed past me, and I couldn't stop myself. I snagged her by the belt loop and tugged her against me. Nuzzling her throat, I breathed her in and let out a shuddering sigh. "I'm sorry."

She melted against me. "Stop being sorry and tell me what's going on in that head of yours. We haven't really spoken since . . . everything. Do you even still want me?"

"D-do I w-want you? Are you k-kidding?" I spun her around so I could look into her eyes. "I w-want you so bad my chest hurts."

"Even if you have to share me?" She didn't mention Asher's name, but I knew that was who she was referring to.

"However I c-can have you."

She raised a hand so she could run her fingers through my hair. "Then what are you waiting for?"

"You. To b-be r-ready."

Her expression was tender. "You don't have to hold back with me."

"I d-don't think I can t-take you w-without taking all of you."

"What do you mean?"

"M-my wolf is so on edge. I'm n-not s-sure I can c-control myself. I'll go t-too far. I'll c-claim you."

"Perhaps we can come to some kind of . . . arrangement? Maybe we take the sex out of this and instead use our connection to be more intimate in other ways." Her gaze burned into mine. "Mates are more than sexual partners in my world. I'm assuming it's the same for wolves."

I nodded. I didn't have a whole lot of experience with other wolves, but I knew that much.

"There's still a lot we don't know about each other. Maybe we start there. Get to know each other properly."

"Like a d-date? Like our d-dinner?"

"Exactly, but with less of my abysmal cooking."

I smiled, my heart flipping with the prospect. Taking her hand, I led her to a table, flipped the chair off the top, and placed it on the floor. Then did the same with the other one. "Sit."

"Yes, Alpha," she answered with a soft giggle and did as I told her.

My cock jerked to attention. I liked the sound of that too fucking much.

Throat tight as need hit me in the gut, I forced out, "Good girl," proud of myself for managing it when I caught her resulting blush.

I strode to the bar and switched on the sound system, turning on some music before I poured each of us a pint. That done, I hurried back and set them down on the table. In a fit of inspiration, I ran to the kitchen and grabbed one of the candles left over from some event and lit the wick, carrying the wax pillar back to our table for two and setting it in the center.

"T-there. Now i-it's a date."

"Will there be dancing?"

"If y-you want."

"I want."

"Now?"

"Not yet. I want to learn all your dark secrets first." She grinned up at me over the top of her glass before taking a sip.

I sat in the chair across from her and leaned on the table. "W-what do you w-want to know?"

"Everything. Were you born a lumberman? Did you come out of the womb with an ax and a beard? What's your most irrational fear? Your favorite memory? Your worst?"

I held up my hands, laughing. "Woah, hold on. S-slow d-down. One at a t-time."

"You asked."

"F-fair enough."

"So, were you?"

"Was I w-what?"

"Born a flannel-wearing lumberman?"

"You m-mean a l-lumberj-jack?"

"That's what I said."

She was so earnest I laughed again. "No, you d-didn't. Y-you said lumberman."

"Potatoes, potatoes," she said breezily, waving a hand and not differentiating between the pronunciations at all. "So . . . about that flannel . . . "

"N-no. I wasn't b-born in f-flannel. I w-was j-just a baby. A n-naked one."

Her cheeks went pink. "Same. Though not a lumberjack . . . lumberjane? Lumbersexual?"

"I d-don't think th-that means what y-you think it m-means."

She balled up her cocktail napkin and tossed it at me. "Fine. We were both born naked. Next question."

"Irrational f-fear?"

"Yes."

I thought for a moment, then shuddered. "Angler fish."

"What? You mean those weird fish with their own lights? But they're so tiny. They can't hurt you."

"How d-do you k-know? Ever m-met one?"

"Well, no. But that's due to the whole bottom of the ocean thing."

"Have you seen th-those teeth? Th-they're big enough t-to bite off something that m-matters. And there's no good r-reason for a f-fish to have its own l-light source. It's unnatural. B-besides, you s-said irrational." Fuck, this was the most I'd spoken to anyone other than Remi in a really long time.

She laughed. "So I did."

"What's y-yours then?"

She didn't even hesitate. "That my belly button will come undone and all my insides will fall out."

I blinked, the sheer absurdity of the comment rendering me speechless. "Jesus."

"I know."

"D-do you worry about th-this a lot?"

"More than I should."

I shook my head. "Huh. Well, w-would it make you feel b-better if I p-promise to hold everything in if it ever h-happens?"

"Maybe?"

"That's a n-no, isn't it?"

She nodded. "I'm reasonably sure I'd have a heart attack and die, so while adorable and sweet, your services would not be required."

I took a drink, worried this date had already taken a disastrous turn. "Favorite memory."

Her eyes went a little glassy. "My brother showing me how to find the North Star so I'd always find my way."

"I d-didn't know you had a b-brother."

"Two."

"Do you m-miss them?"

"Yes. Unbearably." Her voice was so small and sad my heart ached. Fuck. Even the happy questions were dangerous territory. "What's your happiest memory?"

I sighed and sat back in my chair. "W-when we were kids, I c-couldn't talk. S-so Remi and I created our own k-kind of s-sign language. W-we m-made up stories about the p-people we met." Christ, I wished I could get through this without stammering. "He's s-so fucking f-funny."

"He is."

I knew she was too polite to ask what she must be thinking, so I offered her the truth. Or as much of it as I could tolerate. "E-eventually the bullying got s-so bad that I f-forced myself to s-start talking again. I w-was t-tired of seeing Remi f-fight for me. I c-couldn't ever g-get rid of the st-stutter, though."

"Have you always had it?"

"N-no. N-not until the n-night our p-parents d-d-died."

She reached out a hand and rested it on mine as I told her the rest of the story, doing my best to spare her the gory details. "No one should have to see that. It sounds terrible."

"It was." God, I was glad she didn't respond with the classic *I'm sorry.*

She blinked away the tears misting her eyes and cleared her throat. "Well, this failed miserably. We're not very good at lighthearted, are we?"

The song changed as we sat there looking at each other, both wondering what to do next. Thank fuck it was a slow song. Standing, I held out a hand. "L-let's try the dancing."

She joined me, and I let out a breath I hadn't realized I'd been holding. We swayed together, and everything felt right in that moment. She was in my arms and not going anywhere.

"S-see?"

She tilted her face up, brow furrowed.

"W-we *are* fine, sugar. Better than f-fine."

"Thank you, Ben."

"For what?"

She rose up on her toes and kissed me. "For the best date I've ever been on."

"Well, the b-bar was p-pretty low after that d-dinner."

"Hey!" She pinched my ribs. "You said you loved my dinner."

I kissed her. "I did. I love e-everything about you."

Her breath hitched, and she curled into me. "I feel the same way about you."

I held her tight, feeling like for once in my fucking life everything was finally going well. That I was on the cusp of truly being happy.

And it was all because I had my mate in my arms.

Nothing would ever make me let her go.

THIRTY-EIGHT

ROSIE

Tom burst into the bar, tearing his hat off his head as he waved his arms, expression exasperated. "I'm sorry I'm late, lads. There was a dead grizzly on my front porch this morning. I had tae pick it up and get rid of it before I could go anywhere. It was already minging. I didn't want it to get any worse."

"A grizzly? This close to town?" Dick asked as Tom claimed his usual spot next to him.

"Aye."

"That's funny, there was a dead moose on the path this morning when I went for my morning constitutional," Harry chimed in.

Tom chuckled. "My morning constitutional is handled in the loo. Your poor neighbors. Talk about minging."

"I bury it." Harry shrugged, entirely unrepentant. "What can I say? I like the feel of the cool breeze on me arse. And the view ain't so bad either."

"Is it normal for dead animals to turn up so close to civilization?" I asked, pulling Tom a pint.

"Nae, lass. But nothing in this town is *normal* now, is it? Though these circumstances are strange to be sure."

My mind flashed to the three dead deer we'd passed on the way in today. "What . . . circumstances?"

"Well, I don't know about Tom's grizzly, but the moose had his throat torn out. Not a trace of blood around the corpse."

"Aye, no blood in the beast's body, but a gaping wound at his throat," Tom added.

Harry leaned in, his voice going low and sinister. "Just like those bodies they've been finding."

I shuddered and glanced at the door, half-expecting Dallas to burst through and declare another murder.

"I know what it is," Dick said.

Everyone turned their attention to the gargoyle sitting on the far left. No one said a thing as we all watched him drain his pint. He slowly pushed the glass toward me, silently asking for another.

"Oh, for Christ's sake, stop dangling it like a worm on a hook, you petty wee man. What is it?"

I pulled another pint and placed it in front of Dick.

"Thank you, love. Now, as I was saying . . . "

"Ye havenae said a bloody thing since ye opened yer gob," Tom grumbled.

"It's a vampire."

My blood ran cold.

"How do you know?" I asked, trying hard to keep my voice normal even though my pulse pounded loudly in my ears. Any North American vampire would know about Cashel Blackthorne and his family—as would most others. My family name was well-known in all vampiric circles. This was dangerous territory for me. If one of my kind was out there, I would need to be more careful than ever. "You said before the murderer wasn't a vampire."

"Perhaps not those, but these animals? Throats gone, no blood. It seems blatantly obvious to me." Dick shrugged. "Everyone in this town knows what a vampire attack looks like."

"Pffft. It doesn't mean that at all. You're reaching. We would be able to scent a vampire from ten paces." Harry's bravado was paper thin. "It could just as easily have been a ravenous mountain lion who dragged its prey away from the scene."

"Maybe he hasn't come into town. Don't scare the poor girl," Tom chastised.

"You're the one that started it," Dick said, his cheeks burning as he offered me an apologetic glance. "Sorry, love."

My phone gave a little buzz in my back pocket, nearly sending me crashing through the ceiling. I pressed a hand to my chest and gave a relieved little laugh. These three had gotten me all wound up. It had been easy to forget what I was doing tucked away up here, distracted as I'd been by my men. But everything they'd said brought reality back into focus.

Pulling my phone out, I checked the screen.

Asher.

HENRY:

Do the three stooges always make you so uncomfortable? Need a rescue, princess?

I grinned, scanning the space in search of him.

My eyes had just drifted over a man in a traditional buffalo plaid flannel, thick black suspenders over his shoulders, a faded black hat pulled low on his brow. *Bingo.*

ME:

> Going for the modern lumberjack look
> today, I see. Inspired by a certain Mercer
> twin we both know?

HENRY:

> Bentley doesn't have a monopoly on plaid.
> This is a logging town. Lumberjacks are a
> dime a dozen. Makes for perfect
> camouflage.

ME:

> Yeah, you really give off the I-chop-wood-
> all-day vibe.

HENRY:

> I do like to play with wood.

ME:

> I am aware. How long has it been since you
> last . . . played? You and Remi haven't
> talked in a while.

I glanced up in time to see Asher shift in his seat. I couldn't tell if he was uncomfortable with the question or worked up for other reasons.

Pocketing my phone, I set to work preparing a special cocktail for him. I'd been crafting this recipe for the past few days, trying to get it right for the next time he showed his face.

Once it was ready, I sauntered to the table where he was holed up.

"What is this? I didn't order anything." Those eyes of his were so beautiful, I lost myself in them for a moment.

"You have to order something or Ben will put you out on your arse."

He took the chilled glass with a dubious glance, holding the amber liquid up and taking a sniff. "What's in it?"

"A little bourbon, some simple syrup, lemon juice, cinnamon . . ." I waved my hand. "Nothing flashy, but it packs a punch. I call it the Black Hat."

He blinked up at me. "You created a cocktail? For me?"

My heart gave a little twist at the almost awed note I sensed in his voice. It seemed cruel to let him know I modified a recipe I'd found online. Twisting my fingers in my apron, I gave him a tight smile and nodded. "Uh-huh."

Bringing the glass to his lips, he smirked and took a deep gulp. His eyes widened as he swallowed it down, and try as he might, the grimace was undisguisable. He coughed and spluttered, setting the drink on the table and trying to catch his breath.

"It's . . . so . . . good." His words were a pained wheeze as he lied. "I think it burned my esophagus and might eat through my stomach lining, though."

Looking down at the half-empty glass, I winced at the little piece of eggshell I saw floating in the dark liquid.

"Why was it slimy?" he asked, a little thread of concern in his voice.

"I think that might have been the egg."

"Egg?" He gagged, then burped. "Are you trying to poison me?"

"The alcohol gets rid of the bacteria."

Remi's scent enveloped me as he slipped a hand around my waist. "You have to shake it until it's foamy first, baby girl."

Asher's skin turned a sickly shade of green. "Excuse me. I'm going to go die now."

He was up and out of his chair so fast he almost knocked it over. My heart sank. "Bollocks, I thought I had it that time."

Remi pressed a kiss to my forehead. "It's the thought that counts."

"Tell that to poor Asher. Now he thinks I'm trying to kill him."

"Eh, you're hardly the first. I wouldn't worry about it."

"Can you go check on him? I don't want him to be alone if he's being sick."

"Are you asking me to hold your boyfriend's hair back?"

"Isn't he your boyfriend too?"

Remi gave me a searing look. "It's complicated."

Given my situation, first with Gavin, then the demon, and now the three of them, I felt the truth of his words in my soul. "Isn't it always?"

"No, actually. Usually it's pretty fucking simple." He flashed me a quicksilver grin and then kissed me. "Be right back."

I watched him run after Asher before I cleared off his table and took the offending drink to chuck it. "So much for that recipe. Onwards and upwards, Rosie," I muttered to myself.

My wrist tingled as I poured round three for the trio of gargoyles, my gaze ever-watchful for my two men to return from the loo. Thoughts of what they could be getting up to had me pressing my thighs together. There was just something about two sexy men taking care of each other that had lust—and an unnamable emotion—punching me in the belly every single time.

They came into the room from down the hall, laughing and smiling. That was a rare sight. Maybe this would work. Maybe we could all be happy. Maybe I'd finally found where I belonged and could truly start my life now.

I should have known better.

"Forget me already, ma petite monstre?"

I shivered as Pan's smoky voice rolled through my mind. He'd been so quiet lately that I'd almost been able to make myself believe it was over. That he was finally going to leave me alone.

"Come. Now. No one will miss you. They're busy. Excuse yourself and come to me."

I didn't want to. But I also absolutely did. He had me by the throat in a way I couldn't explain. Where did he want me to go? Was I really going to flounce into the woods and let him have me against a tree?

"As tempting an idea as that is, you're overthinking this, ma belle. Upstairs. To your old room. I'll take care of the rest. Don't make me come collect you at that bar. You won't like what happens to them if you do. All those innocent patrons. It would be a shame, really."

A flare of need radiated from the mark he'd given me, and I set down the rag I'd been wiping the bar with before slipping away unnoticed. I probably should have been more concerned about who was going to watch the bar, but where Pan was concerned, logic rarely played a role. The demon owned my soul, or so it seemed anyway. I was helpless to resist him and his whims.

I rushed up the stairs to my old flat, finding the door unlocked. Easing it open, I pushed inside and found a swirling plum and midnight portal. I could just make out Pan's hulking form on the other side, a seductive smile curling his lips.

He didn't say a word, just lifted his hand and crooked one long finger, beckoning me.

Summoning me the same way I'd once summoned him.

My feet moved of their own accord, my pulse a steady throb between my legs.

This had to be the last time, and I'd tell him so. I'd more than paid his price. The end was here for us.

I just hoped he'd let me go.

CHAPTER
THIRTY-NINE

PAN

The instant her foot crossed the threshold separating her world from mine, I grasped her wrist and yanked her to me. Then I released the hold on the portal. The amount of power I'd needed to use to break through this time was much greater than before.

Why?

All it took was one whiff of her delectable scent to understand. Her connection to these *other* men was growing stronger. I was losing her.

The fuck I was.

"Have you been breaking my rules, *mon ange?*"

I breathed her in again, filling my lungs and feeding on her arousal, defiance, and even a tinge of guilt, but she hadn't broken my rules. Not yet. But she wanted to. And we couldn't have that now, could we?

"I'm here, aren't I?"

I tutted, brushing my fingers across her throat before gripping it. "That's not the rule I was talking about. You know which one. Have you let them inside you?"

She tipped her chin up, her tone taking on a haughty,

disobedient edge that made me hard. "I thought you knew everything."

I did . . . to a point. I just loved hearing her confess. Something about collecting her sins, about being the reason for them, tickled me. Robbing innocent creatures of their purity was one of my preferred pastimes. Since meeting her, defiling Roslyn Blackthorne had become my new favorite. My cock stirred at the thought. But I wasn't going to fuck her yet. I was going to make her beg for it first.

"Give me your vein, *ma petite monstre*. Then we can play."

"Why?" she asked, expression wary.

With my mark on her skin and as much blood as I'd taken, my hold on her should be strong enough to overrule any instinctual doubt or fear. The fact that she was even able to question me, to push back, spoke to how strong her bond with the others had grown in my absence. It would seem I wasn't the only one with a claim on her soul. And that just could not stand.

"It's part of the package, lovely one. You come when I call, I take your unspoiled blood, my power grows, and you remain hidden. Everyone you love stays safe."

Something flashed in her eyes. Hunger, perhaps? Her tongue darted out, wetting her lower lip.

"Remove your clothes. Or shall I do that for you? Fair warning, if it's me, they won't survive."

The way her lips curled into a wicked grin had me aching. "I'd rather not have to explain why I returned to work nude, if you don't mind."

Stepping back, I settled myself on the couch, adjusting my swollen length as I did. "Go on, then. I'm ready for the show."

Slowly, she removed each article of clothing and

dropped the fabric to the floor piece by piece. I undid the laces on my leather breeches and freed my cock, giving myself a cursory stroke or two as her body was bared to me. The sight of my ring through her nipple, the memory of giving it to her, sent a tidal wave of feral pleasure cresting through me. I loved seeing the evidence of my claim on her. First my mark. Now that. The woman could deny it all she wanted, but she was mine.

Her eyes widened as she watched me. "I forgot how big you were."

I grinned, all wicked pride, as I flashed her my fangs. "The better to fuck you with."

She blushed, the rosy color staining her from head to toe. "Are you the big bad wolf, then?"

"I'm big and bad, sweetheart. Now get that pretty arse over here and show me how much you've missed me."

For a moment I thought she might resist, but she trained her eyes on mine, and something primal passed between us. I wasn't even using my mark to send arousal through her. I hadn't since that first time when I gave it to her. She wanted this.

She wanted *me*.

"How do you want me? On my knees?"

"No. Stand here between my legs and let me take your blood. You don't get my cock until you ask for it. Until you beg for it."

"Wh-where will you take it from?" Fear scented the air. She didn't want her other men to see.

Reaching up, I flicked the ring I'd put through her nipple. "Here."

The shudder that ran through her had me twitching, precum already beading on the tip of my dick. If I let myself, I could drive inside her now. Let her cunt swallow my length and forget about everything else I was meant to do.

She moved forward, her small body trembling as she took her place between my legs.

"No need to be so shy, *ma petite*. It's nothing we haven't done before. Don't I always make it good for you?" As the question left my lips, my tail grazed the back of her leg before sliding between her thighs and flicking through the damp heat of her cunt, making her gasp.

"Y-yes."

"Now, touch me while I taste your perfect tits. I want your hands on my skin. I'm going to make you come apart with nothing more than my lips and tongue."

I expected her to place her palms on my shoulders, or chest, perhaps. Instead, she slipped her fingers into my hair, then over my horns, driving me wild. I'd killed men for less. A demon's horns were sacred. Every demon's were unique, and they held the traces of their owner's magic. As such, they were always claimed in battle between demonkind, as well as by hunters, and sold on the black market. Or hung up and displayed like trophies. To allow her to touch me there, to enjoy it, was like a faerie allowing their wings to be touched. An act of trust and vulnerability so out of character for me, I didn't even know how to react to it.

I knew what I should do. I should stop her. Remind her of her place. Of the dynamic between us.

But I didn't. It felt too fucking good.

She was going to bring me off before I could stop myself. I groaned as those fingers stroked and explored, my whole body shaking as my balls throbbed with the need for release.

"Enough," I said in a ragged plea.

"Do you like that?"

"Fuck, yes. You must've been made by Lucifer just for me."

"Then why do you want me to stop?"

"Because my cum belongs inside you, or at least painted across your body, not all over my chest." I grabbed her by the waist and pulled her closer so her full tit was in my face. The ripe nipple begged for my mouth.

Without warning, I bit down on the turgid length, drawing her blood until her sugar and spice taste exploded in my mouth. I grunted, sucking hard, taking mouthful after mouthful until she swayed beneath my hold. I only needed a drop to satisfy the requirement of the bloodletting, but I was greedy. I fed from her like a starving man, the rush sending euphoria through me.

"Pan."

Her voice was a breathless whisper, the perfect blend of pleasure and pain. The ring on my finger glowed brightly as soon as her blood hit my lips, and now it burned with power, but still I fed. She was mine. My toy. No one else could have her.

A strange link clicked into place between us. I felt her. A frantic sense of desire and fear, lust and panic, conflicting emotions at war with each other. I'd never kept a human long enough to experience this before. It heightened everything, most especially my sense of ownership. She could hide nothing from me now. I owned every piece of her. Mind. Body. Soul.

Breaking my seal on her nipple, I pulled her astride me, impaling her on my cock without warning. I growled, my voice a gravelly rasp as it washed over her skin. "Oh, *âme soeur*. So perfect." Her inner muscles spasmed as she fell apart around me, screaming out her pleasure as I held her in place. "Fuck me, *mon coeur*. Or I'll make you."

I gripped her hips and canted my own upward, her eyes rolling back in her head.

"I'm so full. You're so big. I can't."

"You can. You know I'm the only one who fits you. You were molded to my cock. You're mine."

Her head thrashed side to side, and I could see the denial forming on her lips, but I lifted her up and slammed her back down on me, robbing her of speech and pulling a wordless moan from her instead.

"Don't you dare lie to me, *mon ange*. Not while I'm inside you. Not when I can feel the truth with each flutter of this perfect cunt."

Her emotions swirled in my mind. She hated me, yet she craved every sensation I drew from deep inside her. But most of all, she wanted to come.

"What do you want, little one? What does the sweet Blackthorne princess want her demon to do?"

Her eyes locked with mine, and my dick pulsed inside her heat. "I want you to use your tail."

I grinned, a slow, cruel curve of my lips as satisfaction sang in my veins. I could give her things none of those other impostors could. She might deny her need for me, but she wanted something only I could provide.

"As you wish," I practically purred.

She slowly rolled her hips, moving up and down my length and sending pleasure racing up my spine. And as she requested, my tail slid over her round arse, trailing along the seam between the globes until I found the tight pucker hidden there.

"You want this? You want me to take both of your tight holes?"

"Yes."

I pulled out of her, much to our mutual disappointment, but it didn't last long. I slid the end of my tail inside her cunt, coating it in her pleasure, before pulling out and reclaiming her. This time in both holes at once.

The sound she made as I took her would live in my mind for eternity. A breathless gasp somewhere between a sob and a shout. Her eyes were wild, her face flushed, damp strands of hair sticking to her skin. She was beautiful in her depravity. Made for me.

"Come, *ma petite*. Squeeze my cock with your cunt. I need it." My words were a harsh rasp as I fought the urge to spill my pleasure.

Her face scrunched in concentration as she focused on giving me what I asked for. She was close, but not quite at her tipping point. Knowing her fondness for pain, I leaned forward and bit her, drawing more of her blood and sending her careening off the edge.

She came with a shout of my name, her nails digging into my skin hard enough to draw my own blood. That was it. I couldn't contain myself any longer. I called out *her* name like she was my saving grace as I spilled inside her.

Breathing hard, I wasn't fully aware of my hands loosening on her hips so my arms could band about her body, pulling her closer. I wasn't one for a cuddle, but here I was, nuzzling her, holding her like she was some cherished pet.

For a moment, she allowed it, her hands gliding over my sweat-damp skin, caressing me, dare I say . . . loving me. But then, as if she realized what she was doing, she stopped, her body going stiff in my arms.

She pulled back, easily breaking free of my loose hold as she moved off my lap.

We both groaned as she slid free of me. I should have

kept my gaze trained on her face. Perhaps then I would have been prepared. Instead, it trailed her ripe curves to watch my cum sliding down her thigh.

I growled, shifting forward to push it back inside her when her words stopped me cold.

"This was the last time."

What was she on about?

"No, it's not."

"Yes, Pan. I hope you enjoyed it. This was the last time you get my body. It's over."

The hell it was. It's not over until I say it's bloody over.

I will never be through with you. The thought startled me, waking my anger. I was not some weak-willed mortal who clung to false ideals of love or devotion. But the thought of letting her go, the thought of losing my little monster . . . it was unspeakable.

I chalked it up to a demon's innate selfishness as I snarled, "Oh? Are you no longer intent on keeping yourself hidden, then? Are you ready to step back into the spotlight? Because I assure you, even now, there are doubts about the legitimacy of your death. The Council has questioned whether your remains were human or hybrid."

Liar, liar, Pan.

Desperate times called for desperate measures, though. She needed to *need* me. I couldn't let her go. I wouldn't. Those fools who lusted after her couldn't give her half the pleasure I did. They didn't deserve to swallow her moans. To breathe in her sighs. To feel the rush of her desire coat them.

Those things belonged to *me*. Just as she did.

Roslyn Blackthorne was mine. She'd signed her soul over to my keeping herself.

No one, not some arsehole wolves or obsessive vampire, fated mates or otherwise, would take her from me.

But they aren't the only ones you need to worry about, are they, Pan? What about . . .

No. I wouldn't even think the name. Not now. Not when I had my favorite toy at my disposal.

My hand snatched her wrist, keeping her as my captive. "You really believe this is the last time I will call upon you?" I dipped my face to her mark, my tongue flicking over the rune bearing my name.

She shivered under the brush of my lips at her pulse point. "I-it's the last time you get my body. I will keep our bargain. Return when you call. But you won't take my body willingly again. If it's my blood you're after, there are other ways."

My grip on her tightened even as her words rang true in the emotions rushing between us. "Oh, but your body *is* the bargain, *mon ange.* Or did you forget? You swore to give me *anything.* I mean to claim it all."

"You already have."

"You're still breathing, aren't you? There's always more to take, so long as that heart of yours continues to beat."

"As I said, tonight you had me willingly. But no more. It's up to you whether you lower yourself to take my body by force. A pathetic demon who can't get his woman to open her legs for him."

I took her chin between my fingers, pinching hard as I lifted her head, forcing her to hold my gaze. "At least you admit you're mine. But it is cute that you think you have a choice. You can say you're unwilling all you want"—I leaned down and licked a path up her neck—"your body tells a different story. That cunt of yours can't lie."

"What my body does isn't the issue. It's what my mind and heart say."

"What does a demon care about hearts, unless it's to feast on them?"

"Haven't you heard? No means no. Even for you."

"What makes you think that will stop me? Demons take what they want. We aren't slaves to morality like humans."

"Perhaps not. But my consent matters to *you*."

I growled low. She was right. I wanted her to desire me, to be soft and open, to welcome me into her. What had happened to me? Too many tastes of her sweet blood had clouded my mind. She was a drug, and I a hapless addict. She'd ruined me when I'd been intent on doing the same to her.

How had that happened? When?

I suppose the answers didn't matter. Only that somewhere along the way it had become true.

Roslyn had sold me her soul, but instead of me making her my captive, she ended up being the one holding onto the end of my lead. She was the master, and I a pathetic lap dog.

The horror of it all made my voice hard and deathly cold. A promise of violence to any smart enough to heed it.

"Go, then. Back to your nothing town. To the men who will only serve to disappoint you. Rest assured, you'll be begging for my cock before you know it. So run from me all you want, little girl. I am the monster under your bed. The one haunting your dreams. You will never escape me. Anything else will be a poor substitute for what you really need. And no matter what you say otherwise, you belong to me, Roslyn. There is nowhere you can go where I can't find you."

I released her wrist and she stumbled away, gathering

her clothes even as I opened the portal. She stepped through without a backward glance, leaving me with an unfamiliar pain deep in my chest.

Rage burned in my veins as her scent surrounded me, as the blood she'd let me take kept me soaring, and all I wanted was to destroy something. Standing, I picked up the heavy stone urn from the table beside me and hurled it at the window, snarling when it bounced off, not leaving a dent. Fucking magic.

I closed my eyes and let my senses search for her. And the first thing I saw was that bloody stammering wolf smiling at her. He would be the first to go. And I would make it hurt.

One did not play with an archdemon and walk away unscathed.

No, they bled for the privilege. Paid for their foolishness over and over again until there was nothing left. She wanted to run from me? I'd take away everything she loved until I was all she had left.

Her only choice.

Her only solace.

Her only.

One way or the other, Roslyn would come crawling back. The state she was in when she came back to me, well, that was up to her now, wasn't it?

CHAPTER

FORTY

BEN

"Good, for a Thursday, this place is a fucking zoo. Are we running a drink special I don't know about or something, boss?" Darla popped her head into the office, her voice frantic. "Nadia is here chatting with that one writer guy. Henry? Do you know him? Anyway, do you think she'd mind hopping behind the bar to help out?"

Who the fuck was Henry? I searched my memory for the name, coming up blank until I pictured him. The writer. The handsome young writer. All broody and lonesome. Oh, hell no. Sharing her with Remi and Asher was enough. I wasn't willing to let some . . . *writer* come in and sweep her off her feet. He'd probably seduce her with romance hero lines like, "I've been yours since the day I first saw you." Or "You are the bane of my existence, but I never want us to part." He probably had a British accent too. The prick.

I needed to get out there and see what the fuck was going on.

"No," I said emphatically, standing. "I'll h-help. She w-worked all week. She d-deserves a n-night off." And that

377

way I could be out there, keeping my eye on this Henry creep. Make sure he didn't try to get handsy with my mate.

Darla tossed me a relieved smile. "Thanks, big man. I feel like I need about six more arms just to pass drinks out. Where's a spider shifter when you need one?"

I shuddered at the thought of a human-sized spider. No thanks.

She echoed my thoughts. "Actually, never mind. That's terrifying."

Following her out of the office, I braced for the cacophony I knew I'd find once we reached the bar. Sure enough, there wasn't an empty seat in the house. Tom, Dick, and Harry were perched on their usual barstools, cheeks ruddy, smiles plastered on their faces. Music blared from the speakers, and laughter filled the space. Even the sheriff was in attendance, a lazy smile on his face as he played poker with his deputy and a few other townies. The bears were here too, the club dominating a corner of the bar, their rowdy conversation bouncing off the walls.

"W-what in the world?" I breathed.

"People must be thirsty."

"M-must be. Wh-where's Remi?"

"Right fucking here."

I twisted around at the sound of my twin's voice. He hefted two boxes filled with booze around the bar, setting them down with a thud.

"'Bout time you got your lazy ass out here and actually did something."

There was no heat in his words, though. He threw me a grin as he restocked the shelves.

I rolled my eyes, snagged a bar towel, and tossed it over my shoulder. "Fuck off." He snickered as I turned toward a couple of girls seated at the bar. "What are y-you having?"

"Um, can you do a pornstar martini?" one of them asked.

What the fuck kind of froo-froo bullshit was that? "No."

She deflated, but I barely gave her any attention. My focus was on my pretty little mate and her . . . companion. I didn't like the way he was looking at her. Not one bit.

"Yes, we can, sweetheart. I'll take care of you," Remi said, shouldering me aside. "Two?"

The two girls nodded, and my brother shot me a death stare. "What are you doing? Trying to run business off?" he muttered under his breath. "Go take her a fucking drink if you need to mark your territory so badly."

I glared at my brother, wondering why he didn't seem to be nearly as affected by the situation as I was. He seemed almost amused. Like he already knew the punchline of some joke and couldn't wait for me to be the butt of it.

"Maybe I w-will," I grumbled, filling a highball glass with ice before grabbing a bottle of Glenlivet and pouring two fingers. Then, having already memorized her preference, I added a touch of water to open it up for her.

My girl knew her Scotch. It was surprising, to say the least, when we did a tasting for the staff and she dropped her knowledge on us all. She even knew the regions and the tasting notes for most of the bottles I'd brought in. Her answer when I asked where she learned it all? Her dad taught her. I felt like an idiot because of course the fae knew about things like this. Most of them originally came from Scotland.

My nerves were shot as I closed the distance between us. Protective instinct reared its head as my wolf snarled inside me when I got a whiff of Henry's own wolfy pheromones. Strong and hungry for her. I couldn't blame him, but that didn't mean I had to like it.

She looked up, beaming at me as I set the glass in front of her. "Hey. I wondered if you'd ever make an appearance."

"Who's your f-friend?" I snarled, my wolf slipping into my voice, making my greeting far less friendly than the one I'd planned. I couldn't help it. Just being around the guy made my fur stand on end.

She giggled, reaching for his hand, and I saw red. "Relax, Bentley. *Henry* here isn't a threat."

The smug bastard smiled at her, then looked up at me, pushing up the brim of his ball cap and winking. The gesture was so familiar . . . I would have sworn I'd seen it before. But I'd never met this guy. I would have remembered the tats if nothing else.

Then he spoke.

"It's not fun being on the outside of the sandwich looking in, is it, Mercer?"

Asher. Of fucking course. I felt like an idiot for not recognizing him sooner.

I sniffed. "You s-smell like a w-wolf. Why?"

He scoffed. "I'm not new here. I'm good at what I do. The fucking best, and *someone* had to be here to keep our girl company."

This asshole. He'd been right under our noses all this time. I'd seen the writer scribbling away more times than I could recall. Not once had I put it together.

"How m-many other yous are there?"

Asher cocked one brow and snorted. "You can't count that high."

A growl rumbled low in my throat.

"Boss man, a little help?"

Darla's voice pulled my attention. I exhaled loudly, torn between the need to help her and the desire to stay by my mate.

"Behave," I warned Asher.

"Where's the fun in that?"

Shaking my head, I leaned down and pressed a kiss to Rosie's forehead before walking back to the bar.

Remi's shoulders shook with laughter as I pulled pints for Darla.

"You kn-knew?"

"Of course I knew. He's been in my ass. I can see through every one of his disguises."

"W-why didn't you s-say something?"

He shrugged. "Not my secret to share." Then he stiffened, his body going on alert. "Who is that?"

I followed his gaze to the table I'd just left, seeing a hulking man standing over Rosie. Her easygoing smile bled from her face as she looked up at him. The hairs on the back of my neck stood on end, alarm bells ringing at the look in her eyes. She was ready to defend Asher. Protect the human. But who was going to protect her?

"Take o-one fucking guess."

"Alexi," he breathed, violence flashing in his eyes.

"That fucking b-bear doesn't k-know when to q-quit."

"Want me to handle it?"

"No. I g-got it."

With the way my instincts had been bouncing all over the place tonight, I was primed for a fight. Anything to restore the balance.

My blood hummed with the urge to shift right here and now so I could protect my mate, and with every step I took, I had to push back the urge to let the beast take control.

"Alexi," I said, willing my words to come strong and sure. "You're not w-welcome here."

The bear slowly turned, his smile sharp enough to cut. "Ah, I wondered when you'd grow some balls."

"Why are you here?" Rosie asked. "You were banned. Do you not know what that word means? Should I explain it to you? I'll speak slowly. You. Need. To. Leave."

His meaty palm was a blur of motion as he grabbed her by the nape and tugged her to him. "I'll leave, and I'll take you with me. We can go for a ride."

Slapping at his arm, she glared up at him, the anger in her gaze a sharp contrast to the sweetness of her voice. "No thanks. I've got plenty to keep me satisfied right here."

"That's because you haven't had a bear."

My body trembled as I fought against the need to shift. "Get your fucking hands off her."

The words were a terrifying rumble, my stutter thankfully falling away beneath my wolf's fury. I wanted to rip the bastard's head off, but I didn't want to risk doing anything that might hurt Rosie in the process. With the way he had a hold of her, anything I did right now might get her as well.

"Outside. Now."

"Is the little stuttering wolf boy going to fight me?"

He was such a cocky, arrogant dick. I might have to kill him. "If I have to."

"You and what pack? You can't possibly think you can take me one on one. One swipe of my paw, and I will gut you like a fish."

My wolf bristled at the insult. "You can try."

"Ben, don't." Rosie's eyes weren't filled with angry fire anymore. Now she was afraid . . . for me. She didn't think I could defend her? I would prove exactly what kind of wolf I was. I was a motherfucking Alpha. The top of the food chain. There was no way I was losing this fight.

"Release her. Now."

Alexi snorted but did as I said, tossing her to the floor.

Rosie whimpered as she hit the hardwood, and my fingers sharpened into claws, ready to tear out his throat. Thankfully, Asher was already out of his seat, helping her up. It was the first time I was actually glad there was someone else as dedicated to looking out for her as I was. It allowed me to focus solely on the asshole in front of me.

The rumbled growl that escaped my throat was a warning, but he wasn't cowed. Alexi grabbed me by the throat, lifting me off my feet as his claws dug into my skin. The coppery tang of blood filled the air as he squeezed, and I prepared to shift.

"Now, now, boys. We don't want any violence here tonight. Our drunk tank can only hold one. Don't ruin a perfectly good evening with murder." Sheriff Walker stood up, placing his cowboy hat on his head and leveling a stare at us as Alexi let me fall from his grasp.

My gaze locked with Alexi's. "Churchyard. Right fucking now."

The bear huffed a laugh and sauntered out of the bar, leaving me with a captive audience.

"Don't go," Rosie whispered.

But I had to. I had thrown down the gauntlet, and I knew he wouldn't stop until I laid him out and shamed him.

"I have to."

FORTY-ONE

GAVIN

This bloody human arsehole just couldn't stay away from my Roslyn, could he? But is he human? The slowly healing burn on my sternum reminded me that perhaps the answer was no. So what was he? The blast of power from his palm seemed to surprise him as much as it had me.

Warlock, maybe? Or some kind of mage?

The answer didn't really matter. Whatever he was, the wankstain wouldn't surprise me again.

I snarled as Roslyn curled in him, leaning on the arm he offered as he led her to his car. It was a different one than the beat-up truck he drove the other night. The branches swayed and groaned as I shifted my position among them, wanting to get a little closer. My vampiric eyesight and hearing were unmatched, but the pull—the primal need— to get closer to her was irresistible. I was a helpless moth to her flame. Driven by my baser instincts. They urged me to reclaim what's mine.

Unable to set foot on the ground anywhere within this ridiculous town's limits without being scented and exposed, I was relegated to leaping from tree to tree. All I needed was a loincloth and some oil, and I'd be bloody Tarzan.

"The things you reduce me to, petal."

But my grousing stopped when I followed their trail back to the Mercer's cabin. I'd found the perfect spots to watch her without them getting wise, but I wasn't sure I could take any more of this. Seeing her with these other men tore my control to ribbons. I was barely hanging on. Thank fuck she hadn't let them inside her while I watched.

I followed as the two of them walked through the house, Roslyn stripping out of her T-shirt until she was in just a thin camisole as she headed for the kitchen.

"What if something happens to him, Asher?"

The distress in her voice had my chest tightening. I wasn't used to being so attuned to or affected by someone else's emotions. Usually the sound of pain—emotional or otherwise—was a turn-on. But not in this context.

Right now, I hated it.

It made me feel out of control in a way I despised, a way I'd fought fang and claw to never feel again.

"He'll be fine, princess. He's an excellent fighter. It's what he does."

She's not a princess, you muppet. She's a damned duchess. My duchess.

She bit her lip. "I know, but . . . Alexi is bound to fight dirty. We should be there in case he needs help."

"Trust me, the last thing he needs is to be distracted by you right now."

"I'm not that distracting."

He pulled her against him and feathered a kiss on her forehead. "Yeah, you are."

The sharp hitched breath that echoed in my ears had

fury building in my mind. I should be the one making her gasp . . . in perfect, delicious pain. These men didn't know the half of what she needed. "Don't let him win you over, petal. Not when I'm so close to having you again," I whispered.

"I know he can take care of himself. I'm just worried about him. Honestly, I worry about all of you." She laid her cheek on his chest and sighed. "I just found you, and it feels like I'm already on the brink of losing you all. I came here to start over in a place where everyone would be safe, and within a few weeks, Ben is involved in a duel, Remi sneaks off to secret meetings where he and Ben come limping back covered in bruises and blood, and you"—she grabbed his hand and held it up—"I come to find, are cursed by a vindictive witch. Not to mention the murders. What happened to the sleepy small town I moved to?"

"Isn't it always the sleepy towns that end up being where shit goes down?" The way he tucked her hair behind one ear had my teeth grinding. "Besides, I had this curse long before I met you. And the Mercers have been in their share of fights. It's part of the lone wolf thing."

"They're not alone."

"They might as well be. Two wolves does not a pack make. Especially in a place like this."

She traced the pattern of ink on *Asher's*—what sort of name is that? Honestly, he'd be better off if his mum had swallowed—hand, following the stars all the way to the middle of his forearm. "It's growing."

He let out a humorless chuckle. "How do you know?"

"I pay attention, Asher. Why has it grown so much? Has something happened?"

Asher's posture changed instantly. I knew that reaction, had employed it many times myself. He was about to brush her off and fucking lie to her face. Something *had* happened. Me. And he was just as shaken by that pretty little light of his . . . the one that damn near electrocuted me.

"How am I supposed to know? It's like I told you the other night. Nearly a decade with no change, and then *boom,* you show up, and it starts creeping up my arm like a fungus."

"Fungus arm . . . sexy." Her shoulders drooped. "So you're saying it's my fault?"

Oh good. Perhaps this idiot would dig his own grave and I wouldn't need to dirty my hands. But then he tucked one finger under her chin and forced her gaze to his.

"No. It's no one's fault but mine and that witch. But I am saying that getting attached to me isn't the same as it will be with Ben or Remi. I've got an expiration date, and by the looks of things, it's rapidly approaching."

Yes. It's so much closer than you know, boy. Though I suppose I could just leave him and let that blasted curse of his rid me of him instead. No need to get my hands dirty that way. Surely not killing one of her would-be lovers should earn a point in my favor with my duchess.

At least until she learned of the wolves. But from the sound of it, there was another murderer running around. I could quite easily pass this whole thing off as a complete coincidence. She never need know of my involvement. One of them would meet his untimely end at my hand, but I would do it in such a way that this other killer would be blamed. It was perfect. Then I could dispose of the other in a similar fashion, and the town would chalk it up as a revenge plan gone wrong. The grief-stricken fool ran off to hunt his brother's murderer and met his own end instead. How poetic.

But in order to keep this plot on track, I had a fair bit of research ahead of me. How were these victims killed? Where were they found?

I heaved an internal sigh. As much as I loved having a solid strategy, I was a bit disappointed at the delay. Still, this would serve me best in the end and give my petal no reason to doubt me when I showed up to comfort her.

No.

To rescue her. I'd be her savior, and she'd never leave me again. Then I'd collect each of her tears. I'd do so with the knowledge she was my perfect submissive, utterly devoted to me. Gifted to me by fate. Mine to defile for all eternity.

My cock ached at the thought of her trembling under the kiss of my whip.

"Soon, my beautiful petal. I'll give you what you need and take everything I want."

Asher's soft groan pulled me out of my fantasy and back into their tender fucking moment. "Don't give me hope, Rosie. I've spent a long time suffocating that flame."

"Yes, well, that was before you met me, Asher Henry. And if you know nothing else, you should know this: I am the most stubbornly determined woman you're ever going to meet. I found you, didn't I? That should prove how good I am at achieving my goals once I set my mind to something. So believe me when I say you're not going to die. Not on my watch."

His expression turned wistful as he brushed a finger down her cheek. "If anyone can do it, princess, it's you."

I gagged at the display of saccharine sweetness. Pathetic.

Roslyn yawned, her eyes tired but body tense. "I don't

know if I want to sleep it all away or wash this stress off me."

"It's my experience that I think more in the shower. Come on, let's lie down for a bit. We'll put something on the telly." His adopted British accent was abysmal, and I sneered. What a fucking donut. He sounded like Hagrid from Harry Potter. But she laughed. My duchess fucking laughed, and I hated him.

I followed them to her window, watching and torturing myself all at the same time as he got onto the bed and she snuggled into his arms. Maybe I could break in and snap his neck before he could defend himself. I decided I would if he did a single bloody thing to make her moan.

Before long, his breathing turned deep and rhythmic, the rise and fall of his chest an obvious indication of sleep. But my petal wasn't at ease. She was restless. Tense. Her legs kicked out, deep sighs escaping her every few seconds.

It didn't take much longer until she eased herself from beneath his arm and stood.

"Shower it is, then." She rolled her head from side to side as she stripped out of her clothes and dropped the fabric to the floor.

My throat tightened, hunger for my wife making my fangs descend. I'd fed—gorged myself, in fact—but nothing would sate me like her.

The bathroom window was small and the glass frosted, which was a right kick in the fangs. But I'd had enough time on the outside looking in. This was my chance. The steam and soap would mask my scent. Her babysitter was sleeping on the job, and she was alone. Distracted. I could take her. I could make her mine again.

Easing the window open, I squeezed myself through, dropping silently to the floor. I could make out her shadow behind the curtain. The ripe curves of her breasts and hips as she lathered her hair. Her sweet voice as she hummed softly to herself.

My cock swelled, begging me to go to her. To pin her to the wall and sink inside her the way I should have done on our wedding night. Fingers flexing, I reached for the simple fabric separating us. I was so close to claiming her again. And this time, I wouldn't let her out of my sight. She'd forget about anyone but me.

Annoyed cursing floated through the window, alerting me to the presence of one of the Mercers. Since I'd watched Bentley storm off with some shifter earlier, I could only assume it was the other cocky arsehole.

Remington.

Of bloody course he'd show up. Interrupting me right when I was about to get everything I wanted. I couldn't kill him now. Not when I didn't have the upper hand.

But it wouldn't be long before I ruined them all.

FORTY-TWO

"F-fucking bear." Ben's pained growl tugged me out of the light sleep I'd finally found curled up on the sofa in Remi's arms.

It had taken three cups of chamomile tea, a shower, and Remi coming home for me to settle. Asher hadn't stuck around after Remi returned, even though we invited him to stay. He'd scratched his neck and sort of blushed, mumbling something about it not being the right time for a sleepover.

"Mmm, go back to sleep, baby girl. It's still early," Remi murmured as I wriggled out of his hold.

"I will. Ben's home. I want to check on him."

"I love how much you care about us." He pressed a sleepy kiss to my arm, the first thing he could find in the dark.

"I'll be back," I whispered, but he was already asleep, breathing deeply and letting out little growls and yips, just like a puppy. I couldn't help running my fingers through his hair and watching him for a second, tucking the memory away to savor later.

Then I wandered down the hall toward Ben's room, the fall of water and muttered curses growing louder with every step.

"Ben?" I called softly, not wanting to sneak up on him.

When he didn't answer, I pushed the already cracked door wider and followed the continued grunts and hisses of pain. Light spilled into the bedroom from the en suite, a soft mist of steam escaping from the open door. As I entered, the scent of blood hit me, a curl of unwanted fascination building in my gut.

"Ben? Are you all right?" I asked as the shower turned off and he pulled the curtain aside, revealing his gloriously naked body. He glistened as the water ran down chiseled muscles, my gaze following the path of its own accord.

"Bloody hell," I breathed, equally surprised by his beauty and horrified by the angry bruises and deep gouges marring his skin.

Grabbing a towel from the rack, he started to dry his hair, his mouth curling up in a lopsided grin that did nothing to hide the pain in his eyes. "L-like what you see?"

"At the moment? I'm a little appalled, actually," I said, crossing my arms and leaning against the door jamb.

His smile disappeared. "Hey."

"I don't like seeing you hurt." I rubbed at my chest, an ache building as my mental tally of his injuries climbed into the twenties.

Wrapping the towel around his waist, he came to me. "I'm f-fine, sugar. Nothing for y-you t-to worry about."

"You're not fine. You're bleeding and battered."

"You should s-see the other g-guy."

"Who won?"

One brow raised in challenge. "Seriously?"

"Yes."

"Me. O-obviously."

"Trust me, if you saw what I saw right now, you wouldn't be inclined to think so."

He tossed me the patent Mercer smirk. "That's only b-because you've n-never seen m-me fight. I d-don't lose, sugar."

Tightening my resolve, I bent down and opened the cupboard under the bathroom sink, searching through extra toilet paper rolls and cleaning supplies.

"W-what are you d-doing?"

"Looking for a bloody first aid kit. You need bandages, stitches even. I don't think a plaster is going to cut it."

"I'm f-fine. Come here."

His warm palm gripped my bicep as he pulled me to standing and forced me to face him.

"L-look." He pointed to his already healing chest. "Give me a f-few m-more minutes, and I'll be good as n-new."

I bit my lip, knowing he was telling me the truth and yet still beyond conflicted at seeing him in pain. "Can I at least give you a Band-Aid? It would make me feel better if I could *do* something."

"H-how 'bout you kiss it and m-make it all better?"

That did things to me. The idea of my lips grazing his heated skin, following the lines of his hips down to the . . . my focus drifted to his thickening erection tenting the towel. *Crikey.*

"Really? You're hurt and somehow still aroused?"

"You're m-my mate. I always w-want y-you," he rumbled.

I knew if I gave in this time, there'd be no stopping at sweet kisses and caresses. We were way past that.

Unbidden, Pan's voice rang through my mind. *"You*

know what will happen to him if you let him inside you. I will ruin him. Is that what you want?"

"Where'd you g-go just now, sugar?" Ben's fingers gently tangled with mine.

"What? I haven't gone anywhere. I'm right here."

He tapped the center of my forehead. "N-not here. Don't lie to m-me." His eyes searched mine. "I c-can't take it when y-you lie."

My lies had started out as a way to protect me. And they weren't lies so much as a new truth. But this was different. I *was* lying. Every moment I didn't tell him about my demon was drenched in deceit.

He deserved to know. Not only about the deal I'd made, but about the price. About the depraved things I let Pan do to me in the name of protection. He may not want me anymore after, but that was his choice to make. I couldn't take the next step with him without coming clean, especially when doing so put him at risk.

"Ah ah ah, ma petite monstre. *That's our little secret, remember?"*

"Not anymore."

"Fine. It's his funeral."

If anything, this time his words only reinforced my resolve. Taking a deep breath, I licked my lips and blurted, "I need to tell you something."

The way Ben's eyes flashed with apprehension made my blood run cold. This was where he cut me loose. Better now than after I gave in to him and let him make me his. I wouldn't survive losing him then.

I pulled him out of the bathroom, leading him to the bed. As we sat together, I had to force myself not to tremble from the fear coursing through me.

"I can't be your mate, Ben."

"Why not?" he said through clenched teeth.

"I came here to get away from something dangerous—deadly even—to save my family."

"I kn-know th-that."

"But you don't know how I achieved it."

His blue eyes found mine, and all I saw there was a genuine desire to understand. "Then t-tell me."

Bloody hell, I was a nervous wreck. My stomach churned, a wave of panic sending nausea curling through me. "The reason I am here is that I faked my own death."

He sucked in a breath. "O-okay. That's n-not so bad."

As if on instinct, my focus went to the mark Pan left on my wrist. One finger gently traced the outline. For the first time, there was no answering tingle in my nether regions, which only made my anxiety spiral. "That's only half of it. I also made a deal with a demon to help me stay hidden. No one can know I'm here. It's of the utmost importance because if it's discovered I'm alive, my family will pay the price."

A myriad of emotions played across the beautiful planes of his face. Surprise. Fear. Anger—though I didn't think the last was directed at me.

As suspected, he fixated on the part that most made me want to squirm.

"W-what kind of d-deal?"

I plucked at the hem of the oversized shirt I wore, staring down at my lap and no longer able to meet his gaze. "A terrible one."

"R-Rosie. I n-need more."

"His price was high, and I was desperate. I gave him my —" I stared at my hands with determined focus, trying to keep myself together as the guilt ate me alive.

"Your b-body?"

"Yes. And my blood. More than once," I admitted, his gaze burning through me with its laser-like intensity. Taking a breath, I forced myself to continue. "Whenever he wishes, actually. He calls on me, and I have to go to him. I need you to know I never would have done it if I wasn't desperate. If I didn't believe it was the only way. If I'd known you and Remi . . ." I sighed. "I guess it doesn't matter, because it's done and I can't take it back."

He didn't even seem to register my words as a low warning growl rumbled from him. "He forces you?"

"No. I go because I must, but I . . . enjoy it. He's never forced me to be with him *that* way. I wouldn't seek him out on my own. I don't feel about him the way I do about you and Remi, or even Asher . . . but I don't deny myself the benefits of that part of our bargain either."

"S-so you've been w-with this d-demon . . . all this t-time? W-why d-didn't you mention i-it sooner?"

"I couldn't. At least, not without breaking our deal and risking my family's safety." I exhaled heavily. "I'm risking so much telling you this even now, but I wanted you to know everything. You *deserve* to know everything before we take this any further. He'll come after all of us, and you're already in his sights simply because of how much I feel for you. He warned me that if I . . . was *with* anyone else, he'd hurt them. He was quite emphatic about it, actually."

He slid his hand over my knee, giving it a slight squeeze at my admission. "Is it s-still g-going on?"

"I put an end to it. To that part of it. I will still have to go when he calls, but he won't take my body again."

A heavy sigh left him as he dragged a hand through his thick hair. "Fuck, sugar. I . . . I d-don't know w-what to s-say. I'm glad y-you t-told me. Gl-glad it's over."

I was so thankful I could honestly tell him things were

done with Pan. Ben and I had been dancing around a relationship for weeks. I couldn't move forward with any of them until we were as honest with each other as we could be. Which was why this last part was so hard.

"That's not all." Ben stiffened once more as I laid the rest of my truth at his feet. "This is the part that will make you see why I'm not your future."

His large palm settled over mine. "N-nothing will m-make me believe that."

"I gave up my ability to conceive. Life for a life, he'd said." Those fingers atop mine tensed. "I know how important it is for shifters to build their pack." I hated the wobble in my voice, but even more than that, I hated his silence. Risking a glance up at his stony expression, I whispered, "I'm barren. I can't give you a family. As much as I want to, I can't be your mate, Ben."

Holding my breath, I waited for a shred of reaction from him. Anything more than this painful stillness.

His touch vanished as he removed his hand from mine, and my heart broke into jagged shards. This was what I deserved; I knew that, but it bloody hurt.

Then, with one gentle finger under my chin, he tipped my head up and turned me to face him. "You *are* my m-mate, Rosie. Whether y-you think you sh-should be or n-not. Kids were n-never in my plans, but I c-can't say I d-don't want them with you. But if it's n-not p-possible, there's n-nothing we can d-do to change that."

Relief and disbelief made my body feel oddly weightless. It was too good to be true. Ben was too good to be true. That, along with the ringing in my ears, made me uncertain I'd heard him correctly. "Pardon?"

"I want *you*, sugar. J-just you. Any w-way I can h-have you."

"Did you miss the part where I said he's going to come after you?"

He smirked, eyes twinkling with mischief. "D-do I look scared?"

"He's. A. Demon," I enunciated slowly. "A big scary purple one. With horns and fangs and . . . and . . . a tail."

"And I'm a f-fucking Alpha. I c-can take him." His shoulders straightened. "In fact, I w-will. You c-can't have a c-contract with a g-ghost."

"I don't think you appreciate how terrifying he is."

Ben quirked a brow. "Are you d-doubting me?"

"No, not at all. I just think you might be underestimating *him*."

"You are the f-first good thing fate ever g-gave me. I'm n-not about to let f-fear stand in the way of finally getting a l-little slice of happy in m-my otherwise fucked life. Y-you belong to me, sugar. *Me*. Not him. Let him come for me. I fucking dare him."

With every word out of his mouth, his voice grew stronger and more determined. His stammer faded at the end as his confidence heightened and he seemed to forget the tightness that so often stalled his words.

He was a man on a mission, and that mission was me.

CHAPTER
FORTY-THREE

BEN

"Ben, I . . ." The way her voice trailed off had me desperate to kiss her. If she couldn't believe my words, maybe she'd believe my actions.

I stood, cupping her face and moving to stand between her legs. "Let m-me love you, sugar." It was as much a request to make love to her as it was me seeking permission to show her what I felt for her. The fear she might shoot me down again had the stutter returning. Fuck.

"But what if something happens to you? I can't lose you to him. I've already given him so much."

Steeling myself, I formed each word in my mind before I let my lips utter them. "You'll never lose me." She exhaled softly, and I could see she was so close to giving in. Brushing my thumbs over the crests of her cheeks, I leaned down, my lips all but touching hers. "None of us know how long we have. I could get hit by a car tomorrow. Don't"— that fucking tightness in my throat threatened to ruin this, so I paused, willing myself to get through the statement— "waste time we could be spending together."

The flicker of fear in her eyes had my heart sinking. Here

it was, the moment she rejected me again. When was I going to give up? Accept that she would never let me in.

Never. She is our mate.

My wolf's primal growl knocked me out of my panic spiral before it could even start, his certainty renewing my own.

She and I were meant to be. Fate had brought us together.

I just needed to help her understand what that meant.

Prepared to do just that, I opened my mouth again, but she surprised me with one sweetly uttered word.

"Okay."

"O-okay?"

"Love me, Ben. I don't want to waste any more time."

A rush of pure animalistic need took me out at the knees, and I knelt at her feet, spreading her thighs open so I could fit between them.

"I love how you l-look in my shirt," I rumbled, my lips already brushing her inner thigh.

"I was missing you," she admitted, running her fingers through my hair and pulling a happy purr from my chest. "It smells like you and Remi. I like to smell you on my skin."

I knew another way to make her smell like me. From the inside fucking out.

Sliding my hands up the outside of her thighs, I held her steady as I kissed and licked my way up to her dripping center. I could smell how badly she wanted me, but fuck, I wanted to try and take this slow. Make it last. I wanted to prove to her how right we were together. But my need for her was painful, and I was worried the moment I sank into her tight cunt, I'd lose it, and this would be over before it really began.

"Wh-what are you doing?" she asked, her words breathy and tight as I nipped her soft skin.

"I like to smell like you too, sugar. What better w-way than to eat you until you come all over my face?"

Her thighs spasmed beneath my hold as her entire body reacted to my statement. "Yes. Oh God, Ben. Yes."

"Don't be afraid to hold on to something. I recommend my hair. I'm really fucking hungry for you." Proud as hell that I got through all that without stuttering, I turned my focus back to her pussy. No more talking. There wasn't room in my mind for control over my speech and my wolf.

I parted her slick folds with both hands, shoving her legs wide using my elbows, then I wasted no time sucking her already swollen clit into my mouth. My name left her lips in a breathy whimper as her hands clenched in my hair and I grinned against her, pleased she'd taken my order to heart.

Taking that as a sign to carry on, I alternated between long licks up her sweet slit and soft nibbles on her clit. She was writhing against me within seconds, hips rolling as she searched for more.

That's it, baby. Take me as you want me. Use me. Make yourself feel good.

As if she could hear the commands, she gripped my hair tighter, pressing my face closer as she ground against me, falling apart as I ate her. I groaned against her, savoring the flavor of her desire for me.

But I wasn't done. I wanted her shaking, begging, desperate for me to take her. My fingers sank into her still pulsing sheath, the heat from her walls making my cock jerk and throb. I was fucking dripping for her. All my wolf wanted was to mount her and fill her with my seed. I didn't care if we couldn't have pups. I wanted to be leaking out of her so everyone would know she was mine.

"Ben," she groaned. "It's too much. It's so sensitive."

"Again," I breathed against her, using my mouth and fingers to bring her off a second time.

"God, what are you doing to me?" Her whine as her thighs clenched around my head had me thrusting into the air, wishing it was her pussy instead.

Mount her, my wolf begged. *Claim her.*

I backed away as the last flutters of her second orgasm faded. "I'm loving you, Rosie. Like I promised."

She ran the pad of her thumb over my lips, collecting her slick and holding my gaze as she lifted the digit to her mouth and licked it clean. "Sweet," she murmured.

Fuuuck. Did she have any idea what she was doing to me?

"Sugar," I agreed, my voice sounding like gravel as I fought against the primal need to sink inside her.

"I want to love you too, Ben. Please?"

Goddamn. Just the thought of her mouth wrapped around my cock had me on the knife's edge of coming. A strange pressure built at the base of my shaft, a heavy ache I'd never felt before.

Give her your knot.

My wolf was right there, barely contained. Frustrated at my inaction.

"Hands and knees," I ordered. "Present for your Alpha."

What the fuck was that? My voice didn't even sound like my own. It was me, but harder, stronger. An Alpha commanding his mate.

She nodded frantically and stood as I got to my feet. As she moved to take position, I stopped her with a firm hand.

"Wait, I want you naked." Gripping the hem of her

shirt, I lifted it from her body, baring her perfect curves. The glint of metal piercing one taut nipple caught my eye and pulled a rumble of pleasure through me. I leaned forward, taking the ring between my teeth and tugging slightly. "This is surprising."

She blushed, looking uncertain.

"I like it." I flicked it with my tongue, and she trembled, a soft moan escaping.

"Me too. Now it's your turn to get naked."

She didn't have to tell me twice. I dropped the towel that was somehow still tucked around my waist, though my cock had nearly punched through the terrycloth with as hard as I was.

Her eyes trailed down, color suffusing her cheeks as her lips parted.

I took myself in my hand, fisting my length and running my palm slowly up and down my cock. Letting her get a good look at every single inch that was about to be inside her.

The way her tongue darted out to wet her lips had precum leaking from my dick.

"Taste it."

Her eyes flared wide, and she sat on the bed once more, leaning in to lick my tip like I was a fucking lollipop.

It was my turn to weave my fingers through her hair and grip tight. I simultaneously wanted to thrust deep until I spilled down her throat and hold still, saving the honor for her cunt.

Yes, sweet girl, lick me. Fuck. I love how your mouth feels on me.

Glancing down my body, I watched her lips as she wrapped them around my crown. I had to grit my teeth against the urge to fuck her mouth.

"No. Get on the bed."

She looked up at me, those big eyes of hers bright with desire. Holding my gaze, the little minx took another inch of me in her mouth and had my toes curling.

Bad fucking girl. You want a spanking for not listening to Daddy?

God, the idea of her letting me be her daddy, letting me take care of her, got me so fucking hard. She needed someone to care for her.

That someone was me.

No one was going to be able to protect her—love her—the way I would. She might have more than one mate, but not even they could take care of her needs the way I could.

"I. Said. *Present.*"

The way her pupils flared told me she loved the dominance of my wolf. She released me with a wet pop and turned to her hands and knees. I gripped her hips, pulling her to the edge of the mattress, and then with one hand on her lower back, I pushed her down so her spine was arched and her ass was up, just the way my wolf demanded.

God, her ass was a ripe peach, ready for me to take a bite. My wolf came to life, making my fingers tingle as claws threatened to emerge so I could hold her more firmly.

I took a long, slow breath, forcing control. I'd claim her with my cock and my cum, but I wouldn't mark her, no matter what my wolf wanted.

"Please, Ben. I need you."

My fingers dug in deeper, her whimpered plea nearly more than I could bear. I wasn't sure I could be gentle right now. I had a feeling the second her heat surrounded my cock, I was going to be done for.

"If it's too much . . ." I started, breathing heavily as I lined myself up with her entrance.

"It won't be."

Uncertainty tightened my throat, but I had to say this. "I know I c-can't knock you up, b-but I'm going in b-bare, sugar. Is that—"

"God, yes, Ben. Please, just do it."

I sank all the way inside her in one measured thrust. It was better than I'd ever fantasized. Hot, tight, so damn wet. I'd thought about this more times than I could count. Woken in the middle of the night, panting and sweating with cum painting my abs after dreaming of this exact thing. Nothing compared to being inside my mate.

Her strangled cry of my name had my wolf taking the reins, the need to fully mount her and rut into her too strong to stop him.

"Next time I'll make you run first."

What? Where the fuck had that come from? My wolf was in control now, and he loved the idea of chasing his mate, catching her, biting her.

Christ . . . so did I.

I wanted all of it. Everything.

Her low moan and flood of slick told me she loved the idea too. She really was perfect for me.

Sliding my hand up her back, I wrapped my palm around her throat and pulled her up until she was kneeling, her skin pressed to mine, her hair in my face as I fucked her deep. It was a constant battle for control with my wolf to keep my strokes measured, but the closer I got to climax, the harder it was. My thrusts grew rough, my grip on her tighter, the voice in my ear louder.

Bite her.

Mark her.

Claim her.

"Come for me, sugar," I said, my lips against the base of

her neck, so close to the spot I'd sink my teeth as I marked her.

My other hand found her clit, stroking, circling, bringing her to an explosive release, and I couldn't help myself. I sucked on her tender skin, canines grazing as I trembled from the effort not to bite down.

"Yes," she whispered, but I knew it wasn't really her giving me permission to do this. She was in a euphoric, pleasure-drenched state. If I took her now, I'd never know if it was truly what she wanted.

I tore my lips from her neck and instead shoved her back to her hands and knees, driving in hard and fast, chasing my own release.

Give her your knot.

I didn't know what that meant, but I was so focused on the build in my balls that I didn't care. It was a deep throb laced with pleasure, different from how it felt when I was about to come. Better.

"Fuck, sugar, I—" I was fucking panting. What was this? "God, it feels so good."

"Ben? Are you . . . getting larger?" She moaned and writhed. "You're stretching me so wide."

I looked down to where I was sliding in and out of her, and she was right. My cock had swollen at the base. The veins running down my shaft pulsed as it grew. And fuck, the sight of her taking all of me was so damn hot, it would be burned in my memory forever.

"Take my fucking knot, mate." The words were all wolf, but all me too.

I slammed into her, locking us in place as my knot breached her entrance and the orgasm hit me. There were no words to describe the sensations racing through me. Blinding pleasure had me shaking, my body tensing as I filled her with my cum. And she screamed my name right along with my own guttural moans.

We both shook with labored breaths as we came down from the high of our mutual release. Lifting my arm, I wiped the sweat from my brow and went to pull away so I could clean her up when I realized just what my knot did. She whimpered, but not in pleasure at the tug.

"Sorry, sugar."

We were locked together. Joined in the most intimate way possible with my cum buried deep inside. She might not be able to get pregnant, but it seemed like my biological imperative was still going to fucking try to breed her anyway. Jesus, that did things to me.

"I th-think we're stuck until m-my knot goes down."

She looked back at me, her face beautifully flushed, strands of hair stuck to her damp skin. "Oh. That's a new one."

"For y-you and m-me both." I leaned forward and pressed a kiss to her lips before I laid us down on our sides, holding her tight and breathing in the combined scent of us. She might not have my mark, but she wasn't going anywhere.

As we drifted to sleep, I heard a soft sigh of my name from her lips, and my dick twitched inside her before my wolf growled, "*Mine.*"

CHAPTER
FORTY-FOUR

ROSIE

My body ached in the most delicious way as I rolled and stretched. "Morning," I murmured sleepily, reaching across the bed to where Ben should have been lying. Instead of warm alpha male, my palm touched cool sheets.

Not only was he gone, he'd been gone awhile. My stomach sank, a twist of unease taking hold. Had Pan come for him while I was asleep?

Bolting out of bed, I picked up my discarded shirt from last night and pulled it on.

Maybe he's just an early riser.

Even as the excuse ran through my mind, I dismissed it. There was early, and then there was whatever had actually happened. I wasn't exactly an expert on the morning after, but I knew what sheets felt like when they'd been slept on, and Ben definitely hadn't spent the night beside me. So where the fork was he?

It was easier to cling to the anger than acknowledge the fear. Because if Ben hadn't ghosted me, Pan must have gotten to him. And I simply couldn't accept that.

The sight of a familiar set of broad shoulders eased something in me until I realized it wasn't Ben who stood at the kitchen counter brewing coffee. Clad in nothing but a pair of boxer briefs, Remi would have been pure temptation if I wasn't so worked up.

"Mornin', beautiful," he said as he turned toward me. "You look . . . wait, what's the matter? Did Ben do it wrong?"

Even through my anxiety, the question made my cheeks warm. "Where is he? I woke up and he was gone. Did something happen?"

"Bentley, you asshole. You finally get what you want and still manage to fuck it all up." Remi sighed and shook his head, taking a big sip of his coffee before setting the mug down and muttering, "One of these days I will be the one who gets to enjoy myself and won't be expected to clean up after my emotionally stunted fucking twin."

Reaching me, he gave me a reassuring smile and placed two big palms on my shoulders, brushing his fingers over the spot on my neck where Ben had been so focused as he filled me. "He does this sometimes. Runs off when everything he's feeling gets to be too much. Clear his head. Find his center. Remember when he did the same thing after he tried to mark you? He's just got to settle his wolf down. He'll be back, I promise. It has nothing to do with you."

"He kept himself so controlled."

"He probably had to. His wolf would have been shouting in his ear for him to mark you and complete the bond. If he gave in to everything he was feeling in that moment, he might have done something you weren't ready for and then hated himself once the fog cleared."

"I didn't realize it would be so hard for him." I felt like the world's biggest tease.

"How could you? You're fae."

I flinched, hating that the lie still existed between us, even if it was a necessary one.

"It's different for shifters. We're primal beasts at our core, and when instinct takes hold, it's the battle of a lifetime to stay in control. Or at least that's how it feels." He flashed me a grin. "We're as new to this mate thing as you. It's just going to take us some time to find our way."

"Am I hurting you? By not letting you mark me?" I bit my lower lip and cast my gaze down, not willing to look into his eyes and see pain there.

"Not gonna lie, it does hurt. But it's more of a gnawing ache in my gut. We won't force it on you, but the bond is right there, just out of reach. It's fucking weird, if I'm being honest."

"Remi . . ." I reached for him and ran my fingers over his jaw. "I want to be yours, but there's a lot you don't know."

"So tell me. Tell him."

I sighed. "I did tell him. Last night, before we were . . . together. I laid as much out as I could. Honestly, I thought he'd throw me out on my arse."

He smirked. "But he didn't."

"He didn't."

While part of me wanted to accept that this was simply Ben working through his issues, another still worried about Pan.

"But, Remi . . . there are people after me. It's not safe to be so connected to—"

His warm palm gripped my nape, gaze searing me as he made me look into his eyes. "I'm telling you right now, he is

415

fine. No one has him. I'd know if something happened to him, baby girl. I'd sense it."

"How?"

Dropping a kiss on my forehead, he released me and shrugged, his cocksure attitude returning. "It's a twin thing."

"If you say so," I said with a sigh, not wholly convinced but willing to put my trust in Remi's certainty. He knew his brother better than I did. If he said this was normal, I could only believe him.

Still . . . it wasn't exactly the way I'd hoped to wake up.

Remi wrapped an arm around me, giving me a hug. "Here, let me make you breakfast. You being upset is putting my wolf on edge. I need to take care of you."

I didn't have the heart to tell him I wasn't hungry. Instead, I sat at the small table and watched as he cracked two eggs into a pan and cooked for me. Something loosened inside me at Remi's confidence. Ben was fine. We were fine. If I would just let myself relax and allow myself to be happy, I could get used to this. I could have these handsome wolves treating me like their queen. Waking up with them both in the mornings would be nearly the perfect fantasy brought to life. All I was missing was one sexy hacker.

The four of us were building a life together. Laying the foundation. I hated that there were still secrets between us, though I had to keep them to ensure all our safety. Eventually we'd get to a place where I could tell them everything. About my past. My family. Gavin. Was I technically still married if Roslyn Blackthorne was considered dead? I didn't think so, but it seemed like something they should know about. Especially if their association with me would put them in the Donoghues' crosshairs.

The memory of Gavin's dark gaze and dominant voice sent a tingle through me. Would I ever be free of him? I shouldn't want him. He was a villain in this story, after all.

～

Remi and I had worked quietly together at the bar all day, serving the few patrons who had filtered in throughout the hours. It was just picking up now that the sun had set, and it being a Friday meant we needed all hands on deck, as it were. Darla was due in any minute. And Ben . . . was still missing.

"Where is he?" I asked, finally putting forth the question that had been lurking just under the surface since our conversation this morning.

Remi shook his head. "I don't know. He should be here by now."

Dread worked its way deeper into my heart. Something wasn't right about this. Ben was the constant. He didn't vanish without a trace. That was me.

The door swung open, and my breath caught as I waited to see my plaid-wearing shifter saunter in. When Dallas's head poked through, I sighed in disappointment.

"Hey, Sheriff," Remi greeted. "What can I get you?"

"This isn't a social call, I'm afraid." His attention settled on me. "Nadia, can you tell me where Bentley Mercer was between the hours of one and five this morning?"

"W-with me?" The question caught me so off guard I stuttered, and the anxiety that had simmered in my belly since waking boiled over. This wasn't Ben disappearing to get his wolf in check. This was worse. So much worse.

Pan, if you hurt him, I will end you.

There was no response. I hadn't expected one. I hadn't

felt Pan's presence at all since I'd made the choice to be with Ben. No trace of his voice in my mind or answering ripple when I brushed my fingers over his mark.

"What's this about, Dallas?" Remi asked, his voice wary.

"There's been another murder, and this time we've made an arrest."

Nausea clutched at me. "Who died?"

His cocked brow said he didn't believe for one second I wasn't aware. "Alexi Barinov."

I gasped.

"Is that why you're here sniffing around, asking questions about my brother? He didn't have anything to do with that," Remi said, instantly going on defense.

"We all saw what went down last night, son. Facts are facts. Those two got into a brawl, and now the bear's dead. Doesn't take much to put two and two together."

Remi balled up a towel and tossed it onto the bar. "Yeah, well, you got your facts wrong. My brother didn't kill anyone."

"He was with me last night," I said again, more insistently this time.

"All night?" Dallas pressed. "Can you confidently account for his whereabouts? Where is he now? When was the last time you saw him?"

The memory of the cool sheets kept me from immediately answering.

"That's what I thought. Your brother's got blood on his hands and no alibi, Remington."

Remi pulled his phone from his pocket and began hurriedly tapping on the screen.

"Who are you calling?" Dallas asked.

"A fucking lawyer."

The sheriff shrugged. "It's not going to help. Ben is our

guy. We've got everything we need now that your little barmaid can't corroborate his story. And even if he spent the night in bed with her, Barinov could have died in the hours prior to his coming home. It's an open and shut case. Your brother's a murderer. And there's no telling how much more of this story I'll be unraveling now that I have him. We've got a serial killer on our hands, and where there's smoke, there's fire." Dallas leveled his gaze at me. "You should be more careful who you let in your bed, little girl. The big bad wolf might eat you up next."

Anger boiled over at his absolutely patronizing statement. I lunged over the bar, careless of the fact that he was a police officer and a lion shifter to boot. "How dare you. Ben didn't kill anyone. He wouldn't. You're on a witch hunt because you can't keep the people of this town safe. Bentley is your scapegoat, not a true suspect. I've seen better police work on the telly!"

He growled at me, a low, terrifying sound that Remi returned as he wrapped his arms around me and tugged me backward.

"I don't care who you are, Walker. You threaten my mate like that again, I'll tear out your throat."

Dallas chuckled, tipped his hat, and turned away. "I'll be seeing you, Mercer. Keep that girl of yours on a leash, or I'll toss her into the cell next to your brother's."

"This town only has one cell," Remi muttered, shaking his head as the sheriff walked out.

The bar patrons stared at us, eyes wide, the small crowd silent as a tomb. I almost wished the gargoyles were here just to break the tension.

"Everyone out. Bar's closed until further notice," Remi shouted, taking me by surprise. I'd never heard such an Alpha tone in his voice.

Almost instantly, the bar emptied, leaving Remi and me alone. I didn't realize I was trembling until he pulled me against him. "It's gonna be okay. Asher will be here soon, and we'll figure all this out."

"Asher?"

"He's who I actually texted. He's on his way."

A small tendril of relief fought for purchase in my heart at the knowledge I'd have both of them with me while we figured out a way to help Ben. Settling my cheek against Remi's shoulder, I nodded and breathed him in.

"There's no way this will stick," he continued, stroking my back and pressing a soft kiss to my forehead. "Asher will prove what we already know. Ben didn't kill anybody."

"And if he can't?"

"Then we'll break him out and run. No one fucks with my pack."

Remi ran his fingers down the length of my spine and pressed our foreheads together.

"Our pack," I whispered.

A soft hum of approval escaped him as he pressed his lips to mine. He didn't stop kissing me even as the door opened and Asher came in.

Except it wasn't Asher. I knew it the moment the vampire's scent filled the room.

"Take your fucking hands off my wife."

FORTY-FIVE

"R*ing around the rosie. Pocket full of posy.*" I threaded her lace knickers between my fingers over and over as I absently stared out the window, watching the hellscape before me.

Broken bits of rock drifted across the bleak gray sky while jets of flame randomly shot up from the cracked earth in the distance. It was a beautiful place, if one dismissed the scent of sulfur, lack of any sort of plant life, and the perpetual gloom. A mirror image of Edinburgh, Scotland, to be specific, complete with a castle on the hill and cobblestones everywhere. Because what was more hellish than bagpipes?

I'd spent most of the 1300s topside, roaming the streets of the old city. The plague doctor uniform gave me so much freedom. I was able to stay in my demon form, not use any power, and still wreak havoc.

Ah, the good old days.

A demon really earned their name in those days. Now everyone was evil. Demons were sexualized and treated like some kind of fetish. No one feared us. No one ran into the night screaming. Humans were all but praying for a monster to come ravish them. All one had to do was look at the romance novels online to conclude that we were no longer formidable foes. It brought to light just how the vampires must have felt when Bram Stoker made them into sex gods. Or was that Anne Rice?

"Well, don't you look like the cat who caught the canary?"

I stiffened and slowly spun around at the sound of her voice. "Ah, Pestilence. I don't recall inviting you over."

"Since when does a mother need a reason to come visit her favorite son?"

"You mean her only son."

Mum lifted one shoulder in a shrug. "Doesn't make it any less true."

"Why are you here? I've got things well in hand."

"Do you?" Her gaze landed on the knickers in between my fingers. "You certainly have *something* in hand."

Ignoring her, I stuffed the lace in my back pocket as I strode to the bar and poured myself a dram of whiskey.

"Human form tonight? What mischief are you planning?"

She tossed her long red hair over one shoulder and flashed me a wink. "Oh, you know, just spreading a little of this, a little of that. So much easier to do when the humans think you're pretty."

"Yes, they are superficial creatures." But then memories of the way Rosie ran her fingers over my horns hit me, and I wondered how true it was. She didn't seem to mind my monstrous visage. If anything, she reveled in it. But Mum didn't need me to tell her things were different these days.

Before my eyes, her body morphed, shifting into a demonic form similar to my own, except for her coloring.

424

She was a pale, sickly green with this odd sheen that always gave her the appearance of being a little sweaty. Somehow I didn't think she'd appreciate being compared to solidified vomit, though that's always what the sight of her called to mind. She had a bit of a complex when it came to her looks. Especially since she was the most putrid out of her sisters.

"So, Auntie War has failed, as you know, and we are on a timeline, Pan. The seals won't stay open forever. But it seems to me you are simply sitting around playing with panties. Where are we with the plan?"

I spun the ring on my finger, drawing her attention as I'd intended. "I've been collecting her blood, as requested."

"Why is it taking so long?"

"It has to be a willing sacrifice of blood, doesn't it?"

She huffed. "Yes. Stupid fucking rules."

"She's been more than willing so far. I've made it nearly irresistible for her. She'll give me everything before this is over."

My mother raised a curious brow. "Good boy, Pan." She held out her hand, clawed-palm up. "Now hand it over so I can begin."

My stomach clenched, and a denial sprang to my lips. "No."

"What do you mean, *no*?" her voice dropped low along with the temperature in the room.

"I can't remove the ring until it is filled, remember?"

She bared her teeth in a poor imitation of a smile. "And when do you think that will be, dearest?"

"Soon."

"It had better be. I'm growing impatient."

"I'm simply setting up the pieces on the board, Mother. It's going to plan, and they'll all suffer."

"That's not your job. You have your part to play. I

suggest you do it and leave the rest to me."

I'd never asked my mother for the specifics of her plot. After all, she was Pestilence. It was pretty obvious what she had in store. Yet, I couldn't help but ask, "And what, exactly, is 'the rest'?"

"Patience. Isn't that what you want from me?" She practically slithered through the room, humming a familiar eerie tune as she came up beside a chessboard that had occupied one corner for as long as I could remember. "*Ashes. Ashes. They all . . . fall . . . down . . .*" Mum stretched out the words to my nursery rhyme, the haunting melody slow and sinister as she flicked over one of the ebony pieces.

She left me without another word.

As if pulled by an invisible tether, I stalked across the room, glancing down at the black figurine lying on the board, surrounded by four knights who were still standing. She'd rearranged the position of the pieces without me being the wiser.

A chill ran down my spine as I lifted the carved stone and cradled it in my palm.

She may not have used the words, but the message left on the chessboard was clear. My mother was going after the queen. Rosie was hers to take.

But the rest of them?

I flung out my hand and sent the four knights flying, the pieces shattering as they hit the floor.

They were all mine.

∾

KEEP READING FOR A SNEAK PEEK OF CLAIMED BY THE SHIFTERS, THE MATE GAMES: PESTILENCE BOOK 2!

SNEAK PEEK: CLAIMED BY THE SHIFTERS

GAVIN

The worst thing I ever did was fall in love with my wife.

What a useless emotion. But how could I have avoided it? She died, and still I yearned. Still craved her scent and ached for her touch. That wasn't me. I didn't need someone to make my twisted heart bloody sing.

Until Roslyn let me have her blood.

She *changed* something within me. Woke a long dormant beast, and now I'd never be free of it—of her. Like a dragon who'd found the most beautiful jewel, I wanted to keep her protected and never let another threaten my treasure. And she was *mine*.

Even if she allowed others to touch her. It wouldn't erase my claim. I got there first. I had her before any of them.

"G-Gavin . . ." Roslyn's eyes were wide, the stain of arousal leaching from her cheeks.

"Is this any way for a duchess to behave, Mrs. Donoghue?" I strode deeper into the bar, forcing myself to stay cool and collected. It was a herculean task with the way that Mercer arsehole was holding on to my wife.

"I'm not a duchess."

Oh, how little you understand, petal. "Oh, but you are. It seems someone had been slowly poisoning my father with colloidal silver. By the time we discovered it, there was nothing for it. He slipped away only a few weeks after *your* tragic demise."

"Wait, this fucker is your husband?" Remington snarled as he held her closer.

"No."

"Yes." I spoke over her, loud and strong.

"Well, which is it? Because it looks a lot like she doesn't want you, buddy." He turned her around to face him, one palm cupping her jaw. "Is this who you were running from, baby girl? Just say the word, and I'll get rid of him for you."

"You could bloody well try."

"You've seen what I can do, Dracula. Don't think I can't take you."

I cocked a brow. "Yes, but you haven't seen what *I* can do."

"What are you talking about? You two know each other?" Roslyn tore herself from his grasp. "You . . . you knew about Gavin?"

"Yes, please. Explain to my wife how we know each other, Remington."

I can't wait to see how you're going to get out of this one, Mercer.

"What's he talking about, Remi?" I loved the accusation in her tone. The uncertainty. That little spark of fear.

The wolf's jaw clenched, his eyes flashing with anger before glancing down at Roslyn.

"Oh my God. Is he your"—she looked at me then back at him—"were you two . . ." She had to lower her voice before she could manage, "*together*?"

"Fuck no! God, nothing like that. I would never lower myself to fucking a vampire."

"First of all, I would be the one doing the fucking, so you meant to say you wouldn't lower yourself to being *fucked* by a vampire. Secondly, you would be so lucky to find yourself under my whip, Mercer. And you know I'd make you beg for it until you were weeping. Don't act coy. I've seen the way your face lights up when you watch me perform at *Iniquity*." I had no interest in the wolf, but I couldn't help goading him after that insult. Let my wife chew on that little morsel.

The way Roslyn's breath hitched had me wondering if her reaction was because of his harsh words or the image mine had conjured. I hoped for the latter.

"Why are you here, Gavin?" she asked, her sweet voice stronger than I'd ever heard it.

"You know exactly why, darling. I'm here to reclaim my wayward wife. The one who left me a shattered man when she . . . died."

She sucked in a breath. "Don't toy with me. You weren't shattered. It was an arrangement, nothing more."

All playfulness left me. "You know that's not true."

"Do I? In some circles, an unconsummated union is grounds for annulment. You and I certainly never joined as a mated pair. You were too busy with Daniel."

Remington's brow quirked at that, but I ignored him, my attention wholly focused on my Roslyn.

The vein beside my eye twitched. "I already explained that to you."

431

"You did not."

"I told you it was over. That's all you need to know."

She crossed her arms, defiance stamped on her features. "That's nowhere near good enough. But even if it were, it doesn't change the facts. We were married to salvage a political alliance between our families. It wasn't a love match. Stop pretending otherwise."

Anger burned up my chest. "It could have been! You left before you gave it a chance. You made me think you were dead."

"Fuck, Rosie, that's messed up."

"Whose side are you on?"

I glanced at Remington, nodding. "Right?"

He growled, glaring at me. "I'm not talking to you, fuckface."

"I did what I had to. I didn't think you'd miss me anyway." Roslyn raised a defiant chin. Oh, the punishments I was going to dole out flashed through my mind. When I got her home . . .

"You are mine." I said it slowly and simply, stating the fact as though it wasn't up for debate.

"Not anymore," Remington said, his chest puffing out and eyes going an eerie blue.

"Enough of this," I snarled. "I don't need your permission to collect what's mine." I blurred over to where they stood, taking Roslyn by the wrist.

"Gavin, no," she protested, trying to jerk out of my grasp, but her hybrid strength was no match for the pure vampiric blood running through my veins.

Remington grasped me by the shirt, attempting to push me back. I bared my fangs at him. "Unhand me, dog."

"She told you to let her go. I suggest you do it unless you want to lose your arm."

"I'm not leaving without her."

"Well, you're sure as hell not leaving *with* her."

It looked like I was going to have to do this the old-fashioned way. A fight to the death, my favorite. Releasing her, I nodded at my wife. "Don't go far, petal. I just have to deal with this stray before we can be on our way."

"Gavin, don't. I love him."

The wolf's face blanked in shock, and I used that momentary distraction to strike, my attack fueled by my rage at her words. She wasn't allowed to love him. She was supposed to love me. If I was cursed with the damned affliction, she sure as hell should be too.

I had him by the throat, his eyes wide and bulging, face already turning a mottled purple as he struggled for air.

"Love hurts, Petal. You should know that by now."

Bloody hell, she had tears in her eyes. It was as beautiful as I remembered.

The thought was cut off by an explosion of pain between my legs that sent me doubling over. "You fucker," I rasped, hands curling over my throbbing balls. "That was a dirty move."

Remington wheezed for breath. "Excuse me . . . for not . . . playing fair when you're . . . trying to kill me. Shall I . . . slap your face . . . with a glove next time?"

"You'd have to be a man of class to be worthy of a proper duel."

He pulled out his phone, holding my gaze with a smug satisfaction I wanted to pummel out of him. "Hey, Siri . . . add white leather gloves to my shopping list."

"Okay, sexy beast. White leather gloves added to your list."

"Seriously, Remi?"

"Not the time, baby girl. I'm in my element."

"Is your plan to annoy me to death?" I groaned, finally able to stand upright. I was going to kill this cocky wolf.

The arse simply smirked and took up a fighting stance.

"Enough posturing. Roslyn, pack your things. Once I dispatch this runt, we are going home."

Remington growled. "Who you calling a runt, Mr. Darcy?" He lunged at me, surprising me with his speed and knocking us both back into a barstool. The spindly piece of furniture shattered under the force of our combined weight, and we tumbled onto the floor in a tangle of thrashing limbs.

"You can call me the Duke of Tears." I rolled us so I was on top of him, pinning him with one arm across his chest as I used my other hand to tug his head to the side, baring his throat. "Because you'll be crying for me soon enough."

The door swung open, revealing a tall figure in a hooded sweatshirt. I recognized his scent instantly, Asher. The cursed hacker who'd nearly burned me to a cinder with his hands. His eyes widened in recognition.

There was a blur of motion in the periphery, my only warning before I was knocked backward, an immense pressure reverberating in my chest.

"I thought that would work. Why didn't it work?" Remington asked, glancing down at the broken-off piece of wood in his hand.

"You tried to stake me!"

"I know! I did stake you. It was supposed to be foolproof. Stupid cheap furniture," he muttered, tossing the broken stool leg to the ground with the rest of the rubble.

It took a second for my mind to catch up on this sudden change of events. I patted my chest, half expecting to find a hole, finding instead a familiar solid weight resting over my heart. Reaching into my jacket, I pulled out the tungsten cigarette case. Not a scratch on it.

"Mother*fucker*, you *would* have a stake shield."

Roslyn gasped from behind the bar where she'd taken shelter from the fight. "Where did you get that?"

~

GRAB YOUR COPY OF CLAIMED BY THE SHIFTERS, THE MATE GAMES: PESTILENCE BOOK 2 TO KEEP READING!

THE MATE GAMES UNIVERSE
BY K. LORAINE & MEG ANNE

ALSO BY MEG ANNE

THE KEEPERS

A GUARDIAN/WARD HIGH FANTASY ROMANCE

THE DREAMER (A KEEPER'S PREQUEL)

THE KEEPERS LEGACY

THE KEEPERS RETRIBUTION

THE KEEPERS VOW

THE KEEPERS BOXSET

THE FORSAKEN

A REJECTED MATES/ENEMIES-TO-LOVERS ROMANTASY

PRISONER OF STEEL & SHADOW

QUEEN OF WHISPERS & MIST

COURT OF DEATH & DREAMS

PRINCE OF SEA & STARS

A STANDALONE MMF ROMANTASY ADVENTURE

GYPSY'S CURSE

A PSYCHIC/DETECTIVE STAR-CROSSED LOVERS UF ROMANCE

VISIONS OF DEATH

VISIONS OF VENGEANCE

VISIONS OF TRIUMPH

THE GYPSY'S CURSE: THE COMPLETE COLLECTION

Also by K. Loraine

~

STANDALONES

Cursed (MFM Sleeping Beauty Retelling)

~

REVERSE HAREM STANDALONES

Their Vampire Princess (A Reverse Harem Romance)

All the Queen's Men (A Fae Reverse Harem Romance)

ABOUT MEG ANNE

USA Today and international bestselling paranormal and fantasy romance author Meg Anne has always had stories running on a loop in her head. They started off as daydreams about how the evil queen (aka Mom) had her slaving away doing chores, and more recently shifted into creating backgrounds about the people stuck beside her during rush hour. The stories have always been there; they were just waiting for her to tell them.

Like any true SoCal native, Meg enjoys staying inside curled up with a good book and her fur babies . . . or maybe that's just her. You can convince Meg to buy just about anything if it's covered in glitter or rhinestones, or make her laugh by sharing your favorite bad joke. She also accepts bribes in the form of baked goods and Mexican food.

Meg is best known for her leading men #MenbyMeg, her inevitable cliffhangers, and making her readers laugh out loud, all of which started with the bestselling Chosen series.

ABOUT K. LORAINE

USA Today Bestselling author Kim Loraine writes steamy contemporary and sexy paranormal romance. **You'll find her paranormal romances written under the name K. Loraine and her contemporaries as Kim Loraine.** Don't worry, you'll get the same level of swoon-worthy heroes, sassy heroines, and an eventual HEA.

When not writing, she's busy herding cats (raising kids), trying to keep her house sort of clean, and dreaming up ways for fictional couples to meet.

Made in United States
North Haven, CT
03 January 2025